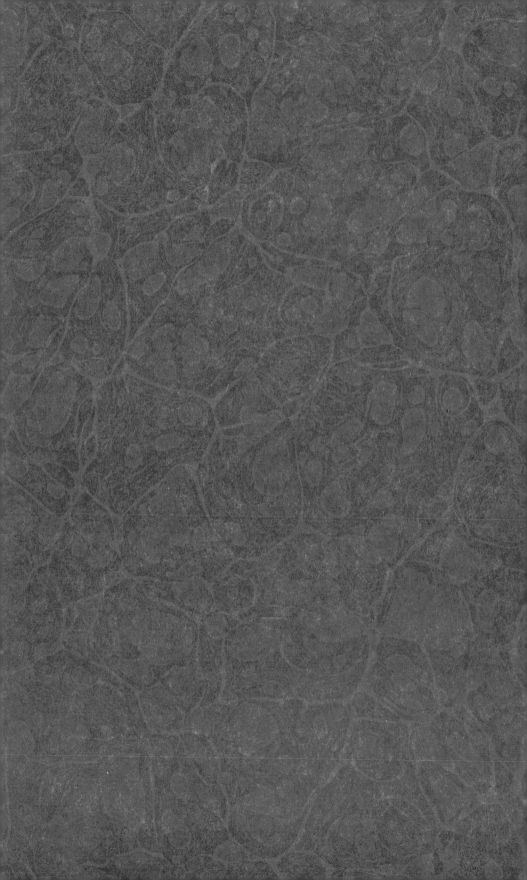

MYSTERY WRITERS
OF AMERICA
PRESENTS

Library of Congress Cataloging in Publication Number: 2014938241
ISBN: 978-1-59474-761-8

Printed in the United States of America
Typeset in Garamond and Stint Ultra Expanded
Designed by Timothy O'Donnell
Production management by John J. McGurk

Quirk Books
215 Church Street
Philadelphia, PA 19106
quirkbooks.com

10 9 8 7 6 5 4 3 2 1

MYSTERY WRITERS
OF AMERICA
PRESENTS

MANHATTAN MAYHEM

EDITED BY
MARY HIGGINS CLARK

1945 2015

70th Anniversary
MYSTERY WRITERS
OF AMERICA

QUIRK BOOKS
PHILADELPHIA

TABLE OF CONTENTS

INTRODUCTION
Mary Higgins Clark
ix

THE FIVE-DOLLAR DRESS
Mary Higgins Clark in Union Square
1

WHITE RABBIT
Julie Hyzy in Central Park
13

THE PICTURE OF THE LONELY DINER
Lee Child in the Flatiron District
31

THREE LITTLE WORDS
Nancy Pickard on the Upper West Side
43

DAMAGE CONTROL
Thomas H. Cook in Hell's Kitchen
73

THE DAY AFTER VICTORY
Brendan DuBois in Times Square
93

SERIAL BENEFACTOR
Jon L. Breen in the Empire State Building
105

TRAPPED!
Ben H. Winters in Chelsea
135

WALL STREET RODEO
Angela Zeman on Wall Street
153

COPYCATS
N. J. Ayres in Alphabet City
167

RED-HEADED STEPCHILD
Margaret Maron on the Upper East Side
193

SUTTON DEATH OVERTIME
Judith Kelman on Sutton Place
201

DIZZY AND GILLESPIE
Persia Walker in Harlem
223

ME AND MIKEY
T. Jefferson Parker in Little Italy
245

EVERMORE
Justin Scott on the Hudson River
259

CHIN YONG-YUN MAKES A *SHIDDACH*
S. J. Rozan in Chinatown
281

THE BAKER OF BLEECKER STREET
Jeffery Deaver in Greenwich Village
295

INTRODUCTION

Mary Higgins Clark

In 2015, Mystery Writers of America celebrated its founding seventy years ago, in March 1945, during the closing days of World War II. The founding group consisted of ten women and men, eventually gaining membership to about one hundred by the end of its first year. I remember when I joined MWA over fifty years ago, only about ten tables were needed at the annual Edgar Awards banquet, a much more intimate affair than today's glittery gala.

Back then, the joke we told was about the man who went to a cocktail party and was asked by another guest what kind of job he had.

"I'm a writer," he said.

"Oh, that's wonderful. What do you write?"

"Crime novels."

Pause. Icy stare. Then the put-down. "I only read *good* books."

That was then, this is now. Today, suspense and crime novels, "thrillers" as the English call them, have taken their place worldwide as an honored and thoroughly enjoyed branch of literature. And MWA has grown right alongside the genre. From its humble beginnings, when those ten authors met in Manhattan to form what would become today's MWA, our venerable organization has grown to more than 3,500 members around the world.

The seventieth anniversary of Mystery Writers of America is a very special occasion. Since its founding, the organization has worked tirelessly to protect and promote mystery and crime writers, working in conjunction with them, as well as with publishers and libraries, to elevate both the genre and its authors. And that is why our tireless former executive vice president and current publication committee chair,

Barry Zeman, and I conceived the idea of a special anniversary tribute collection celebrating Manhattan, where MWA was conceived and created.

Manhattan Mayhem is my third MWA anthology, and although I am proud of each one, this one holds a unique place in my heart. I invited a stellar collection of authors, including those who had previously given their time and talents to my past anthologies and are still active in MWA, as well as writers I have not had the pleasure of working with until now. Each was asked to select an iconic Manhattan neighborhood in which to set a story. The result is a marvelously diverse collection of tales that takes place from one end of the borough to the other— from Wall Street to Union Square, Central Park to Harlem, and Times Square to Sutton Place South, as well as eleven other evocative New York City locations.

Some writers decided to visit the Manhattan of the past, such as N. J. Ayres in "Copycats," a gritty tale of post–World War II cops and criminals, and "The Baker of Bleecker Street," Jeffery Deaver's tale of wartime espionage. In "The Day after Victory," Brendan DuBois chose to write about a pivotal moment in the city's history, V-J Day in Times Square. Angela Zeman selected a different era, the bustling early 1990s, for "Wall Street Rodeo," a story of street hustlers and cons-within-cons that plays out on the street hailed as the financial capital of the world.

Other authors spun stories that encompass many years and, often, decades. Jon L. Breen tells of a series of unsolved crimes that reach back more than half a century in "Serial Benefactor." T. Jefferson Parker takes us on a tour of the darker side of Little Italy's crime families from the 1970s to today in "Me and Mikey." Judith Kelman's "Sutton Death Overtime" combines the perils and pitfalls of mystery-novel writing and the disappearance of a Manhattan socialite whose case is laid to rest decades later . . . or is it? Native Manhattanite Justin Scott weaves one of our most fanciful tales, crossing crime, time, and space to spectacular effect in "Evermore." I also offer a story of my own. "The Five-Dollar Dress" is a cautionary tale about how we may never truly know those closest to our hearts.

But of course, even today, Manhattan is a hotbed of imagined crimes and mystery as well as the real thing. For some of our stories, family is at the heart of a crime. In "Three Little Words," Nancy Pickard reveals the often-spiteful core of the Big Apple and what happens when one woman tries to change it. The mystery-solving mother of series detective Lydia Chin tackles a missing-persons case brought to her by her son in S. J. Rozan's "Chin Yong-Yun Makes a *Shiddach*," while in "Red-Headed Stepchild" fellow MWA grand master Margaret Maron shows a step-sibling rivalry that matches anything adults can dream up. Thomas H. Cook portrays how some family ties can bind to the bitter end in "Damage Control," set in a gentrified Hell's Kitchen, and Persia Walker's "Dizzy and Gillespie" tells of a dispute between neighbors in a Harlem apartment building, with a loving daughter caught in the middle.

All these wonderful stories, and we've barely scratched the surface. Lee Child's drifting modern warrior Jack Reacher makes a stop in the Big Apple in "The Picture of the Lonely Diner," in which just exiting a subway station ensnares him in enough intrigue and danger to fill a novel. A sunny day in Central Park turns dangerous for at least one perpetrator in Julie Hyzy's "White Rabbit." And Ben H. Winters takes us behind the cutthroat world of Off-Broadway theater in "Trapped!"

Our esteemed publisher, Quirk Books, has illustrated each of the stories with maps and photographs from these classic neighborhoods, making *Manhattan Mayhem* a unique tribute and keepsake anthology in honor of a very special organization and an equally special city.

We hope you'll be as pleased reading these stories as we were writing them.

a message from

MYSTERY WRITERS
OF AMERICA

ON THE OCCASION of MWA's seventieth anniversary, we would like to take a moment on behalf of the organization to extend our deepest appreciation to Mary Higgins Clark. Since joining its ranks as a young writer, she has consistently been a tireless champion of MWA, our members, and mystery writers worldwide.

Mary is always ready to lend a helping hand in our endeavors. In addition to many tasks performed on behalf of MWA during her more than ten years as a member of the National Board of Directors, as MWA's national president she served as an indefatigable and peerless leader and spokeswoman for our genre. Mary also took on a small job that lasted for two years, organizing and chairing the 1988 International Crime Congress, a stellar weeklong affair hosting mystery and crime writers from all over the world.

If that were not enough for one individual to give of her time and talent, Mary has also edited three annual MWA anthologies and contributed to many more.

She is a talented and beloved writer, and her outstanding contribution to the genre was duly recognized when she was named MWA Grand Master for her outstanding body of consistently high-quality work produced over her storied career.

Much has changed since Mary first joined our ranks, but she, thankfully, has remained the same gracious, warm, and caring person she has always been, and we are all richer for knowing her. Certainly recognized worldwide as "The Queen of Suspense," around here she is known as "The Queen of Our Hearts."

We offer our deepest and most sincere thanks for Mary's many years of selfless service to Mystery Writers of America and writers everywhere. We hope there are many more to come.

BARRY T. ZEMAN
Chair, Publications Committee

TED HERTZEL, JR.
Executive Vice President

THE FIVE-DOLLAR DRESS

Mary Higgins Clark

It was a late August afternoon, and the sun was sending slanting shadows across Union Square in Manhattan. *It's a peculiar kind of day,* Jenny thought as she came up from the subway and turned east. This was the last day she needed to go to the apartment of her grandmother, who had died three weeks ago.

She had already cleaned out most of the apartment. The furniture and all of Gran's household goods, as well as her clothing, would be picked up at five o'clock by the diocese charity.

Her mother and father were both pediatricians in San Francisco and had intensely busy schedules. Having just passed the bar exam after graduating from Stanford Law School, Jenny was free to do the job. Next week, she would be starting as a deputy district attorney in San Francisco.

At First Avenue, she looked up while waiting for the light to change. She could see the windows of her grandmother's apartment on the fourth floor of 415 East Fourteenth Street. Gran had been one of the first tenants to move there in 1949. *She and my grandfather moved to New Jersey when Mom was five*, Jennie thought, *but she moved back after my grandfather died.* That was twenty years ago.

Filled with memories of the grandmother she had adored, Jenny didn't notice when the light turned green. *It's almost as though I'm seeing her in the window, watching for me the way she did when I'd visit her*, she reminisced. An impatient pedestrian brushed against her shoulder as he walked around her, and she realized the light was turning green again. She crossed the street and walked the short distance to the entrance of Gran's building. There, with increasingly reluctant steps, she entered the security code, opened the door, walked to the elevator, got in, and pushed the button.

On the fourth floor, she got off the elevator and slowly walked down the corridor to her grandmother's apartment. Tears came to her eyes as she thought of the countless times her grandmother had been waiting with the door open after having seen her cross the street. Swallowing the lump in her throat, Jenny turned the key in the lock and opened the door. She reminded herself that, at eighty-six, Gran had been ready to go. She had said that twenty years was a long time without her grandfather, and she wanted to be with him.

And she had started to drift into dementia, talking about someone named Sarah . . . how Barney didn't kill her . . . Vincent did . . . that someday she'd prove it.

If there's anything Gran wouldn't have wanted to live with, it's dementia, Jenny thought. Taking a deep breath, she looked around the room. The boxes she had packed were clustered together. The bookshelves were bare. The tabletops were empty. Yesterday she had wrapped and packed the Royal Doulton figurines that her grandmother had loved, and the framed family pictures that would be sent to California.

She only had one job left. It was to go through her grandmother's hope chest to see if there was anything else to keep.

The hope chest was special. She started to walk down the hallway to the small bedroom that Gran had turned into a den. Even though she had a sweater on, she felt chilled. She wondered if all apartments or homes felt like this after the person who had lived in them was gone.

Entering the room, she sat on the convertible couch that had been her bed there ever since she was eleven years old. That was the first time she had been allowed to fly alone from California and spend a month of the summer with her grandmother.

Jenny remembered how her grandmother used to open the chest and always take out a present for her whenever she was visiting. But she had never allowed her granddaughter to rummage through it. "There are some things I don't want to share, Jenny," she had said. "Maybe someday I'll let you look at them. Or a maybe I'll get rid of them. I don't know yet."

I wonder if Gran ever did get rid of whatever it was that was so secret? Jenny asked herself.

The hope chest now served as a coffee table in the den.

She sat on the couch, took a deep breath, and lifted the lid. She soon realized that most of the hope chest was filled with heavy blankets and quilts, the kind that had long since been replaced by lighter comforters.

Why did Gran keep all this stuff? Jenny wondered. Struggling to take the blankets out, she then stacked them into a discard pile on the floor. *Maybe someone can use them,* she decided. *They do look warm.*

Next were three linen tablecloth and napkin sets, the kind her grandmother had always joked about. "Almost nobody bothers with linen tablecloths and napkins anymore, unless it's Thanksgiving or Christmas," she had said. "It's a wash-and-dry world."

When I get married, Gran, I'll use them in your memory on Thanksgiving and Christmas and special occasions, Jenny promised.

She was almost to the bottom of the trunk. A wedding album with a white leather cover, inscribed with *Our Wedding Day* in gold lettering, was the next item. Jenny opened it. The pictures were in black and white. The first one was of her grandmother in her wedding gown arriving at the church. Jennie gasped. *Gran showed this to me years ago, but I never realized how much I would grow to look like her.* They had the same high cheekbones, the same dark hair, the same features. *It's like looking in a mirror,* she thought.

She remembered that when Gran had shown her the album, she'd pointed out the people in it. "That was your father's best friend . . . That was my maid of honor, your great-aunt . . . And doesn't your grandfather look handsome? You were only five when he died, so of course you have no memory of him."

I do have some vague memories of him, Jenny thought. *He would hug me and give me a big kiss and then recite a couple lines of a poem about someone named Jenny. I'll have to look it up someday.*

There was a loose photograph after the last bound picture in the album. It was of her grandmother and another young woman wearing identical cocktail dresses. *Oh, how lovely,* Jenny thought. The dresses had a graceful boat neckline, long sleeves, a narrow waist, and a bouffant ankle-length skirt.

Prettier than anything on the market today, she thought.

She turned over the picture and read the typed note attached to it:

Sarah wore this dress in the fashion show at Klein's only hours before she was murdered in it. I'm wearing the other one. It was a backup in case the original became damaged. The designer, Vincent Cole, called it "The Five-Dollar Dress," because that's what they were going to charge for it. He said he would lose money on it, but that dress would make his name. It made a big hit at the show, and the buyer ordered thirty, but Cole wouldn't sell any after Sarah was found in it. He wanted me to return the sample he had given me, but I refused. I think the reason he wanted to get rid of the dress was because Sarah was wearing it when he killed her. If only there was some proof. I had suspected she was dating him on the sly.

Her hand shaking, Jenny put the picture back inside the album. In her delirium the day before she died, Gran had said those names: Sarah . . . Vincent . . . Barney . . . Or had it just been delirium?

A large manila envelope, its bright yellow color faded with time, was next. Opening it, she found it filled with three separate files of crumbling news clippings. *There's no place to read these here,* Jenny thought. With the manila envelope tucked under her arm, she walked into the dining area and settled at the table. Careful not to tear the clippings, she began to slide them from the envelope. Looking at the date on the top clipping of the three sets, she realized they had been filed chronologically.

"Murder in Union Square" was the first headline she read. It was dated June 8, 1949. The story followed:

The body of twenty-three-year-old Sarah Kimberley was found in the doorway of S. Klein Department Store on Union Square this morning. She had been stabbed in the back by person or persons unknown sometime during the hours of midnight and five a.m. . . . .

Why did Gran keep all these clippings? Jenny asked herself. *Why didn't she ever tell me about it, especially when she knew I was planning to go into criminal law? I know she must not have talked with Mom about it. Mom would have told me.*

She spread out the other clippings on the table. In sequence by date, they told of the murder investigation from the beginning. In the late afternoon, Sarah Kimberley had been modeling the dress she was wearing when her body was found.

The autopsy revealed that Sarah was six weeks pregnant when she died.

Up-and-coming designer Vincent Cole had been questioned for hours. He was known to have been seeing Sarah on the side. But his fiancée, Nona Banks, an heiress to the Banks department store fortune, swore they had been together in her apartment all night.

What did my grandmother do with the dress she had? Jenny wondered. *She said it was the prettiest dress she ever owned.*

Jenny's computer was on the table, and she decided to see what she could find out about Vincent Cole. What she discovered shocked her. Vincent Cole had changed his name to Vincenzia and was now a famous designer. *He's up there with Oscar de la Renta and Carolina Herrera,* she thought.

The next pile of clippings was about the arrest of Barney Dodd, a twenty-six-year-old man who liked to sit for hours in Union Square Park. Borderline mentally disabled, he lived at the YMCA and worked at a funeral home. One of his jobs was dressing the bodies of the deceased and placing them in the casket. At noon and after work he would head straight to the park, carrying a paper bag with his lunch or dinner. As Jenny read the accounts, it became clear why he had come under suspicion. The body of Sarah Kimberley had been laid out as though she was in a coffin. Her hands had been clasped. Her hair was in place, the wide collar of the dress carefully arranged.

According to the accounts, Barney was known to try to strike up a conversation if a pretty young woman was sitting near him. *That's not proof of anything,* Jenny thought. She realized that she was thinking like the deputy district attorney she would soon become.

The last clipping was a two-page article from the *Daily News.* It was called "Did Justice Triumph?" It was about "The Case of the Five-Dollar Dress," as the writer dubbed it. At a glance, she could see that long excerpts from the trial were included in the article.

Barney Dobbs had confessed. He signed a statement saying that he had been in Union Square at about midnight the night of the murder. It was chilly, so the park was deserted. He saw Sarah walking across Fourteenth Street. He followed her, and then, when she wouldn't kiss him, he killed her. He carried her body to the front door of Klein's and left it there. But he arranged it so that it looked nice, the way he did in the funeral parlor. He threw away the knife as well as the clothes he was wearing that night.

Too pat, Jenny thought scornfully. *It sounds to me like whoever got that confession was trying to cover every base. Talk about a rush to justice.*

Barney certainly didn't get Sarah pregnant. Who was the father of the baby? Who was Sarah with that night? Why was she alone at midnight (or later) in Union Square?

It was obvious the judge also thought there was something fishy about the confession. He entered a plea of not guilty for Barney and assigned a public defender to his case.

Jenny read the accounts of the trial with increasing contempt. It seemed to her that although the public defender had done his best to defend Barney, he was obviously inexperienced. *He should* never *have put Barney on the stand,* she thought. The man kept contradicting himself. He admitted that he had confessed to killing Sarah, but only because he was hungry and the officers who were talking to him had promised him a ham and cheese sandwich and a Hershey bar if he would sign something.

That was good, she thought. *That should have made an impression on the jurors.*

Not enough of an impression, she decided as she continued reading. *Not compared to the district attorney trying the case.*

He had shown Barney a picture of Sarah's body taken at the scene of the crime. "Do you recognize this woman?"

"Yes. I used to see her sometimes in the park when she was having her lunch or walking home after work."

"Did you ever talk to her?"

"She didn't like to talk to me. But her friend was so nice. She was pretty, too. Her name was Catherine."

My grandmother, Jenny thought.

"Did you see Sarah Kimberley the night of the murder?"

"Was that the night I saw her lying in front of Klein's? Her hands were folded, but they weren't folded nice like they are in the picture. So I fixed them."

His attorney should have called a recess, should have told the judge that his client was obviously confused! Jenny raged.

But the defense lawyer had allowed the district attorney to continue the line of questioning, hammering at Barney. "You arranged her body?"

"No. Somebody else did. I only changed her hands."

There were only two defense witnesses. The first was the matron at the YMCA where Barney lived. "He'd never hurt a fly," she said. "If he tried to talk to someone and they didn't respond to him, he never approached them again. I certainly never saw him carry a knife. He doesn't have many changes of clothes. I know all of them, and nothing's missing."

The other witness was Catherine Reeves. She testified that Barney had never exhibited any animosity toward her friend Sarah Kimberley. "If we happened to be having lunch in the park and Sarah ignored Barney, he just talked to me for a minute or two. He never gave Sarah a second glance."

Barney was found guilty of murder in the first degree and sentenced to life without parole.

Jenny read the final paragraph of the article:

Barney Dodd died at age sixty-eight, having served forty years in prison for the murder of Sarah Kimberley. The case of the so-called Five-Dollar Dress Murder has been debated by experts for years. The identity of the father of Sarah's unborn baby is still unknown. She was wearing the dress she had modeled that day. It was a cocktail dress. Was she having a romantic date with an admirer? Whom did she meet and where did she go that evening? DID JUSTICE TRIUMPH?

I'd say, absolutely not, Jenny fumed. She looked up and realized that the shadows had lengthened.

At the end, Gran had ranted about Vincent Cole and the five-dollar dress. Was it because he couldn't bear the sight of it? Was he the father of Sarah's unborn child?

He must be in his mid-eighties now, Jenny thought. His first wife, Nona Hartman, was a department store heiress. One of the article clips was about her. In an interview in *Vogue* magazine in 1952, she said she had first suggested that Vincent Cole did not sound exotic enough for a designer, and she urged her husband to upgrade his image by changing his name to Vincenzia. Included was a picture of their over-the-top wedding at her grandfather's estate in Newport. It had taken place on August 10, 1949, a few weeks after Sarah was murdered.

The marriage lasted only two years. The complaint had been adultery.

I wonder . . . Jenny thought. She turned back to the computer. The file on Vincent Cole—Vincenzia—was still open. She began searching through the links until she found what she was looking for. Vincent Cole, then twenty-five years old, had been living two blocks from Union Square when Sarah Kimberley was murdered.

If only they had DNA in those days. Sarah lived on Avenue C, just a few blocks away. If she had been in his apartment that night and told him she was pregnant, he easily could have followed her and killed her. Cole probably knew about Barney, a character around Union Square. Could Vincent Cole have arranged the body to throw suspicion on Barney? Maybe he saw him sitting in the park that night?

We'll never know, Jenny thought. *But it's obvious that Gran was sure he was guilty.*

She got up from the chair and realized that she had been sitting for a long time. Her back felt cramped, and all she wanted to do was get out of the apartment and take a long walk.

The charity pick-up truck should be here in fifteen minutes. Let's be done with it, she thought, and went back into the den. Two boxes were left to open. The one with the Klein label was the first she investigated. Wrapped in blue tissue was the five-dollar dress she had seen in the picture.

She shook it out and held it up. *This must be the dress Gran talked about a couple years ago. I had bought a cocktail dress in this color. Gran told me that it reminded her of a dress she had when she was young. She said Grandpa didn't like to see her wearing it. "A girl I worked with was wearing one like it when she had an accident," she'd said, "and he thought it was bad luck."*

The other box held a man's dark blue three-button suit. Why did it look familiar? She flipped open the wedding album. *I'm pretty sure that's what my grandfather wore at the wedding,* she thought. *No wonder Gran kept it. She could never talk about him without crying.* She thought about what her grandmother's old friends had told her at the wake: "Your grandfather was the handsomest man you'd ever want to see. While he was going to law school at night, he worked as a salesman at Klein's during the day. All the girls in the store were after him. But once he met your mother, it was love at first sight. We were all jealous of her."

Jenny smiled at the memory and began to go through the pockets of the suit, in case anything had been left in them. There was nothing in the trousers. She slipped her fingers through the pockets of the jacket. The pocket under the left sleeve was empty, but it seemed as though she could feel something under the smooth satin lining.

Maybe it has one of those secret inner pockets, she thought. *I had a suit with a hidden pocket like that.*

She was right. The slit to the inner pocket was almost indiscernible, but it was there.

She reached in and pulled out a folded sheet of paper. Opening it, she read the contents.

It was addressed to Miss Sarah Kimberley.

It was a medical report stating that the test had confirmed she was six weeks pregnant.

MARY HIGGINS CLARK's *books are worldwide best sellers. In the United States alone, her books have sold over 100 million copies. Her latest suspense novel,* I've Got You under My Skin, *was published by Simon & Schuster in April 2014. She is an active member of Literacy Volunteers. She is the author of thirty-three previous suspense novels, three collections of short stories, a historical novel, a memoir, and two children's books. She is married to John Conheeney, and they live in Saddle River, New Jersey.*

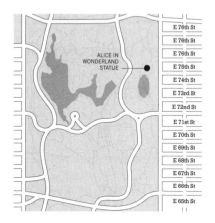

WHITE RABBIT

Julie Hyzy

The young woman sitting on the bench stopped fingering a strand of her white-blonde pixie cut. Startled, she looked up, shielding her eyes from the sun. "Excuse me?"

"I asked if you were recapturing your childhood." The man who had spoken reached down to tap a corner of the book lying on her lap. He had a round face and the sort of little-boy haircut most men ditch long before they hit thirty. Wearing black-framed glasses and a bushy brown beard, he carried a soft paunch and a beat-up messenger bag.

"Interesting reading choice," he said. "Especially considering the view. My name's Mark, by the way."

Stiffening, the young woman clutched the collar of her sweater.

Although most of the benches ringing the popular spot were unoccupied, this corner of Central Park was far from desolate. Tourists clambering to pose with its central attraction—an eleven-foot-tall Alice in Wonderland statue—included three young families and a group of college-age kids eagerly snapping photos and sharing results.

"I don't make a habit of talking to strangers," she said, turning her attention to two toddlers in shiny neon jackets attempting to climb the giant bronze sculpture. Their father leaned against the White Rabbit and squinted at his phone.

"I'm not strange." Mark sat on the bench next to her, settling his bag on his lap. "But your comment makes me curious. Are you?"

She didn't answer.

One of the toddlers, lying prone atop a low mushroom, lost his chubby grip and slid off sideways, landing hard. A split second later, his piercing wails jolted the father into attentiveness. He pocketed the phone and picked up the kid.

Mark pointed and leaned close. "Shouldn't they be in school?"

"Too young," she said. "Listen, I don't want to be rude—"

"Then don't be." He propped one elbow atop the bench back and settled an ankle across a knee. Exhaling loudly, he rested his other hand on the messenger bag. "Relax. We're at a popular attraction in the middle of a busy park on a sunny October afternoon. There's no harm in a little conversation."

She lifted her book. "There is if it keeps me from reading."

"Except you aren't," he said. "Reading, that is."

"What do you think this is?" This time when she lifted the book, she shook it. "A surfboard?"

He drew her attention to the nearby steps, where a young woman hunched over a paperback in her left hand while biting the thumbnail of her right. "*She's* reading." He extended his arm, pointing at a pair of joggers rounding the model boat pond. "They're *not* reading." With an amused look on his face, he said, "Amazing powers of observation, coupled with deductive skill." He spread his hands. "It's a gift."

"I'd say you're full of yourself."

"You wouldn't be the first. Hang on." He pointed again, this time skyward. Lifting his chin into the crisp, twisty breeze, he pulled in a deep breath through his nose. "Did you catch that?" He continued with barely a pause. "That familiar smell, right on time. You recognize it, don't you? Death and new beginnings in one fragrant breath. Worn-away leaves and pristine notebooks. Every autumn it comes, right on schedule. Sometimes it lasts for days; sometimes it's gone before you exhale."

"Very poetic, but that doesn't answer—"

He walked his fingers along the edge of her book. "You've been sitting here for an hour with *Alice's Adventures in Wonderland* on your lap, but you haven't turned a single page."

Her voice rose. "You've been watching me?"

He scratched his neck. "'Watching' makes me sound like a stalker. Can't have that. Let's just say you pique my interest."

"If that's supposed to be a pickup line—"

"It's not. Call me curious. Call me intrigued."

"Call you a weirdo," she said.

He laughed. "Touché. What did you say your name was?"

"I didn't."

"Oh, right. You're being *careful.*" He smirked as he stretched the word out. "You're afraid Mark-in-the-park might tempt you out of your comfort zone. Don't worry," he said with a dismissive wave, "I like knowing people's names, is all. A quirk of mine. I thought you'd be someone who appreciated a little witty repartee." He pushed his glasses farther up his nose. "You don't *look* uptight or fainthearted. Apparently, I made the clichéd mistake of . . . " He touched her book again. "Judging by a cover."

She closed it with a *thump.* "I'm leaving now."

"No, you're not," he said. "You're waiting for something. Or someone. Am I close?"

"My reason for being here is none of your business."

"How about this, then?" He patted the messenger bag. "You won't leave because you want to know what I have in here."

"Why would I care?"

"Let's see." He opened the bag slowly, grinning as he unbuckled the leather strap and peeled it back. Using his thumb and index finger, he reached inside, latched onto something solid, and gently eased it out.

"What are the chances?" he asked as he dropped a copy of *Alice's Adventures in Wonderland* into her lap. Blue hardcover. Gold lettering. Identical to hers.

She jerked in surprise. "What's going on? What are you trying to pull?"

"Whoa, sorry," he said. "Just thought it was a fun coincidence. Nothing more. The only thing I'm trying to pull is a little conversation. Geez."

"No way. What did you do? Run to the nearest bookstore and buy this? You really *are* a stalker."

"Oh, come on." When she didn't respond, he said, "Okay, even if I *had* gone to such drastic lengths, tell me: to what end? You're street-smart, you're savvy. A little paranoid, perhaps, but this is New York, so that can be forgiven. What nefarious plan could possibly be served by my producing this book at this moment?"

She traced her fingers along its gold embossed title but didn't answer.

"Now that you understand my reasons for chatting you up are completely benign, we can begin anew, can't we? Hi, I'm Mark."

She handed back the book. "I'm . . . Jane."

He grinned. "Nice to meet you, Jane." Opening the cover, he flipped pages until he reached an illustration of the Cheshire Cat. "He's my favorite character."

"He would be."

Mark chuckled. "You see there? We've known each other for ten minutes and already we can share a joke. I'm not so terrible, am I?"

Jane didn't answer. The father and two toddlers were gone, as were the photo-happy tourists. They'd been replaced by a dozen kids, all about five years old, who climbed and shouted and raced while two women in matching day-care-emblazoned sweatshirts supervised. On the bench directly opposite, three twentysomething professionals chatted, then raised paper coffee cups in an animated toast that was lost to

WHITE RABBIT · JULIE HYZY

the wind.

"May I?" Mark asked.

It took Jane a second to realize he was reaching for her book. She slammed both hands down. "Don't touch it."

"Sorry." He shrugged as though it made no difference. "I thought I'd compare copyright dates. See which one is older. I didn't mean to offend you."

"They're exactly the same. Anyone can see that."

At that moment an old, bearded man shuffled past. Wearing an overcoat with a frayed collar, he carried a grubby cup and a fragment of creased cardboard. He approached the day-care workers first, earning twin evil-eyed glares before getting shooed away. Unfazed, he turned and made his unsteady way toward Jane and Mark.

He shook his paper cup of change in front of her. The clumsily lettered cardboard sign he held read: *Please share.* Below that: *In pain.* Jane turned her head and murmured, "No, thank you."

Mark pulled a wallet from the messenger bag, drew out a couple of singles, and stuffed them into the beggar's cup. The old guy grunted, then shuffled away to take a seat behind the statue.

"You realize he'll probably drink that donation," Jane said.

Mark shrugged. He pushed up his glasses and resumed paging through his book, stopping to spend an extra second or two at each illustration. When he lifted his head again, he asked, "Why here?" He gestured at the bronze Alice sitting atop a giant mushroom, her cat Dinah in her lap. "And why the book? Any special significance?"

She bunched her sweater's neckline. "Why do you care?"

"Sorry." He lifted both hands. "Didn't mean to touch a nerve. Again. Two adults, same time, same place, same book. Seems like one heck of a coincidence. I know why I'm here. I was curious about you."

"Why *are* you here?" she asked.

"Birthday, if you must know," he said with a grin. "I took the day off from work to do something special for myself."

"Happy birthday," she said with little warmth.

He nodded.

"Is sitting in Central Park with *Alice* the best 'something special' you could come up with?" she asked.

"This year, it is." He turned a few more pages. "I'm making myself a gift of good memories."

"So *you're* here to recapture your childhood?"

"Something like that. Can't help thinking about my dad today. He didn't always know how to connect with his children. But, man, give him a book to read aloud, and the guy turned into a Shakespearean actor with a deep baritone voice. Of course, as a kid, I didn't know what a Shakespearean actor was or what baritone meant—but I can still hear him now." He lifted his copy of *Alice*. "This book was his favorite."

Jane smoothed her pixie cut as though tucking it behind an ear. "Is your father . . . gone?"

"Late last year," he said.

"I'm sorry."

Mark lifted his chin toward the statue where the day-care kids clambered and crawled. "He used to bring us here when we were kids. And read to us. I can't help but associate this place with him."

Jane remained quiet.

Still staring at the kids, Mark said, "This is the first birthday since—" He gave himself a quick shake. "Enough of my melancholy reflections. Tell me what brings you here. I hope your reason is happier than mine."

Jane took her time before answering. "I don't know why I'm here. Not really." She glanced down at the book in her lap, then up at the statue, then at Mark. "I guess the best explanation I can give you is that I came here today for closure."

"That doesn't sound happy."

She looked away. "You know how you always hear about criminals returning to the scene of the crime?"

"Yes."

"How come you never hear about the victims? Nobody talks about their pain—their need to return."

"Oh, I see," he said in a breath. "I'm sorry to hear it. If you don't mind me asking, what happened? Sometimes talking to a stranger can help."

"I thought you said you weren't strange."

"Good catch." He smiled. "So, maybe I lied about my pickup lines."

"Not going to work on me, sorry."

"Fair enough. Forget all that. No silly games. As I'm sure you've noticed, I can talk your ear off. But I'm a good listener, too."

Four times Jane smoothed the side of her pixie, tucking nonexistent hair behind her ear. She bit her lip.

Mark cleared his throat. "Central Park is pretty safe most of the time, and this spot tends to be busy with kids and tourists." He waited a beat. "But obviously it isn't safe enough. Not if you were injured . . . or hurt . . . here."

"Not me." She shook her head and ran her fingers up and down the book's edges. "Do you remember the young woman who was murdered in the park a year ago?"

"Someone was murdered?" His brows came together. "Here?"

Jane pulled in a shuddering breath. "This is hard for me."

"Take your time."

"I'm surprised you don't remember. The story got massive coverage because her father was some bigwig in the police department."

"Oh, wait," he said. "I do recall hearing about that. That was a particularly brutal crime, wasn't it?"

Jane nodded.

"They never caught the guy, did they?"

Jane shook her head.

"I take it you knew her?" Mark asked. "Was she a friend? She wasn't your sister, was she?"

Taking another hard breath, Jane clenched her eyes shut. When she opened them again, she whispered, "I loved her."

"Oh," Mark said. He stroked his beard, glancing from side to side. "You mean—"

"Yeah, I mean what you think I mean. I was in love with her."

"I don't remember her name," Mark said. "I'm sorry."

Jane's body drew in on itself. "Samantha."

"I'm very sorry for your loss." Mark swallowed, looking around again. "How long were you and Samantha together?"

"We weren't," Jane said. "I never got the chance to tell her how I felt."

A group of teenagers arrived in a collection of flailing legs, arms, and shouted profanities. They swarmed the statue, displacing the five-year-olds, who whined their resentment. When one of the young men swigged from a flask, the day-care workers gathered their charges and hustled them away.

Mark drummed his fingers against his messenger bag. "I'm very sorry," he said again. "You said it happened about a year ago?"

"Today," Jane said. "One year ago today."

Mark gave a low whistle. "Now I understand. This is a vigil for your friend. And I interrupted you." He waited a moment and then said, "I can't imagine how hard it must be—I mean, hard to return to the place where she was murdered."

"It didn't happen here. It was deeper in the park," Jane said, "in an area the police said has a sketchy reputation."

"Not the Ramble?" he asked.

"That's it," she said. "I guess it's popular with bird-watchers and for quick hookups. I've never gone in there myself."

"There's a stretch of the Ramble near the lake that's seen a few assaults in recent years. Is that where it happened?"

She held up both hands. "No idea."

Mark scratched his head. "Seems like a pretty bold move on the killer's part. How did he do it?"

Jane made air quotes. "Blunt force trauma, according to the police. They found a tree branch nearby with her blood on it."

"Blunt force. A less grisly way of saying she was bludgeoned to death. I'm very, very sorry this happened to her." Shaking his head, Mark leaned back. "I've watched enough TV cop shows to know that murder is a messy business. The guy who killed her is either some kind of evil genius, or he got lucky."

"Got lucky, I imagine." Jane shivered. She sat up a little straighter. "It does help to talk. You were right."

"Tell me about Samantha."

A nearby shout interrupted them. A policewoman with a determined expression started up the steps, bellowing at the boozing teenagers. The paperback-reading woman didn't flinch—didn't even seem to notice—as the cop strode past.

The teens bounded away before the officer reached the top of the plaza. Two vaulted the low stone wall to the east while the rest scattered north, disappearing into the park.

Jane followed the action. "Cops never catch *anybody* anymore, do they?"

"I don't think she tried very hard," Mark said.

"That's what I mean. They don't really try."

Tranquility restored, the officer took her time surveying the whimsical haven. She made a slow circuit around Alice, reaching out to skim the Mad Hatter's brim.

Jane drew in a deep breath and blew it out. "I met Samantha only a couple of weeks before she was murdered. She worked at the yogurt place next to my office. You know how it is when you just click with someone?"

"I do." Mark smiled. "I feel like that today." He raised both hands. "I'm not flirting. I swear."

Still gazing at the statue, Jane went on, "Anyway, what I felt for Samantha came on in a rush. Exactly like in a romance novel, where a character's life shatters completely, and she knows she'll never be whole again. Not without that other person. I've never experienced anything like it before."

"That's beautiful."

"After Samantha and I talked a few times, I really thought she felt something for me, too. But she was so amazing, it scared me. What if I misread her? I was afraid that if I spoke up, I might ruin everything."

"Go on."

"I started stopping by the shop more often. I could tell she wanted to have a real conversation as much as I did, but every time we came close, customers would swarm in." Jane rested a hand against her chest.

"She had the sweetest White Rabbit necklace I've ever seen."

"Was that her favorite character?" Mark asked. "Or was Samantha chronically late?"

"Oh, no. Samantha was conscientious and considerate." Jane smiled. "I knew she liked to come here on nice days. Always with a book. I think it was her favorite place in the city."

"It helps to talk about her, doesn't it?"

"It's so strange . . . you being here today . . . with that book. It's like a sign, you know? And you really are a good listener." Jane started to run her fingers through her hair but stopped abruptly. She frowned. "I'm still not used to this. I got it done this morning."

Mark placed a hand on the slice of bench between them and leaned in. "You got your hair cut *today?*" he repeated. "On the anniversary of your friend's murder? Wait, don't tell me: Samantha wore her hair like that, didn't she?"

"How did you know?"

"Lucky guess." Mark straightened, regarding her closely. "Beautiful, but I have to ask: why?"

Jane tugged at her sweater. "It's a way for me to feel close to her again." She stared down. "I keep thinking that if I'd only been braver and spoken up, everything would have been different."

"You can't blame yourself for what happened."

"Doesn't matter. It's how I feel." Jane's jaw tightened. "I'd do anything for a chance to go back and make things right."

Mark squinted into the wind. "I have an idea that may help," he said. "Would you like to hear it?"

Jane shrugged, then nodded.

He rubbed the side of his beard. "When you were a kid, did you ever burn secret notes?"

"What are you talking about?"

"It's a thing people did for a while. Maybe they still do. A cleansing, empowering ritual. Sound familiar?"

"Not at all."

"Okay, here goes." Mark sat back on the bench, stretched out his legs, and crossed his ankles. Elbows out, he laced his fingers atop his head and began, "At summer camp, when I was fifteen, the counselors handed out small strips of paper and told us to write down either our greatest fear or something we wanted to change about ourselves. No talking. No sharing. Totally secret. Then, in a solemn ceremony involving lots of positive affirmation, we took turns tossing our scribbles into a bonfire, watching as each one blazed up into nothingness. It felt pretty hokey when the other kids did it, but . . . "

He lifted both hands to the air, then replaced them atop his head and resumed talking. "Anyway, you get the idea. Identifying our deepest fears and then—symbolically—destroying them reminded us that we had power over ourselves. That we controlled our impulses, rather than the other way around."

"Did it work?"

Dropping his hands to his lap, he sat forward. "It did. That's probably why I remember the experience so vividly, even to this day. What an exhilarating sense of freedom. Now, as an adult, I look back and realize that what I really learned was how to compartmentalize. Although I may not be able to incinerate my negative behaviors so easily, I *can* control when and how I deal with them." He waited a beat before adding, "Maybe you should consider a similar symbolic gesture. You know, to deal with your grief."

The area was the quietest it had been all afternoon. Two kids played and giggled. The old panhandler approached their parents and was rewarded with a handful of change.

Jane glanced around. "I don't believe a bonfire would go over well here."

Mark laughed. "Ya think? But there's got to be something we can do. Any ideas?"

"No."

Two squirrels scampered by.

"I've got it," Mark said. "A brilliant idea, if I do say so myself."

"What is it?"

"What if you tell Samantha how you felt? I mean, poured your heart out to her? Wouldn't that give you closure?" Before she could answer, he continued. "Something brought us both here right now for a reason. I think that 'something' wants you to have peace."

"I'm not sure that's possible."

"What if . . . " Mark leaned close. "What if you visit her grave? You can speak from the heart there, for as long as you like."

Jane played with the neckline of her sweater. "She was cremated."

"Oh." Mark fell silent again. A moment later, he said, "Then, what about a quiet place in the park?"

"Here?"

"Not in this very spot, no. But she died in the park, so that makes this a sacred space. Let's find a quiet knoll, a pretty meadow." He tapped a finger against his lips. "Do you know where Cedar Hill is?" Again, before she could answer, he went on, "By the Glade Arch. It's not that far, and once we settle on a location, I promise to give you privacy. Come on." He stood, offering her his hand.

Jane leaned back. "I don't think so."

His face fell. "You don't trust me?"

"It's not that."

"Then what?"

She didn't answer.

"You can't go back in time, Jane, but I promise you can find closure."

She remained seated.

"I think you should do this," he said softly. "I believe Samantha would want you to."

He looked down at her for a few moments before starting around the statue toward the path that lay beyond. She remained frozen for a solid count of thirty. When she finally stood, she hugged her book and whispered, "Closure."

The old man in the overcoat perked up as she drew near. He made a feeble attempt to beg, jangling his cup of coins. She didn't speak, didn't acknowledge him.

Mark waited for her at the path's opening. "Good girl."

She stopped and stared up at him. "I can do this."

They'd walked no more than a hundred yards when she whispered, "Is that beggar following us?"

Mark turned. "Probably hoping I'll cough up another couple bucks."

"I guess," she said. "Doesn't it seem like he's moving quicker than before?"

He laughed. "I can take him."

"I don't know. He makes me nervous."

Mark veered left to cross East Drive, where he abandoned the walking path for the cover of the trees.

"Where are we going?" Jane asked. "I thought we were heading toward Cedar Hill."

"Shortcut."

She followed, hurrying to keep up. "Why are you walking so fast?"

"You want to lose that beggar, don't you?"

They picked their way along the uneven terrain, sidestepping tree roots that rose from the ground like giant knuckles. Twice Jane came close to losing her footing while navigating a rocky patch. "We passed the Boathouse parking lot back there." She jerked a thumb over her left shoulder. "Are you sure we're going the right direction?"

"This way," he said, leading them deeper into the trees. The ground was soft, covered in shifting layers of red and gold. Crisp-edged leaves somersaulted through patches of vivid brilliance where breaks in the canopy allowed the sun's illumination to pass through.

"Are you sure?" she asked, keeping pace.

Rather than answer, he continued to shush and crunch through the quiet piles. "Watch out." He indicated a fallen log, nearly obscured by the leaves in her path.

Skirting it, she tried again. "I think we're going the wrong way."

Mark turned. "Smell that," he said lifting his chin high, drawing a noisy breath. "Decay and deliverance. There's nothing sweeter."

Jane slowed. She glanced from side to side. "We're still headed west. Shouldn't we be going north?"

Mark waited for her to catch up. Placing a hand on Jane's back, he pointed deep into the trees. "There's a lovely secluded spot not far ahead. I think it would be an ideal place for our ritual."

Resisting the pressure of his hand, Jane stutter-stepped. "I thought we were going to the grassy hill," she said in a small voice.

"Too many people," Mark said. "A ritual like ours would attract attention. I know of a quiet place with a sloping rock behind a giant sycamore. A far better setting to pour out your heart."

She stopped. "Where are you taking me?"

"If you truly long to be free, Jane," he whispered into her ear, "then this is your only path." Though his tone coaxed, it was the pressure of his hand on her back that propelled her through the trees. "Right through there."

"Stop." Her body went rigid. "Why did you bring me here?" Jane looked up, down, side to side, like a little bird caught in a surprise cage. Book tight against her chest, she stared past him, shaking her head. "No." The refusal came out hoarse and soft. She tried again. "Please. No."

"See?" He pointed deeper into the dense woods toward a stone outcropping just beyond a massive tree. "You can see it from here. A sacred place, don't you agree?"

Again, Jane shook her head.

He locked a hand on her arm. "Come on, we'll do this together."

"Don't make me go in there."

"Wouldn't Samantha want you to be brave, Jane?"

She sucked in a breath. "How do you know where Samantha died?" Wrenching out of his grip, she didn't wait for an answer. Sprinting back the way they'd come, she'd gotten no more than twenty feet when, with a yelp, she stopped cold.

The old man in the overcoat blocked her path.

Mark shushed through the leaves to join her. "I think the better question is: How do *you* know?"

Clean shaven now, the old man held his missing beard in one hand and a gun in the other. He shook his head slowly but didn't say a word.

"What's happening?" Jane asked him. "What's going on?"

Mark held out his hand. "Give me the book."

"But . . . it's all I have left of her," she said.

"No," Mark said. "It's all *we* have left of her. Give it to me."

Jane loosened her grip on the blue-bound copy and handed it to him.

Mark removed his glasses, placed them in a pocket, opened the book's front cover and read aloud: "To Laura." The corners of his mouth tugged downward. "May life be your Wonderland, Love, Dad."

"I don't know why it says that," Jane said. "Samantha never explained that inscription."

"How could she?" the old man asked. "She was dead when you took it from her." He holstered his gun beneath his coat. "And her name wasn't Samantha. It was Laura."

"Who are you?" she asked.

He opened his collar wide enough to expose the White Rabbit necklace around his neck. "I'm her father, that's who."

"Samantha's father?" Her mouth dropped open. "The police chief?"

"Laura," he corrected again. "And only an inspector."

"He tricked me into coming here." She pointed at Mark. "He's the one who killed her. Who else could have known where she died?"

"Who else, indeed?" The older man asked. "But what I don't understand is how you lured my daughter in here. She never would have come this way on her own. Never."

"*She* followed me. Really, she did." Jane shook her head vehemently. "You have to believe me. I would never have hurt Samantha. She meant everything to me. Everything. I only took her book so that she'd talk to me."

"She followed you in here?" The old man's voice cracked. "Because you stole her book?"

Jane kept shaking her head. "But it turned out she wasn't my Samantha. Samantha would never have pushed me away. She never would have said such terrible things."

"She *followed* you in here?" he repeated as he grabbed the book from Mark's hands. "For this?" Dropping his head, he pinched the bridge of his nose and covered his eyes.

"Don't you see, there's been a mistake." Jane twisted between the two men. "It's him. He did it."

Mark laid a steadying hand on the older man's shaking shoulders. "We were afraid we'd never find who murdered Laura. But you were right," he said to Jane. "Victims return to the scene of the crime, too. Especially when it's their only chance to catch a killer."

"You're the killer," Jane screeched. "She must have told you how she felt about me. That's how you knew I'd be here today." Turning to the cop, she said, "Don't you see? He bought that book to set me up. He's the one you should be arresting."

As the older man snapped handcuffs on Jane's wrists, Mark pulled his book from the messenger bag. He opened the front cover. "To Mark." His voice trembled and his eyes glistened. "Stay curious as life's adventures unfold. Love, Dad." He waited until the older man looked up again. "I've had this book for a very long time, haven't I?"

The cop's jaw was tight. "Long time."

Jane swallowed. "I don't understand."

"My sister's ritual was to read this book at the statue on her birthday every year," Mark said.

"But . . . how could I know that? She wouldn't talk to me."

"Is that supposed to justify killing her?"

"I didn't mean to hurt her," Jane said. "But she got so angry with me. I couldn't make her understand. When she tried to get away, I lost my temper. I only meant to stop her long enough to listen."

"You stopped her, all right."

"I never would have hurt my Samantha," Jane cried. "It was an accident."

The older man faced her with bared teeth and red eyes. "Let's go."

"But *he* promised me a chance to tell her how I felt." Jane's voice was thin and shrill as she spun to face Mark. "You promised. What about my closure?"

"Her name was Laura," the cop said. "And you'll get your closure in court." He tugged Jane by her handcuffs. "Today, we have ours."

Mark gripped the older man's shoulder. "Good to have you back, Dad."

JULIE HYZY *is a New York Times best-selling author who has won the Anthony, Barry, and Derringer Awards for her crime fiction. She currently writes two amateur-sleuth mystery series for Berkley Prime Crime: the White House Chef Mysteries and the Manor House Mysteries. Her favorite pastimes include traveling with her husband and hanging out with her kids. She lives in the Chicago area.*

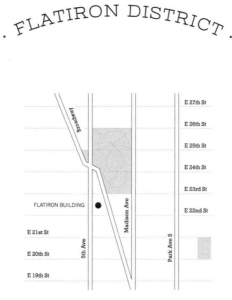

THE PICTURE OF
THE LONELY DINER

Lee Child

Jack Reacher got out of the R train at Twenty-Third Street and found the nearest stairway blocked off with plastic police tape. It was striped blue and white, tied between one handrail and the other, and it was moving in the subway wind. It said: POLICE DO NOT ENTER. Which, technically, Reacher didn't want to do anyway. He wanted to exit. Although to exit, he would need to enter the stairwell. Which was a linguistic complexity. In which context, he sympathized with the cops. They didn't have different kinds of tape for different kinds of situations. POLICE DO NOT ENTER IN ORDER TO EXIT was not in their inventory.

So Reacher turned around and hiked half the length of the platform to the next stairway. Which was also taped off. POLICE DO NOT

ENTER. Blue and white, fluttering gently in the last of the departing train's slipstream. Which was odd. He was prepared to believe the first stairway might have been the site of a singular peril, maybe a chunk of fallen concrete, or a buckled nose on a crucial step, or some other hazard to life and limb. But not both stairways. Not both at once. What were the odds? So maybe the sidewalk above was the problem. A whole block's length. Maybe there had been a car wreck. Or a bus wreck. Or a suicide from a high window above. Or a drive-by shooting. Or a bomb. Maybe the sidewalk was slick with blood and littered with body parts. Or auto parts. Or both.

Reacher half-turned and looked across the track. The exit directly opposite was taped off, too. And the next, and the next. All the exits were taped off. Blue and white, POLICE DO NOT ENTER. No way out. Which was an issue. The Broadway Local was a fine line, and the Twenty-Third Street station was a fine example of its type, and Reacher had slept in far worse places many times, but he had things to do and not much time to do them in.

He walked back to the first stairway he had tried, and he ducked under the tape.

He was cautious going up the stairs, craning his neck, looking ahead, and especially looking upward, but seeing nothing untoward. No loose rebar, no fallen concrete, no damaged steps, no thin rivulets of blood, no spattered fragments of flesh on the tile.

Nothing.

He stopped on the stairs with his nose level with the Twenty-Third Street sidewalk and he scanned left and right.

Nothing.

He stepped up one stair and turned around and looked across Broadway's humped blacktop at the Flatiron Building. His destination. He looked left and right. He saw nothing.

He saw less than nothing.

No cars. No taxis. No buses, no trucks, no scurrying panel vans with their business names hastily handwritten on their doors. No motorbikes, no Vespa scooters in pastel colors. No deliverymen on bikes from restaurants or messenger services. No skateboarders, no roller-bladers.

No pedestrians.

It was summer, close to eleven at night, and still warm. Fifth Avenue was crossing Broadway right in front of him. Dead ahead was Chelsea, behind him was Gramercy, to his left was Union Square, and to his right the Empire State Building loomed over the scene like the implacable monolith it was. He should have seen a hundred people. Or a thousand. Or ten thousand. Guys in canvas shoes and T-shirts, girls in short summer dresses, some of them strolling, some of them hustling, heading to clubs about to open their doors, or bars with the latest vodka, or midnight movies.

There should have been a whole big crowd. There should have been laughter and conversation, and shuffling feet, and the kind of hoots and yelps a happy crowd makes at eleven o'clock on a warm summer's evening, and sirens and car horns, and the whisper of tires and the roar of engines.

There was nothing.

Reacher went back down the stairs and under the tape again. He walked underground, north, to the site of his second attempt, and this time he stepped over the tape because it was slung lower. He went up the stairs just as cautiously, but faster, now right on the street corner, with Madison Square Park ahead of him, fenced in black iron and packed with dark trees. But its gates were still open. Not that anyone was strolling in or strolling out. There was no one around. Not a soul.

He stepped up to the sidewalk and stayed close to the railing around the subway stair head. A long block to the west he saw flashing lights. Blue and red. A police cruiser was parked sideways across the street. A roadblock. DO NOT ENTER. Reacher turned and looked east. Same situation. Red and blue lights all the way over on Park Avenue. DO NOT ENTER. Twenty-Third Street was closed. As were plenty of other cross streets, no doubt, and Broadway and Fifth Avenue and Madison, too, presumably, at about Thirtieth Street.

No one around.

Reacher looked at the Flatiron Building. A narrow triangle, sharp at the front. Like a thin wedge, or a modest slice of cake. But to him it looked most like the prow of a ship. Like an immense ocean liner moving slowly toward him. Not an original thought. He knew many people felt the same way. Even with the cowcatcher glasshouse on the front ground floor, which some said ruined the effect, but which he thought added to it, because it looked like the protruding underwater bulge on the front of a supertanker, visible only when the vessel was lightly loaded.

Now he saw a person. Through two panes of the cowcatcher's windows. A woman. She was standing on the Fifth Avenue sidewalk, staring north. She was wearing dark pants and a dark short-sleeved shirt. She had something in her right hand. Maybe a phone. Maybe a Glock 19.

Reacher pushed off the subway railing and crossed the street. Against the light, technically, but there was no traffic. It was like walking through a ghost town. Like being the last human on earth. Apart from the woman on Fifth Avenue. Whom he headed straight for. He aimed at the point of the cowcatcher. His heels were loud in the silence. The cowcatcher had a triangular iron frame, a miniature version of the shape it was backing up against, like a tiny sailboat trying to outrun the liner chasing it. The frame was painted green, like moss, and it had gingerbread curlicues here and there, and what wasn't metal was glass, whole panels of it, as long as cars, and tall, from above a person's head to his knees.

The woman saw him coming.

She turned in his direction but backed off, as if to draw him toward her. Reacher understood. She wanted to pull him south into the shadows. He rounded the point of the cowcatcher.

It was a phone in her hand, not a gun.

She said, "Who are you?"

He said, "Who's asking?"

She turned her back and then straightened again, one fast fluid movement, like a fake-out on the basketball court, but enough for him to see *FBI* in yellow letters on the back of her shirt.

"Now answer my question," she said.

"I'm just a guy."

"Doing what?"

"Looking at this building."

"The Flatiron?"

"No, this part in front. The glass part."

"Why?"

Reacher said, "Have I been asleep for a long time?"

The woman said, "Meaning what?"

"Did some crazy old colonel stage a coup d'état? Are we living in a police state now? I must have blinked and missed it."

"I'm a federal agent. I'm entitled to ask for your name and ID."

"My name is Jack Reacher. No middle initial. I have a passport in my pocket. You want me to take it out?"

"Very slowly."

So he did, very slowly. He used scissored fingers, like a pickpocket, and drew out the slim blue booklet and held it away from his body, long enough for her to register what it was, and then he passed it to her, and she opened it.

She said, "Why were you born in Berlin?"

He said, "I had no control over my mother's movements. I was just a fetus at the time."

"Why was she in Berlin?"

"Because my father was. We were a Marine family. She said I was nearly born on a plane."

"Are you a Marine?"

"I'm unemployed at the moment."

"After being what?"

"Unemployed for many previous moments."

"After being what?"

"Army."

"Branch?"

"Military Police."

She handed back the passport.

She said, "Rank?"

He said, "Does it matter?"

"I'm entitled to ask."

She was looking past his shoulder.

He said, "I was terminal at major."

"Is that good or bad?"

"Bad, mostly. If I had been any good at being a major, they would have made me stay."

She didn't reply.

He said, "What about you?"

"What about me?"

"Rank?"

"Special Agent in Charge."

"Are you in charge tonight?"

"Yes, I am."

"Outstanding."

She said, "Where did you come from?"

He said, "The subway."

"Was there police tape?"

"I don't recall."

"You broke through it."

"Check the First Amendment. I'm pretty sure I'm allowed to walk around where I want. Isn't that part of what makes America great?"

"You're in the way."

"Of what?"

She was still looking past his shoulder.

She said, "I can't tell you."

"Then you should have told the train not to stop. Tape isn't enough."

"I didn't have time."

"Because?"

"I can't tell you."

Reacher said nothing.

The woman said, "What's your interest in the glass part of this building?"

Reacher said, "I'm thinking of putting in a bid as a window washer. Might get me back on my feet."

"Lying to a federal agent is a felony."

"A million people every day look in these windows. Have you asked them?"

"I'm asking you."

Reacher said, "I think Edward Hopper painted *Nighthawks* here."

"Which is what?"

"A painting. Quite famous. Looking in through a diner's windows, late at night, at the lonely people inside."

"I never heard of a diner called Nighthawks. Not here."

"The night hawks were the people. The diner was called Phillies."

"I never heard of a diner here called anything."

"I don't think there was one."

"You just said there was."

"I think Hopper saw this place, and he made it a diner in his head. Or a lunch counter, at least. The shape is exactly the same. Looked at from right where we're standing now."

"I think I know that picture. Three people, isn't it?"

"Plus the counter man. He's kind of bent over, doing something in the well. There are two coffee urns behind him."

"First there's a couple, close but not touching, and then one lonely guy all by himself. With his back to us. In a hat."

"All the men wear hats."

"The woman is a redhead. She looks sad. It's the loneliest picture I've ever seen."

Reacher looked through the real-life glass. Easy to imagine bright fluorescent light in there, pinning people like searchlight beams, exposing them in a merciless way to the dark streets all around. Except the streets all around were empty, so there was no one to see.

In the painting, and in real life, too.

He said, "What have I walked into?"

The woman said, "You're to stand still, right where you are, and don't move until I tell you to."

"Or what?"

"Or you'll go to prison for interfering with a national security operation."

"Or you'll get fired for continuing with a national security operation after it suddenly got a civilian in the way."

"The operation isn't here. It's in the park."

She looked diagonally across the wide junction, three major thoroughfares all meeting, at the mass of trees beyond.

He said, "What have I walked into?"

She said, "I can't tell you."

"I'm sure I've heard worse."

"Military police, right?"

"Like the FBI, but on a much lower budget."

"We have a target in the park. Sitting on a bench all alone. Waiting for a contact who isn't coming."

"Who is he?"

"A bad apple."

"From your barrel?"

She nodded. "One of us."

"Is he armed?"

"He's never armed."

"Why isn't his contact coming?"

"He died an hour ago in a hit-and-run accident. The driver didn't stop. No one got the plate."

"There's a big surprise."

"He turned out to be Russian. The State Department had to inform their consulate. Which turned out to be where the guy worked. Purely by coincidence."

"Your guy was talking to the Russians? Do people still do that?"

"More and more. And it's getting more and more important all the time. People say we're headed back to the 1980s. But they're wrong. We're headed back to the 1930s."

"So, your guy ain't going to win employee of the month."

She didn't answer.

He said, "Where are you going to take him?"

She paused a beat. She said, "All that's classified."

"All that? All what? He can't be going to multiple destinations."

She didn't answer.

Now he paused a beat.

He said, "Is he headed for the destination you want?"

She didn't answer.

"Is he?"

She said, "No."

"Because of suits higher up?"

"As always."

"Are you married?"

"What's that got to do with anything?"

"Are you?"

"I'm hanging in there."

"So you're the redhead."

"And?"

"I'm the guy in the hat with his back to us, all alone."

"Meaning, what?"

"Meaning, I'm going to take a walk. Like a First Amendment thing. Meaning, you're going to stay here. Like a smart tactical thing."

And he turned and moved away before she had a chance to object. He rounded the tip of the cowcatcher and headed diagonally across the heart of the complex junction, moving fast, not breaking stride at the curbs and the painted lines, ignoring the DON'T WALK signs, not slowing at all, and finally straight into the park itself, by its southwest gate. Ahead was a dry fountain and a closed-up burger stall. Curving left was the main center path, clearly following some kind of a design scheme that featured large ovals, like running tracks.

There were dim fancy lights on poles, and the Times Square glow was bouncing off the clouds like a magnesium flare. Reacher could see pretty well, but all he saw were empty benches, at least at the start of the curve. More came into sight as he walked, but they too stayed empty, all the way to the far tip of the oval, where there was another dry fountain, and a children's playground, and finally the continuation of the path itself, curving down the other side of the oval, back toward the near tip. And it had benches, too.

And one of them was occupied.

By a big guy, all pink and fleshy, maybe fifty years old, in a dark suit. Pouchy face and thinning hair. A guy who looked like his life had passed him by.

Reacher stepped close and the guy looked up, and then he looked away, but Reacher sat down next to him anyway. He said, "Boris or Vladimir or whatever his name was isn't coming. You're busted. They know you're not armed, but they've gone ahead and cleared about twenty square blocks, which means they're going to shoot you. You're about to be executed. But not while I'm here. Not with witnesses. And as it happens, the SAC isn't happy with it. But she's getting pressure from above."

The guy said, "So?"

Reacher said, "So, here's my good deed of the day. If you want to turn yourself in to her, I'll walk with you. Every step of the way. You can tell her what you know, and you can get three squares a day in prison for the rest of your life."

The guy didn't answer.

Reacher said, "But maybe you don't want to go to prison for the rest of your life. Maybe you're ashamed. Maybe suicide by cop is better. Who am I to judge? So my super-good deed of the day is to walk away if you tell me to. Your choice."

The guy said, "Then walk away."

"You sure?"

"I can't face it."

"Why did you do it?"

"To be somebody."

"What kind of stuff could you tell the SAC?"

"Nothing important. Damage assessment is their main priority. But they already know what I had access to, so they already know what

I told them."

"And you've got nothing worthwhile to add?"

"Not a thing. I don't know anything. My contacts aren't stupid. They know this can happen."

"Okay," Reacher said. "I'll walk away."

And he did, out of the park in its northeast corner, where he heard faint radio chatter in the shadows announcing his departure, and a deserted block up Madison Avenue, where he waited against the limestone base of a substantial building. Four minutes later he heard suppressed handguns, eleven or twelve rounds expended, a volley of thudding percussions like phone books slammed on desks. Then he heard nothing more.

He pushed off the wall and walked north on Madison, imagining himself back at the lunch counter, his hat in place, his elbows drawn in, nursing a new secret in a life already full of old secrets.

LEE CHILD *was fired and on the dole when he hatched a harebrained scheme to write a best-selling novel, thus saving his family from ruin. Killing Floor was an immediate success and launched the series, which has grown in sales and impact with every new installment. His series hero, Jack Reacher, besides being fictional, is a kind-hearted soul who allows Lee lots of spare time for reading, listening to music, the Yankees, and Aston Villa. Visit LeeChild.com for info about the novels, short stories, the movie* Jack Reacher, *and more—or find Lee on Facebook.com/LeeChildOfficial, Twitter.com/LeeChildReacher, and YouTube.com/leechildjackreacher.*

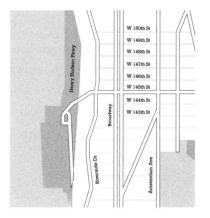

THREE LITTLE WORDS

Nancy Pickard

Priscilla laughed hysterically when her doctor told her she had only a few weeks to live.

When she saw the shocked dismay on his handsome face, she waved away his worry and kept guffawing like a four-year-old who had just heard the funniest knock-knock joke on earth. And, being a preschool teacher, she knew knock-knock jokes and four-year-olds.

Knock, knock. Who's there?

Not me!

Of *course*, she had a rare, virulent, quick-killing cancer.

Of course, she did! It had been that kind of week. Month. Year. *Death could only improve my life,* she thought, and giggled wildly again.

When she finally came out of her initial hysteria and started crying the other kind of tears, her doctor handed her his box of tissues and a long thin notepad. She grabbed both but held up the notepad as she blew her nose.

"What's this for?"

"Some of my patients like to make bucket lists."

"Oh, God," she said, rolling her eyes up to stare at him. "You keep a bunch of these pads in your desk? Sucks to be you! It's life's little ultimate to-do list, isn't it? Buy bananas, but not too ripe. Pick up the dry cleaning, but what for? And forget the super-sized laundry soap."

She giggled and sobbed at the same time.

"I can't die, Sam!" She'd been his patient for a long time; he'd seen her through regular checkups and emergencies. If he called her by her first name, she'd long ago made it clear that she'd call him by his. "I don't even have a prearrangement plan with a funeral home!"

He didn't laugh.

"It's not too late," he said carefully.

"There just won't be much 'pre-' to it, will there?"

"No," he said even more gently.

"It's funny, isn't it?"

"No."

"Yeah, it is. I'll be the girl with only one thing on her bucket list."

"What?"

"Live longer."

He looked as if he might cry.

"I'm sorry," she said, feeling bad for him. Her humor was normally softer; incipient death had given her an edge. "It's not your fault."

"It's not anybody's fault," he said, shaking his head and pulling out a handkerchief to wipe his eyes.

Nobody's fault? She wasn't so sure about that.

What about the pollution she breathed, the chemicals she drank? And what about stress? Couldn't that kill you? Well, yes, it looked as if it could, though she probably couldn't prove that to her stressful employer, her stressful parents, her stressful sister, her stressful boyfriend, the stressful parents at DayGlow DayCare with their screaming stressed-out children, the stressful woman with the stressful dog in the next apartment, the stressful man at the food cart with her favorite hot dogs, not to mention all the pedestrians who bumped into her on streets and taxis that honked at her in intersections.

And doctors who told her she was going to die.

He said, "If drugs aren't going to help you, or surgery, or radiation . . . what do you want to do with the time you have left, Priscilla?"

"I'm only twenty-six," she whispered, all her laughter used up now.

"I know." His eyes filled again, but he forced an encouraging smile. "So your list ought to be a lot more fun than the one my hundred-year-old patient just drew up—"

"A hundred years old?" she said wistfully. "I wish."

"It's not so great. Her big moment was drinking cranberry juice in spite of being allergic to it. Go for it, Priss. Go for more than cranberry juice. Don't hold back. Who knows? Maybe happiness will cure you."

He didn't believe that.

She didn't, either.

But as a way to kill time for the next couple weeks, before time killed her, it did beat shooting herself. She said as much to Sam, which made him grimace.

"May I use your pen?"

He handed one to her and then watched her write three words at the top of the pad. She printed them with force, going over each letter multiple times, so that even from across his desk he could see the thick black letters.

She held them up for him to read:

TELL THE TRUTH

His eyebrows shot up. "I was expecting something more along the lines of, 'Ride a roller coaster' or 'Fly to Paris.'" He gestured toward the pad. "That could cause some damage."

"It could do some good," she countered.

As she left his office, he asked her to check in every day.

"For pain control? Or to know when I ought to go into hospice?"

"Yes," he said, and then he hugged her.

She clung to his white jacket for a moment. "Thank you for telling *me* the truth," she whispered, and then she bravely walked away.

She called him on each of the next three days.

On the fourth morning, Dr. Samuel Waterhouse's tearful receptionist brought in a newspaper that explained why they wouldn't get a call that day.

———— · — · — · ————

The night before, Priscilla Windsor had been stabbed to death as she walked—running was no longer possible—in the late cool twilight along Riverside Drive. The redbud trees would blossom into mauve by the next morning, but she wouldn't see them. She had hoped to live long enough to see spring, but she had also been afraid of seeing it, fearing that it would fill her with unbearable longing for more life. On the night she died, the buds were still wrapped tight as tiny boxers' fists, as if they didn't want to pound her with the bittersweet pain of seeing them open their petals.

Witnesses saw her stumble near the dog park, saw a person in sweats and a hoodie stoop to lift her up, saw them huddle for a moment, saw him set her upright, saw him prop her against a tree, saw him pat her shoulder, saw him continue on his own run. They thought, *Aw, nice guy.* They smiled toward his unidentifiable back as he ran faster than before. When he turned a corner, they remembered to look back at the woman he'd so kindly helped.

They saw her sway, and then slide down the tree, and not get up again.

"Oh, my God," a woman said, pulling her dog closer on its chain.

Other people hurried to check on the fallen woman; there was shock when they saw blood, horror at the knife, then confusion as they figured out who among them should call 911. The Upper West Side of New York City was a neighborhood, and even if they didn't personally know this young woman, they knew they wanted to help her.

"Are you sure it was a man?" one of them asked as they compared notes on what they'd witnessed. "I really thought it was a woman."

"But we're all agreed he was white, right? Or *she* was?"

But they weren't agreed on that, either. Nor on tall or medium height, or stocky or thin build, or even whether the perpetrator had come up to the woman after she stumbled or had in fact caused the stumble. The hoodie was black, gray, red, or navy. There were fifteen eyewitnesses, and the cops joked later that you'd have thought they were all looking in different directions at fifteen different women being killed by fifteen different perps. One eyewitness swore there might have been two people who stopped to "help."

It had the earmarks of a random killing by a random crazy person, people said. She had been in the wrong place at the wrong time. It was the very randomness of it—in a public place, in front of lots of people, on a lovely evening—that made it so frightening. The truth was, they would have felt safer if the killer had specifically, and with malice, set out to kill *this particular woman*, instead of just stumbling onto the easiest person to stab.

———— · —— · —— · ————

Sam Waterford rarely attended the funerals of his patients, and he felt nervous about going to this one. At one such ceremony, years ago, he'd been screamed at by a family, and he didn't want that to happen again. The family filed a malpractice suit the next day. They lost because he hadn't done anything wrong. But ever since, he hadn't wanted to remind other grieving families of his failures, or what they perceived as such.

The church on West End Avenue was packed, reflecting the social status of Priscilla's parents, who were the head of a famous brokerage firm (her father) and the head of an even more famous charitable foundation (her mother). He paused at the back of the sanctuary for a moment and then walked down the center aisle so that he could slide between two couples in a pew near the front. When he glanced to his right, he didn't recognize the stylish couple who had made room for him. But when he faced left, he found a very tanned older woman already grinning at him.

"Dr. Waterford," she said, "do you recognize me with my clothes on?"

"Mrs. Darnell," he said, smiling as if he hadn't heard that joke a million times before. Her first name was Bunny, but he didn't use it to address her. "How are you?"

"I suppose you'll find out at my next appointment."

He smiled again. She was as rich as chocolate torte and as thin as someone who never ate it, which was how she fit into her black Chanel ensemble, a perfect funeral suit.

"Poor thing," she murmured, meaning, he supposed, the deceased and not him.

Then the organ music swelled, and the service began.

He spent it staring at the family and feeling anxious.

He could see them clearly in profile from where he sat. It was easy to pick out the elegant mother, the portly middle-aged father, the older sister who looked like a harder version of Priscilla.

They are remarkable, he thought.

In a packed sanctuary filled with the sounds of soft weeping, the air thick with the awareness of tragedy, they sat rigid and dry-eyed. Mr. Windsor did not put his arm around Mrs. Windsor. The mother never looked at her daughter. None of them wiped away a tear. It was hard to imagine anyone disliking Priss, but it appeared that either her own family was holding in torrents of emotion, or else they loathed the daughter and sister they had lost. He had seen this posture before—in hospitals, on the deaths of patients whose families did not love them.

At the close of the service, Mrs. Darnell said, none too quietly, "Well! Wasn't *that* just the oddest funeral you've ever attended?"

A woman in front of them turned around.

"Strangest ever," she said.

Startled, Sam looked questioningly at his patient.

"What? You didn't notice? They hardly mentioned her! Barely even said her name! Such a lovely girl, so giving and generous, and not a word about any of that. Nothing about her childhood, or even her education—and she went to fine schools, believe you me. I'll grant you, too many funerals these days go overboard into a dreadful sea of sentimentality, but this went too far onto dry land. There's restraint, and then there's looking as if you don't give a damn about your own child! When is the last time you went to a funeral where fifteen distant cousins twice removed didn't get up to speak about how close they were to the deceased, telling all those family stories that nobody else gives a hoot about?"

She was right, he realized. He'd been so wrapped up in theorizing about the Windsors that he'd barely noticed the entire service was nothing but hymns, Scripture readings, prayers, and a quick stiff homily from a minister who didn't seem to have even met Priscilla. That was explained when Mrs. Darnell gossiped on, saying, "This isn't even their church, you know. Maybe they couldn't get in when they wanted to, but I'll bet you this church now has a nice endowment for a new set of choir robes. Or something. But what an impersonal service! Why, even my church lets people get up and lie flatteringly about the deceased, and we're Episcopalian!"

They were rising to their feet, along with the rest of the crowd, when a man's deep voice cried out. "Wait! Wait! I want to say something about her!"

People stopped, stared, looked at each other.

"Uh-oh," Mrs. Darnell said, looking maliciously pleased.

"She was an angel!" the man said. "Is no one going to tell about how she was an angel? Sit, sit! Let me tell you what she did for me!"

"Pakistani, do you think?" Mrs. Darnell whispered.

People sank down again in the pews, a little anxiously, shooting glances toward the family in the front row. Sam watched the sister turn around to check out the speaker, but she quickly faced forward again, as if her mother, seated next to her, had pulled her back. The father's left shoulder jerked hard, once, and that was it. The three of them returned to sitting like statues.

"She must have bought a hot dog from me twice a week, every week, for the whole last year," the man said in a voice that penetrated every corner of the large room. "She said I had the best hot dogs in New York City! And I treated her like I treat everybody—I yelled at her to hurry up, to give me her order, to move along. She smiled at me; I never smiled back. She said thank you, but I never did. Then, the day before she was killed—the day before!—she came early to my stand, and she said . . ." His voice faltered. He pulled out a handkerchief and blew his nose. "She said she'd give me *five thousand dollars* if I was nice to all of my customers for the entire day."

Audible gasps arose from the audience.

"Five thousand dollars!" he said again, sharing the crowd's astonishment and skepticism—even though it was well known in the city that Priss Windsor had once given away a three million dollar inheritance from her godfather.

"A crazy girl, I thought," the man confessed. "But five thousand is five thousand, so I said, what would I have to do? And she said, you have to be kind to people, you have to smile at them, and say things courteously. You have to thank them for their business, and you can't throw things at them!"

He shook his head. "Sometimes, it's true, I hate it when people pay in pennies and nickels. Sometimes, it's true, I throw it all back at them."

He made fast work of the rest of the story. How she gave him half the amount to start, how she had brought a blanket and sat on the grass to observe him, and how she gave him grins and thumbs-up as his courteousness improved throughout the day. And how, at the end of the day, she gave him the rest of the five thousand dollars, and he gave her a free hot dog.

"She was an angel," he said, turning toward the family whose faces had not turned toward him. "She changed my life that day. My wife says thank you, too!"

There was a low murmur of chuckles.

"I just want to say all that, and how sorry I am that she . . . I was so shocked when I saw . . ."

His voice trailed off, and he sat down.

But then he popped back up again.

"Somebody has to speak for the dead!" he proclaimed. "She says, 'Be kind.' Thank you." He sat down again, flushed with exertion and emotion.

Someone else stood up, a pretty young woman.

"He's right, Priss really *was* an angel, and she was funny! I was in a taxi with her two days before she died, and right after we got in, the driver laid on his horn something awful. Priscilla leaned forward and told him that she'd give him a hundred dollars if he didn't honk for the whole rest of the ride—"

There were little explosions of laughter among the crowd of frequent taxi riders.

"And he didn't! When he let us off, he grinned at her and he said, 'So what will you give me if I don't honk for the rest of the day?'"

At that, nearly the entire crowd laughed, the kind of heartwarming, affectionate laughter that makes shocked and grieving people feel better.

"What did Priss say to him?" a man called out.

The young woman turned a trembling smile toward him. Her eyes shone with tears. "She said that she and several million people in Manhattan would give him their everlasting gratitude." Again, the crowd burst into laughter. "And then he said, the driver said, 'Is it okay if I tap on my horn if I need somebody to move back at a stop light?' And Priss laughed and said, 'What? You think fifteen cars behind you won't beat you to it?'"

There was laughing and clapping, but not from the family, Sam noted. Their shoulders did not shake with laughter; they still did not dab tears from their eyes. Whatever was damming them up inside did not give way.

As yet another mourner got up and started to tell a story, Sam saw Mrs. Windsor give a sharp sign to the minister to get his attention. Then she pointed to the organist, making it clear what she wanted.

Almost immediately, the music rose to Bachian heights, drowning out the testimonials. Ushers walked rapidly into place at the ends of pews and began to move the big, and now boisterous, crowd out of the sanctuary.

Shocked, Sam realized he might have just heard evidence of Priscilla Windsor's bucket list: *Tell the truth.* He wondered, *If this was what she did with strangers, what was on her list for people she knew well?*

"Now, that was more like it," Mrs. Darnell said approvingly as they rose to their feet. "Even if Maggie hated it. Did you see how fast she got that minister to move? Oh, well, at least we had a little fun, and that dear girl would be glad, I'm sure of it. You're going to the reception now?"

"No. I wasn't invited. I don't know the family."

"Oh, well, bosh to that. You just crook your well-tailored arm and let me hold your elbow, and I'll get you in as if you live there. I'm assuming Priscilla was your patient, although I know you won't tell me so. You know us better than our husbands do, and that makes you at least as close to her as family. Closer, in the case of *her* family, and don't you ever tell anybody I ever said so!"

Sam smiled at her. "I won't."

A few pews from the exit, he managed to ease away when Mrs. Darnell wasn't looking and lose himself in the crowd. He wanted to chase down the last person who had risen to speak, the one who had been defeated by Bach.

A floral dress, puffy hair, a round face.

He spotted her standing between two younger women, and immediately he intuited whom they might be: teachers at the preschool where Priscilla had worked, a school so unfashionable that it didn't even have a waiting list. They looked unfashionable themselves amid the chic crowd. The older woman looked like somebody a child might run to for a hug.

She didn't smile when he said, "Excuse me."

"Yes?"

"You started to get up, in the sanctuary just now, to say something about Priscilla—"

"Yes."

"I'm sorry you didn't get to. Would you mind telling me what it was?"

"Who are you?"

"Oh, I'm sorry. My name is Sam Waterhouse. I was her doctor."

"Oh." She looked tired, harried, and a lot less huggable up close. "I was only going to say that the children and parents at our preschool adored her. I thought it might bring us some business. Do you have grandchildren?"

He was taken aback by her cold words and sharp eyes—and by her assigning grandchildren to him before his time.

"I have a son in fourth grade."

"Really?" The single word had an amused tone that offended him, as if it tickled her that a man his age could have a child that young. He thought the woman tactless and unpleasant; no wonder her preschool didn't have a waiting list.

"I liked her," he said on Priss's behalf. "I liked her very much. I thought maybe you were going to tell a funny story about her."

She snorted and eyed the young women on either side. What she didn't see was how they eyed each other the moment she turned her attention back to him. "The story I could tell wouldn't be so nice," she said. "I fired her last week." She finally smiled, but it had a smirky edge. "Maybe not the right story for a funeral, hm? What kind of doctor did you say you are?"

"Ob-gyn."

"Oh. I was sure you'd say psychiatrist." She smirked again and walked away.

One of the young women went with her, but the second woman lingered and said quietly, "Don't pay any attention to her. She was always jealous of how much the kids and parents liked Priss more than her. And she's still furious about what Priscilla did."

"What did she do?"

"She read a couple of parents the riot act. Which they *so* had coming!"

"When was this?"

"The day she died." Her eyes filled with tears. "It's so awful, to think her last memory of us was of getting fired, but I think she knew that the rest of us loved her for it. Susan"—she pointed a thumb back over her shoulder in the direction the floral dress had gone—"won't cross our parents for any reason, because she doesn't want to lose their money. It drives us crazy. The parents Priss yelled at used to pick up their kids any ol' time they wanted to, even if they were two hours late, or even later! No call ahead, no making plans with our permission. No consideration for us at all, and their poor kids felt abandoned, even though we lied and told them their mom and dad weren't the jerks they really are."

"And Priss—Priscilla—told them off?"

"Did she ever! It was beautiful! Shocked the heck out of them. And us! They pulled their kids out of the school right then, even though Susan fired Priss in front of them and apologized until I wanted to puke."

"Did Priss say anything to you about a bucket list?"

"Isn't that something people do when they know they're going to die?" Her hands flew to her mouth. "Oh, my gosh. Do you think she had a premonition?"

"No, no, I just—"

"She did say that telling off those people was something she'd always wanted to do. Well, not *always,* but you know what I mean."

That sounded very bucket list–like to him, especially when combined with the incidents involving the hot-dog vendor and taxi driver.

He wanted to ask the young woman a question that was going to sound rude no matter how he phrased it, so he just said it plainly: "Why did Priss go to work there, do you know?"

She smiled a little. "You mean, when she had all this?" She swept her right arm in an arc, indicating the signs of money around them, in the clothes, in the hair colors, in the address of the church, in the limos and cabs waiting at the curb outside.

"I guess I do mean that. And also—" He gestured in the direction of the floral dress.

"Oh, she's nice when she interviews you," the young woman said. "All cookies and teddy bears. You only find out later how she really is. And we never knew about this." Her glance took in the crowd. "We thought Priss was just like us, only nicer." She smiled again, a sweet smile. "All I knew was that she had a degree in early childhood education, and she needed a job, just like us. Well, I guess she didn't *need* one, but she wanted it. I have a theory, now that I've seen all this . . ."

He cocked his head, the way he did to encourage patients to tell him all their symptoms.

"I think she walked into DayGlow DayCare and saw the real situation: a witch of an owner, an unhappy staff, the effect that had on the kids. And she decided she could change it. Change us. I think she went to work there because she was one of those people who makes other people feel good just to be around her."

"And did she have that effect?"

The woman nodded. "Slowly. It was happening. We—the staff— were happier. The kids were having more fun and learning better. Susan was the roadblock, and parents like those two that Priss told off." She started to cry openly. "I'm going to miss her so much."

If she'd been his patient, he would have hugged her.

He hugged her anyway.

———— · — · — · ————

"Are you ready?"

He turned at the sound of Bunny Darnell's voice and told her he was.

"Who was that cute little thing?"

"She teaches at the preschool where Priscilla worked."

"Ah." For the first time, her face and her voice softened. "Priss was a nice child." Then her expression and tone turned wry again. "How she came out of *that* family, I'll never understand." She gave him a slanted look. "Oh, I could tell you stories."

"I wish you would."

"Really? I've *never* heard you gossip about your patients. It's one of the reasons we all go to you, you know. You keep our secrets. Are you going to change my idolatrous image of you?"

"God forbid." He smiled. "But I'm not the one who would be telling the stories, and I wouldn't be passing them along to anyone else."

"Oh." She laughed a little. "Good points. In that case, get in our car and prepare to be shocked."

———— . — . — . ————

But he wasn't shocked. Not by the stories of Priscilla's father's shady business practices, and not by the stories of how her mother lavished big salaries on herself and her staff toadies instead of spending all she should on the charitable organization she led. Even when Mrs. Darnell confided that Priscilla had gotten pregnant at sixteen, he didn't react with surprise.

"You're not even surprised at that?"

"I was her doctor. Even teenagers get stretch marks."

"So you could tell."

He didn't acknowledge her statement.

"Did she tell you that her parents kicked her out of the house? If you must know, she came to me for help. I took her in and gave her spending money. And then, may God forgive me, I left her with my housekeeper and fled to Europe and didn't return until it was over. She put it up for adoption, you know. It was a terribly lonely time for her, I'm sure."

It amused him that she'd said "If you must know," as if he were pressing her to tell him all these things that flowed out as if she'd kept them locked up a long time and was glad at last to say them aloud.

"Why did she go to you for help?" he asked.

She looked surprised at the question. "Well, because I was her godmother. Didn't you know?"

He did know. It was why he'd sat down beside her. "I guess I'd forgotten."

He glanced at her husband, who was driving the Jaguar through Central Park from the west side to the east.

"Then . . ." Sam left his awkward question unasked.

She laughed. "You're thinking of the godfather who left her the three million? That was my first husband, George. It wasn't easy for George to give money away. I nearly had to threaten to kill him if he didn't put her in his will. She was cut out of her parents' will. I wanted her to have something, even if it took her a long time to get it. Then, when George got so sick, I had to tell him, please, she isn't in so much of a hurry for it. But it was too late. He was gone, and she wasn't broke anymore."

"But then she gave it all away."

"I should have realized she might. She didn't want to be anything her parents are, including rich. And she took to heart that Bible verse that causes so many of us anxious nights."

"Which one?"

"The one about how it's harder for a rich man to get into heaven than for a camel to pass through the eye of a needle."

Her husband smiled at the traffic ahead of him.

Sam stared out a window. "Do you think she's in heaven?"

"She'd better be, or what's a heaven for, if it won't take angels?"

"Do you want to end up in heaven?"

"Why do you think we take all those trips to Egypt? I'm searching for pygmy camels."

He laughed. "That's still going to take a very big needle, isn't it?"

For the first time, her husband spoke. "You've never heard of the Seattle Space Needle?"

Sam laughed again. He liked these people.

After a bit, he said, "I understand why you can't stand her parents."

She nodded. "Loathsome people. No mercy. From them to her, or from me to them."

———— · — · — · ————

Bunny Darnell's husband magically found a parking space near the Frick museum, and then he threaded their trio smoothly past a doorman and into an elevator that opened directly into a penthouse apartment.

"Buffet to starboard," Mrs. Darnell advised Sam. "Drinks to port, host and hostess receiving guests amidships, in front of the windows. Will you want a ride back with us?"

"I'll get myself home. Thank you."

"No problem," she said, adding, "as the young ones say, though I wish they wouldn't. Whatever happened to a simple gracious 'You're welcome'?"

She then surprised him by placing a hand lightly on his shoulder to give herself a boost up to kiss his cheek.

"If you're lucky, they won't remember you," she whispered, causing him to turn to her so sharply that he knocked her briefly off balance. Sam grasped her elbow to steady her.

He apologized as people around them stared with concern at her and disapproval at him.

Bunny Darnell looked straight into his eyes and said quietly but firmly, "Don't be sorry for what you've done, Sam."

He stared as she walked away, then he turned blindly toward the windows.

When he could think clearly again, he joined a line of people waiting to speak to the family. All around, he heard comments marveling at the view of Central Park. He looked out over its trees, on toward his beloved West Side, and wished he were there with his wife and son, inside his own happy family, instead of here, intimately, on the East Side, with an unhappy one.

When a white-jacketed waiter went down the line with a silver tray and wine, Sam was tempted, but he decided he'd better keep his wits about him.

———— · — · — · ————

"I was her doctor," Sam told her mother quietly.

"I know who you are," she said coldly.

She'd been his patient, too, years before—right up until the day she'd taken Priss to him for a pregnancy test.

"May I speak to you privately?" he asked.

She stepped back, indicating with a head gesture that he should follow her to the window ledge behind her.

"Excuse me for asking something that will seem none of my business, but did Priscilla speak to you in the days before she died?"

"Speak to us? If you mean, come here without warning after years of saying nothing to us, then yes, she did. If you mean, did she speak the same unspeakable things she said to us years ago, yes, she did. And I'm assuming she spoke them to you as well, or you wouldn't be here asking this question. I have to give you credit, Doctor. Apparently, you have never spoken of them to anyone else, because I think we would hear about it if you had broken your vow of confidentiality. So I will *confide* in you, Doctor, that my elder daughter was a hateful destructive liar, not the saint some people think she was."

He felt his own anger rise along with hers.

He'd intended to ask if she knew about her daughter's fatal condition. He thought it might comfort them to know the killer hadn't taken away a long life from Priscilla, hadn't deprived her of marriage, a career, children, future friends, and meaningful years. The cancer was going to steal all that, regardless.

Now he didn't feel like offering a single word of comfort.

It sounded to him as if Priss had given her family one last chance. She had told the truth, and once again they had rejected it and her.

He leaned in toward her mother. "If you ever want to know the real truth, Mrs. Windsor, I have the baby's DNA. All you have to do is have your husband come in with a sample of his—"

She slapped him.

"Hey, hold up!"

When he stopped his fast walk to the elevator and turned, he was so unnerved that he could feel the blood drain from his face—which must, he thought, make her slap stand out like finger paint on his pale face.

The young woman chasing him down looked so like his late patient that he nearly blurted "Priscilla—"

As she got closer, the eerily strong resemblance vanished; she was younger than Priss, but looked older.

"Ha!" she said. "For a minute you thought I was her, didn't you? I've spooked a whole lot of people today. So much fun. Speaking of which, what'd you do to piss off my mother?"

"I said something she didn't want to hear. You're Priss's younger sister?"

"Yeah, I'm Sydney." She laughed again. "I hope you think of something else offensive to say to my mother. That was very entertaining. Who are you, anyway?"

"I was her doctor."

"Mom's?"

"Well, yes, at one time. But I meant your sister's."

He saw a look of distaste cross her face. "Do you know, if she hadn't given away all that money, I might be three million dollars richer now?"

"What makes you think she'd have left it to you?"

She gave him a sharp look. "And that's your business how?"

When he didn't answer, she said, with a lift of her chin and an unpleasant smirk, "At least she left me her boyfriend. Although, to be honest, I stole him a little earlier than that."

Sam followed her glance to a dark-haired young man slouched against a wall, the sole of his left shoe propped against the gorgeous wallpaper, his hands crossed behind his back as he rested his weight on them. The propped foot made Sam feel like a grumpy old codger;

he realized that his first thought was: *No manners, no respect for other people's property. Figures, for a jerk who'd let one sister steal him away from the other sister.* He felt pained on Priscilla's behalf, but then thought maybe she'd got the better end of that particular bargain. The stolen boyfriend and the thieving sister deserved each other.

"Why didn't your parents hold the service at their own church?" he asked.

"Because our minister might have said nice things about Priss."

"Wow."

"Hey, she's lucky they didn't hire a funeral home."

"All this punishment just for being an unmarried pregnant teenager?"

Sydney shot him a furious look, which he received as an equal match to his own fury at all of them.

"What about you?" he asked her very quietly.

"What *about* me?"

"Your father—"

"Shut up! If you say anything else, I'll slap you, too."

Sydney turned away so fast that her long hair swung across her shoulders.

Seeing hostile looks from people around him, Sam continued on to the elevator and took it down, descending in regal solitude because no one wanted to ride with him.

———— · — · — · ————

Out on the street, Sam checked his phone.

His receptionist had texted: *Cop wants to talk to you.* She had left no name but did give him a number, which he called immediately.

The man who answered said, "Dr. Waterhouse. Thanks for calling me back. I'd like to talk to you about the murder of Priscilla Windsor. Where are you right now, sir?"

"Just leaving the funeral reception at her parents' place."

"Well, that's a lucky coincidence, because I'm waiting outside there. By any chance, are you tall and handsome, with ridiculously great silver hair, wearing a really nice gray suit?"

"I think you have me confused with Richard Gere. I'm medium height, mid-fifties, black suit, graying brown hair."

"Oh, okay, I've got you now. I guess we can't all be Richard Gere. But, really, you're not so far from George Clooney."

"Detective . . ."

"Paul Cantor. Turn left, look ten yards down for a short bald guy in a blue suit that he won't let his wife throw out."

They shook hands, crossed over to the Central Park side of the street, and found a bench, where they sat with their backs to the park and their faces toward traffic.

Without a word, the detective handed Sam a long thin piece of notepaper with Sam's name and office information at the top. Under that were the words TELL THE TRUTH, and then a list with an asterisk in front of each entry.

* ~~Hotdog guy~~
* ~~Dog lady~~
* ~~Taxi drivers~~
* ~~Sydney/Allen~~
* ~~The Awful Parents~~
* ~~The Other Awful Parents~~
* Dustin

All but the last entry had a single line drawn through it, as if each had been taken care of and then crossed off. Additional asterisks followed down the page, but nothing was listed beside them; she had either meant to add more or figured she already had plenty.

"Where'd you find this, Detective?"

"In her fanny pack. Do you have any idea what it is?"

"It's a bucket list," Sam informed him, and then he detailed the facts of the illness that had been set on killing Priscilla until someone took its chance away.

"Ah, some of this explains the funeral," the detective said.

"I think so."

"Hot-dog guy. That was amazing."

"She was an amazing young woman."

"Five thousand bucks. Makes me wish I'd had a chance to be rude to her, too."

Sam laughed.

"You liked her?" the cop asked him.

"Oh, yes. She was a genuinely nice person."

"Who might want to kill her?"

"What? It wasn't a random guy?"

"We have a witness who saw somebody dressed like a runner near her building. Leaning against it, like he was waiting. Straightened up when she came out. Started walking, as if following her. Crossed a street when she did, turned the direction she did, and kept going after her. It didn't look dangerous at the time, our witness says; it looked more casual. But that's a hell of a casual coincidence—that he'd just happen to be hanging out near her building."

"I don't know what to say. Wow. That's"—Sam stared at the traffic going by—"really awful. I can't imagine who—"

The cop shrugged. "I'm thinking it wasn't the hot-dog guy or that taxi driver."

"Yeah." Sam glanced at the detective. "I heard a story you didn't hear. Remember the woman who got up to say something, but she never got a chance?"

"There were people popping up all over the place. I was at the back. I could see all of them. Which one was she?"

"Floral dress. Middle aged. Close to the front."

"What was her story?"

"That she fired Priscilla the day she died."

"She was going to tell *that*?"

"Well, no, she was going to say that all the little kids loved Priscilla."

"Then why fire her?"

"For telling the truth." Sam told the whole story, according to both women, as it had been told to him.

"So that would be 'The Awful Parents,' I guess. But who are 'The Other Awful Parents'?"

"Her own, I think. Or vice versa."

"So that could explain the incredibly impersonal service. I've never seen one like it. All those fancy people there to hear nothing about her, at least not until the mourner rebellion."

"Mourner rebellion." Sam nodded. "That's what it was."

"The mom and dad looked as if they'd wandered into a funeral for a stranger."

"I just got slapped by one of them."

The detective's eyes widened. "What did you do, tell them you liked her?"

"I suggested to her mom that if she ever wants to know for sure whether her husband had molested their daughter, I still have some DNA that could prove it one way or the other."

"Holy moly, Doc. Let's walk while you tell me more."

As they got up to enter the park, the detective pointed to the bucket list. "Who are Sydney and Allen, do you know?"

"Sydney is the sister who hated Priss for giving away three million dollars to charity, and I'm guessing that Allen is Priss's boyfriend who cheated on her with her sister."

"Man, oh, man," the detective said. "Am I ever glad you gave her a piece of paper with your name on it." He laughed a little. "What about this last name? Dustin."

"Don't know," he said, lying.

As they parted, the detective said, "Don't worry. We'll catch her killer the easy way—with surveillance video."

Sam's heart picked up its pace.

He had worried about exactly that possibility.

He steadied his voice: "A camera in the park?"

"No, across the street from her building."

For the first time that day, Sam felt beyond nervous, beyond anxious, and deep into frightened. When he shook hands in farewell, he hoped his palm wasn't as sweaty as he feared it was.

At the last minute, he found the nerve to ask, "Have you looked at it yet?"

"The video?" The cop shook his head. "No, but I hear it's good stuff. See ya, Doc. You gave me good stuff, too. Thanks."

Sam got his breathing under control and then called home just to hear his wife's voice. She was an architect, working from their house.

"How's tricks?" she answered, their habitual query.

"Okay. How are you and Eric?"

They had a ten-year-old son, the light of both of their lives.

He would have been adopted if they'd gone through proper channels, if Sam hadn't put the proper papers under his patient's nose and whisked them away to be shredded after Priscilla signed them. No one was ever supposed to know her baby was a child of incest; Eric was only ever supposed to know that he had been loved by a young mom who couldn't keep him. And when the time came for him to ask about her, she would have vanished into bureaucratic thin air. He would never know where she was, she would never know where he was, and everybody would be happier for it.

Priss had named him Dustin.

Of course, he would be on her bucket list.

Of course, she would want to see him once more before she died, if only from a painful distance. That's what Sam's wife Cassity had predicted when he told her about Priscilla's diagnosis. His wife, so smart, so empathetic, had immediately cried, with desperation and doom in her voice, "She's going to want to see him, Sam! It's going to ruin his life!"

And ours, Sam had realized at that moment.

At first, he'd tried to convince himself that nothing could happen, for Priscilla couldn't find any of the information she might seek; she didn't possess copies of the paperwork and had been too young to know to ask for them.

But he realized that if she were as determined as he knew she was capable of being, she would then come to him, asking for the information: *Where is my child?*

What would he tell her? He could lie, but that would only lead her to an adoption agency that had never heard of her. He could tell her the truth—that he had fooled her and taken her baby—a revelation that could spiral into disaster.

Maybe she'll be happy I did it, he'd tried to convince himself. *Maybe she'll think it's all for the best.*

But what if she didn't? Could they take that chance?

They could lose Eric.

Losing his medical license would be the least of Sam's punishments; losing Eric would be the very worst. Between those two consequences would be kidnapping charges against him and his wife.

"Honey," Cassity said, interrupting his terrified thoughts, "he's still at school. Are you so busy you've lost track of time?"

"I guess so. Speaking of . . . gotta go. Love you guys."

"Ditto, Doctor."

The dog lady couldn't get her terrier to shut up.

The dog barked. His owner yelled at him. The dog barked again because the owner yelled. The owner yelled again because the dog barked. And around and around they went, barking and yelling, all because of a knock on the door.

"Who is it?" she screamed at her apartment door.

"Police!" a male voice called back.

"Oh, for God's sake, Buddy, be quiet!"

As she unlocked and opened the door with one hand, she held onto the dog with her other arm. "Hang on. Let me get his magic collar and he'll shut up. I guess I'm going to have to keep it on him all the time."

The thick-set man in a blue suit stood in the doorway as she picked up the little dog and scurried to her tiny dining room, where she picked up a collar and struggled to get it onto the pooch.

"It's eucalyptus!" she said to the cop at the door. "Just watch!"

Somehow she got it fastened onto the dog.

Buddy started to make a ferocious charge toward the door, opening his mouth to bark, but a second in he stopped barking.

"See?" his owner crowed. "Magic, I'm telling you."

"What the heck?" the blue-suited cop asked as he stepped inside. "Why'd he stop barking?"

"The collar lets out a spray of eucalyptus scent! He hates it."

"I never heard of that. That's amazing. Where'd you get it?"

"My neighbor, that poor sweet girl, gave it to me the day before she got murdered. That's why you're here, isn't it? To ask me about Priscilla? She was lovely. I know Buddy's barking drove her mad. It drove me crazy, too. But she found out about these magic collars and gave one to me."

"I've got to get one for my dog."

"They're expensive, and it doesn't work on all dogs, I hear."

"It sure works on this one."

"Oh, yes. And Buddy's a barking demon."

The cop, who had crouched to take a look, stood back up. "Yeah, I heard him."

"I don't know anything about her getting killed except that it was horrible, and I'm just broken up about it."

"Did she say anything about being stalked or followed?"

"Oh, my word, no. I never heard anything like that. Was that what happened?" She didn't give him time to answer. "I'll tell you what I did hear, though. When she came down to give me the collar, she was jittery, and she told me she was going to do something she wasn't sure she should do."

"What?"

"She told me she'd had a baby when she was only sixteen, and her parents had kicked her out of the house, and by that time it was too late for an abortion, and she'd put it up for adoption, and she was going to try to find the baby and just get a look at him. That's all she wanted, she said, just to see him one time before she died to make sure he was taken care of. She told me she had cancer. Isn't that ironic? That she had only a short time to live anyway, and then some monster kills her and takes away her only chance to see her only child. It's just so sad and awful. She had the worst luck. Seems so unfair for such a nice person. I'll think of her every time Buddy doesn't bark."

———— · — · — · ————

With a shaking hand, Sam laid his keys on the little curved table in the foyer of his home.

"Cassity?" he called out to his wife. "I'm going to change clothes. Then let's go for a run."

"Okay!" she called back from her office.

Minutes later, they met in the foyer, and she smiled a welcome home for him. It looked forced; there'd been a brittle, frantic quality to her since Priscilla's murder. It hurt his heart to see it in her face and hear it when she spoke to him. Only with Eric did she still seem like herself.

She was tall and athletic, with college-shot-putting shoulders and legs that could pound down tracks as if Olympic medals were at stake.

"I'm rarin' to go," she said, though she sounded weary.

She had on running shoes, pants, and a top; her long dark hair was pulled into a ponytail at the top of her head. *She's so beautiful,* Sam thought, *and such a wonderful mother.* They'd both married late and then waited for many fruitless, disappointing years for the child they both wanted. Nothing had worked, but somehow their marriage grew deeper in a situation that would have weakened many others. He loved her fiercely, thought her brave and tender, brilliant and wonderful. He had felt guilty through all the years of trying to have a baby because it was his biology that failed them. When they finally agreed on adoption, enough years had passed that their ages became a problem on applications.

When fate delivered a chance to give her what she wanted so much, and to do what looked like a good deed in the process, Sam had grabbed it—baby blanket, warm baby, and all. And now his heart felt sick as she yelled toward the back of the house, "Eric, sweetie, your dad and I are going for a run, and I'm going to beat him as usual! Don't go play next door without leaving us a note, okay?"

"Duh, Mom!" their son yelled back. "Go, Dad!"

"We love you!" Sam called with an aching heart. "Go over to the neighbors' now, so we don't have to worry about you!" He waited a moment. "Eric? Yes?"

"Okay, parental unit!"

He nodded, turning toward his wife.

"New running duds?" he asked.

She pirouetted in front of him. "You like?"

"Nice on you. Where's your old gray hoodie?"

"In the trash, where it should have been long ago."

"What about those navy sweatpants you love?"

"Out with the hoodie! Too many holes. You ready?"

She jogged past him and was down the front walk before he got the door closed and locked. As he turned toward her, he thought, *They're going to take Eric away. They're going to tell him the truth about how he came to be, and how he came to be with us. He's going to be thrown into the path of those terrible people. I'm going to prison for kidnapping a baby. She's going to prison for killing his mother, who was dying anyway.*

He heard himself making excuses for Cassity.

"Let's run by the river," he said as he caught up to her.

Night was falling, and soon there would be long, dark spaces between the streetlights.

He couldn't allow these terrible fates to happen; and most of all, he couldn't allow Eric to know the truth about himself and his birth family. Even to be left alone in the world would be better than knowing all the horrible things he might otherwise have learned about *both* of his families.

Sam's cell phone rang. He nearly ignored it, but the long habit of being a doctor awaiting the birth of babies made him stop and turn it on while Cassity jogged in place by his side.

"Doc? It's that cop again. Are you near a computer? I want to send that surveillance video to you and have you see if it looks like any of these people on her list."

"Detective, I haven't met them all."

"You've met more of them than I have."

"Okay. Right now?"

"Yeah. Right now, if you don't mind. Or even if you do."

"Wait?" Sam asked his wife.

She nodded, continuing to jog in place.

By the time Sam reached his computer, the e-mail was already there in his inbox. He clicked the video into action and watched while his heart felt as if it was hammering within every cell of his body, as if it might hammer so hard that it could beat him to death.

The quality was poor, but one thing was clear.

The figure in the hoodie and jogging pants was slouching against the wall of a building, with his hands pressed between his body and the wall and his left foot propped against it.

Sam didn't collapse with relief while the detective was still on the phone with him. But when they hung up, he sank down onto the carpet, crossed his arms over his knees, put his face on his arms, and sobbed into them.

His wife came in, saw him, and ran to him, putting her arms around him. "What? Oh, Sam, honey, what?"

"It was the boyfriend. Priss's boyfriend killed her."

His wife collapsed into him, weeping, too.

"Oh, thank God it wasn't you, Sam."

———— · — · — · ————

A week passed before he could tell her the whole truth that he learned from the detective: Priss broke up with her boyfriend when he became scarily possessive and jealous, her sister told the police, and then Sydney pushed him further and further down that path. To turn him against Priscilla and toward herself, she told him about Priss's former boyfriends, increasing the numbers to spice up the story, claiming that one or two were still in her sister's life while Priss was seeing him. Then, to light the final fuse to his wounded ego and growing rage, she said: "And I'll bet she never even told you she had a baby with another man."

NANCY PICKARD's *short stories have won Anthony, Agatha, Barry, Macavity, and American Short Story awards and have been featured in many "year's best" anthologies. She has been an Edgar Award finalist for her short fiction and for three of her eighteen novels. She has served on the national board of directors of MWA and is a founding member and former president of Sisters in Crime. She lives near Kansas City, where she is working on a novel and percolating future short stories. Her favorite short story is "A Clean, Well-Lighted Place" by Ernest Hemingway, because it says everything that needs to be said and evokes deep feeling and understanding, and it does all that (in her opinion) in clean, well-lighted sentences.*

DAMAGE CONTROL

Thomas H. Cook

She'd been found in the dilapidated Bronx apartment where she'd lived for the past seventeen months. It was a basement apartment and had only a couple small windows, but she'd made it darker still by drawing the curtains. It was so dim inside that the first cop to arrive had stumbled about, looking for a light switch. He'd finally found one only to discover that she'd unscrewed all the light bulbs, even the ones in the ceiling and the fluorescent ones on either side of the bathroom mirror. Neighbors later told police that they hadn't seen a single sliver of light coming from her apartment for well over a month. It was as if the terrible capacity for destruction that I'd glimpsed in her so many years before had at last grown strong enough to consume her entirely.

A Detective O'Brien had related the grim details over the phone, the deteriorated condition of her body being the most graphic, the fact that the smell had alerted the neighbors. Then he'd asked me to meet him at the police station nearest my home. "Just following standard procedure," he'd assured me, "Nothing to worry about."

We'd agreed on a time and date, and so now here I was, dealing with Maddox again, just as I'd done so often before.

"So, tell me, what was your relationship with this young woman?" Detective O'Brien asked immediately after we'd exchanged greetings and I'd taken a seat in the metal chair beside his desk. His tone was casual enough, but there was an implication of something illicit in the word *relationship*.

"We took her in when she was a little girl," I told him.

"How little?"

"She was ten when she came to live with us."

That had been twenty-four years earlier. My family and I had lived in Hell's Kitchen when there'd still been some hell left in it; sex shops and hot-sheet hotels, burnt-out prostitutes offering themselves on the corner of Forty-Sixth and Eighth. Now it was all theaters and restaurants, chartered buses unloading well-heeled senior citizens from Connecticut and New Jersey. Once it had been a neighborhood, bad though it was. Now it was an attraction.

"Us?" Detective O'Brien asked, still with a hint of probing for something unseemly. Had I abused this child? Is that why she'd embraced the darkness? Luckily, I knew that nothing could be further from the truth.

"With my wife and me, and our daughter Lana, who was just a year younger than Maddox," I told him. "She stayed with us for almost a year. We'd planned for her to stay with us indefinitely. Lana had always wanted a sister. But as it turned out, we just weren't prepared to keep a girl like that."

"Like what?"

I avoided the word that occurred to me: *dangerous*.

"Difficult," I said. "Very difficult."

And so I'd sent her back to her single mother and her riotous older brother, hardly giving her a thought since. But now this bad penny had returned, spectacularly.

"How did she come to live with you in the first place?" O'Brien asked.

"Her mother was an old friend of ours," I answered. "So was her father, but he died when Maddox was two years old. Anyway, her mother had lost her job. We were doing well, my wife and I, so we offered to bring Maddox to New York, pay for the private school our daughter also attended. The hope was to give her a better life."

O'Brien's expression said everything: *But instead . . .*

But instead, Maddox had ended up in the morgue.

"Did you know she was in New York?" the detective asked.

I shook my head. "Her mother remarried and moved to California. After that, we lost touch. The last I heard, Maddox was in the Midwest somewhere. After that, we had no idea where she was or what she was doing. What was she doing, by the way?"

"She'd been working as a cashier at a diner on Gun Hill Road," O'Brien told me.

"Maddox was very smart," I said. "She could have . . . done anything."

The detective's eyes told me that he'd heard a story like this one before; a smart kid who'd gotten a great chance but blown it.

I couldn't keep from asking the question. "How did she die? On the phone, you just said her body had been found."

"From the looks of it, malnutrition," O'Brien answered. "No sign of drugs or any kind of violence." He asked a few more questions, wanted to know if I'd heard from Maddox over the last few months, whether I knew the whereabouts of any family members, questions he called "routine." I answered him truthfully, of course, and he appeared to accept my answers.

After a few minutes, he got to his feet. "Well, thanks for coming in, Mr. Gordon," he said. "Like I said when I asked you to come down to the station, it's just that your name came up during the course of the investigation."

"Yes, you said that. But you didn't tell me how my name happened to come up."

"She'd evidently mentioned you from time to time," O'Brien explained with a polite smile. "Sorry for the inconvenience," he added as he offered his hand. "I'm sure you understand."

"Of course," I said, and then I rose and headed for the door, sorry that Maddox's life had ended so early and so badly but also reminding myself that, in regard to my finally pulling the plug on the effort I'd made to help her, she'd truly given me no choice.

At that thought, her image appeared vividly in my mind: a little girl in the rain, waiting for the taxi that would take us to the airport, the way she'd glanced back at me an hour or so later as she headed toward the boarding ramp, her lips silently mouthing the last word she would say to me: *"Sorry."*

But sorry for what? I'd asked myself at that moment, for by then she'd had so much to confess.

——— · — · — · ———

"Did you see her body?"

I shook my head. "There was no need. The building super had already identified her."

"Odd that your name came up at all," Janice said. "That she'd . . . talked about you."

My wife and I sat with our evening glasses of wine, peering down onto a Forty-Second Street that looked nothing at all as it had when Maddox lived with us. Night was falling, and below our twelfth-floor balcony, people were on their way to Broadway, among them a few families with small children, some no doubt headed for *The Lion King.*

"So, she came back to New York," Janice said in that meditative way of hers, like a philosopher working with an idea. After a moment, a dark notion seemed to strike her. "Jack?"

I turned to face her.

"Do you think she ever . . . watched us?"

"Of course not," I said, then took a sip of my wine and eased back, trying to relax. But I found my wife's mention of the possibility that Maddox might, in fact, have stationed herself somewhere near the building where we'd all once lived, and where Janice and I still lived, surprisingly unnerving. Could it be that after all these years, she'd returned to New York with some sort of vengeful plan in mind? Had she never stopped thinking of how I'd sent her back? As her life spiraled downward, had she come to blame me for that very spiral?

"It's sort of creepy to think of her slinking around the neighborhood," Janice said.

"There's no evidence she ever did that," I said in a tone that made me sound convinced by this lack of evidence. And yet, I suddenly imagined Maddox watching me from some secret position, a ghostly, ghastly face hatefully staring at me from behind a potted palm.

Janice took a sip from her glass and softly closed her eyes. "Lana called, by the way. I told her about Maddox."

Lana was now married, living on the Upper West Side. Our two grandsons went to the same fiercely expensive private school that both Lana and Maddox had attended; Lana with little difficulty, Maddox with a full repertoire of problems, accused of stealing, cheating, lying.

"Lana and I are having dinner while you're in Houston," I said.

Janice smiled. "A nice little father–daughter outing. Good for you."

She drew in one of her long, peaceful breaths, a woman who'd had remarkably few worries in her life, who liked her job and got along well with our daughter, and whose marriage had been as unruffled as could have been expected.

With a wife like that, I decided, the less she knew about the one time all that had been jeopardized, the better.

"Lana took it harder than I thought she would," Janice said. "She'd wanted a sister, remember? And, of course, she'd thought Maddox might be that sister."

"Lana's done fine as an only child," I said, careful not to add a far darker truth, that my daughter was, in fact, lucky to be alive, that the year Maddox had lived with us had been, particularly for Lana, a year of living dangerously, indeed.

"We were very naive to have brought Maddox to live with us," Janice said. "To think that we could take a little girl away from her mother, her neighborhood, her school, and that she'd simply adjust to all that." Her gaze drifted over toward the Hudson. "How could we have expected her just to be grateful?"

This was true, as I well knew. During the first nine years of her life, Maddox had known nothing but hardship, uncertainty, disruption. How could we have expected her not to bring all that dreadful disequilibrium with her?

"You're right, of course," I said softly, draining my glass. And with that simple gesture, I tried to dismiss the notion that she'd come to New York with some psychopathic dream of striking at me from behind a curtain, smiling maniacally as she raised a long, sharp knife.

———— · — · — · ————

And so, yes, I tried to dismiss my own quavering dread as a paranoid response to a young woman who'd no doubt come to New York because she was at the end of her tether, and the city offered itself as some sort of deranged answer to a life that had obviously become increasingly disordered. I tried to position my memory of her as simply a distressing episode in all of our lives, with repeated visits to Falcon Academy, always followed by stern warnings to Maddox that if she didn't "clean up her act," she would almost certainly be expelled. "Do you want that?" I'd asked after one of these lectures. She'd only shrugged. "I just cause trouble," she said. And God knows she had, and would no doubt have caused more, a fact I remained quite certain about.

And so, yes, I might well have put her out of my mind at the end of that short yet disquieting conversation with Janice that evening as the sun set over the Hudson, my memory of Maddox destined to become increasingly distant until she was but one of that great body of unpleasant memories each of us accumulates as we move through life.

Then, out of the blue, a little envelope arrived. It had come from the Bronx, and inside I found a note that read: *Maddox wanted you to have something.* It was signed by someone named Theo, who offered to deliver whatever Maddox had left me. If I wanted to "know more," I was to call this Theo and arrange a meeting.

I met him in a neighborhood wine bar three days later, and I have to admit that I'd expected one of those guys who muscled up in prison gyms, cut his initials in his hair, or had enough studs in his lips and tongue and eyebrows to set off airport metal detectors. Such had been my vision of the criminal sort toward which Maddox would have gravitated, she forever the Bonnie of some misbegotten Clyde. Instead, I found myself talking to a well-spoken young man whose tone was quietly informative.

"Maddox was a tenant in my building," he told me after I'd identified myself.

"You're the super who found her?"

"No, I own the building," Theo said.

For a moment, I wondered if I was about to be hit up for Maddox's unpaid rent.

"Sometimes Maddox and I talked," he said. "She usually didn't have much to say, but a few times, when she was in the hallway or walking through the courtyard, I'd stop to chat." He paused before adding: "She'd paid her rent a few months in advance and told the super that she was going away for a while. He assumed she'd done exactly that, just gone away for a while, so he didn't think anything of it when he stopped seeing her around."

"She planned it, you mean," I said. "Her death."

"It seems that way," Theo answered.

So, I thought, *she'd murdered someone at last.*

Theo placed a refrigerator magnet on the table and slid it over to me. "This is what she wanted you to have."

"*Beauty and the Beast,*" I said quietly, surprised that Maddox had held on to such a relic—and certainly surprised that, for some bizarre reason, she'd wanted me to have it. "I took her and my daughter to that show."

"I know," Theo said. "It was the happiest day of Maddox's life. She remembered how you bought the magnet for her and put it in her hand and curled her fingers around it. It was tender, the way you did it, she said, very loving."

I gave the magnet a quick glance but didn't touch it. "Obviously, she told you that she lived with us a while."

He nodded.

"Unfortunately, I had to send her back to her mother," I told him bluntly, picking up the magnet and turning it slowly in my fingers. "She told lies," I added. "She cheated on tests, or, at least, she tried to. She stole." *And that was not the worst of it,* I thought.

All this appeared to surprise Theo, so I suspected he'd been taken in by Maddox, fallen for whatever character she'd created in order to manipulate him. She'd tried to do the same with me, but by then I'd seen how dangerous she was and had acted accordingly.

"And so I sent her back," I said. "I'm sure that's what she wanted all along."

Theo was silent for a moment before he said, "No, she wanted to stay."

Perhaps at the very end, Maddox truly had wanted to stay with us, I thought. But if so, that only meant she'd have done whatever she had to do to accomplish that goal. In fact, I decided, that might well have been the reason she'd done what she'd done that night in the subway station.

"She was capable of anything," I told Theo resolutely.

At that point, I actually considered telling Theo the whole story, but then found that I couldn't.

After a moment, Theo nodded toward the refrigerator magnet. "Anyway," he said, "It's yours now."

———— · — · — · ————

"What are you supposed to do with it?" Janice asked when I showed her the *Beauty and the Beast* refrigerator magnet. She made her well-known and purposely exaggerated trembling notion. "It feels like some kind of . . . accusation."

Suddenly it all became clear. "It's Maddox's way of giving me the finger just one last time," I said. "Making me feel guilty for sending her back. But she was the one who made it impossible for her to become a part of our family." I shook my head vehemently. "So, I'm just going to stop thinking about her."

I wanted to do just that, but I couldn't.

Why? Because for me, it had never been "to be or not to be, that is the question." It was what a human being learned or failed to learn while on this earth. For that reason, I couldn't help but wonder if Maddox had ever acknowledged in the least what I'd hoped to do for her by bringing her into my family, or if she had accepted the slightest responsibility for the fact that I'd had to abandon that effort. With Maddox dead, how could I pursue such an inquiry? Where could I look for clues? The answer was bleak but simple, and so the very next day I took the train up to the Bronx.

Maddox had lived in one of the older buildings on the Grand Concourse. I'd gotten the address from Detective O'Brien, who'd clearly had more important things on his mind, a girl who'd starved herself to death no longer of much note.

Theo was in the courtyard when I arrived. He was clearly surprised to see me.

"Have you rented out Maddox's apartment yet?" I asked.

He shook his head.

"Would you mind letting me see it?"

"No," Theo answered casually.

He snapped a key from the dangling mass that hung on a metal ring from his belt. "They're coming to clear out her stuff tomorrow."

"Did she have a diary, anything like that? Letters?"

He shook his head. "Maddox didn't have much of anything."

This was certainly true. She'd lived sparely, to say the least. In fact, from the drab hand-me-down nature of the furnishings, I gathered that she'd picked up most of what she owned from the street. In the kitchen I found chipped plates. In the bedroom I found a mattress without a bed, along with a sprawl of sheets and towels. When she'd lived with us, she'd been something of a slob, and I could see that nothing in that part of her personality had changed.

"That day you told me about," I said to Theo after my short visit to Maddox's apartment, "the day we all went to see *Beauty and the Beast*. Did she say why she thought that was the happiest day of her life?"

Theo shook his head. "No, but it was clear that it meant a great deal to her, that day."

I remembered "that day" very well, and on the subway back to Manhattan, I recalled it again and again.

It wasn't just that day that returned to me. I also recalled the many difficult weeks that had preceded it, causing a steady erosion in my earlier confidence that Maddox would adjust well to New York, that she would succeed at Falcon Academy and, from there, go on to a fine college, her road to a happy life as free of obstacles as Lana's.

At first, Maddox had been on her best behavior, though in ways that later struck me as transparently manipulative. She'd complimented Janice on her cooking, Lana on her hair, me on my skill at playing Monopoly. On the first day of school, she'd appeared eager to do well; she had even seemed proud of her uniform. "It makes me feel special," she'd said that morning, and then she flashed her beaming smile, the one she used on all such occasions, as I was soon to learn, and that I'd taken to be genuine, though it wasn't. But the dawning of this dark recognition had come slowly, and so, as I'd walked Maddox and Lana to their bus that first school day, then stood waving cheerfully as it pulled away, I'd felt certain that I now had two daughters, and that both of them were good.

——— · — · — · ———

Janice was still at work when I returned home after making my bleak tour of Maddox's apartment. I was already on the balcony with my glass of wine when she came through the door. By then the sun had set, and so she found me sitting in the dark.

"I went up to the Bronx today," I told her. "To Maddox's apartment."

She looked at me with considerable sympathy. "You shouldn't feel like you failed her, Jack," she said quietly.

With that, she turned and headed for the bedroom. From my place in the shadows, I could hear her undressing, kicking off her dressy heels, putting away her jewelry, and then the sound of her sandaled feet as she came back onto the balcony, now with her own glass of wine.

"So, why did you go there?" she asked.

I'd never told anyone about that day, and I saw no reason to do so now. "I was just curious, I suppose," I said.

"About what?"

"About Maddox," I answered, "Whether she ever . . . " I stopped because the words themselves seemed silly. Even so, I couldn't find more precise ones. " . . . ever became a better person."

Janice looked puzzled. "Maddox was just a child when she left us, Jack," she said. "It wasn't like she was . . . formed."

But she hadn't just "left us," to use Janice's words. I'd sent her back, and I couldn't help but feel that Maddox must have known why, must have understood what had become so clear to me *that day*.

It had come at the end of a harrowing eight months of difficulty, and even as I'd bought the tickets for *Beauty and the Beast*, I'd suspected that my options were becoming fewer and fewer with regard to Maddox staying with us.

There'd been the continually escalating problems at Falcon Academy, where Maddox had repeatedly made excuses for the accusations hurled against her. She'd never intended to steal Mary Logan's fancy Mont Blanc pen; she had simply picked it up to give it a closer look, then mistakenly dropped it into her own backpack, rather than into Mary's. And, after all, didn't those two bags look similar, and hadn't they been lying side-by-side in the school cafeteria?

Nor had she lied about how she'd gotten hold of Ms. Gilbreath's answer sheet for an upcoming history test, because it really had fallen out of the teacher's pocket, and she'd seen that happen and meant to give it back immediately, but she was already a long way down the hall, and so, well, wasn't it only natural that she tucked it into the pocket of her skirt so that she could give it back to her at the end of the school day? And anyway . . .

Maddox had manufactured explanations for everything that came her way, most of them vaguely plausible, as she must have realized, a fact that increasingly worked against her in my mind. It wasn't just that she lied and stole and cheated; it was that she did it so cleverly that, in every case, the charge against her emerged with that fabled Scottish verdict: "Not Proven." For was it not possible that an answer sheet might fall from a teacher's notebook . . . and all the rest? Listening to her exculpatory narratives, I began to feel like Gimpel the Fool in I. B. Singer's famous story. Was I, like Gimpel, a man who endlessly could have the wool pulled over his eyes? In secret, did Maddox laugh at my credulity in the same cruel way that the villagers mocked Gimpel?

I'd been in the throes of just that kind of searing analysis of Maddox's character as I'd stood in line at the box office. But there was an added element as well. Maddox and Lana had lately begun to quarrel. A room that once seemed plenty big enough for two young girls to share had become, over the past few months, an increasingly heated cauldron of mutual discontent. There were arguments over where things, particularly underwear, were dropped or left to dangle. Crumbs were an issue, as were empty bottles; Lana the neatnik, Maddox the slob. I'd endured shouting and crying from Lana, sullenness from Maddox, but at each boiling over I'd refused to intervene. "Work it out, you two," I'd snapped at one point, and I expected them to do exactly that.

Then, suddenly, and for the first time, our home life was rocked by violence.

It was a slap, and it occurred as the culminating act of a long period of building animosity between Lana and Maddox. The shouting matches had devolved into sinister whispered asides at the breakfast and dinner tables, little digs that I simply refused to acknowledge but that, over time, produced a steady white noise of nasty banter. Gone were the days when Maddox complimented Lana's hair or when Lana even remotely pretended that she considered Maddox her sister.

And yet, in many ways, as Janice sometimes pointed out, they were behaving exactly like a great many sisters do. My wife had never gotten along with her older sister, and I knew that the same could be said of countless other siblings. Still, I had wanted harmony in my household, and the fact that the relationship between Maddox and Lana had become anything but harmonious produced a steady ache in my mind. The truth is that, on that day, as I stood in line waiting to buy those tickets, I felt wounded, perhaps even a tad martyred by the conflict between Maddox and Lana. After all, was I not a man who had selflessly taken in another person's child and who, rather than gaining a spiritual pat on the back for the effort, reaped a daily whirlwind that was tearing my home apart? And that, just the night before, had finally erupted in an act of violence?

Had I not heard that slap, I might never have known that it happened. But as soon as did I hear it, all notion vanished of my no longer intervening in the disintegration of my family life.

The door to their room was open. They were now sitting on their respective beds, Maddox with both feet on the floor, Lana lying facedown, her head pressed deep into her pillow.

When she raised it, I saw the fiery red mark that Maddox's hand had left on her cheek.

"What happened?" I asked from my position in the doorway.

Neither girl answered.

"I won't leave this room until I know what happened," I said.

I walked over to Lana's bed, sat down on it, and lifted her face to see the mark more clearly.

Then I stared hotly at Maddox. "We *do not* strike each other in this family," I snapped. "Do you understand me?"

Maddox nodded silently.

"We do not!" I cried.

Maddox whispered something I couldn't understand. Her head was down. She wouldn't look at me.

"No matter what the reason," I added angrily.

She lifted her head. Her eyes were glistening. "I mess everything up," she said softly.

Suddenly, I found that I couldn't buy one bit of it, neither her tears nor her weepy self-accusation, which, however vaguely, had the ring of an apology. *No,* I decided, *you have fooled me all along,* and with that grim realization, I abruptly believed that all the accusations against her were true, all her explanations false. She had played me as a con artist plays a mark. I was her pet fool.

And yet, despite all that, I knew I would not send her back.

No, there had to be a way to help Maddox.

Besides, there was plenty of time.

And so, in an effort to reset everything, I decided that we should all take a deep breath, give it another go, do something together, something that spoke of sweetness and kindness and the power of a human being to look beyond outward appearances.

That was when I thought of *Beauty and the Beast.*

———— · — · — · ————

Lana was already seated at a small corner table when I arrived at the restaurant. She was dressed to the nines, as usual, with every hair in place. Her life had gone very well. She had a good job and a good marriage, with two nice little boys who appeared to adore their parents. From childhood down to this very moment, I told myself as I sat down, she'd gotten everything she'd ever wanted.

Except a sister.

It was a thought that immediately brought me back to Maddox, to how right I'd been in removing her from the circle of our family.

I brought up none of this latest news, of course, and we chatted about the usual topics during our dinner: how her work was going, how the boys were doing, upcoming plans of one sort or another. We'd already ordered our end-of-meal coffees when she said, "Mom told me you've been thinking about Maddox."

I nodded. "I suppose I have."

"Me, too," Lana said. "Especially that day."

"The day we went to *Beauty and the Beast*?" I asked.

Lana looked puzzled. "Why would that day be special?"

I shrugged. "Okay, what day do you mean, then?"

"The day Maddox hit me."

"Oh," I said. "That day."

"The thing is, I provoked her," Lana said. "I was just a kid, and kids can be cruel. I see it in the boys. The things they say to each other." Tentatively, I asked, "What did you say to her?"

"I told her that she was here because nobody wanted her," Lana said. "Her mother didn't want her. Her brother didn't want her. I told her that even you didn't want her." She paused and then added, "That's when she slapped me." She lifted a slow, ghostly hand to that long vanished wound. "And I deserved it."

I wondered if Lana had come to blame herself for my decision to send back Maddox. If so, she couldn't have been more wrong. It wasn't anything Lana had done that decided the issue. The blame had always lain with Maddox.

"Maddox had to go," I said starkly, still too appalled by the evil I'd seen in the subway station to reveal what had truly convinced me to send Maddox back.

The thing that struck me as most odd now, while Lana sipped nonchalantly at her coffee, was the sweetness that had preceded that terrible moment. *Beauty and the Beast* had come to its heartbreaking conclusion, and, along with the rest of the audience, we were on our way out of the theater, Lana on my right, Maddox on my left. As we approached the front doors, Lana suddenly bolted ahead to where items associated with the show were on sale. Maddox, however, remained at my side.

"I liked it," she said softly, and with those words, she took my hand in hers and held it tenderly. "Thank you."

I smiled. "You're welcome," I said as my heart softened toward her, and I once again harbored the hope that all would be well. Lifted by that desire, I stepped over to the counter and bought two refrigerator magnets. I gave one to Lana, who seemed much more interested in the

T-shirts, and the other one to Maddox.

"Thank you," she said softly. "I will always keep it."

She turned toward a couple who were exiting the theater. They had a little girl in tow, each holding on to one of the child's hands.

"That's what I want," she said in that odd way she sometimes said things, looking off into the middle distance, speaking, as it seemed, only to herself. "I want to be an only child."

By then, Lana had made her way to the theater's front door. "Can we go to Jake's, Dad?" she asked when we reached her.

Jake's was a pizza place in the Village where we tended to have dinner on those days that we found ourselves downtown and didn't want to rush home to cook.

I looked at Maddox.

"Jake's okay with you?" I asked happily.

She smiled that sweet smile of hers. "Sure" was all she said.

The subway was only a few blocks away. We walked to it amid the usual Times Square crowd, at that time a curious mixture of vaguely criminal low-life and dazzled tourists.

On the train, I sat with Maddox on one side and Lana on the other, a formation that continued as we exited the train and made our way to the restaurant. During the meal, Lana spoke in a very animated way about *Beauty and the Beast,* while Maddox remained quiet, eating her slice of pizza slowly, sipping her drink slowly, her gaze curiously inward and intense, like one hatching a plot.

We were done within half an hour. The restaurant was near Washington Square, and so, before returning home, we strolled briefly in the park. Lana glanced up as we passed under the arch, but Maddox stared straight ahead in the same inward and intense way I'd noticed at the restaurant.

"You okay?" I asked as we left the park and headed for the subway.

Again, she offered me her sweet smile. "I'm fine," she said.

We descended the stairs, then one by one we each went through the turnstiles and headed down the long ramp that led to the uptown trains. We were about halfway down when I heard the distant rumble of our train heading into the station. "Come on, girls," I said and instinctively bolted ahead, moving more quickly than I thought, as I realized when I turned to look behind me.

The train had not yet reached the station, but I could see its light as it emerged from the dark tunnel. On the platform, perhaps ten yards behind me, both Lana and Maddox were running. Lana was skirting the edge of the platform, with Maddox to her left, though only by a few inches. I looked at the train, then back at the girls, and suddenly I saw Maddox glance over her shoulder. She must have seen the train barreling out of the tunnel, for then she faced forward again and, at that instant, leaned to her left, bumping her shoulder against Lana's so that Lana briefly stumbled toward the pit before regaining her footing, as if by miracle.

I heard Maddox's voice in my mind: *to be an only child.*

The little girl who'd been the object of Maddox's murderous intent was now a grown woman with children of her own, and I had only to look across the table to reassure myself that I'd done the right thing in sending Maddox away. To have done otherwise would have put Lana at risk. Other children had done dreadful things, after all, and that searing episode in the subway station convinced me that Maddox was capable of such evil, too. She had declared what she'd wanted most in life and then ruthlessly attempted to achieve it. I had no way of knowing if she would make another attempt, but it was a chance I wasn't willing to take, especially since the intended victim was my own daughter.

"Maddox had to go," I repeated now.

Lana didn't argue the point. "I remember the day you took her to the airport," she said. "It was raining, and she was wearing that sad little raincoat she'd brought with her from the South." She looked at me. "Remember? The one with the hood."

I nodded. "That coat made her look even more sinister," I said dryly.

Lana looked at me quizzically. "Sinister? That's not a word I would use to describe Maddox."

"What word would you use?" I asked.

"Damaged," Lana answered. "I would say that Maddox was damaged by life."

"Perhaps so," I said, "but Maddox had done some damage of her own."

"Meaning what?"

"Meaning that she stole an answer sheet at Falcon Academy," I said. "One of her classmates saw her."

"You mean Jesse Traylor?" Lana laughed. "He just got caught himself. Cheating on his taxes." She took a sip from her cup. "Jesse was the school apple-polisher, a tattletale who would have done anything to ingratiate himself with the headmaster."

Cautiously, I said, "Even lie about Maddox?"

"He'd have lied about anyone," Lana said. She saw the disturbance her answer caused me. "What's the matter, Dad?"

I leaned forward. "Did he lie about Maddox?"

Lana shrugged. "I don't know." She glanced toward the street where two little girls stood outside a theater. "She apologized, by the way," she said. "Maddox, I mean. For slapping me. Not a spoken apology." She looked as if she were enjoying a sweet memory. "But I knew what she meant when she did it."

"Did what?" I asked.

"Nudged me," Lana answered. "It was a way we had of telling each other that we were sorry and wanted to be sisters again." She smoothed a wrinkle from her otherwise perfectly pressed sleeve. "After we had pizza at Jake's," she said. "In the subway. We were running for the train, and Maddox gave me that hostile look she used when she was joking with me, and then she just nudged me, and that was her way of saying that she was sorry for hitting me, and that she knew I was sorry for what I'd said to her." She looked at me softly. "And since we were both sorry, things were going to be okay."

With those words, Lana finished her coffee. "Anyway, it's quite sad what happened to Maddox." She folded her napkin and placed it primly beside her plate. "The way she never got her balance after she left us." She smiled. "And so she just . . . finally . . . stumbled into the pit."

"Into the pit," I repeated softly.

Shortly after that, we parted, Lana returning to her husband and children, I back to my apartment, where, with Janice out of town, I would spend the next few days alone.

I passed most of that time on the balcony, looking down at the tamed streets of Hell's Kitchen, my attention forever drawn to families moving cheerfully toward the glittering lights of Times Square, fathers and mothers with their children in tow, guiding them, as best they could, through the shifting maze. I saw Maddox in every tiny face, remembered the tender touch of her small hand in mine, her quiet "Thank you," for the little refrigerator magnet she had returned to me; the last bit of kindness I'd shown before sending her out of our lives forever.

Had she been a liar, a cheat, a thief? I don't know. Had I completely misunderstood the little nudge she'd given Lana that day as the two girls raced for the train? Again, I don't know. What children perceive and remember years later can be so different from what adults know . . . or think they know. Perhaps she'd already been doomed to live as she did after she left us, and to die as she did in that bleak, unlighted space. Or perhaps not. I couldn't say. I knew only that for me, as for all parents, the art of controlling damage is one we practice in the dark.

THOMAS H. COOK *is the international-award-winning author of more than thirty books. He has been nominated for the Mystery Writers of America Edgar Allan Poe Award eight times in five different categories, and his novel* The Chatham School Affair *won the Best Novel Award in 1996. He has twice won the Swedish Academy of Detection's Martin Beck Award, the only novelist ever to have done so. His short story "Fatherhood" won the Herodotus Prize for best historical short story. His works have been translated into more than twenty languages.*

THE DAY AFTER VICTORY

Brendan DuBois

It was seven a.m. in Times Square, New York, on Wednesday August 15, when Leon Foss slowly maneuvered the trash cart—with its huge wheels and two brooms—along the sidewalk near the intersection of Seventh Avenue and West Forty-Sixth Street, shaking his head at the sheer amount of trash that was facing him and the other street sweepers from the Department of Sanitation. He had on the usual "white angel" uniform of white slacks, jacket, and cap—which was stiff and felt new—and never had he seen so much trash. It was almost up to his knees.

Traffic moved slowly through the square—Packards, Oldsmobiles, old Ford trucks making deliveries—tossing up plumes of torn paper, tickertape, and newspapers that had been tossed around with such glee the day before, on V-J Day—Victory over Japan Day—the end of the war.

His eyes darted along the sidewalk, taking in the Rexall Drugstore, a bar, a restaurant, and a joint called Spike's Place. It had dark windows and an unlit neon sign overhead, and a small alcove with a closed door.

A few pedestrians were moving along the cluttered sidewalks, but it seemed like most of New York was taking the day off after yesterday's events, the biggest party since . . . well, since anyone could remember. And what a party, and he had missed every single second of it. Instead, he had listened to NBC Blue via his RCA radio in his third-floor walk-up in Washington Heights; he had no interest in catching the subway south to join the party. He had sat there in the tiny room, smoking a Chesterfield, listening to Truman's flat Missouri twang go on and on, nothing like FDR's cultured way of talking. Months after FDR's death, he still missed That Man's voice. . . . As he had smoked that cigarette yesterday and listened, his phone rang.

"Leon?" had come a woman's voice.

"Yes, Martha, it's me," he had said, speaking to his sister. In the background were sounds of machinery. Martha worked at a war plant out on Long Island. "How are you doing?"

"Taking a break, wondering how much longer I'll have a job. Are you listening to the radio?"

"Yes."

"It's finally over, then, isn't it."

"That's what they're saying."

"Leon . . . you're too old to keep at it. Let it go. It's all over now. Please, stop working."

"Martha, it was nice of you to call," he had said. "Don't be late going back to the assembly line, okay?"

And he had hung up and smoked the Chesterfield and listened to Truman some more.

Now he started with his morning's work, taking the big broom, pulling stuff off the sidewalks so the larger street sweepers could pick it up. Paper, broken beer bottles, broken gin bottles, copies of the *Daily News* and other newspapers, with their EXTRA headlines. *Sweep, sweep, sweep.* More torn pieces of paper. A uniform cap for a Marine. He picked it up, looked inside the brim, saw a hasty scrawl of some kid's name on a piece of cardboard stuck behind the plastic. He walked down the sidewalk a bit, carefully placed the hat on top of a blue and white mailbox, just in case the boy came back later to retrieve it.

Just in case.

Broom in hand, he went back to his cart to see another sanitation worker standing there, older, heavier, his white uniform stained. His face was covered with black bristle, and Leon figured that, in the rush to get to work this morning, he forgot to shave.

"Hey," the worker said.

"Hey," Leon said right back, and the worker said, "Christ, who the hell are you? You don't belong here. I know all the regulars."

Leon lowered his broom, went back to work. "Look around, Mac. More trash here than any other place in the world, and it's gotta be cleaned up." *Sweep, sweep, sweep.* "I usually work on Staten Island. Boss called me yesterday, said to get to Times Square this morning, and here I am."

"Oh." Then the guy leaned over and peered into Leon's cart, and damn, Leon almost had a fit at that. But the guy leaned back without noticing anything and said, "Shit, you must have just started."

"That's right."

The other sweeper started pushing his cart and stopped. His head rose to take in all the tall impressive buildings rising up from Times Square. "Greatest city in the world, ain't it?"

"No argument here," Leon said.

"Think about it. All those cities around the world, bombed, flattened, or occupied. London, Paris, Berlin, Moscow, Tokyo. Only one city didn't get hit. Ours." The man spat on the ground. "I spent a couple of years in Civil Defense. Got an armband and a white helmet. Did some drills about how to do first aid and put out incendiary bombs. Also knocked back a few beers. Christ, we was lucky. You know, I'm not much of a religious guy, but it makes you think God spared us, you know?"

"Good point," Leon said, still working.

"All those lights back on, rationing ending, the boys coming back. My boy, too . . . he was stationed over in Belgium, and he'll be back home soon. This place is gonna jump in the years ahead. Mark my words! Jump!"

Leon gave the guy a cool brush-off smile. "Yes. Jump."

The worker shrugged, started pushing his cart. "See you around, bud."

"You, too."

And when Leon turned to keep on sweeping, there was a man standing in the alcove of Spike's Place, smoking a cigarette.

Leon froze, and then he went back to work.

Sweep, sweep, sweep.

——— . — . — . ———

More paper, more broken glass. There was a growling hum of a street sweeper at work on the other side of the square. Tickertape, some pages torn from a phone book. A woman's pale pink brassiere. And then, a woman's pale pink panties. A matching set? Maybe. He sure hoped they slipped off some pretty girl in a moment of delight and happiness that all the killing, wounding, and soldiers being made prisoner was over. That those long days of dreading the phone call, the knock on the door, the telegram delivery, the casualty lists in the newspapers, all those days were now, finally, behind you.

Sweep, sweep, sweep.

He paused in front of Spike's Place, where the man was standing, still smoking a cigarette. He looked sharp, late twenties, early thirties, maybe. Nice shiny black shoes, dark gray slacks, and dark blue blazer. White shirt and a real snazzy tie, a snappy fedora. He looked at Leon and then looked away. Leon leaned on his broom. "Hey," he said.

The guy grunted back. "What a party, huh?" Leon said. "Biggest party in the world. Were you here?"

The guy smiled for a flash. He had nice white teeth against a tanned complexion. "Nope. Was at some private function. Whooping it up."

"Ah, good for you," Leon said. "More high class, more fun, I bet, than hanging out here in the streets." He spread out his arm. "Here, it was jammed to the damn gills, you know? Could hardly walk around. Lots of people drunk and fighting; some of the girls kissing. Years from now there'll be newsreels and photos, all saying what a great place it was . . . and they'll skip over the fights, the bad breath, the drunks throwing up on your shoes."

"Yeah, I guess."

Leon stood up from his broom and started to work. *Sweep.* And then stopped.

"Hey," he said. "I know you."

The guy took another drag. "No, I don't think so. Don't think we ever met."

"No, no, I never forget a face," he said. "That's what my wife, Donna, said, before she died a couple of years back. I never forget a face."

The man just stood there, looking slightly put off, and then Leon snapped his fingers. "Got it! I've seen your photo a couple of times. You're Sonny Delano. Am I right?"

Delano smirked. "What, you a cop under that garbage man costume?"

Leon smiled back at him. "You think I'm a cop, Mister Delano? Ha, that's a good one . . ." He took another sweep. "Don't mean to be any trouble . . . it's just that, well, hell, it's you, Mister Delano. Over the past years you've been in the papers a lot, you know? You got pinched at least a dozen times, and each time you walked, am I right?"

Same smirk on the younger man's face. "That's right. DA and coppers could never make anything stick."

"Good for you," Leon said. He picked up his broom, knocked it against the edge of the curb. "Hard to believe, you know? Nearly four years on, and now it's over. War is done. Peace treaty to be signed in a couple of weeks. Funny thing, ain't it."

"Whaddya mean, funny?"

Leon leaned against his broom once more. "Think about it, Mister Delano. Day before yesterday, if you were a Jap sailor or soldier, you could get killed, just like that." Leon snapped his fingers for emphasis. "Now, no more killing. The war is over. In less than forty-eight hours, you went from being a target to something else. Same for you, too."

"Huh?"

"Well, no offense, Mister Delano, but you know . . . the stuff you were involved with . . . I mean, the stuff the coppers and the newspapers said you were involved with. Selling sugar and meat on the black market. Stealing rubber tires. Making fake gas coupons. A couple days ago, I bet, the coppers were still on your trail. But the war's over now. I read that, pretty soon, all this rationing is gonna be over. You'll be in the clear. You must feel pretty good about that. All the stuff you might have done during the war, well, you're in the clear. Who's gonna bother you about all that?"

A funny little grin, a puff from his cigarette. Leon said, "So. What are you going to do now, Mister Delano?"

He brushed some dust from one of his coat sleeves. "Who knows. The war over, lots of opportunities for sharp guys to make a buck. Guys coming home with money in their pockets, looking to get married, make babies, get new homes. Yeah, there's gonna be a big boom coming, you just wait and see."

"And you'll be there, making a buck, right?"

"You know it."

Leon went back to work for a few seconds. *Sweep, sweep, sweep.* He caught Delano's eye again. "You know, no offense, you look pretty healthy. Good shape. Why weren't you in the service?"

Delano's eyes narrowed and seemed to turn from neutral to freezing cold. "I was exempt," he nearly spat out. "Four-F."

"Oh. A doctor said that, huh?"

"Yeah. I got a bad ticker. The hell business is it of yours?"

"Sorry. My wife told me I always yapped. You know, you did what a lot of other guys did, am I right or am I right? You see that story last year, how the entire Penn State swimming team, they got medical deferments, too? Hey, that's how the system was rigged. Some guys went out and served, and other guys, they could pull strings and stay home."

"Way of the world, pal."

"I guess so."

Leon swept up the sidewalk, leaving Spike's Place behind him. His breathing was raspy, and his head ached. Too much coffee, cigarettes, and thinking last night had kept him up. *Sweep, sweep, sweep.* He worked his way back down to Spike's Place, where Delano was still waiting. Of course, he was still waiting. Leon was counting on it.

"Some job you got there," Delano said.

He shrugged. "It's a job. You know, I got kicked out of my other job because I was too old, too slow. But I like to keep busy, I like to contribute."

Delano grunted. Leon said, "Look at this city, will you? Best city in the world. You know why it works? For the most part, people get along, look out for each other, cooperate. Oh, they do business and make money and build things, but I'd like to think, for the most part, that people are honest, like to live on the straight and narrow. That's how it works. That's the only way it can work."

The man looked at his watch, moved his feet impatiently, looked at his watch again. Leon chose his next words carefully. "But there's always the parasites, the sucker fish, the ones who ride along and get something for nothing, or for little. Like the draft dodgers, the hustlers, the thieves . . . like you."

The ice-cold look in those killer eyes had come back. "It's time for you to get back to work, trash man."

Leon said, "You ever hear of Bataan?"

"Who the hell hasn't?"

"Lots of people have already forgotten it," Leon said, the words coming out hard. "My son was there, fighting for the Filipinos, fighting for the U.S., fighting for *you*, Mister Delano. Don't you feel any sense of . . . oh, I don't know, *thanks* for what he and hundreds of thousands of others did? Respect? Guilt?"

Delano tossed his cigarette butt to the ground. "Clean that up, old man, and leave me the hell alone. I'm meeting someone important this morning."

Leon reached over with his broom, caught the cigarette butt, swept it back to him. "I bet you are. Let me guess. Ty Mulcahey, right? Connected with the dockworkers union. Was going to meet you because, pretty soon, lots of troop ships are going to come through this wonderful harbor, and you and Ty wanted to see what kind of action you could get from all those ships and soldiers coming here."

Delano stepped out of the alcove. "How the hell did you know that?"

Leon smiled, leaned on his broom. "You're gonna love this, Mister Delano. You see, I never did tell you what I did before I came here today as a broom sweeper. I worked for the government. Department of Justice. When I started, it was called the Bureau of Investigation, but now you and folks listening to the radio know it as the FBI."

———— · — · — · ————

He wondered if Delano was going to make a break for it and was happy to see the guy stay in one spot, like he wasn't about ready to back down. "What . . . the . . . hell?"

"Got friends in the field office here, pulled a couple of strings— hey, just like you—and got word to you that Ty Mulcahey wanted to meet you here at Spike's Place. But Ty's not coming. He's probably sleeping off a drunk over at Hell's Kitchen. Nope, Ty didn't want to meet you, but I sure as hell wanted to."

"You got nothing."

Leon laughed. "Hell, tell me something I don't know! Me and the boys in blue here, we've been chasing you for years, right up until I was forced out on retirement. Just like Tom Dewey and Frank Hogan, the DAs. Even the Little Flower called you New York's Public Enemy Number One last year. He wanted to do to you what he did to Lucky Luciano, arrest him and line him up to get deported, but it never panned out. So here you stand, still a free man. Feel pretty good about yourself?"

More trucks and cars rumbled by. Some horns were honked in a joyful fashion, signaling no more war, no more death, no more waiting to hear bad news.

Leon said, "Cat got your tongue? For real? Let's talk about real. The last thing I ever heard from my boy"—and damn it, right then, his voice broke, and he hated sounding like a weepy old man—"was a letter from him, sent before Bataan fell. I must have read and reread that one sheet of paper a thousand times over the year. Never heard anything else. Then MacArthur invaded the Philippines and the main POW camp was liberated back in January. I waited, and I waited, and then I got that telegram from the Red Cross. You know what it said?" Delano started to walk away, but Leon got right in front of him. "It said my Jimmy had died one month before the camp was freed. One month. Thirty damn days!"

Leon's throat constricted again. "So, I'll let you be. Only if you answer one question."

"I don't have to answer a damn thing, old man."

"Maybe. But maybe it'll be in your best interest to answer, sonny. Maybe you answer this question, I leave you be, so you can keep on being a parasite."

Delano tugged at his jacket, straightened his flashy necktie. "Ask your damn question."

Leon nodded. "Ever since Pearl Harbor, ever since that day . . . you ever feel sorry, or guilty, about what you did? How you lived off the war, how you let other sons and fathers take your place? Sons and fathers who might have bad eyes, or flat feet, or bad hearing, but were still called up and drafted because they didn't have your connections, your way of doing things. You ever feel guilty about that?"

Delano reached into an inside jacket pocket, took out a pack of Camels and a gold lighter. He lit off the cigarette, took a deep puff, and returned the cigarettes to his coat; he did the same with the lighter after snapping it shut with one satisfying *click*.

"No," he said, smirking. "Not for a goddamn minute. I lived and those dopes died, and that's all right by me."

Leon just nodded again, went back to his trash cart, reached down inside, and from a crumpled-up paper bag—the bag the sanitation worker had thankfully overlooked—he took out a .45-caliber Colt model 1911 pistol with a tube silencer screwed onto the end.

"Wrong answer," Leon said, pointing it at Delano's chest.

BRENDAN DuBOIS, *of New Hampshire, is the award-winning author of seventeen novels and more than 135 short stories. His latest novel is* Blood Foam, *part of the Lewis Cole mystery series. His short fiction has appeared in* Playboy, Ellery Queen's Mystery Magazine, Alfred Hitchcock's Mystery Magazine, *the* Magazine of Fantasy & Science Fiction, *and numerous anthologies, including* The Best American Mystery Stories of the Century *(2000) and* The Best American Noir of the Century *(2010). His stories have twice won the Shamus Award from the Private Eye Writers of America and have earned three Edgar Allan Poe Award nominations from MWA. He is also a* Jeopardy! *game-show champion. Visit his website at BrendanDuBois.com.*

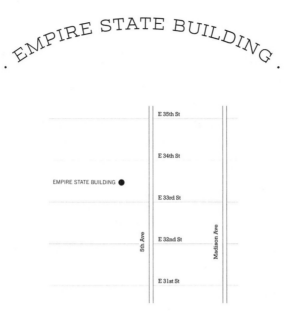

EMPIRE STATE BUILDING

E 35th St

E 34th St

EMPIRE STATE BUILDING ●

E 33rd St

5th Ave

E 32nd St

Madison Ave

E 31st St

SERIAL BENEFACTOR

Jon L. Breen

To start with, I'm a centenarian, Sebastian Grady by name, and still fully marbled. My current address is Plantain Point, a retirement home on the California coast with a lot of residents from the entertainment world. To give you an idea, the president of our association is called the Top Banana, though most of the vaudevillians have died off.

As you can imagine, I've seen many younger generations come of age, and the current lot don't seem too anxious to make the transition to adulthood. Don't ask me if I blame them.

Evan is my favorite great-granddaughter. I never expected to be so fond of a girl with a guy's name, but in this century of yours—mine was the last one—I guess one size fits all. I hadn't seen her since she was an infant when she turned up one day to interview me for a school ge-nealogy assignment, I being the oldest relative available. But once the paper was done and graded, she kept coming back. She seems to enjoy my company.

She's a mature sixteen by current standards. In some ways, she's typical of her generation, including being constantly connected to ev-ery portable communication device that comes along, but she's a smart girl, rarely says "like" except as a verb expressing approval or a prepo-sition with a discernible object. She has an active social life, some of it with live people, does sports, gets good grades, loves puzzles, and likes a challenge. Her mind is always on the move. I'd unhesitatingly back her in a timed Sudoku contest.

On one recent visit, we were sitting on my eighth-floor deck look-ing out at the Pacific Ocean. Family news and current events exhaust-ed, I said casually (but with an ulterior motive), "I've got a puzzle for you, honey."

"Great. What is it?"

"There's a list of sentences I want you to look up for me, tell me what they mean, where they came from, what they have in common, if anything. You can go on the Internet for this, look 'em up on Giggle or Garble or whatever it's called. Shouldn't take you long."

She gave me that big, braced-teeth grin that always melted my heart. She knew I wasn't quite as ignorant as I pretended to be. She'd taught me to use the Internet when she was eight years old; I have my own computer, and Plantain Point has Wi-Fi. "Does this have any-thing to do with one of your investigations?"

"What are you talking about?"

"Gramps, I know you're an amateur detective."

"No such thing, except in books."

"Don't forget I've read all your memoirs."

Just the published ones, and there were some unpublished ones I hoped she'd never see. Maybe when she was older.

"Okay, you got me. There *is* a mystery connected to this list, and I'll tell you all about it when you've identified the items."

I passed it over, neatly printed in my still steady hand:

Massachusetts is a long way from New York.
She'll start upon a marathon.
You don't even know a hazard from a green.
You can't stop the weather, not with all your dough!
She got herself a husband but he wasn't hers.
That ain't the highest spot.

"Any of that ring a bell?" I asked.

"Nope, not at all. So what's my deadline?"

"Try to get it done while I'm still alive."

"Gramps, you're full of it."

"Get it done, and I'll tell you the wildest story you ever heard, and every word of it true."

"I'll be back with the answers tomorrow," she promised, and I knew she would. In the meantime, I let my mind drift back to the only century where I really felt at home anymore.

———— · — · — · ————

Now that I've passed a hundred myself, my old buddy Danny Crenshaw doesn't seem quite so amazing as he used to. He only made it to ninety-four. But the last time I saw him, 1978 it was, same year he died, he seemed as happy and busy as ever.

I first met Danny in the late 1920s. He was among the Broadway headliners lured west by the advent of talking pictures. A little guy with tons of nervous energy, he always played younger than his age and never seemed to change much as the years went by. Multitalented as Danny was—actor, singer, dancer, songwriter—they never seemed to know how to use him in pictures, and he was homesick for New York.

"Seb," he said to me one day in the studio commissary, "you heard the latest about the Empire State Building? They're going to have a mooring mast for dirigibles. They'll be able to load and unload passengers 1,250 feet above the street."

"Sounds like a goofy idea to me. What about the wind?"

"They've got all that figured out."

"Okay," I said. Of course, it didn't work in the end, but smarter guys than me thought it could.

"Seb, I gotta get back to Broadway. I want to perform for people I can see and hear, not just a bunch of studio technicians. And I want to see that building."

By the time King Kong took Fay Wray to the top of Al Smith's folly only to be shot down by airplanes, Danny was back in Gotham City to stay. Over the next years, I'd pay him a visit whenever my work took me to the Big Apple, see him onstage when he was working and at home when he was resting. I was usually there on Classic Pictures business, that being my main employer in those days, and those times I was on my own, not nursing some pampered actor, I'd stay at a not-quite-deluxe hostelry the studio had a special deal with. It was within walking distance of the much classier Hotel McAlpin at the corner of Broadway and West Thirty-Fourth Street, where Danny lived for decades as a permanent resident. His upper-floor quarters were luxurious enough to suit his success, but he'd picked the place for its view of the Empire State Building, just up the street.

It was sunny in Manhattan one day in early 1946 when I walked from my hotel to the McAlpin. Passing through the heart of the Garment District, I dodged those huge clothing racks pushed along the sidewalks by New Yorkers in a hurry. Like the taxicabs, they somehow negotiated the chaos to get where they were going without mishaps.

The McAlpin had been the biggest hotel in the world when it was built in 1912. Impressive as the three-story lobby was, decorated in Italian Renaissance style, filled with marble and murals depicting women as jewelry, the most dazzling sight was the basement Marine Grill, where Danny, between shows at the moment, had invited me to a late lunch—as a celebrity resident, he had an in with the management. The food was undoubtedly fine, but all I can remember of the menu was the oysters—Danny loved oysters, another thing he missed on the West Coast. The whole room, with its curving ceilings, was decorated in colored terra-cotta, and I'll never forget the spectacular murals showing the history of the New York harbor. I was especially impressed by the depiction of a four-funnel ocean liner.

"Has that been here since they opened?" I asked.

"Sure, I think so," Danny said.

"Is that ship by any chance the *Titanic*? I mean, what an irony. *Titanic*, 1912."

"I think they actually opened in '13, had a sort of preview party for VIPs at the end of '12. And relax. That's the *Mauretania*."

As we ate, Danny told me about the military plane lost in the fog that had crashed into his beloved Empire State Building the year before. He also rhapsodized about the show he would open in later in the year, produced by Belasco.

"David Belasco?"

"No, Elmer. David's dead. You'll meet him later. Elmer, I mean."

When we got upstairs to Danny's apartment, it was late afternoon. He said he'd invited a few friends to drop in and meet the visitor from Tinseltown, and he was sure his wife would want to say hello. She'd be back any minute. The number of Danny Crenshaw's wives (four or five, I think) was not unheard of in show business. More unusual, to the end of his life he still seemed to like all his exes, and as far as I knew, they felt the same about him.

This one's name was Mildred, and, looking back, I think he may have loved her the most, though she drove him the craziest. Like all Danny's wives, she was lovely, and like most, she was taller than he was. Her bright, carrot-colored hair was her most striking feature, but her mild manner contradicted any redhead stereotype. She entered the apartment that afternoon loaded down with shopping and not expecting to find company, but I guess knowing Danny she was always ready for it. She was stylishly dressed and coifed in the fashion of the times: a brimmed hat with flowers at the front and a bow at the back, shoulder pads, gloves, clutch purse, nipped-in waist on a form-fitting skirt to just below the knee, ankle-strap shoes with wide heels. She greeted me cordially, and the gathering grew from there.

The first drop-in guest was a tall and wispy fellow with a little mustache. From the casual intimacy with which Danny and Mildred both welcomed him, I had the impression he was a frequent visitor. "Seb, meet Jerry Cordova," Danny said. "My old partner in the Lunchtime Follies."

"What's that?" I asked.

"It was a spin-off of the Stage Door Canteen. We'd go out and entertain the workers during their lunch hours at defense plants and shipyards."

"I got paid a pittance," Jerry said, "but Danny did it strictly for the war effort."

"What a sucker, huh?" Danny said with a wink.

"Headliners worked for free," Jerry explained. "I'm not a headliner."

"One of these days, you'll be another Gershwin!"

Next to arrive was Rosey Patterson, a theatrical agent and an old pal of mine—in our respective roles as herders of actors, we'd been indirectly involved in an early-1930s murder case right there in Manhattan. He wasn't quite as compactly built as Danny, but he was just as hyper, always on the move. I remember thinking it might be a strain on the nerves to be around both of them at the same time. Rosey embraced me in the best show business fashion and said he wanted to tell me about a great detective story he'd just read. But there were two tall men filling the doorway right behind him, and I don't think he ever got the chance.

The older one, who had the muscular frame of a body builder, gripped my hand before waiting to be introduced and said, "So you're Seb, Danny's Hollywood connection. I'm Elmer Belasco." He gestured to the younger man. "This is my worthless son, Arthur."

"Not totally worthless," Arthur said. "I'm a new father. Baby girl. Fresh out of cigars, though."

"You fellows related to David Belasco?" I asked.

"When it suits us," Arthur said. "Back in the twenties, when dad worked for Flo Ziegfeld, he figured the name helped him."

"Didn't help at all," Elmer said. "The opposite, if anything."

"More likely he reminded Ziegfeld of Sandow the strongman," Rosey said.

Apparently, these spontaneous gatherings were a regular thing to Mildred. She knew we'd be drinking and gossiping and catching up and drinking—how we drank back then—and that what began in the late afternoon would likely extend into the evening.

It was Jerry Cordova who made it a party. He resembled his late hero George Gershwin in one respect. If he entered a room with a piano—and Danny Crenshaw wouldn't be without one—he would be asked to play, and if he wasn't asked, he'd do it anyway, singing along in a reedy voice something like Cole Porter's. Shortly after he got there, he sat down at the keyboard unbidden, as if this were why he was invited, and maybe it was.

Arthur Belasco was just twenty-two. He was starting to make inroads as an actor on Broadway, though his father constantly grumbled that he had no talent. Father and son were always sniping at each other, with insults that sounded pointed but presumably weren't to be taken seriously.

"I had to find some way to get into the family business," Arthur said. "The old man here insisted. Medical school was a dead end, he said."

"He could do less harm on the stage than in the operating room," Elmer retorted. It sounded like a practiced routine, and everybody took it as harmless kidding. Except for Mildred, who had a pained look on her face every time father or son launched a zinger.

In later years, remembering Mildred, Danny would say, "She was the kindest, sweetest person God ever put on earth. Imagine a dame with no sense of humor putting up with a joker like me for as long as she did. Mildred was a bleeding heart, full of empathy, but she couldn't see nuances."

That day in 1946, I witnessed an example. Jerry Cordova had launched into "Who Cares?" from *Of Thee I Sing*, written by the Gershwin brothers deep in the Depression. Mildred listened with apparent appreciation and joined the applause when he was finished.

"That was great, Jerry," she said, "but I've always hated that song."

"Oh, dear, I've offended my hostess," he said.

"No, don't be silly. It's a nice tune, but I hate the lyrics. They're nasty, uncaring, mean spirited."

"How so, Mildred?" Rosey Patterson inquired.

"You'll be sorry you asked," Danny said.

Mildred said, "It's that line that goes 'Who cares if banks fail in Yonkers?' Well, a lot of banks failed in the Depression. We had to go to war to get out of it. When I hear that, I think about all the people I knew and those I didn't know who had money in those failing banks, who maybe lost everything. How could you not care that banks failed in Yonkers or anywhere else?"

"I've tried to explain this," Danny said with a mock long-suffering expression. "Baby, the people in that song are trying to get through difficult times, like we all were back then. They depend on the power of their love to see them through. Whatever happened, they could handle it because they were in love. That's the point. It's called a love song, see? It's got nothing to do with people who lost money in banks that failed."

"Well, it's just not right to be so cavalier about it, that's all," she said. "Play something else, Jerry."

"Give me a minute while I run through all the lyrics in my head," the pianist said.

Everybody laughed. Mildred didn't—she seldom did—but she was a good enough hostess not to throw a wet blanket on the evening, even providing an improvised meal from a nearby deli when it became apparent nobody was going anywhere till well after nightfall.

I'm sure we covered a lot of subjects that night. Did we touch on peacetime transition, the bomb, our relationship with the Soviet Union, prospects for the returning veteran, President Truman's job performance, the Yankees and the Giants and the Dodgers? Maybe. But these were Broadway folks, so mostly we talked about Broadway. Could Tennessee Williams duplicate his great success with *The Glass Menagerie*? Opinions were mixed, but most thought he couldn't. How did Maurice Evans's current production of *Hamlet* stack up against his predecessors'? Rosey Patterson swore nobody ever topped Barrymore, but Danny made a case for Gielgud as the dean of Danes, and Mildred mentioned Leslie Howard. Who was the greatest composer of Broadway musicals? Jerry loyally argued for Gershwin, others countered with Jerome Kern or Richard Rodgers, and Elmer Belasco shocked everybody by insisting it was Kurt Weill. Was Adele Astaire really a greater talent than Fred? Danny said so with a straight face, and a lot of old-timers agreed with him, but when he claimed Gummo was the funniest Marx Brother, I doubted he was serious.

One topic was inevitable for theater people that particular day. I was surprised we'd been there for two or three cocktails before anybody mentioned it.

"So, I guess you all heard about Claude Anselm," Rosey said.

Heads all nodded.

"What happened exactly?" Arthur Belasco said. "I mean, was he murdered?"

"Papers say he was mugged," Rosey said. "Back alley thing late at night. He'd been to see some avant-garde artist who was staying with all the other bohemians at the Chelsea Hotel down in the Village."

"Anton LeMaster," Danny supplied. "Anselm wanted to get him to design a set for his next production, thought his surrealistic style would fit the creative concept."

"More important," Rosey said, "he'd work cheap."

"Yeah, old Claude would have made a lot of promises, appealed to the vain artist's ego and the starving artist's wallet. I think somebody had warned LeMaster what a bastard Anselm was, and he'd turned him down. Not two blocks from the Chelsea, somebody clubbed Claude to death."

"The poor man," Mildred said. "I know what he did to people, but even so."

"Nobody here's going to mourn that guy," Jerry Cordova said, picking out the melody of "I'll Be Glad When You're Dead, You Rascal You" but sparing us his Louis Armstrong imitation.

"Most hated man on Broadway," Danny said.

"In the running, anyway," Rosey said. "Who cheats my client cheats me. And he didn't just cheat actors. He cheated backers, playwrights, theater managers—and always got away with it. Wanted to add a scenic designer to his trophy case, I guess."

"I used to see Anselm on the golf course," Elmer Belasco said. "Never played a round with him, thank God."

"Too good?" Arthur kidded. "Dad can hit the ball a mile, but you should see the yardage he gets on his putts."

"Hey, why don't you go learn your lines or something and not smart off at your elders?"

"What do you mean? I've memorized the whole play."

"It's true," Elmer told us. "Kid has a photographic memory. He could do *Hamlet* for you right here if he'd ever learned how to act. Anselm was as bad a golfer as the kid is an actor. Couldn't play worth a damn, but for some reason he kept at it. I think he looked for opponents who were even worse than he was. Or were motivated to pretend they were."

"Too bad some anonymous mugger got him," Danny mused. "Lot of people on Broadway wish they could have done the job."

"I can just see the full obits in the papers tomorrow," Rosey said. "'Broadway's lights grew a little dimmer with the shocking death of a beloved man of the theater.' And they'll be able to get plenty of quotes from mourners who are secretly cheering."

Elmer nodded. "Scoundrels die, but deals live on."

Rosey had a mischievous gleam in his eye. "Here's an idea. Let's say I was the person who bumped off Anselm, revenge on behalf of my clients and all the bastard's other victims. I wasn't seen, covered my tracks, managed to make it look like a routine mugging."

"Congratulations," Jerry said, playing a snatch of "For He's a Jolly Good Fellow."

"Yeah, great, but I think I'd feel something was lacking."

"What do you mean?" I asked. Rosey loved to have a straight man to feed him cues.

"It wouldn't be enough that the guy was dead. I'd want to claim credit."

"And get yourself fried in that nice comfy electric chair they got up at Sing Sing?" Danny asked.

"No, I'd do it indirectly and anonymously. It wouldn't be necessary to put my own name on it, but I'd want the world to know he was executed on behalf of Broadway and all the people whose careers and lives he stomped on."

"And once you did that fine gesture, would you be able to stop at just one?" Arthur Belasco asked.

"Yeah," Danny chimed in. "I can suggest some other vermin in our fine theatrical profession that are just as deserving."

I hadn't contributed much, not being a Broadway insider like these folks, but now I decided to go along with the gag. "Rosey, it's an attractive idea, but you have to think this through. The mistake those clever murderers in books make is getting too cute for their own good. Gilding the lily. Giving the supersleuth a way to get at them in the last chapter. Why provide a deliberate clue that could be traced back to you?"

Rosey shrugged. "Anonymous letters to the cops or the press maybe. I'd give myself a name. The Stage Door Avenger?"

"Naw, the newspapers would do it for you, and they'd come up with something better than that," Danny said.

"Jack the Ripper named himself," I pointed out.

"Let's get to the important stuff, Rosey," Danny said. "Who'd you pick as your next victim?"

Mildred had been silent through all of this. Now she raised her hands as if in surrender. "Fellows, I just hate this kind of talk. Can we change the subject, or can you play something else for us, Jerry?"

Jerry launched into a medley from *Show Boat*, and that was that.

The next day, a cryptic message in all capital letters appeared in the personals columns of all the evening papers, and there were a slew of them in New York at that time: "YOU DON'T EVEN KNOW A HAZARD FROM A GREEN." At the time, nobody knew what it meant or had any reason to connect it to the death of Claude Anselm. By the time anybody made the connection, three more Broadway scumbags had died.

As I knew she would, Evan turned up the next day with the answers. When I kidded her about visiting two days in a row, said they'd have to put her on the payroll with the nurses and maids and social directors and therapy dogs, she rolled her eyes impatiently.

"I did them in the order you listed them. Is the order significant?"

"Not really, but go ahead and do 'em that way."

"Okay. 'Massachusetts is a long way from New York.' That one threw me for a while. I kept getting bogged down with driving distances between cities in Massachusetts and New York, but then I remembered an obvious trick to using a search engine. To get the exact words, you put the whole phrase in quotation marks. Then it was easy. It's a line from a song called 'Lizzie Borden' written by Michael Brown. Wasn't Lizzie Borden a famous murderer, Gramps?"

"Many people think so, if murderers can be famous."

"At that point, I thought the other lines might have to do with murderers, too, but they didn't. Pretty soon I knew what they had in common. They're all from songs in old Broadway shows. I took down some more relevant information about each one, not knowing what was important and what wasn't, and I made a little chart for you." She handed me a sheet of paper.

EVAN'S CHART

QUOTE	SONG	SHOW	COMPOSER	SINGER	DATES/NOTES
"Massachusetts is a long way from New York"	"Lizzie Borden"	Leonard Sillman's *New Faces of 1952*	Michael Brown	Ensemble	Royale Theatre, May 16, 1952–March 28, 1953
"She'll start upon a marathon"	"A Pretty Girl is Like a Melody"	*Ziegfeld Follies of 1919*	Irving Berlin	John Steel (tenor)	Opened June 16, 1919, New Amsterdam Theatre, June 16–December 6, 1919*
"You don't even know a hazard from a green."	"Mr. Gallagher and Mr. Shean"	*Ziegfeld Follies of 1922*	Music by Al Shean; lyrics by Ed Gallagher and Bryan Foy (uncredited)	Gallagher and Shean (some sort of comedy team)	New Amsterdam Theatre, June 5, 1922–June 23, 1923**
"You can't stop the weather, not with all your dough."	"The Cradle Will Rock"	*The Cradle Will Rock*	Marc Blitzstein	Howard DaSilva	Windsor Theatre, January 3, 1938; Mercury Theatre, February 28–April 2, 1938***
"She got herself a husband, but be wasn't hers."	"The Ballad of Jenny"	*Lady in the Dark*	Music by Kurt Weill; lyrics by Ogden Nash	Gertrude Lawrence	Alvin Theatre, January 23, 1941–May 30, 1942
"That ain't the highest spot."	"Come Up to My Place"	*On the Town*	Music by Leonard Bernstein; lyrics by Betty Comden and Adolph Green	Nancy Walker	Adelphi Theatre, December 28, 1944–February 2, 1946

*Suspended about a month by Actors' Equity strike.

**Team had earlier performed song in vaudeville, 1920.

***Directed by Orson Welles. First performance, actors in audience rather than onstage.

"Great work, Evan, very thorough. What did you think of the songs?"

She made a face. "I just read the lyrics for most of them. In that Gallagher and Shean thing, one of them doesn't know what the game of golf is called and is ridiculed for it by his partner, but his partner thinks it's called lawn tennis. Did people think that was funny in those days, Gramps?"

I shrugged. "I guess you had to be there."

"Now," she said, "when are you going to tell me about the Broadway Executioner?"

"How do you know anything about that?" I really was surprised, but she quickly reminded me why I shouldn't have been.

"Did you think I could Google all those song lyrics and not find out they were clues in a serial murder case? References kept turning up in the results lists."

"Then I suppose you must know all the rest of the details, too."

"No, I wanted to get the list back to you today, and I figured you could tell me more about the murders than the Internet could."

"A rare compliment. Well, here goes." I began with a description of that spontaneous party in Danny Crenshaw's apartment. Then I gave her a brief account of the deaths that followed.

"The second victim was Monique Floret. I never saw her, but I'm told she was a beautiful woman and a lousy actress. Sometimes affected a French accent, they tell me, but she came from New Jersey; don't remember what her real name was. She was notorious for breaking up Broadway marriages."

"Some hobby," Evan said, "but how long could you keep it up?"

"In Monique's case, she had quite a run. One night she'd gone dancing at the Savoy Ballroom in Harlem. That was a great place, Evan, class all the way, home of the lindy hop and the jitterbug. For a long time, it was the one truly integrated nightspot in Harlem. The Cotton Club catered to white audiences but didn't welcome black faces except onstage. The Savoy welcomed everybody. They had continuous music, two bandstands and two big bands, one playing while the other one was on break. Back in the 1930s, there was a famous Battle of the

Bands between Chick Webb's orchestra and Benny Goodwin's, a black band versus a white band for a mixed audience that loved the music and didn't care who was playing, as long as they were good."

"So, this Monique was murdered there?" Evan asked, cutting to the chase, as usual.

"No, it was later that same night. Plenty of witnesses saw her there dancing, but they couldn't say if she'd been accompanied when she left or had been alone, which wasn't likely in her case. Her death was written off as a suicide, jumping in front of a subway train. But that same day, before her death even happened, the personals columns carried the message: 'SHE GOT HERSELF A HUSBAND, BUT HE WASN'T HERS.' People who noticed it probably thought it was part of some creative but subtle advertising campaign. Nobody figured murder, least of all the police."

"And who was the third one?" Evan prompted.

"Xavier Esterhazy was a fashionable director who was notorious for his casting couch, exploiting young hopefuls. Of both genders, actually. Sort of the mirror image of Monique Floret. He had made plenty of enemies, and not just for his sexual sins. He was found frozen to death in a snowdrift after the big post-Christmas blizzard of 1947. In his case, the message in the papers the day he was found was 'YOU CAN'T STOP THE WEATHER, NOT WITH ALL YOUR DOUGH.'"

"That was a long time between victims."

"Yes, and the next one didn't come along until summer 1949. Ned Spurlock was a sleazy producer who'd had a couple of mild hits but made most of his money by overselling shares in shows and pocketing the difference when they flopped."

"Can you do that?"

"You can, but again, how long can you get away with it? He was under investigation by the district attorney's office at the time he was shot to death. His body was found abandoned in one of those clothing racks I used to dodge when I walked through the Garment District. It was clearly murder this time, but the weapon was never found, and the case remained unsolved. The message in the personals the day it happened: 'SHE'LL START UPON A MARATHON.'"

Evan said, "On the others I can see the connections. A terrible golfer, a husband thief, the weather quote for a person left in a snow-drift. But what was the point of this one? Did it have something to do with the New York Marathon? My friend Gwen has run in three L.A. Marathons and wants to run in that one, but her mom doesn't want her to go. Was the place they found his body somewhere on the marathon route maybe?"

"Nope. New York Marathon didn't start 'til 1970. But one of Nat Spurlock's lucrative flops was a musical that closed out of town called *Boston Marathon*."

"Weren't the police suspicious by this time?"

"If they were, they never admitted they had a serial killer on their hands. Some true-crime writer made the connection around 1950, published a book about it, and came up with the Broadway Execution-er tag. He got half the details wrong. It was a crummy book, what we'd call in Hollywood an exploitation job, but the name stuck, and the case still turns up in books about unsolved murders."

"Wait a minute, Gramps. We have two quotations left. What about them?"

"I'll get to that. First, I have to tell you about another visit to Danny Crenshaw."

——— ·—·—· ———

Every time I visited Danny at the Hotel McAlpin after that, we'd talk about the case. We had one of our most interesting postmortems one day in late 1951, around the time the Broadway Executioner took a curtain call. Danny was still busy, doing a lot of television now. He groused that live TV combined the worst features of legit and pictures, but he seemed to thrive on it nonetheless.

"Seb," he said, "you remember that little get-together we had here around the time of the first murder?"

His I-don't-know-what-number wife peered into the living room. This one was named Suzy, blonde, cute, '50s fashionable, and funny as hell, or at least Danny thought she was. "Hey, can I join you guys? I love murder talk."

"Sure, honey," he said. "But this is serious."

"I can be serious," she promised.

"I've got a little theory about those murders," Danny said. "You remember who was there, Seb?"

"Sure, I think so."

"You in touch with any of them?"

"No. Rosey Patterson's the only one I knew well, and I haven't seen him in years."

"Rosey used to drive me nuts," Danny said. "All that excess energy got on my nerves."

I smiled. Danny had the same effect on people.

"Anyway, they're all still around. Rosey doesn't run around like he used to, but he's held on to some big-money clients. Elmer Belasco's pretty much retired but still in good health, as far as I know. His son Arthur finally took his dad's advice and gave up acting. Got into behind-the-scenes work. Last I heard, he has a job on some show in preparation, satirical revue with young unknown talent. Jerry Cordova works for a record label, and I still see him around once in a while, at parties, doing his Gershwin number. As for Mildred—"

"Poor Mildred," Suzy sighed. "How she ever put up with you, I can't imagine."

"You know her?" I asked.

"Sure," Suzy said. "We have lunch once in a while to compare notes. Sometimes we think all Danny's ex-wives ought to get together, expand our horizons. How many are we now, Danny?"

"You're no ex-wife, baby. Never will be."

"So, what's Mildred doing?" I asked.

"Good works," Danny said. "Her new husband could buy and sell me a hundred times over. Anyway, let me get to the point. We'd talked about Anselm's death, and somebody mentioned what a lousy golfer he was. Then the next day that first message hit the personal ad columns. Then three more murders, three more messages. All the times after the first, the message ran much closer to the crime, not two days later. Sometimes the messages had to have been placed before the murder even happened. So what does that mean, Seb?"

I had a hunch what he was getting at, but I wanted to hear it from him. "I don't know. What's it mean?"

"The Broadway Executioner murders were hatched in this apartment, that's what. I don't know who killed Anselm. Maybe a personal enemy, maybe a random mugger. But somebody at that party got the idea for a series of do-gooder murders of theatrical villains. They put that ad in the papers, whether they'd done the original killing or not, and then they continued on the same path and had a lot of crazy fun doing it. Somebody in this room that day took that idea and ran with it. Maybe Jerry. Maybe Elmer. Maybe Arthur. Maybe Rosey." He smiled now. "Maybe me. Maybe you. Maybe Mildred."

"No, not Mildred," Suzy said. "She'd have killed you next."

"Yeah, probably." Danny was obviously obsessed with the case. He'd even checked out alibis for his roomful of suspects—how he managed to do that, I'm not sure. Unfortunately for his theory, none of them could have done all the murders, according to his charts. Elmer and Rosey were both out of the country at the time of the Floret killing. It was hard to see how Mildred could have physically managed the Esterhazy job, and I couldn't see her in the serial killer role anyway. Arthur was in London when Esterhazy died. Jerry was working in Florida when Spurlock got his. As for me, I was in Hollywood the whole time. Danny didn't mention his own alibis. For a minute I wondered if he was going to confess. He didn't.

Danny was taking his detective work very seriously, but I wasn't. I wasn't even sure the Broadway Executioner existed, though how some opportunist could have entered those pointedly appropriate ads in the personal columns before the fact, short of psychic powers, stumped me.

That same day, maybe while we were kicking around theories, the Executioner was up in Cape Cod taking his fifth victim, Justin Gentry, an aging matinee idol best known for getting supporting players, stage hands, directors, dressers, and anybody who annoyed him fired.

He'd even tried to dismiss the playwright on one production. Died in a boating accident, but what about that newspaper personal item that said "MASSACHUSETTS IS A LONG WAY FROM NEW YORK"?

———— · — · — · ————

"So," I said to Evan, "that finished out the career of the Broadway Executioner, at least as far as I know."

"But that isn't all. What about the last one, about the highest spot? Who got killed to that melody?"

"As far as I know, nobody."

"Then why was it on the list?"

"Because there's a little more to the story."

———— · — · — · ————

Danny had retired from the stage, but he was still doing occasional TV, on videotape now, when he died in 1978, right around the time they were turning his beloved Hotel McAlpin into an apartment building. At least he wasn't around to see the Marine Grill torn up and replaced by a Gap store a dozen years later. In one of our last conversations, Danny noted that Max Bialystock in Mel Brooks's *The Producers* could have been inspired by Ned Spurlock, though much more amusing and less villainous. Danny never lived to see the stage musical with Nathan Lane, but he loved the movie with Zero Mostel.

Life went on, and for years I didn't think much about the Broadway Executioner. Lots was happening. My eighties may have been busier than my seventies. It was only a couple years ago, a happy centenarian living out my days at Plantain Point, that I thought about the mutual interest Danny and I had in those killings, and I considered taking a crack at solving them, just as an intellectual exercise, of course. And so I did, after a fashion.

I'd put together certain clues and got a very rickety theory that sounded good to me, but it might not convince anybody else—and certainly wouldn't fly in a court of law. Besides, all my suspects from that long-ago New York cocktail party were dead. Weren't they? Well, not quite. Arthur Belasco, Elmer's son, had put together quite a career as a Broadway producer—an honest one, I should add—in the last quarter of my century. He was still working and still vigorous, as why shouldn't a young man barely in his eighties be, and he'd come to California on a book tour, promoting his newly published memoirs. Plantain Point has a lot of showbiz residents, and I suggested to our energetic young program director, always looking for diversions for her geriatric charges, that she call Arthur's people and arrange for him to drop in during his California visit, give a little talk maybe, sell and sign some books. Once he was in town, I called his hotel and invited him to pay me a little visit while he was here.

Some people change less than others with the years, and I could see in Arthur's wrinkled face the brash twenty-two-year-old I'd met back in 1946. He remembered me, too, though we hadn't seen each other since. He glanced around at all the entertainment memorabilia in my living room and said it brought back memories. I wanted to bring back one particular memory over a glass of Remy Martin XO.

When he noted a signed photo of Danny Crenshaw in my rogues' gallery, I said casually, "I guess you remember that get-together at Danny's place, back in 1946?"

"Vividly. Hotel McAlpin. It's now called the Herald Towers. They tore out those incredible murals in the basement restaurant. I think they're in a subway station now. Can't argue with progress, can we?"

"We can, but progress won't listen. Did you put anything in your memoirs about that day?"

"No, there was nowhere to go with it, so it wound up on the cutting room floor, as you Hollywood types might put it. We did write it up, though. My daughter Eleanor helped with the book, and that day was so imprinted on my memory that I was able to reconstruct it pretty much word for word onto a tape recorder. Didn't miss a thing."

"As I remember, Eleanor was just a baby at the time. But she joined the family business, too, didn't she?"

"In a big way. She's a better actor than her old man, as my father constantly reminded me. Does plenty of TV, plays, pictures."

"But about that day in Danny's apartment. I know you have a great memory, but I doubt if you can remember every conversation you've had and every social event you've been at since World War II."

"No, but that one was unforgettable. Especially a little colloquy between Danny and his wife and Jerry Cordova about an old Gershwin song. Eleanor really enjoyed that part."

"Any chance you or she could send me a transcript of your notes on that party? I might have a use for it."

"Sure. Be happy to. Why the special interest, Seb?"

"I think that was when you and your dad hatched the Broadway Executioner murders."

Arthur Belasco's eyes widened, then narrowed. He looked around for a moment like a hunted animal. Then he intoned, his voice dripping with menace, "Seb, I don't know what you think you know or how you know it. But if you hope to still be breathing when I leave, we need to come to an understanding." His hand had moved to a bulge in his jacket pocket.

"You can't get away with it," I said. "You're not going to shoot me in my own apartment."

"There are other ways," he said, a gleam of madness in his eyes. "I'm an expert at that, aren't I?"

I'd kept a straight face as long as I could. I laughed at him. "Your dad was right. You are a lousy actor."

Then he laughed, too, and pulled out a pipe. "I had you for a second, though, didn't I?"

"Maybe for a second," I agreed.

"Well, for a second, you had me, too. I heard about Danny's crazy theory, you know, and maybe there's something to it. But the old man and me as the murderers? Very far-fetched, and I'm glad you don't really think that."

"Oh, but I do," I said. "Arthur, you and I both know the chances of getting anybody charged with a series of crimes the police don't even admit were crimes after all these years is zero, and there's nothing to prove my theory in a court of law. We also know that no matter what I say, you have nothing to fear from me and have no reason to pull out your roscoe and ka-chow it at me this pleasant afternoon. But I'd be happy if, just between us, you could admit what happened and tell me how you brought it off."

"You've got a lot of nerve," he said, still taking it as a joke. "First, tell me what your evidence is."

"Okay, here goes. First, look at the songs. Two of the ones that carried clues were in productions of the *Ziegfeld Follies*, and we know your father worked for Ziegfeld in that period."

"Uh-huh. So what?"

"How about this? Most of the songs, except for the Irving Berlin, were from lesser Broadway composers. No Gershwin, Porter, Rodgers, Kern. Instead Shean, Blitzstein, and Brown. But one song was by Kurt Weill, and he was your father's choice as greatest Broadway composer."

"Philo Vance and Charlie Chan would have thrown that one back."

"Okay, but look at the alibis. Elmer couldn't have committed all of the murders. You couldn't have committed all of the murders. But *between* the both of you, you could have done them all. You and Elmer joked about his wanting you to join the family business. Could it be that he asked you in on this project as well?"

"Oh, if he'd been a serial killer, he probably would have. Great family man, my father. You got anything else?"

"The clue on Ned Spurlock referred to somebody running a marathon. The connection wasn't as immediately obvious as some of the others. But Ned Spurlock and Elmer Belasco both worked on a flop musical called *Boston Marathon*."

"I remember that one. It died in Boston, where else?"

"Maybe Elmer had been one of Ned's victims."

"Well, he hated him enough. Still, that's pretty thin."

"Oh, it'll stay pretty thin, but I did save the best clue for last. The line about Massachusetts and New York came from a show called *New Faces of 1952*, which didn't open till May of that year. In late 1951, when the murder of Justin Gentry occurred, you were working on a satirical musical revue that would introduce young talent. Sounds like *New Faces* to me."

"It was. I'm proud to have worked on that show. Incredible cast. Paul Lynde, Eartha Kitt, Carol Lawrence, Alice Ghostley, Mel Brooks. But what was your point?"

"Just this. Before it opened, when it was still in preparation, how many people would have known the lyrics to that Lizzie Borden song? Somebody involved with the production would. Whoever put that line in the personal columns to foretell Spurlock's murder had to have been involved with the show before it opened."

"That one's a little better, Seb, I have to admit. But you're still talking through your hat. How do you know how long that song was in gestation before the show opened and who else might have heard the lyrics? The author might have been singing that at Broadway cocktail parties for a year. Jerry Cordova might have been playing it, for all we know."

"Okay, it's speculation, but I don't expect to satisfy anybody else. I just want to satisfy my own curiosity. So, why don't you just admit to me that you did it? You and your father."

Arthur shook his head. "Sorry to disappoint you, Seb. Your theory is clever. Rosey Patterson would have loved it. But my dad and I weren't murderers." After a moment's silence, he grinned slyly. "We could have done it, though, and if we had, it wouldn't have been a crime. It would have been a public service. Remember that book O .J. Simpson did?"

"Where he said he didn't do it, but this is how he'd have done it if he did it?"

"That's it. Just for fun, I'll use my imagination and do an O. J. number for you on the Broadway Executioner murders."

"Starting with Claude Anselm."

"Oh, that one would have been Dad's alone. Assuming, that is, that it was really part of the series at all, and not just an anonymous mugging, like everybody thought. Dad hated Anselm's guts. He'd worked with him, knew how he operated. He could have stalked the guy and killed him and left the scene knowing he'd never be suspected. But let's say I found out about it. Maybe I saw him just after the killing, spotted something that tipped me off. Maybe he was disposing of the weapon. A bloody golf club would be appropriate. So, I'd get him to tell me the truth, and he'd make me agree to stonewall it. Certainly, I'd have had no problem with the morality of the thing. Then Rosey's brainstorming on it might have inspired us. Dad had done it once. Why couldn't he do it again, especially with me helping him? Put that line about Anselm's lousy golf game in the personals the next day. It was no great trick to place a classified ad anonymously in those days. Then after that, we'd make it harder on ourselves, give ourselves a challenge. Sort of predict the murder to the papers before we actually committed it. Maybe I had this desire to show my dad I really was a good actor, that I could put on a fright wig and do a righteous killing and cover my tracks. Hey, this makes such a good story, I almost wish it really had happened this way. So, let's see, what was the next one?"

"Monique Floret."

"Ah, yes, that bitch. That woulda been mine alone. I would have altered my appearance so I wouldn't be recognized, easy for an actor. 'Even a crappy one,' I hear my dad saying. Blackface maybe? No, I wouldn't risk that in Harlem. But add a moustache, comb my hair a different way, dab on a little gray to make me look older. I'd have gone to the Savoy, danced with her to the alternating bands—"

"How'd you know she'd be at the Savoy?"

"Made a date by phone to meet her there, used a phony name, dropped a few famous ones she'd know to make me look like an insider, pretended I could help her career or something, said my wife didn't understand me. Monique couldn't resist that stuff. She'd tried to frame my dad one time. Didn't know that, did you? It would've killed my mother, but he got out of it before it boiled over. Then I'd have left the Savoy with her, walked the streets looking for my opportunity, pushed her in front of a train in the subway station."

"It wouldn't be crowded enough at that time of night. It sounds risky."

"Having embarked on this plan, you think we were worried about risky? Anyway, I'd have had a chance later if the platform wasn't nearly empty. I had to do it that night, you know. The message was already in all the papers, and you don't pay to advertise a show and then cancel it."

"How about Esterhazy?"

"That would have been Dad's. I wasn't even in town at that time. Esterhazy loved cloak-and-dagger stuff. If Dad had called him and arranged to meet him somewhere secretly, in some cheap and anonymous hotel room, he'd come even in a blizzard, wouldn't tell anybody about it. I'd learned something about drug actions during my short stint in medical school, and that would come in handy faking a natural death. Telling Dad how to do it could have been my contribution. Dad would have drugged him, carried him out by a back exit, and buried him in the snow before he could wake up. Cause of death: freezing."

"Quite a job for a man of his age."

"Seb, you remember how strong my father was, and Esterhazy was the size of a jockey. He could have done it."

"What about Spurlock?"

"Hmm, yeah, that was a tricky one, wasn't it? Shot to death, weapon never recovered, cops had to know it was murder. How the hell would we have done that one?"

"You mean you're stumped?"

"No, no, give me a minute. This is fun, isn't it? We'd have got together on Spurlock, too. Once again, Dad was in a position to arrange a meeting surreptitiously, maybe in a hotel near the Garment District."

"The McAlpin, maybe?"

"That'd be an appropriate gesture, I admit, but probably more of a down-market place, not so conspicuous. So, let's see. I acquired a garment rack and filled it up with long overcoats so the body could be concealed there later. I stationed it in a secluded spot among the trash cans behind the hotel. Meanwhile, Dad was in charge of shooting Spurlock, getting him down a back stairway unseen, and helping me hide the body. We might have tried to hang the guy up in one of the overcoats, but that probably wouldn't work. Whoever pushed the rack to the spot where it was found would have noticed its unusual weight, so he had to be the murderer or his accomplice. Those racks are so commonplace on the streets in that area, any single one is about as noticeable as Chesterton's postman. I'd have done the pushing, looked for a spot to disappear quickly, then abandoned the rack, leaving the cops to find the body and wonder. Dad could have disposed of the gun any number of ways."

"That leaves Gentry."

Now Arthur gave me a broad satirical smile. "You'll need a séance to answer that one. I was nowhere near the scene, so my dad must have handled it by himself. Let me just say he was an experienced sailor and very able, despite his advanced years. He could have found a way. So there you have it. That's how we might have done it—if we'd done it."

"But you didn't do it."

"Heck, no."

"Now, still speaking hypothetically, if you'd done all this, so successfully, with nobody suspecting, why would you have stopped?"

"Gee, I don't know. Maybe we planned more that never came off. I'll bet there were some we wanted to do but couldn't find a way to do them safely."

"Safely for yourselves?"

"For innocent bystanders. We were never safe. That was part of the thrill. We might have wanted to do another in tribute to Danny, whose party was responsible for our whole crime wave. What better way than to send some deserving scoundrel off the top of the Empire State Building to be squashed on the street below? Hard to bring off, though, and we couldn't have the victim take out some poor pedestrian. That would make us murderers rather than public benefactors, wouldn't it? But if we'd been able to do the Empire State Building job, we'd have had a great line for the newspaper ads, from *On the Town*. It's where the sailor on twenty-four-hour shore leave reads in his old guidebook that he should visit the Woolworth Tower for the best view of the city, and the lady cab driver points out to him, 'That ain't the highest spot.'"

"If all this had happened, do you think anybody might have found you out?"

"Not the cops or some true-crime writer, that's for sure."

"Somebody closer. Your daughter Eleanor. She's a Broadway person, too."

"She's gone from ingénues to leading ladies to mother parts to old crones, and she's seen all the theatrical mendacity we did. Good word, mendacity, *Cat on a Hot Tin Roof.* It wouldn't have shocked her, and she wouldn't have given us away. If any of this had happened, you understand. Let me have another glass of that brandy, will you, Seb?"

We parted on friendly terms that day. Had Arthur indirectly confessed to the Broadway Executioner murders, or was this just a game two old codgers had been playing to while away the time? Arthur has since died, too—and he'd seemed so healthy and vigorous that day he came to Plantain Point. So no one at that gathering of Danny's survives, except me.

If all it amounted to was another way to bond with my favorite great-granddaughter, that was okay with me. Evan developed an interest in the music of long before her birth, started listening to original cast albums on whatever her current listening device was, branched out into big bands, swing music, jazz. That was what I'd really been hoping for when I sent her after those old songs.

Then one morning I read in one of the dwindling print newspapers the obituary of a Wall Street investment banker, Edgerton Makepeace, who had blood all over his hands during the financial crisis but was never prosecuted for anything, of course. Not quite in the Bernie Madoff class, but close. He'd backed some Broadway shows, but, more to the point, some Broadway people had lost a ton of money with him. He'd died by drowning in the East River during a visit to the South Street Seaport, a sort of nineteenth-century nautical theme park with a fleet of historic ships. It crossed my mind that the Executioner might be back at it, next generation this time, the little daughter and memoir collaborator, Eleanor Belasco, maybe with an accomplice of her own. I soon dismissed the idea.

But that very day, Evan showed up for one of her regular visits in a state of high excitement.

"Gramps," she said, "it's gone viral; it's being tweeted and retweeted in record numbers—"

"Try speaking English," I said.

"It's all over the Internet, and nobody knows where it came from."

"What is?"

"WHO CARES IF BANKS FAIL IN YONKERS?"

JON L. BREEN *is the author of eight novels, two of them shortlisted for Dagger Awards, and over one hundred short stories. His most recent book is* The Threat of Nostalgia and Other Stories. *A long-time reviewer and columnist for* Ellery Queen's Mystery Magazine *and* Mystery Scene, *he has won two Edgar Awards for his critical writings. A resident of Southern California, he nevertheless loves New York.*

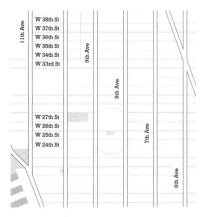

TRAPPED!
A MYSTERY IN ONE ACT

Ben H. Winters

SETTING

Studio L, an unremarkable rehearsal studio in a warren of unremarkable rehearsal studios, collectively known as the Meyers-Pittman Studio Complex, located on the sixteenth floor of a tall nondescript building in Chelsea, a couple blocks south and one long avenue over from Port Authority. The walls are mirrored; the floor is marked with tape; tables and chairs are clustered to represent the location of furniture on the real set.

Downstage right is a props table, laden with all manner of weaponry. The play in rehearsal is the Broadway thriller "Deathtrap" by Ira Levin, and the table displays the full range of weaponry called for in that show, viz., "a collection of guns, handcuffs, maces, broadswords, and battle-axes."

CAST

PATRICK WOLFISH, the stage manager, wears black boots, black clothes, and a black attitude. He sits scowling with arms crossed, projecting the combination of administrative prowess and social awkwardness that is the hallmark of technical personnel.

ELSIE WOODRUFF, the director, is young and smart. While others speak, she nods and furrows her brow, as if she's evaluating their ideas to rate them on a scale of one to four stars. When *she's* speaking, she gestures a lot, as if she feels she must constantly be directing everything.

LEWIS CANNON, the fifty-something actor playing Sidney Bruhl, wears sunglasses indoors and has an unlit cigarette behind his ear. He talks slowly, with the pompous self-regard befitting a star much bigger than he is.

MARCUS VOWELL, the good-looking young actor playing the good-looking young playwright Clifford Anderson, is theatrical, even for a theater person. He is very butch to look at, with well-muscled arms and a prominent jaw, but his affect is high camp, in that way that is utterly delightful for the first thirty seconds or so.

DETECTIVE MA WONG works homicide for the New York City Police Department. Her manner is no-nonsense, in sharp contrast to the abundant nonsense all around her.

TRAPPED!

At rise, DETECTIVE WONG is standing thoughtfully beside the props table, turning a page in her notebook. After a moment, a second pool of light opens far upstage right, discovering PATRICK WOLFISH seated in a chair, his crossed arms signaling irritation and displeasure. Their conversation has an impressionistic feel, as both speak directly to the audience.

WONG: "Deathtrap." That's a play?

PATRICK: Yes. It's a play. About a murder. Actually, it's a play about a play about a murder. "A young playwright sends his first play to an older playwright who conducted a seminar that the young playwright attended." That's the description of the play within a play, but it's the same as the play. Both plays are called "Deathtrap." Very meta. The twist—actually, the first of the twists—

WONG: *(raises her hand)* I just wanted to confirm that it's a play.

PATRICK: Yes. It's a play.

WONG: So that explains the weapons.

PATRICK: Yeah. It's in the stage directions. "The room is decorated with framed theatrical window cards and a collection of guns, hand-cuffs, maces, broadswords, and battle-axes."

WONG: Can you quote the whole play?

PATRICK: It's my job.

WONG: You're the stage manager?

PATRICK: Yes. It's my job to know the script. Also to organize and manage rehearsals, to ensure a safe and productive working environment, to—

WONG: *(raises her hand)* I just wanted to confirm that you're the stage manager.

PATRICK: Yes.

WONG: And you've worked with the producer Otto Klein in the past?

PATRICK: Nine shows and counting.

WONG: Well, just nine. Mr. Klein has been beaten to death, re-member, Mr. Wolfish? His body was found this morning stuffed between the snack machine and the . . . *(She refers to her notes.)* The Dr. Pepper machine.

PATRICK: Right. Yeah. I know.

(WONG fishes in her pocket and holds up a cell phone.)

WONG: And do you know what this is?

PATRICK: It's a phone.

WONG: It's Mr. Klein's phone. Would you read this text, please?

(She holds it higher; PATRICK leans forward and squints, reading the tiny screen.)

PATRICK: But—but I didn't send this. Why would I send this?

WONG: I had the exact same question.

PATRICK: But I didn't send it. Seriously. I lost my phone yesterday.

WONG: Where?

PATRICK: Here. During rehearsal!

WONG: So. Someone with your phone texted Mr. Klein, asking him to arrive an hour early this morning, and then when he did, that person bludgeoned him to death and left his body slumped behind the Dr. Pepper machine. But it wasn't you, because *(making a big show of checking her notes)* you lost your phone. Yesterday.

PATRICK: *(standing up)* Yes. Yes! Well, obviously I *didn't* lose it. Obviously, someone stole it. The murderer!

WONG: Would you sit down, please?

PATRICK: *(still standing)* Ask my husband. Ask Peter! When I got home from rehearsal last night, I was looking all over for my damn phone. Ask him!

WONG: Great idea. Where is he right now?

PATRICK. Right now? He's working. He's an actor.

WONG: Is he in a rehearsal?

PATRICK: No, no. He's—he's not in a show right now. He was up for a swing in *Honeymoon in Vegas*, but the choreographer on that hates him.

WONG: So, where is he?

PATRICK: He's busking. Riding the A/C train, singing Gilbert and Sullivan.

WONG: All right. I'll send someone out to find him, and we can get this thing cleared up. *(She takes out her phone to make a call.)*

PATRICK: Look. Detective. Detective. I've never killed anyone in my life.

WONG: In that case, you're free to go.

PATRICK: Really?

WONG: Sit down, please.

The lights dim on PATRICK *as he reluctantly sits, but stay illuminated on* WONG, *who, after murmuring instructions into her phone, shifts attention to upstage left, where a new pool of light finds* MARCUS VOWELL, *overwrought and overemoting.*

MARCUS: I just—I just—I mean, I *can*not believe it. Dead? Klein is *dead*? He can*not* be dead. I mean, I feel like he is literally right here in this room right now.

WONG: Actually, Mr. Vowell, we're still awaiting the coroner's van. Mr. Klein is out there next to the Dr. Pepper machine, if you'd care to see him.

MARCUS: Oh, my God, no thank you. I could *not* handle that. It's just *so*, so sad and *so*, so weird. I've never known anyone dead before. My friend Rigoberto was extremely sick once, and he was *sure* that it was cancer. He said goodbye to all of us, one by one, and then the doctor told him it was indigestion, and he just had to chew his food more. *Such* a close call. *So* scary.

WONG: Mr. Vowell, who was present at rehearsal yesterday?

MARCUS: Yesterday, yesterday . . . Okay, let's see. We were rehearsing act two, scene two. It's *such* a good scene. Sidney gives his whole shocking speech and then he looks at Clifford and he goes, "I'm out of dialogue. Your go." And then Clifford—that's me, I'm playing Clifford—*such* a good part—I go, "I'm hoping you'll take pity on a pretty face." I love that line. Love it! It's *such* a good play.

WONG: I've never seen it.

MARCUS: Oh.

WONG: I don't see a lot of theater.

MARCUS: That's a shame.

WONG: I saw *The Lion King*.

MARCUS: Oh! Wasn't it *so* gorgeous? Wasn't it just *amazing*?

WONG: Eh. Lions? Singing? I didn't buy it. So, who was present at rehearsal yesterday?

MARCUS: Right, right, right, right. Okay. Me, obviously, plus Lewis Cannon, he's playing Sidney. You've heard of him.

WONG: No.

MARCUS: Okay, well, he's an actor. And then Patrick Wolfish, of course, he's the stage manager. And Elsie, the director, and Mr. Klein. The producer obviously doesn't have to be at every rehearsal, but he is always around. Like, always. But now he's dead—I just can't *believe* that he's dead—it's just so, *so*—

WONG: Sad, yes, you said. Marcus, did you get a message like this one last night?

(She holds up the phone, as before.)

MARCUS: *(Reading, puzzled first and then horrified.)* No. Wait— wait. Oh, my *God*. Patrick killed Klein! Patrick killed him! This is *insane*! He *murdered* him? The stage manager did it? Why would he *do* that?

WONG: Good question. Any idea why Mr. Wolfish would have wanted Mr. Klein dead?

MARCUS: No! Klein was terrific. He was a *marvelous* man! He was marvelous! Everybody loved him. *Everybody.*

(The lights dim on weepy MARCUS, and, downstage left, we find ELSIE WOODRUFF.)

ELSIE: He was a monster. A total monster. If I were making a list of the worst people in the world, I would go, first Klein, and then the guy from the church that pickets soldier's funerals because God hates gay people. Or maybe Bashar Al-Assad would be second. And then the funeral guy, third. But *definitely* Klein is first.

WONG: So you're glad he's dead, Ms. Woodruff?

ELSIE: I didn't say *that*. Death sucks. But I'm not rending my garments about it, is all I'm saying. He was a bad producer and a bad human being.

WONG: Why, then, did you choose to work with him?

ELSIE: Well, Detective, have you ever heard of money? It's thin and green and you need it to pay for things. I live in a Williamsburg walk-up that costs me two grand a month. I need to work. Besides, I love this play. Klein was a moron, but an Off-Broadway revival of *Deathtrap* was a solid idea. Some other people disagreed.

WONG: Oh? And which people were those?

(Lights down on ELSIE and up on PATRICK, who huffs.)

PATRICK: I made no secret of that opinion. Reviving *Deathtrap* was a bad decision. It was a sentimental favorite of Klein's, but it has zero chance of connecting with a contemporary audience.

WONG: And why is that?

PATRICK: It's dated, for one thing. Carbon copies? Electric type-writers? Home phones?

WONG: You don't think a modern audience knows what a home phone is?

PATRICK: Well, of course they do. But it marks the piece. It makes it feel stuffy and small. I told Klein, let's do something that matters. I told him, you want to do a thriller, let's do Martin McDonagh. Or let's do a Belber. Let's do a Sarah Ruhl. Let's do *Hamlet*, for God's sake!

(Lights switch back to ELSIE.)

ELSIE: *(rolling her eyes)* Does he think there's no outdated referenc-es in *Hamlet*? When was the last time you ate funeral meats, Detective? When was the last time you were hoisted by a petard?

WONG: What?

ELSIE: Exactly. Just for the record, I'm not surprised that Patrick killed him.

WONG: I didn't say that he did.

ELSIE: What?

WONG: Do *you* think that artistic differences constitute sufficient cause for murder, Ms. Woodruff?

ELSIE: No. *(suddenly feeling cornered)* Why?

WONG: *(turning a page in her notebook)* How was your working relationship?

ELSIE: With Klein? Why? What have you heard?

(Lights down on ELSIE and up on LEWIS CANNON. He peeks over the top of his sunglasses, as if relating a great secret.)

LEWIS: Did they get along? No, ma'am, they did *not* get along. They certainly did not. And listen, I've seen a lot of friction on a lot of sets over the years, and this was bad. This was very bad.

WONG: Sorry, wait just a moment. Your name is Mr. Cannon, is that correct?

LEWIS: *(incredulous)* Uh, yes? That's a joke, right? *(Off WONG's look.)* No? God, that's *embarrassing*. For you, I mean. Embarrassing for *you*. But okay. That's fine. Yes, my name is Lewis Carlin Cannon. I have won Obies. I have won Drama Desk Awards. *(Off her look, again.)* You do not know what those things are, and I am *horrified*. Listen, darling, I was Nicely Nicely last year.

WONG: What is that?

LEWIS: *Guys and Dolls?* Roundabout revival? *(sings a little)* "I got the horse right here . . . " No?

WONG: I don't like theater.

LEWIS: Oh, no?

WONG: Whenever I watch a play, I think that if these people were really good, they'd be on television.

LEWIS: You better be careful, sweetheart. Someone around here might kill *you*.

WONG: So. You said that Mr. Klein's relationship with the director, Ms. Woodruff, was a bit tense.

LEWIS: Tense? Tense is not the word. This was brutal. This was like—well, I'll tell you, one time I was working at the Public, with Tony—that's Tony Kushner—and we're rehearsing, and I'm giving him some little suggestions—

WONG: Excuse me. *(WONG takes out her phone.)* Hello?

LEWIS: And George—George C. Wolfe, that is—he gets very agitated by this side conversation, and things are getting *very* hot—

WONG: Sorry, Mr. Cannon, just a moment—

LEWIS: And then Stritchie comes in—that's Elaine Stritch, I called her Stritchie—

WONG: Please, stop talking now.

(WONG listens to her phone for a moment while the lights dim on LEWIS and find PATRICK.)

WONG: My officers are having some trouble locating your husband. Can you give us more of a description?

PATRICK: He's a six-foot-tall man with a beard, singing "Poor Little Buttercup" on the A train. I think you'll find him.

WONG: We're doing our best, sir.

(Lights down on PATRICK as WONG turns to ELSIE.)

ELSIE: We didn't have a bad relationship. He just had a bad presence, okay? That's all.

WONG: What do you mean by a "bad presence"?

ELSIE: I mean, when he was present, everything was bad. He would stand behind me while I was trying to direct, making these small agitated noises. Actors are tiny people. They are fragile. They need to be brought along gently, like ponies. I would say, "You're doing great, you're almost there . . ." And there would be Klein, standing behind me, huffing on an unlit cigar, making everybody palpitate. He was ruining the show, and when a show tanks, the producer goes on to another show. But the director? The director is the captain. The director goes down with the ship.

WONG: So, the production was going poorly?

(ELSIE opens her mouth to answer, and the lights switch over to LEWIS.)

LEWIS: Yes. A disaster! That's why I was trying to get out.

WONG: Excuse me?

LEWIS: This was the *worst* train wreck I've ever been involved in, and I was once in a musical about a train wreck called *Train Wreck!* which was a total train wreck. Although Alan—that's Alan Cumming—

WONG: Mr. Cannon?

LEWIS: Alan brought his usual joie de vivre to the role of the coal shoveler. He and Sutton—

WONG: Mr. Cannon? What did you mean by "get out"?

LEWIS: Oh. It's nothing. I had . . . another offer. Another opportunity.

WONG: And what do you mean by "trying"?

(Lights shift to MARCUS, who gasps.)

MARCUS: Oh, my God, *of course!* I forgot all about that! Yes, he got a call—it was right in the middle of rehearsal. Monday, maybe? Tuesday? He got off the phone and . . . oh, my *God*, it was *Lewis*. Lewis Cannon killed Klein! That *monster!*

(Lights shift to ELSIE.)

ELSIE: Yup. Yes. I was there when he got the call. We were in the middle of the heart attack scene, end of act one. It's high drama, big emotions, and Lewis's phone rings and he *takes it. (sighs)* Actors. I'm telling you.

WONG: Go ahead, please.

ELSIE. He's on his phone, and his eyes get wider and wider, and you just know he's going to get off the phone and say something enormously egotistical and self-regarding. You can just tell.

(Lights shift to PATRICK.)

PATRICK: He just goes (*does a very good Lewis impression*), "Three words, folks. Gypsy. Broad. Way."

WONG: And what was your reaction?

PATRICK: I told him that Broadway is one word, and then I said, "Back to work, folks."

(Lights shift to ELSIE.)

ELSIE: After rehearsal, he went to Klein, who of course was a monster about it. He refused to let Lewis out of his contract. Absolutely refused. Stood there puffing on his disgusting cigar just going, "No, no, absolutely not." I told Klein, just let him go play Goldstone; he'll be terrible in this show if he feels handcuffed, pardon the pun. *(Off WONG's look.)* There are handcuffs? In the play? Oy. Listen, the point is, Klein thought that Lewis's celebrity, exceedingly minor though it is, was the only thing selling tickets.

(Lights back to LEWIS, who takes off his sunglasses and stares balefully at WONG.)

LEWIS: Fine. You got me. I wanted out. I shouted about it a little. So that means I killed the guy? What am I, Sweeney Todd all of a sudden? *(Beat.)* He's a murderer. In a play. Skip it.

(Switch to MARCUS, who is back in full overwrought mode.)

MARCUS: I mean, I just can't *believe* it. It's *crazy*. First, it was the disgruntled stage manager, and now it's the fading Broadway star. It's like *everybody* is killing Klein!

(Switch to ELSIE.)

ELSIE: You know what it's like? It's like one of those old Broadway thrillers! *Gaslight. Dial M. for Murder. Mousetrap.* That whole genre, which Levin was totally paying tribute to with *Deathtrap*. Someone gets killed, the audience gets clues along the way, but the solution is always more complicated than it seems. And there's always a policeman of some sort. Usually a dull, plodding sort of person. No offense.

WONG: That's okay.

(Switch to LEWIS.)

LEWIS: Hey, can I make a little suggestion, here, Detective Wong? You want to know who killed the guy, maybe start with the person who literally said the words, "I could *kill* that guy."

WONG: And who was that?

(Switch to MARCUS, who looks up from his crying and takes a long pause before speaking.)

MARCUS: Yes. Technically, yes. Yes, technically, I said that. But not like *that*. I didn't say it like, "I am *going* to kill him." I said it like, "I *could* kill him!" As in, like, "You're exasperating me!" Haven't you ever said you wanted to kill somebody!

WONG: No.

MARCUS: But surely people have said it about *you*.

WONG: Excuse me?

MARCUS: Nothing. Forget it! I did not kill Mr. Klein. I didn't—I couldn't!

WONG: Because . . . ?

MARCUS: Because . . . because . . .

WONG: Yes?

MARCUS: *(leaping from his chair)* Because I *loved* him. And he loved me, too. He couldn't say it, Detective, but he did. It was clear every time I looked into his eyes. He would say, "Good morning, Marcus," but what his heart was saying was, "I love you, I love you, I love you!"

WONG: Interesting.

MARCUS: Interesting? I lay bare my soul and all you can say is "interesting"? Are you not human, Detective? Have you no soul? This man and I shared a hidden passion, smoldering in our breasts like the living coals of a fire, and all you can say is "interesting"?

WONG: Very interesting.

MARCUS: Oh, for God's *sake*.

WONG: Will you sit down, please? *(MARCUS complies, slowly, while WONG checks her notes.)* I had understood that Mr. Klein was married.

MARCUS: Yes. Right. "Married." To a "woman." His "wife" is a "makeup artist" and she "travels frequently."

WONG: May I take your quote marks as indicative of skepticism?

MARCUS: He was in the closet, is what I'm saying. He was way back in the back of the closet, with the winter hats. Which was totally infuriating. Hello? The twenty-first century has arrived, Mr. Klein! You work in show business, Mr. Klein! And not television, either. In the *theater*. It's New York! It's Chelsea! Go ahead and be gay!

WONG: So, the fact is, then, that you confessed your love to him, and he turned you down.

MARCUS: I guess so. I guess if all you care about is "facts," then yes.

WONG: Excuse me. *(WONG takes out her phone and listens for a moment.)* Well. Well. Okay, then.

MARCUS: What? What was that?

(During the following, the various pools of light melt away into a general wash, and we find the cast members, in their various positions, around the room. WONG turns her attention back to where it started, to PATRICK, while the others watch.)

WONG: Well, we found him.

PATRICK: Peter? *(visible relief)* Thank God.

WONG: And . . . he doesn't know anything about any missing phone.

PATRICK: What?

WONG: Peter told my officer that your cell phone was definitely in your possession yesterday evening. He says that you were sending and receiving texts all night.

PATRICK. What? But that's—that's impossible.

MARCUS: Oh, my *God!* Patrick killed Klein! *Again.*

PATRICK: But—but I didn't. I didn't kill him. I've never killed anyone. My phone—my phone was stolen—

WONG: So you've said.

ELSIE: I am going to write such a great play about this.

LEWIS: So, the mystery is solved? We can leave now?

WONG: Not quite.

ELSIE. It's old-fashioned, sure, but producers will love it. Small cast. Virtually no set . . .

(PATRICK leaps for the props table, grabs a battle-axe.)

PATRICK: No one is going anywhere!

ELSIE: . . . shocking denouement.

WONG: *(unruffled)* I thought those were all props.

PATRICK: Not all of them. My research revealed that constructing a fake battle-axe would cost as much as buying a real battle-axe. I also got real police handcuffs from an online auction site, rather than paying through the nose for fakes. *(He swings the axe menacingly at WONG.)* I'm a great stage manager.

WONG: *(drawing her service weapon)* Put that down, please. I've called my officers, and they will be here any minute.

PATRICK: But I didn't kill him! Why would I? He was my ticket!

WONG: He was your what?

LEWIS: Yeah. What does that mean?

PATRICK: It means I've been stealing from him, you dummy.

WONG: What?

PATRICK: Why would I kill him when I've been robbing him blind for years?

ELSIE: *(taking notes)* Oh, this is fantastic.

MARCUS: Stealing! Oh, my *God!* Patrick is a thief! An embezzler! Hm. Actually, I guess that's not as bad as a murderer.

WONG: You'd best explain yourself, Mr. Wolfish.

PATRICK: What's to explain? I've been submitting phony receipts. Raiding the petty cash. For years. Years! Klein is a dope who doesn't pay attention, and that's been my livelihood for a decade and a half! Why do you think I wanted him to do a show that might draw a paying audience! Peter and I just bought a house in Hudson, for God's sake. If Klein is dead, how will I pay the mortgage?

(A booming, merry voice sounds from offstage.)

KLEIN: Yes! How?

(The door of the studio swings open. Enter OTTO KLEIN, beaming, drinking a Dr. Pepper.)

KLEIN: How, indeed?!

LEWIS: Well, I'll be damned.

ELSIE: Another twist!

(MARCUS runs to KLEIN and hugs him fervently.)

MARCUS: You're not dead! You're not dead! This is *so* amazing. He's not dead, everybody!

KLEIN: No, I'm not, kid. Though I got one hell of a crick in my neck. *(To WONG.)* Listen, next time I die, remind me to do it in a hammock.

WONG: You got it.

PATRICK: But—but—I don't understand—

KLEIN: Of course, ya don't. But I been wise to you a long time, Patrick. I just needed to hear you say it! And more important, I needed to get it all recorded on my phone. *(He holds up his iPhone and grins.)* You'll be offering your next round of explanations to a judge.

PATRICK: And—but— *(He wheels toward WONG.)* Don't cops have better things to do than aid in this sort of—of—playacting?

WONG: I wouldn't know. I'm not a cop. I'm—

ELSIE: Wait! Ooh! Wait! Let me guess it! You're his *wife*!
WONG: Bingo.

(WONG and KLEIN embrace.)

ELSIE: I *love* it!
MARCUS: Well, color me corrected. Not gay at all! Straight and married to a fake policeman! God, I love this cit—ahh!

He screams as PATRICK charges past, tossing aside the battle-axe and leaping at KLEIN in a fury. KLEIN and WONG move to defend themselves, but LEWIS smoothly intercepts PATRICK, drops him with a hard left to the chin, grabs the handcuffs from the table, throws them on PATRICK, and sits on him. Everybody applauds.

ELSIE: Wow.
MARCUS: Bravo!
KLEIN: Well done, Lewis. Well done and thank you.
WONG: *(getting off her phone)* The real police will be here momentarily.
KLEIN: Good. Very good! Boy, this all worked perfectly.
PATRICK: This isn't fair. This isn't fair, goddamn it! I was trapped. Trapped!
ELSIE: *(to LEWIS)* So, wait. Are you an undercover cop or something?
LEWIS: No. Are you kidding? God, no. That's all from the play *Harlem Streetlights*, which I did with LAByrinth at the Bank Street in—God, was it ninety-two? Ninety-four? *(Everybody has immediately lost interest. They begin to yawn or take out their phones.)* Anyway, Stevie—that's Stephen Adly Guirgis; I call him Stevie—he handpicked me for the role, and Stevie said that in the interest of verisimilitude ...

(The curtain falls as he keeps talking.)

THE END.

Dedicated to Erik Jackson, man of the theater

BEN H. WINTERS *is the author, most recently, of the Last Policeman trilogy, which won both the Edgar Award and the Philip K. Dick Award for distinguished science fiction. He is also the author of* Sense and Sensibility and Sea Monsters, *a* New York Times *best-selling satire, and* The Secret Life of Ms. Finkleman, *an Edgar-nominated middle-grade novel. Before doing any of these those things, he was for many years a lyricist and librettist. He lives in Indianapolis and at BenHWinters.com.*

WALL STREET RODEO

Angela Zeman

"Mr. Emil Bauer, I'd hoped to see you here. Especially today."

I had rubbed against a hunchback this noon. Accidentally, of course. I'd never be so crass as to touch the poor fellow on purpose. Besides, everyone knows the luck comes from an accidental touch. Thus, you understand my excitement. Then I positively tripped over little James here, who dropped his five-dollar bill right in my path! Don't tell ME that's not luck! So, I hustled him and his cash right here. To Emil's spot. "Please meet my friend, newly minted, you might say, heh, in this neighborhood." I flourished my hand toward the child. "Mr. James Conner."

Emil glanced fuzzily at the boy. "How old is it?"

The kid bowed slightly, tattered though he was. "Eight years, sir."

"Ah. Vell brought up," Emil muttered, sounding like a growly dog. He wriggled closer to the statue's base, shredding the seat of his old pants on the rough cement. I don't know which took me aback more, the kid bowing or Emil growling.

Emil rearranged some phlegm in his throat and said to me, "Mr. Slick Nick! You are vell?"

"Just Nick, please. As well as you see me, so kind." I snapped out my words, showing teeth for a smile. Emil's eyesight was too poor to catch my true expression. I *despised* that moniker, stuck on me by some low rabble I no longer acknowledge. Jealousy, that's all it was. Breathing deeply to calm myself, I managed to soften my smile.

"Zo, Mr. James." Old Emil squinted at the small boy, then dropped his gaze to the five spot in the boy's outstretched palm. "Ah. Dis is for me?" He didn't reach for it. His gnarled hands stayed folded atop the old cane he held upright between his knees. The dough had triggered a memory, and as his watery faded eyes began to blink, Emil forgot he had an audience. Money did that to him. A five spot or a penny, no difference, and his mind would drift back to long-ago better days.

I'd warned the boy he'd do that, but not to worry. I frowned. He didn't *look* worried. Maybe he believed me, or maybe . . . "Kid . . . you *sure* you're not a Murphy? Y'look like one."

The boy shrugged but avoided my gaze. Sure sign of a lie. I studied him, my toe tapping the bricks. Hm. Some Murphy had assuredly given him that distinctive shade of red hair. His mother, possibly. Thousands of Murphys filled the tenements, like barnacles on a barge. Dear God. I'd better treat him decently. No amount of money was worth the risk of upsetting Murphys. I shivered.

I myself, though not Irish, heavens no, have spent some few unlucky nights outside, to which I credit my most admirable virtue: acceptance of all men, no matter their circumstances. Besides, Jamey, who swore he was not a Murphy, had money. And I did not. Which was why I troubled to make his acquaintance and drag him over to Wall Street.

"Is this story worth a fiver?" James asked me with what I had to admit was an admirable sneer for an eight-year-old. He'd obviously had dough chiseled out of him before. His palm was already drooping toward the safety of his jeans pocket.

I faked a scowl at him: "A cynic at your age? Tsk, tsk!"

"I don't even know you!" He scowled back at me. Were I not so kindly natured, I'd say the boy actually snarled. I patted his cute round head, then wiped my hand on my trousers. Pests abound in our beloved New York, especially in spring.

I snagged his arm and peeled open the sweaty fingers, then pushed the hand back at Emil again. "It's worth a fiver just to get him started," I muttered to James. "Trust me." I stroked my straggly goat's beard and turned my moral back on the implications of a stranger telling a very small boy to "trust me." I'd been a small boy once, too. A wry echo of my mother's voice said in my head, *"But never so sharp as this one."* Mothers. What do they know? Then I flinched, as if her ghost was hovering near with a rolling pin in hand.

We had to get old Emil to open up. Spare dough was rare these days, except among fat guys wearing diamond stickpins, who were more likely to swipe yours than share theirs. A gaggle of skinflints, to a man.

"Look here, Emil. This boy wants to hear the barmaid and the roller skate story. Don't you, James?" The boy nodded somewhat doubtfully but then repeated, " . . . Roller skates?"

(*Hooked!* . . .) I touched my hankie to my eye to catch a falling tear over the gullibility of precious little tykes. Aw. Then I stuffed the rag out of sight. I've never understood the unfailing draw of roller skates. Baffling.

"You won't regret this!" Pretending Emil had agreed, I hurried around to perch on the step next to the fellow. He liked to sit on the bottom steps of the Federal Building, dozing his old age away at the feet of the Father of Our Country. Well, not the father of mine, no indeed, but why quibble? George Washington, forever bronzed for the enjoyment of pigeons. In Emil's position, he could lean his arthritic back against the sun-heated pedestal and keep a fond and comfortable eye on the Stock Exchange across the way.

"Emil used to work there." I pointed at the exchange. "Before his, um, early retirement."

James peered askance at the old man, whose mounds of threadbare tweed-draped corpulence seemed permanently bonded to the pediment holding up George. "Why'd you retire early, Emil?" His young voice seemed a bit rougher than it should for a tyke of his age. *Interesting. Did he possibly smoke? No. I refused to believe it.*

After a silence, Emil answered. "To experience the glory of a thirty-year vacation, dear James. Near a river. The air was healthier there."

James and I glanced at each other at the same moment. I knew better, and James did not believe him.

As my mouth opened to beg James to let it go, he blurted, "Sing Sing?"

Emil nodded.

"How much did you steal?"

Emil shrugged. "I can't remember. I'm old now."

"Poor fellow." I turned aside from Emil and mouthed to James: "*Three hundred g's.*"

James's eyes narrowed. He mouthed back at me, "*For that, he got thirty years?*"

I made a face. "*Took it from the wrong fellow.*"

James remained standing, but at eight, he was level with us, like a trio huddled round a burning oil drum in sleety weather. "So cozy!" I exclaimed. "All friends together, right, James? May I call you Jamey?" Emil swayed away from me as if the question was indelicate. Jamey gave me the fish-eye but nodded, willing to get along, probably due to the cash.

I leaned toward Jamey. "To be clear," I whispered harshly, "if he remembers where he stashed his goods, I'll be happy to reimburse your fiver. The rest is *mine*. Got that?"

His shoved his head toward me on his twiggy neck. "We'll see," he snapped.

I could've bitten him. But fortune smiled on Jamey, and Emil spoke up.

"Everybody vants to know about ze roller skater, poor lass," mused

Emil in his high, slightly hoarse voice. He smacked his dry lips and eyed me. He must've calculated the contents of my wallet by the holes in my coat, because he instantly sighed and looked away. "*Ein bisschen bier* vould be pleasant."

I couldn't deny it. My beard was dripping like a wet rag. So unattractive. "April weather," I muttered.

Emil settled his haunches more comfortably on the step and then looped his hands around his knees. He let his cane drop onto the broad sidewalk in front of us. Jamey leaped to retrieve it, but I shook my head at him. "It's Emil's game," I muttered behind my hand.

Jamey looked at me, puzzled for only a second. He moved to make more room to allow Emil's game to proceed, if it should happen. Shrewd child.

I'd seen Emil's game in action and figured it was yet another reason why he spent his days on these steps, leaning on President Washington. Bankers and brokers were not just of the toffee-nosed "how dare you!" breed, but also usually flush. If they perchance tripped or, even better, fell over Emil's cane, to a man they would bash and kick the poor old guy in revenge for injuring their dignity—that most fragile of body parts. That is, until Bull stopped the show and made the victim empty his pockets to soothe Emil's pain. Then Bull would shove the patsy to move along, and he and Emil would split the haul. Speaking of . . .

A vast shadow cast itself over us.

"Hey, Bull," said Jamey.

"Ah, heh, you know each other, what a surprise!" I used my best party voice.

Jamey shot me a patronizing look. "Everybody knows Bull."

He meant this Wall Street Bull, who I'm fairly certain is human. The other one weighs seven thousand pounds and doesn't move, although he seems ready to: gouging and snorting, his bronze horns lowered threateningly. Tourists had fallen hard for the Wall Street "Charging" Bull. His creator, the artist Arturo Di Modica, had parked him right in front of the exchange one night last Christmas, like a present under the big tree. City Hall had demanded the "gift's" removal. But tourists speak loudly with dollars. I heard the city refused to buy the Bull from Di Modica but, to keep the tourists happy, will soon shift him—the bull, not its creator—to Broadway in front of the small Bowling Green Park, but facing uptown. Both he and the copper we called Bull . . . well, certain resemblances, that's all I'll say in mixed company.

Emil shivered as his sun disappeared, then he glanced up to view the Bull blocking all light. Emil's face glowed with delight! "Bull, my boy! Sit down!" (As if the Bull could fold his vast bulk and perch on a narrow step. Sometimes Emil doesn't think things through.) "I'm just about to tell these two gentlemen about the roller skates!"

Bull nodded, as if impressed. Even his thin lips curved at the ends as if trying to remember smiling from his younger days. "Yeah? That's a good story. You'll like it, Jamey. Mind if I hang close 'n hear it, too?"

The Bull was big, as his name implied, and he also pursued the occupation implied—he was Wall Street's cop. The NYPD kept the other Wall Street posts in rotation, but for some reason, Bull was permanent here. Maybe because he was due to retire soon? Just a guess. His name also fit perfectly, because if anything happened that he didn't like, he'd beat the living bejeesus out of you. Never laid a fist on me, I assure you. But like some, the Bull couldn't get enough of Emil's stories. I figure that's why he's never more than twenty feet away from the old man. Touching, isn't it?

The Bull, displaying rare affection, patted Emil on the shoulder. "Thanks, but I gotta stay standing, Emil. In case. You know. Duty."

Oh, yeah. The Bull—protector of Wall Street—had to be ready on his feet to chase down wind-blown umbrellas or give directions to tourists.

Emil nodded in grave sympathy. "Always duty first, Bull. God bless you."

I turned my head, suddenly happy I'd missed lunch.

"Enough of this. A stack of chores're waitin' for me."

My eyebrows shot up. Was Jamey making demands? Of Emil? Of me? Kid had moxie. A bit of pride tickled my chest.

Jamey folded his arms, the bill still crumpled in his fist. He braced his thin legs and stuck out his chin. Kid meant business.

Bull's eyebrows rose. He winked at Jamey. "He's serious, Emil. Jamey delivers his mother's mending every day over to the club girls. That's how they get on."

Emil smiled at Jamey. "I'll try to hurry, then, son. A good boy."

I patted Jamey's shoulder. "All will become clear soon. Trust me." Oh dear. I hated that phrase. "Give Emil the fiver."

He almost didn't . . . then he did. If he weren't only eight, I'd have been fearful of crossing him in business. Thankfully, he *was* only eight.

Emil took the bill, sniffed at it.

I cleared my throat. "It's a bill, Emil. Not something to eat."

Emil bobbed his head gently. "Habit. Different times." He chuckled at himself, then stretched his long arms and filled his lungs with air, and finally began. "Zis young woman—"

I interrupted, "Long time ago, right Emil?" Bull frowned at me, but I didn't care. Emil needed direction.

"Oh, yass. Long ago. Forty years, I am tinking. Her name vas Rose. Because of her hair, I'm sure *you* understand." He directed this at Jamey, who nodded as he shoved grubby red bangs out of his eyes. "See, this young lady vas truly a lady, believe me, but as ve all must do things to keep da beer on the table, so did she. She verked in a musical bar, and instead of valking around, she roller-skated on the vooden floor. It vas a novelty of da time."

Jamey gasped. "Really? I'da liked to seen that!"

Emil leaned forward and grabbed one of Jamey's paws. "A good son like you, I vould not lie." He settled back again and sighed. "One day, she, uh . . . she died."

I almost fell into the street. "She didn't *die*. She married you. Remember, Emil?"

Emil looked at me, eyes unfocused for a few moments. Then they cleared. "Yass. You are right. Da lovely Rose consented to be my vife. She retired her skates and verked to make a good home for us. Ve both hoped for a son." His voice trailed off in sadness. "Like zis dear boy . . . "

"And you had several, didn't you?" I prompted. Bull frowned at me again. I lifted my hands to him, meaning, somebody has to keep him on track. Bull nodded. He knew about the loot lost somewhere in old Emil's memory, and he knew I did, too. So he stayed pleasant and waited for more of the story to unfold.

"What were your sons' names, Emil?" That might help, if he remembered them all.

"Mmm . . . " Emil looked at his feet. Thinking. I hope.

"Walter?" I started him off.

"Nah, not Valter, Giselle vas da first."

"That's a girl's name," Jamey stated flatly. He looked at me. "I know that much."

"Yes, indeed," agreed Bull. He nudged me with a toe. "Actually, Emil had all girls."

I brushed dust from my shins resentfully. "Nix that. How would you know?"

"Of course Bull vould know!" said Emil, frowning at me. The frown faded. And when Bull sighed, I knew Emil's memory was again derailed.

"Sorry I mentioned it," I told Bull. And meant it.

Bull rocked on his massive feet and murmured to Emil, "Alice." That galvanized Emil. "Yass, yass! Alice, my luffly Alice."

He smiled up at Bull, who said, "She was very lovely. Who else do you remember?"

Emil breathed deeply, making an effort to remember for Bull. "V—um—Vanessa. Yass. Ah, my luffly Vanessa, she loved to dance, like her mother." The memory evidently made him happy.

Bull shifted. "So Emil, how many daughters were you and the beautiful Rose blessed with, huh?"

Emil shook his head. "So long ago. Seven little girls we had. Little girls with pretty red hair and dresses. Shoes, dey needed. Dere feet, they grew and grew. Like the girls themselves." He sighed. "Dey were angry with me always. Always needing stockings, school books I could not afford. . . . This is vy I hire my services to dem. Over dere." He tipped his head toward the exchange. "I vas a very good accountant," he added heatedly.

Okay. Now we were getting somewhere. I cleared my throat. "I'm sure. And now your girls are lovely, lovely grown-up women. Aren't they, Emil?" Subtle. Nothing heavy handed. I felt proud of myself.

But Emil shrugged. "I don't know . . . "

Jamey tilted his head. "Sure you do. You're the papa, you had to raise them and then marry them off so some other guy would buy their dresses and food. And then you get grandbabies."

I stared at Jamey. "Full of surprises, you are, kiddo."

Emil's wrinkled old mouth puckered. Something was bothering him. I leaped in, hoping this would lead us to the *right* memories, the ones we wanted to hear. "So. Now. As Jamey said, your lovely girls all married handsome gentlemen—" I had to pause as Bull gave in to a fit of coughing, which sounded suspiciously like laughter. He finally settled down, red faced. "All done?" I asked him politely. He nodded. I returned to Emil. "So, they all married, did they?"

Again Emil shrugged. "I don't know."

Jamey stepped closer. "Why don't you know? They're your family. Right?"

Emil gave Bull a frightened look. He reached for his cane, his big hands fumbling and shaking. Jamey picked it up and handed it to him. Emil snatched it angrily. "I don't know because I don't know. If I know, den I must know what it is your Slick Nick and Bull want to hear. I don't *want* to remember!"

Bull and I tried to hush him, but Jamey wouldn't quit. "Don't you live with your family?"

Emil turned, head trembling violently. "No, no. I don't know."

"Then who takes care of you? You're sorta clean, ya don't live on the streets, that's clear enough. And look at the fat on ya. Somebody must keep you fed. Who?"

Emil stared wide-eyed down at Jamey. "I don't know." Despite his frail wobbles, he tried to go around Jamey.

But Jamey planted his fireplug body in front of him. Emil growled at him, but the kid didn't seem worried. His words sounded stern. "Look. You don't dump your family. You seem okay to me, for an ex-con. Families gotta take you back, anyway. 'At's why you got family, Ma says."

Emil stopped suddenly and peered at the little boy. He never wore glasses, but I'll bet he needed them. "Your ma says dat?"

Jamey nodded vigorously.

"Do you—do you—have a papa?" Emil asked Jamey.

Jamey tilted his head. "Sure. Every kid's got a pop somewheres. Ma says so, anyway."

"Ah, ah, zo, he does not live in ze same house with you?"

Jamey shook his raggedy hair. A no, I presume. "He's too busy, Ma says. I think he ran off. In fact . . . well, I just think it's good he's gone. Good for Ma, I mean. And us."

"Us?" Emil inquired.

Jamey nodded. "Me an' my brothers."

Emil leaned on his cane. He wobbled, the cane wobbled, but in spite of all that movement, he appeared to be thinking. I rushed up to his side and touched his elbow.

"Emil."

He jerked his arm away from me but stayed where he was. Okay. Maybe still thinking.

"Mr. James," he suddenly said. "May I go home with you today?"

Jamey seemed taken aback, but he shrugged. "Sure. Near dinner time anyway. Ma always makes enough for an army. From habit, she says."

And while Bull and I stood watching, the two shuffled away arm in arm, going east on Wall Street. I wanted badly to follow, but how to lose the well-muscled person at my side?

We stood together and watched the two figures until they turned north on a side street and disappeared from sight.

"Ah, well, Bull. Nice seeing you again."

Bull glanced down at me, a wide grin on his face. "I'll bet." He strolled off. To do his duty, no doubt.

I waited until I decided Bull was too far away to notice, then I ran as fast as I've ever run in my life, trying to catch up to Emil and Jamey. I darted in and out of all the side streets, nothing. Nothing in sight for me to follow. Damn it, nothing!

———— · — · — · ————

The next morning, no obliging hunchback strolled my way. Nor any stray dough, either. I held down a curb in front of a strip club—quiet at this time of the morning—and tried to come up with a new plan. I kept in mind that just possibly, possibly, I still had some luck left over from yesterday.

Just then, whistling from a tortured songbird pierced my sensitive ears—and then I recognized it as some theater production's theme song. Jamey strode right behind me, lips puckered. His arms were holding a huge cloth bag—his mother's collected chores for the day, I guessed.

He didn't stop. Obviously, the dear boy hadn't seen me. I jumped up, patting dust from the seat of my trousers. "Jamey! I say, Jamey, old son!" He paused, saw me, and then turned around and waited for me to catch up. "Hiya, Slick," he said.

I took a moment to unclench my teeth. "Dear boy. I'm so sorry Emil never finished his story about the roller-skating lady. Ah, perhaps . . . perhaps we might try again today?"

"Why? Find some money somewheres?" The wretched boy laughed.

I stood and looked at the kid. He didn't move. I didn't move. He looked odd, a peculiar gleam sparkling in his eyes. Still, neither of us moved or even spoke. Finally, he sighed. "Gotta go, Nick. Sorry." He began backing away from me, tilted his head in a goodbye motion, and then turned and resumed his cheery progress across Forty-Second Street.

Suddenly, he turned and shouted, "Mr. Emil won't be at Wall Street today."

"Why not?"

"Just thought I'd save you a useless trip. Mr. Emil found more, uh, interesting places to be, see?"

"No, I *don't* see!" I turned my back on the kid and strode off. *But I saw, all right.*

I heaved a sigh and set off eastward. It's said to be peaceful by the river. Who'd said that—oh, yes, Emil. There must've been a river somewhere near Sing Sing. I might as well try to calm myself. Because I knew Emil, like the Dangerous Bull (take your pick of Bulls), would also no longer be found on Wall Street. I'm no child; everything had become instantly clear to me . . . well, after seeing Jamey again. The expression on his face had said it all, and I got it, as they say in the crude popular vernacular.

As I sat on the edge of the seawall, legs dangling, watching the gaily painted tiny tugboats push and haul the monstrous barges up and down the East River, I suddenly realized the first clue I'd bungled. That scarlet hair. I'd ignored my own intuition, never wise! The second clue: Bull's unusually (to me) extensive knowledge of Emil's daughters. Third clue . . . well, in no certain order . . . Emil said if he remembered his family, he'd be compelled to "know" what everyone wanted him to remember. *That* was a big clue!

The biggest clue of all—Jamey said his *ma* had said a family must take one back, *even if coming home as an ex-con.* Remembering how hard that had flattened poor Emil . . .

But my very first mistake? The luck from the hunchback had clearly been meant for Jamey. Emil's grandchild. One of many, I'd wager. Rose had, no doubt, bequeathed her girls with her own brilliant shade of red hair, and Emil had stolen to try to support them all. And through Jamey, Emil finally discovered he would still find a welcome among his family.

I stood up, smacked the dust from my trousers yet again, and strolled up toward the beautiful sailing ships anchored there, letting the breeze and the sights restore me. But I still wondered: which daughter had Bull married? And when Emil "remembered" for the good of his wonderful, beloved family in these hard times where he'd stashed his stolen goods, would Bull turn the lovely old man in?

Nah.

ANGELA ZEMAN *claims that wit never dies in her stories, but other life forms must fend for themselves. Her work spans several subgenres. In 2012 Otto Penzler reissued her first novel,* The Witch and the Borscht Pearl, *plus a collection of related short stories as e-books and print-on-demand books. She is published by Mysterious Press,* Alfred Hitchcock Mystery Magazine, *and various anthologists. She is a member of Mystery Writers of America, International Thriller Writers, Private Eye Writers of America, and the International Crime Writers Association/North America. Learn more about her and her work at AngelaZeman.com.*

COPYCATS

N. J. Ayres

"The stinkin' rat finks have our uniforms on! They're sending our troops the wrong way!"

Voices didn't travel far in the tree cover or under the sledgehammer sounds of explosions. Sergeant Sam Rabinowitz watched as Private Jacobs jumped out of the Jeep and tore up to him to say it again. "Hold on, Private," Rabinowitz said.

"A truck driver just told me that!" Jacobs had been assigned a forward position to support an intersection with a fellow MP. Their squad's mission was to direct Allied troop traffic south of the Belgian city of Bastogne.

Sergeant Rabinowitz ordered the squad to fall out. He knew rumors in wartime were often used as strategy by both sides. He had his men park their gear on snow and heaps of fallen branches, then permitted them to pop the hood of the Jeep so they could warm any drinkable liquids by setting their tin cups around the engine.

Rabinowitz sat with Maroney, the radioman, on a large low rock. Communication had been pretty well shot—static, then five words, then two, then static, then nothing. While Maroney worked, Rabinowitz slid his bayonet out of its scabbard on his belt, sliced off a hunk of salami he had in his pack, and offered it to Maroney before he cut a piece for himself.

Wet had entered a separation in Rabinowitz's boot. The ache was almost smothered by numbness, a sign that it could turn to frostbite. He tried to ignore it. The whole platoon had suffered many more serious casualties than swollen toes in the advance along the eighty-mile front, later named the Battle of the Bulge for its geography.

Private Mike Kelley shoved back into the group from a piss run, along with another soldier they hadn't seen before. The new man said he was headed back to the front after being separated from his squad. Sergeant Rabinowitz asked where he was from and a few other things, and then he turned his attention back to his communications grunt.

Within hearing distance of the sergeant, Private Kelley offered the new man his half tin of coffee. So, when the soldier smiled his thanks and tapped the bottom of the tin with a certain remark, it was all over. The soldier said, "Up your bottom."

"Up your bottom" instead of "bottoms up."

Private Jacobs never swore. He was raised Orthodox. But after subduing the German fink and stripping him of his stolen fatigues and tying his wrists and ankles, Izzy and Mike Kelley shuffled him ten yards out from the encampment and sat him on a fallen tree. Then Sergeant Samuel Rabinowitz cored out the enemy's heart with the Colt Commando .38 that had belonged to Alfred Herschel Rabinowitz in World War I. Rocking from one foot to the other, Izzy said he wished he could have done the job. The führer himself had ordered any enemy soldier caught in a German uniform executed on the spot. What was good for the goose, Sergeant Rabinowitz said. His squad members went on with their business, but with a fresher fear in their eyes.

———— · — · — · ————

It was only five years earlier that Sammy Rabinowitz and Mike Kelley had sat in Izzy's bedroom listening to the jazz guitar of Eddie Condon on twelve-inch 78s while putting together model airplanes, these boys whose fourteenth birthdays were all less than six weeks apart. Mike said Eddie Condon was deaf in one ear, and Izzy said he was crazy. How could he play like that, then?

Sammy's model was a B-17 Flying Fortress his uncle with the shakes had given him. He also surprised Sammy with the latest issue of *Model Airplane News*. The other boys were jealous of Sammy's good fortune and wouldn't crack a page. Izzy just plopped the magazine on top of a beat-up issue of *Air Trails* on the bed next to the card table.

Izzy and Mike Kelley had only gliders to work on. Izzy told Sam they found the glider kits in the alley behind Mr. Gessel's toy shop on Orchard Street. Mike sent Sam a shake of his head that Izzy didn't see. It wasn't the first time their friend had lifted something that wasn't his.

The apartment was on the walk-up's fifth floor, his bedroom window shoved up for air. The problem started when Izzy's mother came home from work early from the laundry on Avenue B that afternoon. When she opened Izzy's door and smelled what she smelled and then looked at the bottles on the table, she went bananas. The labels said *Airplane Dope*. To her, that was what Benny Goodman's drummer got arrested for, that what's-his-name Gene Krupa, who had sleepy eyes and regularly dropped his sticks in the middle of a song.

Izzy was sitting on the far side of the table. That meant he was out the door last, catching a volley of slaps on his head and shoulders from his mama. Even the sound of feet pounding down the stairs didn't mute the noise from Mrs. Jacobs as she tore apart her son and daughter's room, the little girl who had to sleep perpendicular at the foot of Izzy's bed because her own room was so small. When the boys reached the sidewalk, Sammy spotted the glint of two glass bottles exiting Izzy's window, scoring the clear blue sky while floating on the high wails of that *meshuga* woman.

The boys ran over to Tompkins Park and collapsed on the grass, laughing. That is, until Sammy Rabinowitz said what he stupidly said. "Izzy's mother is a dope. Izzy's mother is d-o-p-e-y!" He said it and said it, caught up in the giggles.

So Izzy naturally had to bust him one. Then Sammy busted him back but was quicker, turning Izzy's nose and lips a meaty, swollen red. Maybe it was time. Maybe they had worn each other out from their differences before. From that day on, Isadore Jacobs and Sammy Rabinowitz avoided each other as much as they could, trading mild insults when they passed in school or on the street.

———— · — · — · ————

Seventh Precinct in the Lower East Side was the next-to-smallest precinct in Manhattan, but it was the neighborhood, and Sam was glad to walk a beat there when he was nineteen, watching out for old people and shopkeepers and little kids who played too long in the dim light of dusk. It's where his father had been a cop and an older cousin, too, both in the 1920s.

Sam's father died at age thirty-nine, when Sam was sixteen. His mother's sisters were at the apartment after the funeral. His mom said to one of them she wanted to go be with Arnie, she couldn't live without him. Sammy sat in a dark corner, his elbows on his knees and his face in his hands until that moment. He raised his head up, and his mother caught his eye. "Oh, no, Sammy," she said, "I didn't mean it. I won't ever leave you! Not for a long while, God willing."

It was up to him then to find some way to bring in money to help. His mom sewed for people but had a problem with her legs and couldn't sit very long. Sam made deliveries for shopkeepers all around the neighborhood. As time went by, he somehow didn't get drafted, and he didn't enlist. He wanted to be a cop, and that was it. Heroes and protectors had to be among civilians, too, didn't they?

But lately, every time Sam-the-Cop Rabinowitz went into Katz's Deli on the corner of Houston and Ludlow, not only did he see the walls covered with pictures of movie and theater people, but he also saw a single sign that ripped at his conscience: SEND A SALAMI TO YOUR BOY IN THE ARMY. It kept buzzing his brain when he was on the street.

All along the wall behind the food counter hung salamis, long and short, fat and thin, hanging by the ends of their casings, even during the days of rationing. There's always a way to get around restrictions, especially if you live in the right city. The aromas from steaming bins of pastrami and corned beef and hot dogs on the grill drew in people from the sidewalk who didn't even know they were hungry until then. That November of 1944, Sammy purchased four salamis and brought them home and asked his mother to send them to the troops. "What," she said, "I should know how to do this?"

The next afternoon while on his beat, he made up his mind. He saw Izzy Jacobs and Mike Kelley through a window of a soda shop, each devouring a charlotte russe. Mike always set aside the maraschino cherry for the last bite.

Sam went in, rattled up a chair, and rode it in reverse with his arms on the back. As if no time had elapsed since graduation, he said, "Hey, guys," and looked at his watch. "At three o'clock, I'm going down to the induction center to enlist. Who's coming with?"

Neither Izzy nor Mike had walls to paint or deliveries to make or machines to stitch leather for shoes. Jobs were hard to come by. Bosses got away with paying women less than the men they replaced, and women were feeling the glow of their own paychecks for a change. Sam's call to enlist was an easy persuasion. The three set off to the recruitment center.

———— · — · — · ————

At Camp Gordon training camp, southwest of Augusta, Georgia, the young recruits found another from their neighborhood: Tino Caruso. His house was at Avenue D and Sixth. That gave him a direct shot into the East River Park if he wanted, where there was no noise from kids playing stoop ball and stickball in the streets and girls playing potsie on sidewalks. Sam liked recalling a day he'd wielded a broom handle to smack a high-bounce spaldeen missile with such muscle it took out a basement window across from Izzy's place: instant home run. But the tinkling glass and the holler from inside had all the kids running down Avenue C, right in the middle, weaving around cars whose drivers laid on their horns. It was all fun, but once in a while he'd like a walk in the park . . . maybe with a girl.

The boys all made it through Military Police Corps combat training. Sam got stamped sergeant because of his city police experience, brief though it was. Izzy and Mike did okay, too. Tino Caruso was a bit of a dawdler, the last one over the obstacles, the last one to hand in written work. They requested codeployment and were surprised when they got it.

On the third day south of Bastogne, Sergeant Samuel Rabinowitz trudged through two-foot snow alongside Private Caruso. Manhattan winters saw snow, yes, but here Sam's bones quivered from the cold and the constant explosions and shrieks of strafing and the grind of engines above, which was not Allied cover but German Stutkas concealed by a white lid of clouds. The enemy had fuel to fly while Allied aircraft sat dry-docked on tarmacs with near-empty tanks. It was later learned that the English-speaking Germans in stolen uniforms did more than misdirect traffic and cut communication lines. They raided critical supply lines: rail cars, trucks, warehouses.

That day when Sam and Tino slogged along a barely visible road, they saw a high rock face ahead where they could take a breather. Just before reaching it, there was a *crack* and something grazed the right side of Sam's face. He swiped at his cheek with the back of his glove, then saw Caruso stumble but regain his feet and point to what Sam had already judged was a sniper's nest in a tree thirty yards away. In a flat two seconds, the shooter was meat on the ground. When Tino turned to say thanks, Sam understood that what had popped onto his cheek was the better part of Tino Caruso's nose.

———— · — · — · ————

Caruso lived, of course. All the guys from the Lower East Side who codeployed lived. After the war's end, they burrowed back to their neighborhoods. Sam stayed with his mother for the time being. She could use the help and he could save for the day, whatever that might be. He snagged a Seventh Precinct badge again, which didn't happen for every former officer coming back from the war.

He was grateful but soon restless. He couldn't help but think of a certain something: in the snowy woods of Belgium, he had ordered an enemy soldier wearing a hijacked American MP uniform to be shot for giving wrong directions and switching road signs to send soldiers off to nowhere. Not that Sam wanted to be making a decision like that today, but here, on wheeled or foot patrol, he spent his days slapping citations through drivers' windows and writing up accident reports.

So much had changed. Conversations centered on labor disputes. Unionized longshoremen had picketed, forcing hundreds of jobs to go idle. Fifteen thousand city elevator operators refused to punch buttons to take people up to their apartments and offices. Then the tugboat crews struck. The Irish and Italians were fussing at each other more than ever, who knew over what. Many more Jews were moving on from pushcarts, succeeding in their small businesses and relocating their families to classier suburbs.

And small crime was thriving—if you could call it that. The top district attorney was trying to fight it, placing more undercover cops to bust up prostitution, the numbers games, the creeping narcotics trade. But as of now, Samuel Rabinowitz could only walk his beat, chalk tires to see how long a car had been parked at a space with a posted time limit, and keep an eye out for no-goodniks prowling for something to lift.

———— · — · — · ————

A year passed, and the better part of another. He took to going to temple after not attending for a long, long time. There he met a girl named Ruth. She loved him. He tried loving her.

One afternoon he and Ruth took a table at Katz's Deli. It wasn't until their order came that he noticed Izzy and his sister two tables over. The sister, holy joe, had she ever changed. She was what, seventeen, eighteen, now? Sally. That was her name. Sally. And there was that sign: Send A Salami To Your Boy In The Army. Yellow, just beyond Sally Jacobs's light-brown, curl-sprung head. A crown it could be.

Sam brought Ruth over to say hello. Izzy invited them to sit, bring their food. The rest of the time at that table, Sam did not register Ruth in his consciousness at all.

Ruth saw. Afterward, Ruth complained. Ruth walked.

In a week Sam and Sally strolled streets together to look in windows, and one Sunday they went to a movie called *Gentlemen's Agreement*. The story had a New York City journalist, Phillip Green, becoming Phillip Greenburg so he could understand anti-Semitism. Sam and Sally talked a lot afterward about the masquerade. She could never do it, fake who she was on whatever side, while he kept saying you do what you must for a cause.

And, of course, he thought about, but didn't tell her about, the fake MP in the woods south of Bastogne sitting proudly on a fallen tree, chin up, spine straight, lips moving in praise to the God or führer he loved, so that her newest suitor, Sammy Rabinowitz, could aim a muzzle at his chest and blow out the young German's heart.

———— · — · — · ————

Sam was off-duty, out of police uniform, and at another favorite place for breakfast, tearing into a bagel loaded with cream cheese and sliced salmon and onions, two kinds of pickles on the side. He picked up a newspaper from the seat of the chair opposite and was reading it when Izzy and Mike Kelley walked in. Sam rarely saw anyone from the old days. Now he'd seen Iz twice in two weeks.

Sally had told Sam her brother didn't really like it that she was dating him. "Izzy can be funny about things," she said. Iz thought Sam had it too easy. Easy—Sam's father dead early, Sam out busting his hump for jobs to help out his mother, once in a smelly butcher shop.

Mike headed over to his table. He still sported a crew cut, his red scrub looking good atop a body that had gained the right weight. His pants bore a sharp crease, as always, and his shirt, you could go blind from the white. "They let you off the beat?" he asked. "Don't they know you'll just go stir up trouble?" Not too funny, but Mike always tried.

"They let a horse out of its stall sometimes," Sam said. "What's buzzin', cousin?" Mike said he was selling furs out of his uncle's shop in Stuyvesant.

Izzy, he could be Sad Sack from the comics, slouchy as he was. He gazed at the banner on the newspaper that Sam still held in his left hand and said, "Don't tell me you read that piece of toilet paper."

Sam shrugged and didn't explain.

Izzy's face pinched. He said to Mike, "Let's order. We have things to do."

They got their orders bagged. On the way out, Izzy gave Sam a look that should have bothered Sam, but the effort would take more energy than what his caffeine boost had yet imparted. Good old Mike: at least he mouthed a "sorry."

Sam folded the newspaper and laid it on top of the next table, masthead boldly showing. It was his first look at the *The Daily Worker*, the rag that had disrupted more than one family and set of friends.

The next time Sam went out with Sally, she told him how crabby her brother was after seeing Sam in the deli. "It was that newspaper you were reading," she said.

"He thinks I'm not serious about you, is all. I'll go have a talk with him. When's he home?" Her brother still lived with their mother, although they'd moved downstairs to the first floor. The next day on his lunch break, Sam rang the two-chime bell.

When Izzy opened, he paused and then said, "Get your filthy Commie feet out of here." He leaned left, and Sam could see a yellow something move between the door hinges. The door opened wider so Izzy could show him he was gripping his old stickball bat.

"She's safe with me, Izzy."

"You like your stinkin' knees? You like walking around in your cop suit? Tell you what. Keep walking. The direction you came from."

Sam left, but for Izzy's mother's sake. She was sitting on the green couch by the front window, holding back the lace curtain. Sally told him their mother's doctors said she'd had a nervous breakdown. The father lived a separate life two apartments over. Mrs. Jacobs's gray hair hung in strings past the collar line. Her mouth was the shape of a staple.

———— · —— · —— · ————

Six months later, Sam got a transfer to the Ninth Precinct. He'd still be pressing the bricks for a while, but in a larger area. If things worked out, he was told, he might get to work investigations, with a small pay pop. He let that desire be known from the start, but he knew it could be a year before it happened.

Still, now each day on the way to the Ninth squad room, he'd be singing the latest song, maybe "Buttermilk Skies" or "Prisoner of Love." And when he went to visit Sally in the apartment she took with a girlfriend and the girlfriend stepped out, he'd try singing to her like Dick Haymes did with "Till the End of Time," he was that happy.

Sally had snagged a job as a telephone operator, and though she hated leaving her mother, she was tired of sleeping on the couch and needed time away from a needy parent. Her place was only twelve blocks away, and Mom would be all right with Izzy still at home. To make Sam laugh, she'd put on fake operator voices and tell him far-fetched stories. One night after doing that, he said, "You're making a hurtin' turtle out of me, if you don't marry me." First time he ever said it.

"Hurtin' turtle? That don't even rhyme," she said, and then she got buried in laughter. It took two more proposals before he got her to say yes.

———— · — · — · ————

Sam's sergeant called him in and told him there was a major hoodlum named Harry Gross putting the bite on dozens of storekeepers and bar owners. "If we don't stop him, he'll be mayor before we know it."

A funny one, and Sam laughed but could see how true it could easily be. The sergeant said he was giving Sam a transfer. "Detective Brian Hirsch over in Investigation needs more men to bust this guy. There are written tests and a probationary period, of course, but then you're good to go." He said Sam caught Hirsch's notice when Hirsch assisted an undercover officer in a numbers bust with two precincts involved, and Sam was one of two cops handling crowd control. Hirsch liked his deportment and, when he checked, his record. Sam didn't even know who the detective was, but he gave his sergeant his thanks, along with his regrets. And when he left the building, he threw a kiss to the sky.

The weeks went by fast. Sam aced the tests; why wouldn't he? He bragged to Sally. They talked about a wedding date for fall.

———— · — · — · ————

Detective Hirsch leaned in across the cluttered desk that wasn't even his, wasn't anybody's, just a desk with everybody's junk on it. This man who looked like Sam's own father, with a hairline that was almost a memory and the rest of it Brilliantined so shiny it was close to blue; hazel eyes that could drill out any lie you ever thought you could get away with; and hands that should've belonged to a guy lifting wrestlers two at a time out over the ropes.

"Graft," Hirsch said. "Too many of our guys got dirty hands. I don't know about you, but I didn't pin on this badge so I could have a side job taking cash from criminals. You with me on this?"

An easy yes from Sam.

"There's a gonif who, shall we say, perpetrates persuasion for Harry Gross."

Sam nodded and asked, "Knee-capping, rib-pounding, like that?"

"Knuckles, knives, kicks to the jewels," Hirsch said. "Just like Gross doesn't do it himself, this guy has gorillas, too. One of these days a client's gonna get capped, and Gross and his henchmen will be candidates for the electric cure. I'd like to send a message to Gross before he gets any bigger for his britches. This gonif working for Gross; he wears scarves and floppy hats to conceal something that happened to his face. Spotters say you can tell because it's waxy-like. The nose is not the same size every day. Some days he's Jimmy Durante, some days he's Pacific Islands."

"Wait. A guy with a fake nose?"

"Right. He—"

Sam said it slowly: "Tino Carlo Caruso."

Detective Hirsch said, "You know him?"

"I might."

Not Tino, damn it. Not the Tino who got his crotch stuck on the barbed wire in basic because he slid under the wire instead of on his stomach. Was it the war? Was it what happened the day of the sniper? Or had Tino always been on the brink, and Sam just didn't know it because the two weren't reared in the immediate vicinity of each other? Cops on the take was one offense. But Tino, from the neighborhood— at least sort of—put an ache in Sam's gut in a different way; as if Sam were somehow responsible for him, *had* been responsible for him on a Belgian road one toe-curling winter. That cursed day, Sam had told him to keep a glove clamped on his face until they reached a medic. Had Tino been saved for this?

The only thing impeding Hirsch's plan now was that Sam knew Caruso. That meant no undercover on this plan.

———— · — · — · ————

All the same, Sam was getting ready for If and When. He pushed weights and ran track and was the first to split the leather on the gym's new punching bag. He'd learned hand-to-hand in military training camp and underwent a skim of personal combat in police academy, yet every Sunday he paid an instructor in Chinatown for a private three-hour class in *pa-kua*, the Chinese battle art featuring eight animal movements. His favorites were the lion and the snake. His reflexes and timing were impeccable, and he advanced through the belt rankings quickly.

One Saturday morning, Sally got him to go to a new temple on Fourteenth that Izzy had joined. Sam pretended to like the droning lay cantor, the very young rabbi, the short ladies telling him how handsome he was. But it was hard for him to hear anything while in the pews because of Izzy, five rows up, reciting loudly, davening like a man with fumes on the brain during prayer. He didn't know if Izzy saw him there.

Sally was taking classes at City College and had to study, so she and Sam necked in the car she'd just purchased and regretted already, and then he drove her home.

Sunday he took a bus to where Izzy worked at a tire store. Sam knew the street the shop was on. Parking was tight even up to the apron of the shop, and he had to approach between cars. Izzy was outside, signing a paper for a deliveryman who brought a tire that now leaned against Izzy's shin. When the guy left, Izzy looked after the truck a moment, and then he took the tire to a car on the far side of the shop door. He unlocked the trunk with a key, lifted the trunk gate, and put in the tire; he shut it and looked around again. Sam was already stooped between cars. It was too noisy on the street to talk to him there. He would wait until Izzy was back inside.

A mechanic came in from the garage at the same time Sam pulled open the shop door and asked Izzy if that was the tire delivery. Izzy said no. The mechanic left grumbling.

When Izzy faced the front and saw Sam, he said, "You would come here?"

Sam waited a beat and then said, "Why'd you do a thing like that, Iz?"

Izzy tipped his head down, looked this way and that at the floor, then met Sam's gaze and said, "Shut your face, oh-holier-than-thou."

"Iz, Iz. You need extra dough? I can—"

"Not from you."

"You can't do that, Iz, come on."

"Maybe it's not what you think."

"Maybe it is," Sam said.

Did he have the thing right, though? What if Izzy intended to deliver the tire to someone else, and it was a different tire the mechanic was expecting?

A customer came in. Sam hung around reading wall charts and tire labels. The man paid a balance from work previously completed, telling Izzy to be sure to thank his boss again for letting him run a tab. When the customer was out the door, Izzy stayed behind the counter. He said, "I got one question."

"Fire it up," Sam said.

"Are you or are you not a stinkin' rat-fink Communist?"

"Look, Izzy, that's not it, and you know it. Some things, they just come to you. You don't mean for it to happen. Sally and I love each other, we really do. It's been a year. No. Seven months, two weeks, and three days I've known it was her. I'd like you to be my best man, Iz. Will you do that for us? Day before Valentine's Day, Sally says, so I won't forget the anniversary. Do that for us, Iz?"

The color dropped from Izzy's face. He reached under the counter and brought up an oil-smeared tire iron, laid it on the counter slowly, and said, "How you like them apples, Sergeant?" Sergeant—with a level of contempt in his voice you'd expect from a bad stage actor. And sure, Sam would know about bad theater, because Sally had him take her to plays uptown, so they could claim some culture, too.

———— . — . — . ————

Like tonight. Tonight he and Sally would hop the subway, grab a dog off a cart, and go see *Annie Get Your Gun*. Afterward, they would steer around the corner to a hot spot for a drink. Sam's mother had been helping Sally with a sewing project. She wouldn't say what; he only knew it was a dress. On the subway, Sally held a giant shawl tight around her so Sam couldn't see, but when they got off and she spread open the soft-cream shawl, the sight near knocked the wind out of him. The design bared the shoulders, pinched the waist, flowed down to a boat-collar moat at the top of the hips, and then drove a waterfall of ruby red to just below the knees. On her feet were black heels with red silk roses on the tops.

After the play and a short stop for cheesecake at the end of the block, they walked toward the subway. The air was perfect. You could see the stars even through the sign glare. Sam wished he could conjure the night to go on longer than the ten hours it was meant to be. But when he spotted a police call box two feet down an alley on the way to the subway, he apologized but said he wanted to phone in because Hirsch liked that.

When she saw him come back from the call box, Sally said, "You have to go now, don't you? Go, baby. I can get myself home just fine."

"Nope. I'll take my goodnight kiss on the steps, thank you."

He tried showing spirit the whole way to Sally's place, but he knew his body odor was growing, and he kept his arms to his side. In front of her door he kissed her deeply, let her go in, and waved goodbye through the glass. Then he took himself to the scene of the crime: the old tenement apartments on Avenue C, where Sally's brother Izzy and her mother lived. He didn't know what was going on exactly, but he sure didn't want her there.

———— . — . — . ————

Number 216.

Detective Hirsch threaded his way down the sidewalk and up the stoop, where barrier rope stretched across the front of the handrails. He showed his ID to the beat cop, then saw Sam approaching and waited. Other cops were keeping away the googly eyes and one female tenant coming home from a shift job. Nothing to see but cop cars on the street.

Inside was another matter. Inside was blood in moats along the hardwood floor between the walls and carpet. Speckled lampshades and pictures. A blotch of blood had soaked into the shoulder of the light-green couch near the window, where Mrs. Jacobs had held back the curtain the last time Sam saw her. The white doilies were off the headrest and one arm.

Izzy's body lay in the kitchen. At the moment Sam came up, the photog was snapping a close-up of Izzy's face, where a V-shaped cut had been made near his mouth all the way to the cheekbone. Detective Hirsch said that kind of slice was usually meant for chumps in prison, the scarring designed as a dead-sure label for a snitch. It was "off" to have it carved on a corpse. "You taking notes, Rabinowitz?"

Sam had his notebook out, but had only entered the brush-blood on the doorjamb of the apartment. His head felt full of gelatin. Those weren't watery eyes, oh no. That wasn't sour gag in his throat.

Iz. Stickball Iz. Model airplane Iz. Comrade-in-arms Private Isadore Jacobs. Soon to be brother-in-law Izzy. How could it be? Sam's thoughts raced to Sally. How could she endure this? He held her in his mind as if he held her in his arms, as if the power could transfer. God help her if anyone told her before he did.

Detective Hirsch led Sam down the hallway to the bedroom, pointing out smears at elbow level. "He was dragging her. Look here at the marks on the floor," he said, pointing to black marks. Old lady Jacobs always wore lace-up witch shoes with black soles.

In the room, Hirsch nodded toward the bed where Mrs. Jacobs lay on her stomach in the middle, head over the side as if searching for something that fell on the floor. Sam could see the side of her face, so he knew it was her, though her hair was tinted red, not the gray as he'd last seen it. Tinted because her mood had improved so much, and Sally had gone over and helped her mother do it, and they almost did it to her own.

Detective Hirsch said, "Come closer." Sam did, near the legs of Mrs. Jacobs, and knew what he was supposed to see, and didn't want to. Hirsch shone his flashlight on her flank, where pale red bruises had formed under smears of blood and feces.

———— · — · — · ————

When Sally buzzed to let Sam in, she was still in her nightgown. With Sam was Sally's aunt, who lived in Brooklyn. Sally flicked her glance between them but didn't need to say a thing to know she was about to absorb a horror. They guided her to the couch, and the two sat with Sally and then told her, and took turns cradling the child she became.

———— · — · — · ————

Sam was parked in a room by himself at the station, a closet that had been turned into a place where officers could write reports. Detective Hirsch wanted him to have no distractions. He told him to write down the name of every person he thought Isadore Hadwin Jacobs knew, from kindergarten to Krautland.

Izzy's father had also been informed, of course, and was told to come to the station the next day for an interview, but Sam doubted he was involved.

Sam kept asking Detective Hirsch if he would please have someone check on Mike Kelley to make sure his friend was all right. *Why wouldn't he be?* Sam asked himself, even as he kept seeing Mike and Izzy, Izzy and Mike in most every memory flashing in.

———— · — · — · ————

Because Sam's mother had gone to Florida for a wedding of a childhood friend, he was able to bring Sally over to his apartment that night. They lay in his bed while she talked and cried, and then they got up and he fixed her something to eat, and they talked, and they lay back down and talked some more. Next to Sam's bed was a pull-down shade with a chomp at the side. He didn't remember how it got there. The moon filled it, and the gray shadows of its face seemed to be laughing at him. They slept. He woke with Sally kissing him. It didn't take long before he entered her, and afterward he was saying "I'm sorry, I'm sorry," and she was whispering, "No baby, I wanted you to, I wanted you to."

She got up to go to the bathroom. Back in bed, she said she was bleeding. Again he said he was sorry. She said nothing this time.

Despite himself, he fell back to sleep. As dawn was glowing through the hole of the shade, he felt Sally's warm breath and then her lips on his and heard her say, "Hold me again, Sammy; you have to hold me, or I can't live."

———— . — . — . ————

Pain from feeling helpless can be worse than from a thing over and done with, like watching a sick person die versus the death itself. Every day that passed without an answer to who killed Izzy and the mother slapped Sam in the face. He had his own precinct's assignments, and Sally required much of his off-hours time, so he pestered the detectives in Precinct Seven every other day, until he suspected they conveniently weren't there to answer. He'd seen Mike Kelley at the services and tried to talk with him, but all Mike did was walk around inside and outside like an ice pop with the color drained out.

A month to the day after the murders, two men in a basement game room on East Thirteenth were rubbed out. One was a gopher for the owner, the other a regular player. The owner lost only a finger from a pistol shot. He said he knew from the get-go it was mobsters imitating the St. Valentine's Day Massacre. The dogs, he called them, wore fake cop uniforms, pretending to bust his joint. "I saw dirty shoes coming down the steps. Then this one mope had a button off. Our cops don't dress like that." Proud of NYPD cops even while he broke the law. He ordered them out with an unloaded shotgun from a shelf, and that he shouldn't have done.

Detective Samuel Rabinowitz and a probie wrote it up, the probie drawing the scene with templates that had cutouts for arrows and rooms and bodies. Sam asked the owner if he could remember anything else. "Yeah, there was this one, hung back by the stairs. He had a crew cut and red hair. Very pale, like an albino. He was screaming while the shooter grabbed my money and Jimmy was moaning on the floor. I loved that Jimmy, like a son he was. I'm gonna make pig-slop out of them that did it, soon as I can."

———— · — · — · ————

Was Mike Kelley the only redhead with a crew cut in the borough of Manhattan? Of course not. But Sam's impulse was to go with what you know.

He took a jog off his assigned route after looking up the fur store Mike's uncle on his father's side owned. Mr. Kelley had to buzz him in—so many walk-away thefts going on, he explained. Mike was in the back; he'd get him.

Mike and Sam stood squeezed between two racks of furs. Sam's nose itched. He barely even had to open his mouth when Mike, after being sure his uncle was out of earshot, said, "Not here, Sammy." He told Sam to meet him in Tompkins Square Park. "That giant elm in the center? The one, you know, half of it's dead from beetles? Nine o'clock. It's dark by then."

Under a light pole, the light further helped by a full moon, Sam eyed Mike's boots as the men sat down on the bench. "Fancy wear there, partner."

"Pampa boot. Cost a few pennies, yeah."

He was going to comment on Mike's shirt, too, but Mike beat him to it to criticize his own. "Hawaiian now? Stylish. Police work must be good to you."

They nodded affirmative to each other and looked across the pathway at the silhouettes of a girl and guy making out on the grass. "You need to go break that up?" Mike asked. "Oh, you don't have your badge on."

"Mike. What you got to tell me?"

"I wasn't there."

"You wasn't where?"

"That game room that got shot up. Somebody told me someone saw a redhead. It wasn't me. I heard."

"You seen Tino Caruso lately?"

Mike got up and went to the edge of the walkway. All of a sudden he started doing jumping jacks. He said for Sam to come join him and laughed stupidly.

Sam went over and grabbed him by the back of the collar and shoved him back onto the bench. "Izzy. What happened with Izzy? You know. I know you know."

Mike's face shone from a burst of July sweat. His eyelashes were pale smiles from the side. But Mike wasn't smiling, and in a swift motion he lowered his head, and put his hands to his face, and silently sobbed.

Sam got it out from him. Tino Caruso had had Izzy wiped. The mother wasn't supposed to be part of it. When Mike heard Mrs. Jacobs had been violated besides having taken a pistol shot to the back of the head, he disappeared for two days, later making an excuse that he tripped on a curb and knocked himself out, and spent those days in a hospital unidentified. That explained the bruises from banging his head against an alley wall, the reason his eyes were ringed in green and black. "He'll bump me off too, he knows I talked to you."

"Doesn't he live around here? Why'd we come here, then?"

"Uptown, near Stuyvesant. He's loaded now, from rip-offs. He works for a big guy named Harry Gross. Some he does on his own, on the side."

"Why in hell did you get involved, Mike?"

"The take-down on Thirteenth, he made me come along. I swear I didn't know what was going to happen."

"And why'd he do Izzy? Why carve up his face like that?"

"Tino didn't do it himself."

"I don't care about that. I want the guy who did it. His name?"

"He goes by Hambone. Izzy flapped his yap about Tino's new career. Somebody talked to somebody. That somebody was a cockroach. He told Tino. I'm scared like I never been, Sammy. What'll I do?"

"You have to go down, Mike, you know that."

"Pop me now, Sammy. They send me upriver, I'm meat for the taking." Then he sank to his knees and cried so hard, no sound came out. Sam pulled him sideways and squeezed, telling him it would be all right, although of course it wouldn't be. Again, nothing was the same. Nothing ever would be.

Sam walked Mike to the street, where they were going to go their separate ways. Then Mike said he was sure he saw Hambone's car drive slowly by. Hambone, the muscle for Tino. The one who cut up Izzy and maybe got nasty with Mrs. Jacobs. A groan came out of Mike, right before he turned and puked in the grass.

Sam had his handkerchief out for him when he rose back up. "You're coming with me."

When he got Mike to the station, Detective Hirsch convinced the captain to put him in a safe house in Queens until he could be used in a courtroom for state's evidence.

When he lifted his cigarette from the ashtray, Hirsch's fingers made the cig look like a toothpick. Sam wished he had those damn fine weapons. He told Hirsch that Mike Kelley said that Tino meant the game room disaster to be strategic, to send a message to all his suckers.

"Tino's IQ can't lift a fly off a feather. I can locate him before anyone else can. The piece of dirt acting as his muscle is Fishel Gross, a nephew of mobster Harry. He goes by Hambone. Let me put the word out that I maybe want in on Tino's action. We set it up, we take him down."

Detective Hirsch raised his voice to tell Sam to stay out of it until he could put a team together. "For now, you're under orders to cool it." Sam left the meeting with an ache in his gut. He liked Hirsch. He liked the job, his brothers, his badge. *Don't do this,* he kept telling himself.

He'd already found out from Mike that Tino's routine on Thursdays after eating out was to go home, call up a girl, do their business, and have her gone by midnight so he could fall asleep reading Captain America comics with his Magnavox radio set to WMCA. Clockwork.

Sam recalled that was the one thing Tino was good at.

The night air was stifling, windows open everywhere. Sam studied the building to locate where Tino's window would be. He took the fire escape on the north side. Some people kept wooden sticks in the window so it would open only so far. Not Tino. He must feel invincible, Sam thought. He stepped through, not even a curtain or drape to push aside, right into his bedroom.

Tino's weapon lay on the side table where anyone could lift it. Sam tucked the gun in his waistband and then leaned down to clamp a hand over Tino's mouth. He almost drew back. The man slept with his nose on—Groucho glasses hooked to a nose, without the furry eyebrows. Did he wear those with his lady visitors? Maybe they thought it was cute.

He covered Tino's mouth to wake him up, then made him sit in a chair. Tino, naked except for shorts, kept wrapping his torso with his arms as if he'd never been in a military shower. Sam told him he could put his clothes on in a minute. Sam sat on the edge of the bed with his gun on his leg and decided he wasn't going to lay it all on Tino right there, right then, but he did say, "It wasn't your nose you lost, Tino. It was your heart."

Tino's face was scarred beyond what the rifle bullet had done. He must have had some failed surgeries that affected his cheeks; hence, the casual comment about it looking waxy.

"You don't know," Tino said.

"I know plenty." Sam stood and walked a few steps, faced him, and asked, "Were you always a creep, Tino? If not for the war, would you have ever killed a friend and molested an old lady?"

"I didn't do any of that!" Tino's eyes shifted just a fraction of a second.

That's when Sam felt a shadow-pull, a flutter-fall of instinct, the way the mystery alert in the Belgian woods had given him the awareness to cancel the intent of a sniper.

Just so, here in Tino's bedroom, from nowhere came the warning. Sam moved his back to the wall.

When Fishel "Hambone" Gross, in socks and shorts, took two

steps in with a pistol out chest-high, Sam grabbed his forearm and, with the butt of his service revolver, chopped Hambone's weapon out of his hand. Then he twisted the big man's left arm back to force him down, kicking the firearm into the wedge of the door. But Hambone's nickname held for a reason. He was big and stubborn.

Tino flustered about the apartment, tugging on pants and a pullover and finding a different nose in his top drawer, while Sam had to perform maneuvers to put the Hambone down, not wanting a fired round to pierce a wall or floor. At last, he fought handcuffs on him, but only after rendering a side-kick to his knee. To Hambone's whining and prone figure, Sam said, "*Nana korobi, ya oki,*" and in English, "Seven times down, eight times up" but then added, "my ass!"

He asked Tino, still by the closet, "What, you have him sleeping over? Bad luck for him. Is there a woman in there, too? Any other surprises?" Tino shook his head no. Sam made the two men go into the living room and motioned them to sit in chairs. Hambone had to shuffle-hop to get there, groaning all the while from pain in his knee. People noises came up through the floorboards. Someone else banged on a wall, the demand from neighbors to settle down.

A glance around the room brought Sam to a telephone. He shifted his firearm to his left hand and picked up the receiver, but he'd been distracted by the noise and took too long to dial, and in a flash Hambone's cuffed arms noosed Sam's arms to his side.

Pain yet forced out Hambone's groans, but he managed to haul Sam back to the bedroom and the open window. Sam tried tripping him on the way, but the irony of Hambone's knee displacement and subsequent footfalls worked against him.

Even through the action, Sam saw Tino rise from the chair, quietly open the door, look back, and exit.

Wearing Officer Sam Rabinowitz like a bib, the two-man act tumbled backward through the opening. When they hit the fire escape grating, Sam used the jolt to rotate and free his arms. The big man struggled to his feet, bringing Sam with him. Handcuffed as he was, he clenched his hands like a club. Sam used a sweeping circular motion to divert the blow, and in so doing he cartwheeled Hambone over the low rail. He heard a *splat*, soon followed by a spiraling yowl from cats mating and a far-off siren's wail.

Officers found the second body on the other side of the building, where the stairway to the roof deck had been the conduit to convey a forlorn Tino Caruso to his inglorious end.

The arguments weren't serious between Sally and Sam about whether Honora should come before Isadora, or Isadora before Honora. Sally won out, saying it would be Honora, after her mother: Honora Isadora Rabinowitz. And she told the nurse in the hospital the next one would surely be a boy, and his name could be Aaron Samuel or even Aaron Alfred Samuel Rabinowitz.

Buds on a bunch of pussy willows tied with pink ribbon were a gift from Detective Hirsch. The stems sat in a clear vase on the sill. Sun shafts hit the glass and marbleized the wall and ceiling. When the nurse came in for Sally's meds and saw the satisfied looks on the couple's faces after the naming situation was settled, she said, "You two look happy as cats in a creamery." And so it was, and so it continued to be for fifty more playful, worrisome, down and up years.

N. J. AYRES *earned an MWA Edgar Award nomination for a story in another of Mary Higgins Clark's anthologies (*The Night Awakens, 2000*). She has published three forensics-based novels featuring former Las Vegas stripper Smokey Brandon, a book of poetry, and numerous short stories. For over twenty years, Ayres (Noreen) wrote and edited complex technical manuals for engineering companies in Alaska, California, Texas, and Washington. Learn more at NoreenAyres.com.*

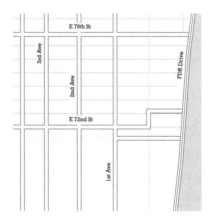

RED-HEADED STEPCHILD

Margaret Maron

"Are they twins?"

The first time Abby heard that question, she and Elaine were eight years old and they were scrambling onto the Alice in Wonderland sculpture in Central Park. It was July, and she still remembered how warm the smooth bronze mushroom had felt to her bare legs and how sunbeams glistened on Elaine's long straight hair as she elbowed her way past Abby to get to the Cheshire Cat first.

"Don't push your sister," KiKi called up to them.

"She's not my sister," Elaine muttered.

"I'm sorry," KiKi said, turning to the young woman whose toddler tugged at the Mad Hatter's jacket. "Did you ask me something?"

"Your daughters," said the toddler's mom. "Are they twins?"

The woman hadn't heard Elaine's disavowal of sisterhood, but Abby lingered by Alice's bronze shoe to hear KiKi's answer.

"They do look alike, don't they? The blonde one's mine, but the redhead's my fiancé's daughter."

———— · — · — · ————

Abby had cried when Dad first told her. "A stepmother? Like Cinderella?"

"Don't be silly, Abby," he'd said. "She's certainly not going to make you scrub floors or sit in ashes. You'll love KiKi, and she's ready to love you. Besides, you already know Elaine from school. A new mother *and* a new sister. It'll be fun."

Fun? She barely knew Elaine. Even though she was only three months younger, Abby's October birthday had kept her from starting kindergarten till she was almost six, so Elaine was a year ahead of her at the Clymer School for Girls.

"Please," she begged Aunt Jess, her dad's older sister and the woman who had cared for her after the mother she could not remember died. She felt her whole world was turning upside down. A stepmother. A stepsister. A new apartment. "Let me stay with you."

"I wish I could, darling, but your dad wants to make a new home for both of you. Besides, you're only moving across the park to the East Side, not Easter Island. We'll still see each other whenever you like."

Later that evening, though, lying sleepless and miserable, Abby heard Aunt Jess say, "You'd better not let KiKi treat her like a red-headed stepchild."

Dad laughed. "Hard to promise that, Jess. Abby *is* a redhead, and she *is* going to be KiKi's stepchild."

"You know what I mean, Daniel. You get so tied up with your work, you sometimes forget you even have a daughter."

"Which is why it'll be good for her to have KiKi. She likes being a stay-at-home mother."

"Except that she didn't stay home, did she? Where were her daughter and her husband when you two were having your intimate little evenings together?"

"I won't dignify that with an answer, Jessica, and if you want to keep seeing Abby, I expect you to keep your opinions of KiKi to yourself."

———— · — · — · ————

"Are they twins?" asked the bridal consultant when KiKi arrived at her first appointment with Elaine and Abby. Her divorce was now final, and the late-summer wedding was to be small and intimate, with the two girls as her only attendants.

"They *do* look like twins, don't they?" KiKi said, but her indulgent smile was for Elaine, who had immediately zeroed in on a purple organza. Even at eight, Abby could see that the color fought with her own thick curls, which were more carrot than strawberry. "I hope you don't mind, sweetie? Sisters have to learn to compromise."

Except that compromise always seemed to require less from Elaine and more from Abby.

KiKi gently explained why Abby and her dad needed to move from their comfortably shabby apartment in the West Eighties to a more modern building on the East Side. "It wouldn't be fair to you and Dad to move into my tiny apartment, just as it wouldn't be fair to Elaine and me to move in with you and your aunt. Too many old memories for all of us. Much better to make new memories together, don't you think?"

But Elaine got her way there, too. That first night in the new apartment, she had drawn an imaginary line down the middle of their bedroom. "The window's mine," she said, "and you can't look out of it."

Abby could not have cared less. The view of that quiet tree-lined street with its sleek modern apartment buildings was boring, and it only made her more homesick for the scruffy charm of the Upper West Side.

When Aunt Jess discreetly probed, Abby had to admit that KiKi tried to be fair. "But Elaine makes such a big deal out of things, it's easier just to let her have her way. Most of the time, it really doesn't matter."

Then there was the problem of Abby's hair, which was so thick that she couldn't yet manage all the tangles herself. KiKi soon lost patience trying to brush it out, and two weeks into the school season that fall, she had Abby's bright orange curls clipped short at the beauty salon. Aunt Jess had been furious the first time she saw the results, and Dad had scowled.

"Fine," KiKi had snapped at him. "Let her grow it back, and *you* brush her hair every morning."

It was their first fight.

———— . — . — . ————

After three years, people no longer asked if they were twins.

By the time Abby was eleven, her hair had begun to mellow into auburn, but it was as thick and curly as ever and still short. Elaine's was like a shining golden waterfall, and almost long enough to sit on. She was already into a training bra and boys, and she sneered at Abby's flat chest. No Browning boys had yet tried to touch her there as they tried to touch Elaine, who would giggle and slap their hands. Elaine's hips were also rounding into womanhood—rounding a bit too much in KiKi's eyes. She soon banned all sweets from the house.

"If it's not in the house, none of us will be tempted," she said, running a rueful finger along her rigorously maintained waistline. She herself had resisted temptation ever since she hit puberty, and it was clearly time for Elaine to learn that lesson, too. She spoke to the dietician at the Clymer School, and they worked out special menus for Elaine's lunches and snacks. To KiKi's frustration, her daughter's extra pounds did not melt away, not even with exercises devised by her own personal trainer.

Dad had been grumpy about the new regime. He liked a dish of ice cream at night, but if Elaine couldn't have ice cream, neither could anyone else, even though Abby had inherited his metabolism.

"Don't tell KiKi," he told Abby when they occasionally sneaked out for a hot fudge sundae at Serendipity.

"I won't," Abby promised. She had become good at keeping secrets and had never tattled about the stash of jellybeans hidden in Elaine's dresser.

"Thank God you inherited my brains, too," Dad said as a storm raged in the next room between Elaine and KiKi over a poor school report. "I can't afford two sets of tutors."

As it was, Abby's grades were so good that she was chosen to help some of the younger students with their reading skills, but no sooner had she settled into a routine with a new child that fall than one of the teachers pulled her aside. "Make sure that Whitney keeps her wooly cap on and that you two don't touch heads."

When Abby lifted puzzled eyes, the teacher whispered, "Head lice. You don't have to worry as long you're very careful when you sit together and she reads to you."

There had been a brief outburst of head lice at Clymer the year before. Hoping to squelch fears before parents started looking at Chapin or Spence, the headmistress arranged for a doctor to give a PowerPoint presentation in the great hall to assure everyone that the nits didn't springboard from head to head without physical contact, and that there was nothing dirty or shameful about the creatures. "As Clymer parents, I hope you will encourage your daughters to be kind to their afflicted classmates," the headmistress told them. "Lice are no respecters of privilege or wealth."

Wealth was something that Clymer parents understood, and privilege was a given. Tuition at that exclusive private girls school was higher than at most universities, so when Elaine started scratching her head a week or so later, KiKi was horrified and Dad was outraged. "Dammit, KiKi! Forty-five thousand a year and that school gives her lice?"

He was not the sort of man who ever dealt with spiders in the bathroom or roaches in the kitchen, and Elaine's condition completely unnerved him. Despite KiKi's indignant protests, he immediately sent Abby back to the West Side to stay with her aunt Jess until Elaine had been nit free for a full week.

Abby knew there was no danger of her catching the lice as long as she and Elaine didn't share hairbrushes or head gear, but she was too happy to argue, especially since Dad came to dinner at least twice a week. It was like old times, and when she hugged him goodbye, he seemed wistful about leaving.

Halloween came and went before he let Abby return to what she still called the new apartment. She had heard all about the tedious two-hour comb-outs with a fine-toothed metal comb, the only way to remove nit eggs from a hair shaft short of picking them off one hair at a time.

"Three hundred dollars a session," Dad grumbled to Aunt Jess. "And her hair's so long, it took three sessions."

"Couldn't KiKi do the comb-outs?" asked Aunt Jess.

"I didn't want her touching the damn things. What if she got them?" He shuddered at the very thought.

Yet by Thanksgiving, KiKi discovered more lice in Elaine's hair, even though Elaine swore she hadn't worn anyone else's hat, used another's brush, or touched heads with anyone when she posed for group pictures with the friends who were now forbidden to invite her for sleepovers.

Dad threatened to sue the salon that had treated the first infestation, and they agreed to do another series of comb-outs for free if Elaine's hair was cut short. This time, Elaine's tantrums didn't work and her long, golden, lice-infested tresses were due to meet the hairdresser's scissors that very afternoon.

"I'm sure you're glad to be leaving," KiKi said sourly as Abby zipped up her backpack while Elaine lay on the other bed, scratching her head and sobbing loudly. "Maybe if you're lucky, you'll get to have Christmas there, too."

Abby didn't respond. The constant bickering between the two adults wore on all of them. Tempers were frayed. Dad alternated between disgust and indignation because of those insects in Elaine's hair, but the bills KiKi ran up on their credit cards didn't help, either. Abby heard him accuse her of marrying him for his money. KiKi was by turns defensive of Elaine and angered by his attitude.

"Your father's been totally unreasonable about all this. I know you and Elaine have had your differences, but if you're not afraid of getting them, why should he act like it's the plague?"

At the door, Abby paused. "I'm sorry, KiKi," she said and gave her stepmother one of her infrequent hugs before ringing for the elevator.

"I so wish you were both going to be here for Christmas," Aunt Jess said as Dad finished putting the lights on her tree.

"Don't say it if you don't mean it," her brother said grimly.

The new apartment was not a happy place these days. Somehow, Elaine's lice seemed to have migrated to KiKi's head, and he'd begun sleeping on the couch in his home office for fear of getting them himself.

Nevertheless, because of tears and promises and probably sex, too, Abby thought scornfully, Dad met her at the school as winter break began and told her that the lice were completely gone. They would be spending the holidays on Manhattan's East Side after all.

Abby nodded and handed him her backpack. "I need to say good-bye to one of the little kids I've been tutoring," she said and hurried back into the building.

Luckily, the lower-school girls were still struggling into their coats and mufflers, and they were glad for her help. In all the happy chatter about Santa Claus and what they were going to get for Christmas, no one noticed as Abby lingered with six-year-old Miranda Randolph, who was due for her second comb-out the very next day and was used to having her hair picked at.

Abby carefully transferred three adult nits and several eggs to the small pill bottle she had started carrying last fall. With a little luck, this Christmas present for Dad would be the final straw in the bundle she had already piled onto the camel's back.

MARGARET MARON *has written thirty novels and two collections of short stories. Winner of the Edgar, Agatha, Anthony, and Macavity Awards, her works are on the reading lists of various courses in contemporary Southern literature. She has served as national president of Sisters in Crime and of Mystery Writers of America, which named her grand master in 2013. In 2008 she received the North Carolina Award, the state's highest civilian honor. Vist her at www.MargaretMaron.com.*

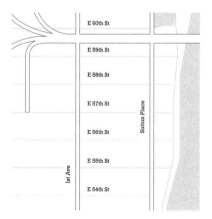

SUTTON DEATH OVERTIME

Judith Kelman

Dinner that night at Café Autore featured veal milanese, three murders, a drug bust, and a heist by the audacious jewel thief "Diamond Slim."

Reuben Jeffers, a doughy reporter from the daily online tabloid *A-List,* scratched notes on a spiral-bound pad. His pinched eyes bounced from that to his iPhone. "Cool idea, Joe! Love your books. Dig in soon as they come out." Jeffers had promised to be a fly on the wall of this venerable monthly gathering of top New York mystery writers, but his presence seemed more like a fly in the soup.

"Ah." Aside from the dozens of volumes in his four popular detective series, handsome lantern-jawed Joe Ransom was a man of meager words.

Not so the reporter. "Must say, this Diamond Slim character sounds like your best yet. Imagine, a robber so rail thin, he can hide in plain sight. Slip through tight spaces like a light beam. Has to be computer generated, right? Or green-screen technology? Don't tell me. Anyhow, brilliant. When did you come up with him?"

"Eighty-two."

L. C. Crocker, ponytailed and bespectacled, looked down his eagle-beak nose. He was no fan of Jeffers, who had placed his latest police procedural at the top of an *A-List* roundup entitled "The Worst of Crimes." The YouTube takeoff "L. C. Crocker Shlock Shocker" had gone viral. Still, Colleen O'Day, the brightest star in their glittery firmament, had asked L. C. to bury the hatchet (though not, as he'd gleefully suggested, in the reporter's skull) and let him do a story on the group. Almost no one said no to Colleen.

"Remember, Jeffers. Anything we say about works in progress is off the record."

The reporter cocked his finger and fired an imaginary round. "Sure, L. C. Gotcha."

"And stash that damned phone! No tweets, no posts. *Capisce?*"

"Gotcha."

"Love the Diamond Slim series, Joe. Can't wait for this one." Stephanie Harris, an affable FBI agent turned true-crime writer, gazed over the battlefield of sauce drips and fractured breadsticks at the regal presence across the table. "Now to you, Colleen. We've missed you! What have you been working on?"

The grand lady spoke in a conspiratorial hush. "Remember the Bitsy Grainger case?"

"Vaguely," said Tony Baker, impish author of nightmare-inducing horror tales.

L. C. tapped his tented fingers. "Was that the psychiatrist whose patient slipped strychnine into her chai tea latte?"

"That was Dr. Betty Barringer. Bitsy Grainger was the young woman who vanished in the early seventies."

"Sorry. Doesn't ring a bell," said Tonya Finerman, a winsome twentysomething whose novel *Done to Death* had been optioned by Spielberg and sold for a seven-figure advance.

"Of course, it doesn't." Jeffers sniffed. "Seventies were way before your time, Tonya. Ancient history, really."

"Maybe so," said Colleen. "But history can be fascinating, especially stories that lack a definite ending. Absent a complete narrative, we fill in the blanks. That's human nature. I believe it's also the reason many of us are drawn to writing."

"Beautifully put," said Stephanie.

"Gotcha. Not going to argue, Ms. O'Day, especially with someone who has permanent parking at the top of the *Times* list. But why that case? Why now?" The reporter twirled his Uniball, summoning another Maker's Mark. "Why you?"

"Not easy questions to answer, Mr. Jeffers. Bitsy was a friend of mine, so of course I was terribly upset when it happened and troubled by her disappearance for many years. But in time, the worst sting of memory fades.

"Then, last October, after that freak early snowstorm, I began thinking about the case more and more, turning it over and over in my mind.

"One night, Bitsy Grainger came to me in a dream. She was caught in a ferocious blizzard, hunched in a tattered camel coat. Matted fur around the hood obscured everything but her eyes. Howling wind swallowed her words. But in the warped logic of dreams, I heard her clearly. 'Help me! Somebody. Please!' I called out. I struggled to get to her. But the storm kept forcing me back. There was nothing I could do.

"I awoke to the sound of my own screams. My throat was raw, heart stammering. It took a few moments for me to separate that horrid dream from reality. But once the fog of sleep lifted, I realized there was something I could do. I could base a book on Bitsy Grainger and solve the mystery of her disappearance at last."

"You mean make something up," Jeffers said.

"Of course I could, if need be. I write fiction, after all. But I've been studying the case for months, and I've figured out what became of her."

"For real? Or you trying to build a buzz?" Jeffers leveled his pen and chuckled. "Clever girl. So what's the story you came up with? Who was this Bitsy Grainger person? And what kind of name is Bitsy anyway? Sounds like a one of those silly mix dogs: a poobrador or, maybe, a cockerdoodledoo."

Colleen ignored him as she would a nasty smell. Her story unspooled against the chicken scratch of Jeffers's pen. "Bitsy was a lovely person, beautiful inside and out. When she went missing, the press infested the Grainger's Sutton Place neighborhood. They skulked in the bushes. Rooted through the garbage. One reporter posed as a gas company repairman to get into the house. Another tried to bribe their housekeeper. Bitsy's husband finally went into hiding to escape them. They had no boundaries, no decency. They acted as if everything was fair game."

"All due respect," Jeffers said, "everything *is* fair game. Sure I don't have to remind you about the public's right to know."

"And I'm sure *I* don't have to remind *you* of your right to remain silent," L. C. said. "So remain the hell silent, will you? Now, go on, Colleen, my dear. You were saying."

"I couldn't get my mind around it. How could a bright, talented young woman with everything to live for simply vanish? It defies expectation, logic, even the laws of physics.

"I met Bitsy two years before it happened. My husband, James, was a resident at New York Hospital, working impossible hours. We were living on a shoestring in a tiny apartment on Fifty-Fifth and First. I'd always dreamt of becoming a writer, but at that point, I doubted it would ever come true. Whatever I sent out came back with one of those form rejection letters. Every publisher used different words, but the message was always the same: *Dear Contributor, Thanks for letting us have a look at your precious baby. Unfortunately, we find him homely and unacceptable, so we're sending him back wrinkled and covered in coffee stains.*

"Our real baby, Sam, was only a few months old, and the poor thing had miserable colic. He slept fitfully and screamed blue murder when I tried to set him down. He was happiest outdoors; so I'd take him out first thing in the morning in one of those baby carriers you strap on. We'd walk for hours, miles and miles.

"Most days, I'd head east. The city was in terrible turmoil back then, with a dismal economy and soaring crime. There were endless reports of muggings, drive-by shootings, break-ins, rapes. By comparison, Sutton Place felt like an oasis of safety and calm. Stately high-rises. Elegant townhouses. Glorious private homes and manicured gardens lined the narrow streets between Sutton and the East River. Charming pocket parks perched at the foot of the Fifty-Ninth Street bridge. People sat there on slatted benches, reading, watching boats pass, taking the sun.

"Early one mild autumn morning, I set out as usual with Sam. We'd gotten a few blocks from our building when suddenly a chill wind whipped up. The sky filled with ominous clouds and split with lightning. Rain began to fall, a few fat drops that soon spawned a drenching downpour. Startled, I ducked down the steps and sought shelter under the arched overhang at the entrance to a townhouse, but there was no escape from the driving storm. I was too afraid to knock. It was so early. I imagined the owners groggy with sleep, hearing a noise and mistaking me for an intruder. Grabbing a loaded handgun, moving stiffly, silently toward the door.

"Sam awoke with a start and started shrieking. I tried to soothe him, but he was inconsolable. And who could blame him? Poor little thing was saddled with a hopelessly inadequate mother. Why hadn't I listened to the weather report? Why wasn't I prepared? What was wrong with me?

"Just then, the door opened. Bitsy Grainger appeared in a white silk robe. She was barefoot, with no makeup and tousled copper-streaked hair, but stunning nonetheless. Pale and full lipped, and the most remarkable eyes: moonstone gray tinged with the tiniest shimmer of blue.

"Her home was beautiful, too. Jewel-toned oriental carpets, fresh white flower arrangements in towering crystal vases, antique furnishings, stunning works of classical art. Mere blocks from our dingy little cluttered apartment, and we'd landed in another world.

"Despite the ungodly hour, she was incredibly gracious. 'Oh my. Y'all are soaked. Come on in. Hurry up now. You'll catch your death.'

"She scurried around, collecting towels, fresh clothes, even a tiny blue stretch-suit that was exactly Sam's size. They were for the son she hoped to have someday, she said with a coy, dimpled smile.

"The rain had let up by then, but Bitsy insisted I stay and have coffee. On the black granite island in the kitchen perched a spectacular red enamel-and-chrome machine. At the press of a button, a grinder crushed beans, dripped heated water, and out came rich espresso capped with foam. With great delight, she told me that her husband, Harold, had ordered the contraption as a surprise because he knew how much she adored cappuccino. I don't think I'd even heard of cappuccino at that point, but it was delicious, sprinkled with cinnamon and powdered chocolate. 'Heaven, right?' she said. That was one of her favorite expressions.

"The morning had turned from disastrous to delightful. How fortunate I felt. Meeting this miraculous stranger. Finding refuge from the storm in her glorious home. Best of all, the moment Sam laid eyes on her, he stopped crying as if someone had flipped a secret switch. He giggled and cooed and flirted, all honey and smiles. Truly, it was love at first sight. Bitsy cooed and flirted right back, 'Look at you, Mr. Big Stuff. Bundle of sugar, that's what you are.'

"For months after that, Sam and I saw Bitsy nearly every day. She would fall in beside us as we strolled through the neighborhood, always with cappuccinos in to-go cups, for her and for me. 'Well, would you look who's here! Hey, handsome. How's my little heartthrob today?'

"She was so easy to talk to, funny and open and utterly without airs. From the way she looked and lived, you would have thought she was to the manor born. Turned out she was a preacher's daughter from a flyspeck town in Mississippi. Her moonstone eyes went cloudy as she described summers there. Swampy heat laced with starving mosquitoes. 'Myrtle is barely a wide spot in the road. One gas station, one stoplight. Poor little excuse for a church with barely enough lost souls to fill it. Easy to find, though—drive straight to nowhere and make a left. Wasn't the best place for a girl like me who liked fun and lots of it. Of course, Mama and Daddy saw things differently. They thought I should focus on study, church, and chores. I'd sneak out of all three and go off with my friends: tattooed boys with big-hog Harleys and dreamy girls like me who thought they had everything figured out at sixteen.'

"She told me she'd fallen in love with Ray Adlen, a strapping nineteen-year-old dropout. He'd proclaimed his love and promised to be with her always. Said they were pretty much engaged, which made everything between them all right.

"Bitsy could see the future clearly. She would marry Ray. They'd live in one of the big cities like New York, Paris, or Waukesha, and she'd become a singer. Either she'd star in Hollywood musicals, like *Breakfast at Tiffany's*, or sing with a band. Maybe both. And of course, she'd make records like Annette Funicello. She'd always had the best voice in her school, always been picked as female lead in the play. Ray adored anything with wheels, and he had a knack for fixing motors. He'd have a garage and a car dealership. They'd make tons of money. Do whatever they pleased.

"When she turned up pregnant, her daddy didn't fall on his knees and pray, like he always said you should when there was trouble. He loaded his Remington Woodmaster and went after Ray. Threatened to blow his head off if he ever set foot near Bitsy again.

"She was desperate to see Ray. Every chance she got, she dialed his number, but no one picked up. Their friends were no help. No, they hadn't seen Ray. No idea what he was up to. Soon as they heard from him, they'd tell him to call. 'I figured they were scared of Daddy,' Bitsy told me. 'Most everyone was. Sundays when he preached, even the little babies went bone still with stretched-out eyes.'

"Still, she was sure Ray would come for her. After all, he'd promised. Forever never changed. They'd run off, have their baby, and . . . cue music, cue Hollywood ending.

"Bitsy's parents kept her a virtual prisoner in the house. Her father forced her to polish the faded linoleum over and over, as if that might wipe out the stain on her soul. He preached at her constantly, raving about hellfire and brimstone, willing spirits and weak flesh.

"Her mother said nothing. 'Momma would get this empty look. All she did was sit on the porch swing in her faded blue dress, humming that song she loved: *'Moon River, wider than a mile . . .'*

"Bitsy had to get away. She stole fifty dollars from the secret stash her mother kept behind the frozen okra, and she packed a suitcase. Soon as she could, she grabbed her things and ran. She was sure Ray would be at the creek, where all her friends hung out on hot days like this. And there he was, behind a clump of bushes, doing what engaged people did with her best friend Wanda.

"What followed was a blur. Somehow, Bitsy wound up on a Greyhound bus to New York. The next night, she arrived at the bustling Port Authority Terminal with a broken heart, a terrible bellyache, and nowhere to go.

"Bad men were on her, as she put it, like ticks on a hound. Thankfully, she knew enough to get away from them, from there. She slipped into the first church she came to and curled up between rows of pews. Hours later, she awoke in wrenching pain. Blood everywhere. The air rang with the scream of approaching sirens. Strangers hefted her onto a gurney and rushed her to the emergency room at St. Luke's. Bitsy thought she was dying, being punished as her father had predicted for her sins. She'd never heard of a miscarriage.

"Once it was over, a hospital social worker came around full of questions. How old was she? Where were her parents? Where was home? Did she have insurance? What kind of insurance did she have? Bitsy's instinct was to make up a story. She claimed she was nineteen, though everyone said she looked younger. Her husband had gone away with his Army reserve unit (like Ray sometimes did). He'd be home in a couple of days. Meantime, a friend named P. J. Clarke was going to look after her at 915 Third Avenue. Bitsy had seen that name and address in an ad on the endless bus ride to New York. Sure, they had the army insurance, but her husband had the card. She promised to call with the numbers the hospital needed as soon as she could.

"Amazingly, the social-work lady believed her. She kept inventing whatever stories she needed to keep from getting caught and sent home. No way could she ever go back to Myrtle. Daddy would kill her. Ray didn't love her anymore. Maybe he never had.

"She knocked around, earned a few bucks, and found people here and there who were willing to put her up. She discovered all kinds of things in garbage cans and on the street: discarded food, gloves, even a thick green wool sweater with a puffy snowman on the front. It was ridiculous but warm. She imagined her friends laughing their heads off when they saw her in it, but she quickly marched the thought out of her head. They didn't exist anymore. Neither did home.

"A week after Christmas, she wandered into a noisy bar one night to escape the cold. People were drinking and laughing, coupling up. In the shadows at the rear, a scrawny, bearded guy in a work shirt was playing a beat-up spinet. After *Stardust*, he segued into her mama's favorite song. *Moon River, wider than a mile* . . .

"Bitsy drifted toward the piano. So much was running through her head: loneliness, longing, the stifling weight of her shattered dreams. She didn't realize she was singing aloud until the manager came over, a wiry man whose name badge read CHAS. She feared he'd kick her out, maybe call the police. Instead, he said he liked her voice. Was she looking for a gig? His regular singer hadn't shown up, and he could use her. How she grinned at that memory. 'Heaven, right?'

"After that, things changed quickly. Bitsy had the look, and she was a quick study. She shed the drawl, learned how to move and play to the audience. Once, I coaxed her to demonstrate. Sam erupted in a baby belly laugh when she assumed the sultry look and smoky voice.

"She developed a following. After a while, she was able to ditch the roommates and rent a place of her own. One thing led to another, and by the time she reached her early twenties, she was singing at the Plaza and at private parties for the rich and fancy. She had entrée to amazing events, a closetful of gorgeous gowns, and suitors galore. Bitsy could hardly believe what had happened to her life, much less make sense of it. She felt like Cinderella, certain the fantasy would shatter at the stroke of midnight. She was dazed by her good fortune but convinced it couldn't last."

"And then, *poof*," said Jeffers, launching an imaginary bird.

L. C. mimicked the gesture. "Poof." But tragically, the reporter failed to disappear.

Jeffers scowled. "Jeez, L. C. The lady is trying to tell her story. Go on, Colleen. What happened next?"

"Bitsy met Harold Grainger at a private film screening. There was an instant attraction, but she was reluctant to get involved. He was decades older, widowed, with a grown son and a daughter. Since Ray, she'd had trouble trusting anyone. She worried about the age difference and the baggage both of them had. But above all, she worried about the giant gulf between their worlds. Bitsy had told Harold where and what she'd come from, but he didn't seem to take it seriously. Someday he was bound to realize that she was, as advertised, a head-shy hayseed, and move on.

"Harold pursued her. They became friends and, eventually, more. By the time I met Bitsy, they'd been married for three years. They'd had a fairytale wedding at the Carlyle and honeymooned on a private motor yacht off the Dalmatian Coast. As a wedding gift, Harold had bought the townhouse on Sutton Place and hired a top designer to furnish it. Bitsy described all this with the bewildered delight of a child who'd gotten the actual pony on Christmas morning.

"I so enjoyed our time together. But as things happen, we went our separate ways. Sam outgrew his colic and began napping like an angel twice a day. I wrote while he slept, and miracle of miracles, I started getting encouraging notes from editors instead of the form rejection slips. Those were followed by my first acceptance, a short story in *Ellery Queen*.

"James's mentor at the hospital accepted the job as Department Chief at UCLA. He let us sublet his sunny two-bedroom in Turtle Bay for a pittance. I still kept an eye out for Bitsy when I took Sam out in his stroller, but we rarely connected. When I did run into her, we'd say a quick hello. We'd talk about getting together, but it never happened.

"Months later, I found an engraved invitation under our door. Tucked in the envelope was a note in Bitsy's flowery handwriting. Neighbors were hosting a party in Harold's honor, and she wanted us to come. The Broughtons lived in the largest private home on Sutton Place, a four-story brick Georgian that had been built for J. P. Morgan's daughter Anne.

"James and I debated about whether we should go. We'd be ducks out of water among Harold's millionaire friends. We had nothing reasonable to wear around people swaddled in haute couture and Harry Winston. But in the end, we decided to accept. After all, Bitsy had embraced me as a friend. She'd been so kind to me and little Sam. How could we turn her down?

"My sister Maureen and her husband, Frank, had made a killing in commercial real estate. She insisted I borrow her favorite dress, a full-skirted floral by Oscar de la Renta. Maureen lent me matching shoes and a Judith Leiber minaudière in the shape of a red rose. I felt like a princess. And James was my prince, dashing in his rented tux.

"The evening was unusually warm for early April, with a light lilac-scented breeze. Waiters in white coats served champagne and canapés in the garden overlooking the East River. Huge tug-drawn barges lumbered by amid darting powerboats. The low wrought-iron railing around the periphery was laced with tiny lights. A string quartet played the loveliest music: Brahms's *Double Concerto,* Pachelbel's *Canon,* and Haydn's *Emperor.* Amazing how the details stick with me. Bitsy's disappearance cast the evening in amber.

"Harold's children were there. Trey was a harsher, brasher version of his father. On his arm was a gum-cracking blonde in a gold lamé mini-dress and sparkling stiletto heels. Harold's daughter Marissa showed up solo in jeans, a sloppy white shirt, and cowboy boots. Both acted icy and contemptuous: a study in filial resentment.

"I was taking in the alien habitat and exotic species when I spotted Bitsy in the shadow of a towering oak, staring toward the river. I hesitated, thinking she might want a moment alone, but something drew me to her.

"When I asked if she was all right, she turned and fixed me with those moonstone eyes. 'You're so lucky to be a writer, Colleen,' she said. 'You get to decide where your stories will go.'

"I told her that wasn't entirely true. Sure, I got to imagine and test possibilities. But stories have to make sense. There has to be consistency, believability, and internal logic. A writer can't simply wander as she pleases, not if she wants to produce something publishable that readers will accept. And sometimes, I get stumped. I have no idea what comes next, can't even envision how to tie things up. Until I do."

Jeffers chuckled. "Nothing like a fat check at the end of the rainbow to get those juices flowing, right, Colleen?"

L. C. silenced him with a poison eye dart.

"Soon after that, we were invited in for dinner. Bitsy hugged me, which had never been her way. And she whispered in my ear. 'Bless you, my friend. Bless you and your darling little Sam.' Then she went off to find Harold. James and I made our way inside together.

"As we took our seats, we had a frantic call from Rachel, Sam's babysitter. She'd turned her back for an instant, and the baby had taken a spill. I could hear his pained screams in the background. James and I raced home and rushed him to the ER at Lenox Hill. They checked him thoroughly, closed the cut on his forehead with Krazy Glue, and sent us home. Everything was fine. Or so we thought.

"Late the next day, Harold called, frantic. Had I heard from Bitsy? Did I have any idea where she might be? He hadn't seen her since the party. After dinner, the men had gone to the library for cognac and cigars. After a while, Bitsy had poked her head in to say goodbye. She was tired. She was going to bed.

"When Harold got home about an hour later, their bedroom door was closed. He didn't want to disturb Bitsy, so he slept in the guest room. By the time he awoke the next morning she was gone. Their room looked exactly as they'd left it after dressing for the party. Wrappings and tags from her red chiffon Halston gown lay crumpled on the velvet settee. Pots of makeup, brushes, and crystal perfume atomizers with tasseled caps were strewn on the vanity. No one had slept in the bed.

"I tried to reassure him. Maybe she'd gone for a walk and lost track of the time. Bitsy loved to wander. But deep down, I knew something was wrong.

"Three days later, the story broke in front page headlines: "Millionaire's Bride Missing." The picture plastered underneath was from their wedding: Bitsy's radiant face, moonstone eyes fixed on the boundless future. A massive investigation followed. Flyers were posted everywhere: *Have You Seen This Woman?* Harold offered a $100,000 reward for information leading to her safe return.

"Her disappearance sparked endless speculation. Maybe she'd been murdered, her body tossed in the East River and dragged by the vicious currents out to sea.

"Maybe she'd been diagnosed with a lethal illness and gone off to die alone. Maybe she'd run off with another man, or gotten embroiled in a criminal enterprise. Some embraced the theory that an obsessed admirer had kidnapped her. Why wouldn't her looks, talent, and fortuitous marriage be punishable by violent demise? Tongues wagged about a secret addiction, mental breakdown, or suicide. But weeks turned to years, and still no ransom demand, no body, no suicide note, not a single credible lead.

"As time passed, the case was shunted to the back pages and, eventually, ceased to be news. A few years later, a book, *Little Girl Lost*, came out about the disappearance. The author claimed that Bitsy had taken up with a charismatic cult leader and was living off the grid in the Adirondacks. Investigators found no evidence that such a cult existed and nothing to bolster the convoluted theory. Obviously, the writer had hoped to capitalize on a lurid story. Nevertheless, press around the publication stirred everything up again. For a while, Sutton Place was unwilling host to yet another media circus. But thankfully, after the book was discredited, the furor died a natural death.

"I understood Harold's decision to stay away. For a long time, I avoided the neighborhood, too. Then one morning, while Sam was at nursery school, I forced myself to walk to Sutton Place and take a look at their townhouse.

"Someone was keeping up the place. Salvia and snapdragons bloomed in the window boxes. The lawn had been mowed; the bushes trimmed. The leaded glass windows sparkled. When I peered inside, I was shocked to find everything unchanged. Through the archway that led to the kitchen, I caught a glimpse of Bitsy's precious coffeemaker. A china cup perched beneath the spout, as if she were about to brew a cup of her beloved cappuccino. Still, the emptiness was palpable. No one lived there. Not anymore.

"A few weeks later, James finished his residency. He joined an internal medicine practice in Greenwich, Connecticut, and we resettled there. My first novel vanished without a trace, but the second became a surprise best seller. Knopf offered a three-book contract with a bigger advance than I'd ever dared to imagine. We put a down payment on the Lake Avenue house.

"Our family continued to grow. After Sam and our daughter Lillian, we had the twins, Lucy and Patsy, and then Robert came along, our little caboose. Those were busy, crazy times, but also full and fun. I wouldn't have traded a day of it.

"Once the whole brood was grown and launched, James and I bought the apartment on Riverside Drive. I loved the idea of a pied-à-terre in Manhattan, and we wanted a river view, but any time the broker suggested I look at a listing on the East Side, I refused. I wanted to stay away from Sutton Place.

"And I did—until last fall. I'd agreed to speak at a fund-raiser for Literacy Partners. My publicist had arranged everything. Until I was in the car on the way, I had no idea the event was to be held in a penthouse down the block from where Bitsy used to live.

"We'd left extra time because of the snow, so we arrived a few minutes early. I asked the driver to take a slow loop around the neighborhood. And I was glad I did. Avoidance did not erase reality. Bitsy's disappearance was a tragic fact. I'd do better to confront it than try to pretend it hadn't happened. Soon after that, I became preoccupied with the case and realized I needed to write about it.

"I didn't return to Sutton Place until I was deeply into the story. By then, I'd traveled to London to meet with Harold's business partner, Richard DeWitt, and to France to see his brother Gregory. Several of Harold's friends had retired to Florida, so I spent a couple of weeks in Palm Beach and Key Biscayne.

"Harold's children live in the flats of Beverly Hills. Both of them are over sixty now. Trey is twice divorced, with two adult daughters, engaged to a very young, very beautiful actress. Marissa and her partner, an artist named Eloise, own an art gallery on Rodeo Drive.

"None of them had seen Harold in many years. After Bitsy's disappearance, he'd settled in Costa Rica. He'd lived a simple life in relative seclusion. A decade ago, he suffered a massive stroke and died instantly. He left everything to a charitable trust dedicated to preserving Caribbean rainforests. Trey and Marissa hired big gun lawyers to challenge the will, but they lost.

"My last stop was Bitsy's hometown. Myrtle, Mississippi, is tiny. Population five hundred. Everyone knows everybody and everything, and everyone was eager to talk. Bitsy's father had died years earlier, but I met members of the Baptist congregation where he used to preach. Reverend Yudis had always liked his whiskey, which he took—naturally—for medicinal purposes. He'd started hitting the bottle harder after Bitsy ran away. One night after many too many at Gus's Tavern, he rammed his pickup head-on into a Kia carrying a family with two little boys. No one survived.

"I spoke with a man named Brent Gregorio. He ran the soybean farm that had been in his family for six generations. He'd gone to high school with Bitsy's mother, Jenny Lou. Crying shame what had become of her, he said: mean drunk of a husband, miserable life. Years after Bitsy ran off, Jenny went missing. Her body turned up weeks later, floating in the creek. The coroner ruled the drowning accidental, but Mr. Gregorio was convinced she'd committed suicide.

"A retired teacher named Bobbi-Jo Cline had been Bitsy's English teacher at West Union High. She remembered Bitsy as pretty and well-liked, but strangely serious at times. Two of Bitsy's best childhood friends, Nora Bea Strang and Clara Addison, described her the same way. They'd be having fun, doing each other's hair, talking nonsense, and then for no reason she'd go glum. Both of them now have gray hair and grandkids. Only Bitsy stayed frozen in time."

Jeffers was jotting faster now, stopping at intervals to reach down and tap something on the iPhone he had hidden poorly in his lap.

"At that point, I'd exhausted all my leads in Myrtle. On the morning I was scheduled to fly out, a woman named CeeCee Adlen called my cellphone. She'd heard I was in town, asking around about Bitsy. She'd moved to Jacksonville years earlier, but she'd made the three-hour drive to see me. I agreed to meet her at the diner and changed to a later flight.

"CeeCee had plenty to say, all bad. Her son Ray had fallen for Bitsy back in high school, and they'd been sweethearts. CeeCee had always known the girl was a two-bit phony. She'd tried to talk some sense into Ray, but he'd been blinded by the pretty package. He'd been such a good boy. But after that 'little slut'—her words—took off on him, he fell apart. Got into drugs. Started stealing to support his habit. He'd been in and out of prison since. One week after he was last paroled in '04, he was shot to death in a bar fight. Left a wife and four kids. Bitsy was to blame. No matter that she'd been out of Ray's life since high school. People see what they want to see."

Jeffers chuckled. "Tell me about it."

"The story was coming together. I knew the book would work, but I wasn't satisfied. I needed to revisit Bitsy's home. Places can yield crucial secrets if you know how to look.

"My assistant Erin is a crack researcher. She helped me dig through property records downtown. The Graingers' townhouse has changed hands six times. Three years ago, it sold to the current owners: Caroline and Ryan Matthews. Over the following week, I left several messages on their voicemail, asking if they'd agree to a short visit. All I needed was to walk through the rooms on the main floor. But they didn't respond.

"I understood, of course. Why would they want their home associated with such a tragic event?"

"Gotcha. Bad for property values; good if they want to be on a city tour for lovers of creepy things," Jeffers said.

"I can imagine what else would be on that itinerary," L. C. said with a pointed glare.

"So, what happened?" Tonya said.

Stephanie chimed in, "Did you reach them? Did you get to see the townhouse?"

"I left one more message, inviting them to call my publisher. Graham would confirm I was a legitimate writer, not some kook. Still, I heard nothing. So I resigned myself to finishing the book without the visit. Instead, I'd walk through the neighborhood, see what I could from the outside. And that's what I did last Thursday."

"I had a lunch date with an old friend at Felidia. After we parted company, I headed toward Sutton Place. As I walked that short distance, the sky darkened and it started to drizzle.

"Standing across the street, I stared at the townhouse. A stuffed bear sprawled facedown in one of the flower boxes. A double stroller lolled against the stair rail. By then, it was raining harder, but I barely noticed. I was drawn closer, crossing the road.

"As I reached the curb, a ginger-haired sprite rushed out to rescue Teddy and the stroller. Spotting me, she did a cartoon double take. 'Oh, my goodness! Can it be? Are you Colleen O'Day?'

"'I am. Please forgive the intrusion.' I admitted it was wrong of me to show up after she didn't return my calls. It was her home, her absolute right to refuse to open it to a stranger.

"She frowned. 'You called? I never got the message. But you're welcome, of course. Come in. Please.'

"She settled the stuffed bear on a child-sized maple rocker and plopped the stroller in the back hall. 'I'm Caroline Matthews, Ms. O'Day. What a thrill it is to meet you. You're my all-time favorite writer! Are you checking out our place for a new novel? How exciting would that be?'

"What I told her was true, but vague. I was basing a story on a cold case from the seventies. I was planning to set part of it in a townhouse like this one, but the identifying details and exact location would be disguised. She said she'd be delighted to help.

"Of all things, *she* was apologetic. 'So sorry about the mix-up,' she said. 'Our regular nanny is out with pneumonia, so our old nanny has been helping out a bit. She must have picked up your voicemails. She stashes things in the strangest places: under the sink, behind the changing table. Nanny Beth has always been a little scattered about stuff like that, head in the clouds. But she's great with the kids. Think Mary Poppins, only American and old. Plus, she's part of the family. Believe it or not, she was my husband's nanny.'

"She's upstairs bathing little Sammy right now. Messiest eater ever! Think Jackson Pollock, only with yogurt and mashed peas. Which reminds me, I'd better run up with Boo Boo bear, or he'll never go down for his nap. Please, Ms. O'Day. Make yourself at home. Look around all you like.'

"Everything had changed. Their furniture was modern: French blue Saarinen egg chairs and that red sofa modeled after Mae West's lips. The place brimmed with happy clutter: toys everywhere, safety grates hugging the stairs. They had three small boys, the oldest two in preschool. I could hear the baby, chortling and splashing. Nanny Beth hummed in the background, a familiar tune I couldn't quite place. How pleased Bitsy would be to have her home full of so much life and exuberance. I could imagine what she'd say, *Heaven, right?*

"But that was all. The townhouse served up no sudden flash of insight. I called upstairs to thank Caroline Matthews, and left.

"As I was about to hail a cab, I had another idea. I headed down the block, past what used to be the Broughtons' house, where I'd last seen Bitsy. A year after her disappearance, the family donated the property to the United Nations. It's been home to the Secretary General ever since.

"The windows were blackened in the scrawny NYPD security booth out front. I turned the corner to escape those unseen eyes. And there I stopped. Through a stand of Japanese privet, I caught a glimpse of the garden.

"The sight propelled me back to the night of the party. I hear the ghost strains of Pachelbel's *Canon* over the growling rumble of a passing barge; the crystalline clink of laughter and champagne flutes. A hint of lilac rides the silken breeze. Elegant guests mingle beneath a gibbous moon. I see Bitsy standing off in the shadows, staring at the tides. She turns and fixes me with her mesmerizing eyes. *You're so lucky to be a writer, Colleen.* She leans in and hugs me. And with that, everything falls into place. I'd had the answer all along."

Jeffers scowled. "Huh? I don't get it."

"Thankfully, a cab came by. I phoned my brother-in-law on the way. My sister Maureen lost her battle with leukemia a year ago, and poor Frank has been horribly depressed. He barely eats, rarely goes out.

"I could hardly contain myself, but I didn't want to say anything, even to Frank, until I made sure my theory was true. I told him I needed to check on something of Maureen's for my book, and he waved me toward their room.

"Frank hasn't been able to part with Maureen's things. Everything is as she left it. I found what I was after right away. And there it was in black and white."

Jeffers scratched behind his ear. "I still don't get it."

"When Bitsy hugged me that night, she slipped a note into the pocket of Maureen's beautiful dress. And there it remained, yellowed with age. I'll never forget the words: *I can't bear the lies anymore. I don't belong and never will. This has to end now, tonight. I've studied the tides. The river will take me where I need to go. Please tell Harold I'm sorry. Tell him I had no choice.*

L. C. pulled a breath. "She killed herself? Wow. I didn't see that coming."

Jeffers's eyes bugged. "Bitsy Grainger offed herself? You're sure?"

"At least we finally know what happened." Colleen raised her wineglass. "To Bitsy Grainger. She took the only way she could see to end her suffering. Rest in peace."

The whole group joined the solemn chorus. "To Bitsy Grainger."

Jeffers stood abruptly. "Excuse me a sec. Nature calls."

"Off the record, Jeffers. You hear me?" But the reporter hurried toward the men's room, tapping away. L. C. sputtered in disgust. "That wormy creep. He's going to tweet the end of your story. He's going to post it all over creation and claim it's his. I'm going to go flush him and his damned phone."

Colleen set a hand on his. "It's okay, L. C. Truly. Let it go."

"But he's a lazy, nasty, unethical jerk. He doesn't care what he steals or who he hurts."

"And he'll get just deserts: a life sentence with himself."

The next morning, Colleen bundled against the morning chill and hailed a cab to Sutton Place. She took a final stroll through Bitsy's old neighborhood and then headed toward the charming patisserie she'd discovered on First Avenue. Their cappuccino was world-class.

She perched on a bistro chair at a tiny table in the rear and placed her order: Bitsy's favorite drink and a croissant. Then she plucked the iPad mini from her tote.

Reuben Jeffers's scoop had garnered the lead in today's edition of *A-List*. "Missing Beauty Mystery Solved!" The piece recounted all the details Colleen had hoped to see: Bitsy's childhood in Myrtle, Mississippi; her betrayal by Ray Adlen and his downward spiral; Harold's move to Costa Rica and his children's lawsuit over the terms of his will. Best of all, they included a manufactured replica of the suicide note Colleen claimed to have found. Jeffers had swallowed her story whole and spat it back unverified. Unscrupulous though he was, he should have known better. Colleen wrote fiction, after all.

But there was no going back. Jeffers's story would be reposted in predictable perpetuity, and it would gather the heft that passes today for truth.

Colleen's order was ready. She checked to be sure the time was right, paid, and stepped outside.

Near the corner, an old woman hunched against the chill in a hooded camel coat. She appeared to be homeless. "Can you help me, please? Can you help—"

Colleen approached. "Here, my friend. For you." She passed the croissant and cappuccino.

The woman cradled the cup and took a sip. Her wrinkled eyes narrowed with pleasure, but Colleen still caught a hint of moonstone gray.

"Bless you, my friend," she said and sipped again. "Heaven, right?"

JUDITH KELMAN *is the award-winning, best-selling author of seventeen novels, three nonfiction books, dozens of short stories, and hundreds of articles and essays for major publications. In 2008 she founded Visible Ink, a unique writing program at Memorial Sloan-Kettering that enables all interested cancer patients to reap the benefits of written expression with the one-on-one help of a volunteer writing mentor. She lives in New York City.*

DIZZY AND GILLESPIE

Persia Walker

Faded glory. That's how I'd describe Mama's apartment. At least, that's what I'd say when I was feeling generous. When I wasn't, I'd say it was a dilapidated piece of shit. But Mama loved it. Loved her seven big rooms, all sprouting from that tunnel of a hallway like branches from a tree. High ceilings, hardwood floors, and a maid's quarters. Not really a living room, but a parlor and a dining room, with nearly floor-to-ceiling windows. Sounds grand, don't it?

Built in 1910, that place was meant for the wealthy. But that was then and this was now and it was old—past old. It exuded sadness and disappointment. It stunk of mildew and dust, of ancient asbestos and long-dead vermin. The high ceilings leaked streams of filthy water, the tall walls were buckled, and the floor was treacherous with slivers.

Mama wasn't blind to all the problems. She simply didn't care. The place had been her home for nearly forty years. She had grown up during the Depression, dirt poor and hungry, in a rambling broken-down farmhouse. Determined to get ahead, she left Virginia when she was fifteen and grabbed a Greyhound bus for New York. That was in 1932, when the whole country was still struggling and chances for a colored girl with a ninth-grade education were next to nil. She had gone to work in Long Island, as a maid in the homes of moneyed white folk. Not often, but sometimes, she would talk about their grand homes. And sometimes I'd wonder: did this place of faded grandeur remind her of the homes she'd worked in? Maybe in her eyes, the dull floors still shone and the sagging walls were still ramrod straight.

Mama was ninety years old. She had lived in Harlem for some seventy-odd years, and she was still proud to be there, in the legendary mecca of black folk. Nowadays, a lot of black Harlemites were heading back down South, where life was slower and money went further. But you couldn't tell Mama that. She still believed that Harlem was the *only* place to be.

She was especially proud to be in Hamilton Heights. It was a historic landmarked district, with rows of stately townhouses and stone terraces. It was home to an ethnically diverse community of actors, artists, architects, professors, and other intellectual bohemians. Certainly, parts of it were lovely.

"This is one of the nicest neighborhoods in all New York City," Mama would say.

Then I'd say, "But I'm not complaining about the neighborhood. It's this building."

And that, of course, was a bald-faced lie. 'Cause I was most definitely complaining about both.

The gentrification that had hit Central and East Harlem had pretty much left West Harlem alone. At least our little part of it. That stretch along 135th and 145th Streets, between Broadway and Amsterdam? It was sad. Cheap landlords, run-down tenements. There were a couple of good restaurants along Broadway, but they were probably going to close soon. The atmosphere of an open-air drug market had certainly calmed down, but sometimes it felt like the dealing had just gone underground.

Then, there was the other Hamilton Heights. It was gorgeous. Convent Avenue, Hamilton Terrace, Sugar Hill: they were stunning— but they had *always* been stunning. Until fairly recently, they'd been among Harlem's best-kept secrets. Even with as well-known a place as City College being on Convent Avenue, Hamilton Terrace, for example, escaped general notice. It was a forgotten enclave. A city apart. Even the air over there was different.

Over there. That's how I thought of it. That was over there. And this was over here, where the people were holding on by the skin of their teeth.

"Well, if you don't like it, leave," Mama would say.

And I would sigh. Because we both knew I couldn't. Not without a decent job and not without her. My dream was to earn enough to get us both out of there, but she didn't want to go.

"This is my home," she'd say. "When I die, it'll be yours, and you can do with it whatever you damn well please. But for now, it's mine, and the only way I'm leaving is when I leave this world."

"Don't talk like that."

"Why not? It's gotta happen sometime," she'd say, and then add, with a rueful smile, "It's got to."

She had a weak heart—weak, but determined. You could see it on her echocardiograph how her heart would hesitate, then give a little flutter and pump, hesitate, then flutter and pump. It amazed her doctors, and it worried me. But it only bewildered Mama. Sometimes, I'd hear her in her room, crying. Why did she have to keep on living when so many of her friends were gone? *Why?*

It wasn't just a matter of being left behind. It was that she couldn't do what she loved doing. Not anymore. She couldn't entertain, give her dinner parties. She was known for her sweet potato pie. Everyone in the building had gotten one at one time or another, usually to welcome them or congratulate them, or just to make them feel better. She loved cooking and going down the hill to the grocery store. But of late, she had become too weak to do either. She had taken to sitting in her room, in the dark, for hours.

I blamed the apartment. It was killing her.

It wasn't just the dirt, the stench, and the roaches. It wasn't just the bathroom ceiling that collapsed without fail every six months, showering down filthy rocks, rotten wood, and cracked plaster.

It was the mice.

Oh, the mice!

They were everywhere. You could hear them skittering through the walls, see them scampering across the floor. Our living room was their highway. One evening, as I rested on the couch, I set a glass of water on the floor. Next thing I knew, a mouse was raised up on all fours, taking a sip. One day Mama left a sweet potato pie on the stovetop to cool. She turned to the sink to wash a spatula and turned back just in time to see a mouse making a beeline for her pie. Man, oh, man, was he making tracks! But he sure put the brakes on when he saw her. She stared into his beady little eyes and he stared right back. Who was going to make the next move?

She was fast, but he was faster. She went to whack him with the spatula, but with a flick of his tail, he was gone. Dove right into the stove, she said, down through an eye. "That sucker jumped right into a warm oven, like it was home. Made me wonder what else was hiding in there."

She told me the story over dinner. That pie had gone right into the garbage, and dinner that night had come out of a can.

Disappointed, I said, "If you won't move, then at least do something about the mice."

She knew where I was going.

"I'm not gonna get no cats. I hate cats. Just hate 'em. They are *not* coming into this house."

"But—"

"This is *my* house," she reminded me. "Mine! Do you hear? And I say no cats."

And that was that.

Until Martin Milford moved in. Of course, at the time, we didn't know nothing about no Martin Milford. All we knew was that the walls of our apartment were suddenly vibrating and a river of mice was coursing through our walls. The place echoed with the sound of a buzz saw. I couldn't tell whether it was coming from upstairs or downstairs. I tried to ignore the commotion at first, but then it got so bad, I had to check it out. I ran upstairs to the apartment above us. Nothing unusual was going on there, so I headed downstairs to the ground floor.

The door to the apartment below us was open and I could see that someone was doing some major renovations.

That someone would turn out to be Milford. He was tall and lanky, with watery blue eyes, thin blonde hair and a short scraggly beard. Reminded me of an aging hippie. He had on a dingy white T-shirt and dust-covered jeans, and he was using an electric saw to rip out a wall. He stopped when he saw me, unhooked his dust mask. As soon as he heard that I was his neighbor, he smiled and shook my hand. I had been prepared to fuss, but he disarmed me by being so friendly and all. He immediately started telling me about himself.

Was a photographer, he said, a freelancer. Had moved up from "below Ninety-Sixth Street."

One of those, I thought. Didn't think Harlem was good enough 'til loss of a job or income forced him to reconsider.

"Look here," I said, gesturing toward his saw, "you—"

"I am so glad I found this place. Been looking for a real long time."

"I understand, but—"

"Lived on the street for a while. When I got this place, I couldn't believe it. Just hadn't had no luck, you know?"

Yeah, I knew. I was barely making ends meet, going from one survival job to another. It was the height of the so-called Great Recession and I was earning just enough to cover expenses.

"Look—" I began again.

"Sold my Harley to get the down payment." He shook his head.

"Never thought I'd have to do that. It's just that things got so bad, I . . . "

"I know, I know," I said, finding it hard to stay angry. "But look here, I wanted to—"

"Landlord said he'd give me a good deal if I took this place as is. It's a bit more work than I thought it would be, but I'm enjoying it. Living room's gonna make a great studio."

I glanced down his hallway. He had all the room doors open. The sunlight was streaming in. He'd already relaid the hallway floor. The new planks gleamed in the late afternoon light. I had to admit, he was doing good work, the kind of work I wished we could do on our place. I looked back at him. He seemed like a nice enough man, and I knew what it was like to have dreams.

"You're going to do a whole lot more?"

"Naw, nearly finished. I think I'll be done in just about a week. Why?"

I just waved it away. "Never mind."

⸻ · — · — · ⸻

The renovations didn't go on for another week, or two or three, but four. A whole damn month.

I tried to talk to him a couple times, but each time he grew less and less sympathetic. "The noise is driving us crazy," I would say. "The dust is coming up in puffs through the floorboards. And the mice. The noise isn't just driving us crazy; it's driving them crazy, too. They're all over us."

"But you can't blame me if you've got mice."

"I said—"

"I know what you said. You can't tell me what to do in my apartment. I'm not stopping my renovations just for you."

I had told myself to keep a cool head, so I bit back what I *really* wanted to say and stayed polite. "Look, I don't want to fight. Just tell me, how much longer?"

"For however long it takes," he said and slammed the door in my face.

I knew he didn't have a permit for the changes he was making, and I thought about reporting him more than once. The city inspectors would've shut him down but quick. If it had been the landlord, I would've dropped a dime in a minute. But you don't do that to another tenant. Not in Harlem. Tenants should always stick together.

So Mama and I swallowed our aggravation over the noise—and the mice. Clearly, Milford's renovations were driving the mice to literally climb the walls. Their population had doubled. And they were having babies. You could hear them squealing. I went out and bought rat poison, but then Mama said not to use it. The mice would eat it, crawl into some little hole and die. Then their rotting little corpses would stink up the place.

Good grief!

We didn't even bother with mousetraps. We'd tried them before. Either the mice weren't interested, or if they were—and this was the worst part—they got caught in them, but didn't die. You'd walk into the kitchen in the middle of the night and find one of them very much alive and kicking. And that meant you'd have to kill it yourself. Not for Mama, and certainly not for me.

So, I kept pushing the idea of getting a cat, but Mama held out, *No, No, NO!*

That is, until the day she found mice in her bedroom, playing on her sheets. Suddenly, she didn't want just one cat, but *two.*

The next day, I got them, rescues from the animal shelter. Dizzy and Gillespie. They were the cutest little things. Fast, too. And hungry. Those mice were gone within days. Fine with me.

Fine with Mama.

But not fine with Milford.

Soon, we heard a knocking on our door. Milford looked exhausted. "What's wrong?" I asked.

He had mice, he said. Not just a few, but hordes of them.

"They got into my bedroom closet, my kitchen cabinets. I found a dead one in my bathtub the other day. And yesterday, I was trying to do a photo shoot, you know, in the living room, and a mouse ran right across the client's feet. She walked out, and now she won't pay me."

"I'm sorry to hear that, but—"

"So, I'm wondering if you guys were doing something—"

His gaze dropped and his eyes widened. I glanced down and saw Dizzy and Gillespie, standing guard at my ankles, staring up at him.

"Cats!" Milford said.

"Obviously."

"You've got to get rid of them."

"S'cuse me?"

"I said, you have got to get of those . . . *things.*"

I couldn't believe his nerve. "Ain't happening. They're my mother's cats, and they are here to stay."

And they really had become *her* cats. I had been the one to push for them, but she was the one they took to. And she took to them. It was Mama who came up with the idea of naming them Dizzy and Gillespie, after the great jazz musician of the 1940s. It was Mama those two cats cuddled up to at night. It was her they loved, and it was clear that she loved them. She had found renewed strength to go down the hallway to the kitchen. She couldn't stand long enough to cook, but she could feed her cats, all the time fussing about "how you've got to feed them just right." Then she would come sit in the living room with me and watch them play and get into mischief. She would laugh and clap her hands! She said she used to be afraid of cats, but she wasn't afraid no more.

"They something else," she said. "So pretty, and so sharp! Why, they understand everything I say!"

We'd tried every medicine under the sun to bring down Mama's blood pressure; they'd all failed or caused bad side effects. Dizzy and Gillespie got it down to normal in a week. Between the mischief that made her laugh, the purring that soothed her nerves, and the security of knowing she could sleep in a mouse-free bed, those cats had brought Mama more joy and better health than I could've imagined.

So, no. We were not going to get rid of them.

"Why don't you get cats of your own?"

"Hell, no!"

He said he was going to take it to the landlord.

"Do that," I said. "He don't care. Saves him the cost of hiring an exterminator."

Then I shut the door and gave Dizzy and Gillespie good ear rubs.

Mama wanted to know what was going on.

"I thought you said he was a nice man," she said when I told her.

I shrugged. "Seemed like it."

She sighed. "If he's the type of folks moving up to Harlem these days, then . . . " Her voice trailed away.

"Then what? You wouldn't be saying you want to move, would you?"

"No," she said. "It's them I'm talking about. They the ones gonna have to go."

———— · — · — · ————

Two days later, Milford was back at our door. Mama was the one who answered.

I watched from down the hall as he bowed and handed her a bouquet of flowers. "I'm sorry," he said, "I don't know what was wrong with me. I had no right to say what I said."

Mama accepted the apology, and the flowers. After he left, she turned to me and said, "Well, well, well. I guess he's not so bad after all."

"C'mon, Mama. You know what happened as much as I do."

"The landlord gave him a piece of his mind?"

"Of course, he did."

The next few days were quiet. I put Milford out of my mind and went back to worrying about work. For the time being, my concerns about Mama were eased. Her health had stabilized. Her depression had lifted. She talked about Dizzy and Gillespie all the time, about how sweet they were, how smart they were, how they were just about the best cats of all time.

Then one day I came home from another useless interview and found Mama sitting in the living room, holding Dizzy. I knew right away that something was wrong. Dizzy was real still and, Gillespie was sitting at Mama's feet, meowing.

"Mama?" I put a hand on her shoulder.

"She's gone," Mama said.

Dizzy's little mouth was open and her body twisted. She must've died in agony.

"What happened?"

"I don't know." She looked up at me, and the grief in her eyes made my heart constrict. "One minute she was healthy and happy, as frisky as you please. The next, she was having a fit of some kind. Then she started vomiting, and before I could do anything, she was . . . like this."

Dizzy was still so small she fit into a boot box.

"Don't put her in the garbage," Mama said.

"I wouldn't do that. I'll take her to the vet tomorrow."

"We'll go together."

"Okay."

But the next day when I came home to pick up Mama, she was in no state to go anywhere. She was sitting in her bedroom, and this time it was Gillespie she held.

Mama had taken Dizzy's death hard enough, but Gillespie's really floored her. She was heartbroken.

I couldn't understand it. "Two healthy cats don't just up and die like that." I asked her if she wanted the vet to do a necropsy, but she said not to. "Leave well enough alone."

I said I would, but I couldn't. I asked the vet what had gone wrong. She had a one-word answer.

"Strychnine."

In other words, rat poison.

I was stricken. This was my fault. I told Mama, "They must've gotten ahold of what I bought. I'm so sorry. I thought I put it all away. But I guess I didn't."

I hoped for a scolding word, but she said nothing, just sat there wrapped with grief. Over the next two days, she went back to sitting in the dark. "This is twice this has happened to me," she said. "I ain't never gonna let it happen again."

She wouldn't say what she meant by that. Just told me to clear out everything belonging to the cats.

"I don't think that's a good idea," I said. "Even if Dizzy and Gillespie are gone, their smell might keep the mice away, at least for a little while."

But her mind was made up.

"Get rid of it. All of it. Then scrub the place clean."

So I did.

Within days the mice were back. Mama's depression deepened and her blood pressure soared.

The doctor was worried. "If we don't do something, then . . . " He let silence fill the blank. "And it could happen soon, real soon."

I tried to talk to her about getting another pair of cats, but she wouldn't hear of it.

"No," she shook her head. "Never again."

I didn't know what to do, so I put my arms around her and hugged her. "It's gonna be okay, Mama. It's gonna be okay."

For a several seconds, we just held each other, sitting in her room. Then she said something.

"What?" I asked.

Her voice was hoarse. "It was my fault," she whispered, "my fault they died."

"What?"

"It was me."

I shook my head. "I don't understand."

She didn't answer.

Then understanding dawned. I covered my mouth in shock. She had killed them. She had killed Dizzy and Gillespie. I couldn't believe it. I didn't want to believe it. But then I searched her eyes, and saw not just the grief, but the guilt.

"You—? It was you? But why? I thought you loved them. I—"

"I don't know." She shook her head. "I don't why I—I just . . . " Her eyes pleaded with me. "I think I just . . . I just wanted to be a good neighbor."

"What does that mean?"

But she couldn't answer. She was gone, withdrawn into her own world.

"Mama?"

She turned from me, wringing her hands.

"I . . . I know I can't bring them back," she said, "but I'm gonna make it right. I'm gonna make it right." She kept saying that. She wouldn't talk to me except to say that.

I was so hurt and angry, I didn't know what to do. How could she have done something like that—that hateful? Kill two helpless cats? Cats she loved? And how could she ever think she could make it right? I didn't want to be around her. I had to get out of there. I grabbed up my coat and my bag, fled down the hall and out the door.

I walked for hours, wondering what I was doing with my life. And I didn't go home that night. I stayed with a friend, trying to swallow the anger, trying to understand. I so wanted to move out. But I was trapped. I couldn't afford another apartment, and she couldn't live on her own. We were stuck in that apartment together, with the stench and the mold and the mice.

I took another step back. Here I was, a grown woman, and all I could think about was running away from home. How crazy was that? All night I thought about it. By morning, I was exhausted, but I had decided.

No matter what, she was my mother and I loved her. As long as she was staying, so was I.

——— ·—·—· ———

Coming up the hill from the train station, I saw police cars, an ambulance, and a crowd standing outside our building. It was my mother. I just knew it was my mother. She had fallen or had some other mishap, and I hadn't been there to help her.

I ran the last few yards to the house and pushed my way through. The lobby was packed with neighbors and cops telling them to get back.

"You've gotta let me through," I cried. "I'm her daughter! Her daughter!"

The cop gave me a strange look and asked me what apartment I lived in.

"Twenty-four."

"That's not the one." He jerked his thumb over his shoulder, and that's when I saw what I would've seen to begin with if I hadn't been so panicked.

Milford's apartment door stood open. A paramedic came out, stripping off his rubber gloves. He said something to one of the cops. I couldn't read his lips. I didn't have to. His expression said it all.

"What happened?" I asked the cop.

"Did you know him?"

"Sort of. I mean, yeah. He's my neighbor." I glanced back at the open apartment door. They were carrying Milford out on a stretcher, in a body bag.

I couldn't believe it. Milford, *dead?*

"What happened?" I asked again.

"We don't know yet. But look," he said, "why don't you give me your name and apartment number in case we need to talk to the neighbors."

"Sure," I said, and gave him the info. "Now, look, I really need to get upstairs. My mom's up there. She's old, and frail, and she needs me. I—"

"Okay. Fine. Just make sure you go straight up."

"I will."

———— · — · — · ————

Later, I'd remember sensing an odd emptiness, a telltale stillness the moment I let myself in. But at the time, all I could think about was sharing the news about Milford.

"Mama?! Hey, Mama!"

No answer. I checked her bedroom, which was right next to the front door, didn't see her, and ran down the hallway, calling out for her. The bathroom door was open. She wasn't in there. Not in the kitchen either.

But she *was* in the living room, sitting in her rocking chair. Her eyes were closed, as though she had fallen asleep, and loosely clasped to her breast, in hands gone slack, was a photograph.

"Mama?"

There was no answer.

"Mama?"

———— ˙— ˙— ˙ ————

That night, after they had taken her away, I sank down on the sofa. Unable to think. Unable to cry. All I could think about was how she had died alone. Despite all my efforts, all my promises to be there for her, in the end I had left her to die alone. And I kept seeing her, clasping that picture, an image of her in her rocking chair, smiling, holding two plump cats, Dizzy and Gillespie, one under each arm. I had taken pictures of her and pictures of the cats, but none together.

Finally, I dragged myself to bed. I closed my eyes, but I couldn't fall asleep. After about an hour, I got up and went down the hall to Mama's room.

The door was closed. I paused, took a deep breath, then gripped the doorknob and went in. I don't know what I expected—or what I feared—but whatever it was, it didn't happen. I didn't break down. I didn't shed a tear. I was too wound up for it, and maybe too afraid to let go.

Mama's pills were there, on her dresser, lined up like little soldiers. All of them, except the sedatives. I checked each bottle, checked them again. Where were they? They should've been there. I had just filled her prescription the other day. Everything else was there, but the sleeping pills.

Then I knew. I understood where all those pills had gone.

Mama's heart hadn't simply given out. She had decided she was tired of living . . . and knowing she planned to go, she had sent Dizzy and Gillespie along ahead of her. *It was my fault,* she'd said, *my fault they died.* It was crazy, but in a crazy kind of way, it made sense.

That's when the tears came, when the realization hit. I had failed her so completely, to help her, to restore her hope, to get her out of there. I had failed her utterly.

———— · — · — · ————

The death certificate issued by the powers that be simply listed heart failure. It did not mention sleeping pills. Maybe they hadn't bothered to check. Maybe they had just seen a very old woman and assumed she had died of natural causes.

It was a simple funeral, just the way Mama had said she wanted it. Despite her belief that she was all alone, she still had quite a few friends in the neighborhood. They showed up, many of them as frail as she was. They were all kind and supportive, and I thanked them for the love they'd shown her.

That evening, one of them stopped by. It was Mr. Edgar. He lived two floors up, and although he was in his eighties, he was often out and about. I suspected he was sweet on Mama.

"I just wanted to return this." He held up one of Mama's pie plates.

"Oh, thank you, but when did she—"

"The other day. She asked me to go to the store for her. I said I would if she would make me a pie."

"Really?"

"You mean, you didn't know? She didn't make you one? 'Cause I bought enough for two."

Slowly, I shook my head. The fact that my mother found the energy to make it down to the kitchen and bake two pies surprised me no less than the fact that she had asked Mr. Reese to buy the ingredients instead of asking me.

I thanked him and started to close the door, but he stopped me.

"Just one more thing," he said. "Some cops came by to see me. Asked some strange questions."

"About what?"

He shrugged. "It's probably nothing for you to worry about. But they might stop by here."

I thought it strange that he was so vague, but I didn't push the matter. He turned around to go, but then caught himself and came back.

"I can't believe I nearly forgot this." He reached into his jacket pocket and brought out a small bottle. It was Mama's missing sleeping pills.

"Your mother gave me these the other day. I happened to mention that I wasn't sleeping well, and she told me to take them. I said I didn't need all of them, but she insisted."

I accepted them in a daze and closed the door. Mama's sleeping pills. She hadn't committed suicide. She really had died of heart failure. I started down the hall but found myself standing outside Mama's door instead. I thought about Dizzy and Gillespie, and how much she loved them.

Then I thought of that picture.

I had buried it with her. I wished I hadn't. Partly because it would've been good to have: a reminder of all-too-brief happy days.

And partly because I wondered who had taken it. I knew I hadn't. I tried to picture it, study it.

I remembered my surprise at finding it. Surprise because I didn't know she had it. Because I didn't even know it existed. And because . . . well, it was a *Polaroid*.

Who in the world still uses Polaroids?

The doorbell rang again.

I thought it was Mr. Edgar or another of Mama's neighbors. Instead, it was two detectives. They held up their badges and introduced themselves as Jacobi and Reiner.

"Yes?"

They asked about Milford, about what kind of relationship I'd had with him.

"None. I barely knew him."

"You didn't get along, right?" That was Jacobi. His gaze slid up and down the hallway, then returned to me.

"What's this all about?"

"Where are your cats?" Reiner asked.

"My cats?" I looked from one to the other. "They're both dead. Why?"

"You like to cook, to bake?"

That was Jacobi. He made a move to step around me, to walk down the hall. I stepped in front of him.

"Not really, no."

He brought his eyes back down to me and I planted my feet, refusing to budge. He didn't like that. He gave Reiner a nod, as if to say that some suspicion had been confirmed.

Reiner asked, "How did your cats die?"

I didn't answer.

"We heard that you suspected poisoning," he went on.

"And that you thought Milford did it," Jacobi added.

Actually, that thought hadn't occurred to me. Maybe it would have, if I hadn't been so quick to assume that I'd done it by accident, or if Mama hadn't indicated that she'd done it by intent.

"Why exactly are you here? It couldn't possibly be to investigate the death of two cats."

"Depends," Jacobi said.

"On what?"

"On whether it was a motive for murder," Reiner said.

"Murder?"

"Turns out Milford died from strychnine poison."

"Really?" I said, keeping my voice calm.

"Yeah, really." Jacobi studied me. "Turns out it was in a sweet potato pie."

"And you think I baked it?"

"Did you?" Jacobi asked.

"No."

"You sure about that?"

"Very."

"What about your mother?"

"What about her?"

"We heard that she's famous for her sweet potato pie."

"Then you must've also heard that she died."

That took the wind out of their sails. A bit.

"When—"

"The same day Milford died. While the paramedics were downstairs trying to save him, my mother was up here, dying."

"Why didn't you call for help?" Reiner asked.

"I wasn't here. I had gone out. When I got back, there was that mess downstairs, that circus about . . . him. And your cops wouldn't let me through. By the time I got upstairs, she was gone."

They didn't have an answer for that. They asked me if they could look through the place, and I said no. They warned me they'd be back. I didn't care. They couldn't pin Milford's death on me, and they knew it.

———— . — . — . ————

I went back to Mama's room. I had remembered one more detail. One more reason why that photograph bothered me: the date stamp in the lower right-hand corner.

It was for the day Dizzy died.

Who still uses Polaroids?

Photographers. That's who. They use them for test shots.

Milford. He must've been in our apartment.

"It was my fault," she said, *"my fault they died."*

Something inside me twisted in pain. How could I have gotten it so wrong? She hadn't killed those cats, but she *had* let the devil in the door. She had wanted to be the good neighbor, so she had given Milford another chance, and he'd used it to poison Dizzy and Gillespie.

In killing them, he'd killed her, too. Losing those cats had pushed her over the edge. Sure, the doctor had said it was heart failure that killed her, but he might as well have written heart*break*.

"I can't bring them back," she'd said, *"but I will make it right."*

And she had.

She would've still been alive if Milford hadn't killed those cats— and he would have been, too.

———— · — · ————

Two months later, I got a good job, and four months after that I'd saved enough to move out. The neighborhood was changing. Columbia University was building a new campus nearby, and everyone was saying how the rents were going to rise. All my friends were telling me how lucky I was to have Mama's apartment, how I shouldn't give it up. That the landlord would have to fix it up or buy me out. But I couldn't take being there. I couldn't stand it.

It took me days to clean the place out, to empty it of forty years of papers. While doing so, I found an old picture that, from the looks of it, dated back to the 1940s. It was of Mama, all done up. She was seated in a garden, nuzzling two small cats. I was surprised. She'd said she always hated cats. I turned the picture over and found a note on the back: *Me, with Cab and Calloway. Just before they died in March of '45.* Cab and Calloway?

"This is twice this has happened to me," she'd said. So, Mama had had cats before, and they had died mysteriously, too.

I felt a new welling of sadness, of loss, bittersweet.

I set that picture aside. I saved it and, that evening, I took it with me to my new place. It got a special spot on my dresser top, right next to a picture of Dizzy and Gillespie, and a picture of Mama and me.

I miss you so much, I thought. But then I took a step back and looked around and it hit me once again. I did miss her, but I sure didn't miss that old apartment.

I sat down and took it all in. *My new place. My new place. My very own, new place.* I said those words out loud, repeated them over and over. I had finally done it. I had moved into one of those townhouse apartments on Convent Avenue, and it was all I'd imagined it to be.

I gazed out my window and sighed.

It was good, so very good, to finally live "over there."

PERSIA WALKER *is a diplomat, former journalist, and the author of acclaimed crime fiction. Her three historical mystery novels, all set in 1920s New York, are* Harlem Redux, Darkness and the Devil behind Me, *and* Black Orchid Blues. *She is a native New Yorker, speaks several languages, and has lived in South America and Europe.*

ME AND MIKEY

T. Jefferson Parker

The first thing my cousin Mikey does after high school is he takes his graduation money from the family and runs off to California. The money was for him to fly back and see the old country, maybe get in touch with his roots or some such thing. Those would be in Reggio, Calabria, but Mikey goes the other direction, all the way to Hollywood. This was in 1972. He was eighteen and skinny, with one of those hippie shag haircuts, and—you gotta love this—he thinks he's got musical talent. He took his guitar.

I'm only two years older than Mikey, but I'm the one had to get him back to Little Italy. He was crashing in Hollywood with a guy he used to jam with in school. The guy's family is tight with us LiDeccas.

So it's no secret where he was. Mikey never got basic stuff like that, like how to do a thing without the whole world knowing about it. It was like he was born with part of his brain missing.

"You made a mistake," I explained to him in the terminal at LAX. "You have responsibilities, Mikey. Who do you think you are?" I couldn't pay full attention to him with all those L.A. women around. Blondes. Miniskirts. I miss the seventies.

Mikey nodded and looked like some dog you'd kick just because he expected it. "I was looking for something to say."

"What's that supposed to mean?"

"But I don't know what it is yet."

"Me, neither. So, you do what you have to do, Mikey—Jesus."

In New York we got back to business, which was LiDecca Brothers Food. Just so you know, it was founded in 1921. It was fish and seafood at first, then we got into produce and dairy. And whatever else needed doing. Me and Mikey's job was servicing the vending machines. We had them in five boroughs and parts of Jersey. Mostly they were candy, snacks, and sodas, but some were hot coffee and tea, which meant cups to reload and unsold product to dump and creamer going bad.

Mikey was a perfectionist, a time-waster. By the end of the day I wanted to kick one of those hot beverage machines to pieces. I had a woman friend out in the Bronx I'd see while Mikey fussed around, making sure everything was shiny and clean, and she made the job more than tolerable.

Some days after work we'd go to Mikey's house on Grand. It was an older place, with a piano in the family room and always beer in the fridge. Mikey's little sisters, they were the skinniest, loudest girls you could imagine, but they were kinda funny, too, and they'd bring us the beers. Christina, his mom, liked me, and I could never figure why. She played the piano. She made the best cannoli I ever ate. But she had her rules. One was, if you talked about the mob or made guys, she'd smack you hard on the cheek and send you out. June, the year before, I said something about Joseph Colombo getting what he deserved, and that's exactly what she did to me. Kinda hurt, but it mostly made me feel small and mad.

One day Mikey closed the doors of the family room on all of them and pulled a big roll of cash out of his pocket. "I'm going to California for a year. I'm gonna play music and get famous."

"Where'd you get the money?" I asked.

"Pop. We had a talk about me taking off with the graduation money for Italy. I'm gonna pay it all back. But then Pop surprised me. Told me he understands dreams because of the single-A ball he played for Philly. He only lasted a year because he couldn't adjust to the off-speed stuff."

"Yeah, yeah, we know all that."

"But the point is he took a year to play the game and try to make it happen. He knows I have this dream to play music and be famous, so he's giving me a year off to do it. At the end of that time, maybe I've made it big. And if I haven't, I'll be able to come back to LiDecca Brothers, work my way up. And this money is to get me started in music."

I felt some anger, I'll admit it. I always liked my Uncle Jimmy—Mikey's dad. My own pop would never do that. Never. We don't have dreams in our line of the family. We have responsibilities. "Well, lucky you, Mikey."

"You come out and visit anytime you want."

"I'll stay here and do my job. And I'll be moving up in the business while you're out in California goofin' off."

Mikey looked at that wad of cash, then put it back in his pocket with a little smile on his face. I could see he was happy to be getting out of Little Italy. He was always a sensitive type. When we were young, he didn't like the way the family was, the way you had to read between the lines. My dad, Dominic—Mikey's uncle—he used to tell me the lines were bullshit and the truth was between them. When we were young, we didn't ever get a direct answer to a direct question. Most questions we didn't get an answer to at all. I got it back then that there were two worlds. One was where I lived every day, and it was okay. Women pretty much ran it. The other one was the real world, though—and I got that I might get to know it slowly, over years and years, and maybe not completely, ever. The men's world. It wasn't talked about directly when me and Mikey were young.

So, for example, Pop went up to Attica on a trumped-up rap, but we—his own kids—didn't know what the rap was. Or one of the Maglione cousins went missing one day, and no one ever saw him or talked about him again. Or Nick, the playboy great-uncle that always had the custom suits and all those beautiful women hanging on him, well, one day we heard that someone had stuffed one of his suits with fish to make it look like Nick was inside, then arranged the suit on the sidewalk outside his favorite seafood restaurant, and no one ever saw him again, either. Shit like that would make Mikey bug-eyed and pale, send him into hiding in his room.

Me? It made me want to be a part of it.

———— . — . — . ————

With Mikey gone, I moved up. Found I could service the vending machines faster without him and his everything-had-to-be-perfect attitude. Which left me spare time for my girlfriends and for me and Pop's side business, which was selling Italian wines to Manhattan restaurants. We had some people back home that could get us the cases for less than other importers, so we kept our prices down and delivered good product. There was also some creativity regarding the labels, but not so anybody would know, except for the occasional pain-in-the ass connoisseur, but those types were never any trouble. Also stuffed in the crates of wine, we got knock-off watches and purses still actually made in Italy back then, so perfect you couldn't tell 'em from the real thing. We moved tons of that counterfeit stuff into New York, month after month. This wasn't the crap you saw on the street; this was the crap you'd pay full retail for in a Midtown store.

Mikey called me almost every week. He wasn't having any luck with the music. He had a waitress he was shacking up with, the singer in his band. He told me he overheard her and the other guitar player talking one night and realized they were just keeping him around for his money. Made me want to fly out right that second, choke those two punks for taking advantage of my little cousin, but you know, I was just as mad at Mikey for letting them do it. See? Another one of those things he just never got: don't let *anybody* push you around. You push first. You push harder. This is not a playground, never was.

He tells me how he's trying to write songs and learn his craft, but how you can go into any coffee shop or bar on Sunset and every waitress there can write and sing, and they know all the music producers by first name, and the guy slapping the burgers is a friend of Frank Zappa, and Zappa's gonna produce his first album, and how amazing it was to be in a city where everybody had talent.

Then one night he calls late, I mean four in the morning late for me, and he's drunk and talking about this party he went to and this songwriter who played piano and sang that night. Warren something. Mikey tells me how he realized he had no talent and nothing to say, so why is he doing this to himself? He sounded relieved. He sounded almost happy.

Two weeks later, he was back in Little Italy.

----------- · — · — · -----------

Of course, I pretty much ignore him, because you don't leave your family, then come back and loaf around like you own the place. Sure, his mom and pop and sisters fall all over him. The neighborhood, they seem to think he's a hero, back home from some big adventure. He'd cut the girly hair and gained some weight, so maybe he looked a little better, but to me he was still the same gutless pretty boy he always was.

My old man and his old man tell us to get an apartment together now that Mikey was ready to pledge himself to the family again, maybe actually learn the business. It was a decent place on Mulberry, four floors up and a small view of the bridge. It had bedrooms at opposite ends of a living room and kitchen, like it was built for people who don't like each other, the way I didn't like Mikey. He was family, though. And I was stuck with him.

I had girls coming over from the hour we got the keys, but Mikey was workin' hard to get into the pants of an old family friend, Regina Strogola; okay-looking, a tough chick who usually got what she wanted. You ask me, he was too good to her right from the start.

One night I'm done with this girl, third time for me and she's still feeling it, so we have a talk, and I go out where Mikey's watching TV in the living room. I leave the bedroom door open. He and I look back at the girl in my bed, and she's got one of those inviting looks on her face. A blonde, of course, hair spread all over my black satin pillow.

"All yours, you want some," I tell Mikey.

"Gina's on her way."

"So?"

"You know."

"You don't know nothin'. We got some work to do later tonight."

"When?"

"When you're done with Gina," I say. "So, don't take too long."

———— · — · — · ————

I drove my Impala. We crossed the Williamsburg Bridge and went into Queens. It was a hot night, and my air conditioner was shot.

"What are we doing?" Mikey asked.

"Pest control," I said. "My sister Julie bought a car from a guy out here, and now he won't give her the money back."

"What's wrong with the car?"

"She don't like it, Mikey. I talked to him on the phone, but he won't listen to reason. Already got himself an Eldo. Don't have the money now. A black. You know."

"You made him an offer he *could* refuse."

"Yeah, yeah, shut up about it."

Me and Mikey had seen that movie at least a dozen times. Best movie they ever made 'til *Scarface*. The violence was right on, especially how Sonny takes care of Carlo. Mikey tried to tell me the flick was about honor and commitment and loyalty, and all that was fine with me, but when they got Sonny at the toll booth, it made me want to pick up a tommy gun and start blasting away myself.

Mikey didn't like it that, in that movie, it always came down to the money. To business. Welcome to the real fuckin' world, I told him. I also told him that business could *be* personal, that it didn't have to be all one or the other, that the movie oversimplified that issue.

In Jamaica, I drove alongside the expressway. It was all Rasta this and that, every block. You could smell the ganja burning. It was hard to find the right street through my dirty windshield. Finally, I did, and I drove by the address, and sure enough, there's a late-model Caddy Eldo, black and gleaming with white sidewalls, exactly like you'd figure for a black dude.

I drove past and parked along the curb and watched a minute. "We're gonna detail his car for him."

"How?" asked Mikey.

"Monkey see, monkey do." I swung open the trunk and we put on the ski masks and got the bats. The new aluminum ones. "Come on. This'll be fun."

We crossed the street and came up on the car from behind. There were lights on in the house, but I didn't care. I smashed the left brake light, then the turn signal. The aluminum made the plastic explode. The Caddy's back windshield took more hits because the safety glass cracked in place but didn't blow up like the plastic.

By then Mikey was on the other side. I only glanced at him, but he was slugging away like a pro. I was whacking the driver's side door when the porch light came on and a big black dude in gym trunks and flip-flops came running down the stoop with a baseball bat of his own, the old-fashioned wooden kind. He stopped short and looked at me.

I said, "Give me the money you stole for that piece a shit Mercury, and we'll stop."

"That money helped buy the Cadillac you wreckin'."

"Up to you, man."

"You be sorry."

He came at me in a funny-looking way, sideways kind of, with the bat cocked over his shoulder. I stepped back like I was confused, then ducked in and took out his kneecap. He yelped and caved in both at once, and I let him have it with the bat. Over and over. Then I thought I'd be like Sonny and kick him, so I did that, too. He was bleedin' and yellin', and I couldn't believe the weird charge of adrenaline going through me. Felt like a river of electricity. Like something I could ride all the way to the moon and back.

"Finish the Eldo!" I screamed at Mikey.

"It's finished! It's done! Let's go!"

I kicked the man once more in the face and told him, "Next time, you give the girl her money back."

All he could say back was "Uck ou," which made me laugh, so I kicked him again and headed for the car.

Mikey drove. I talked the whole way back to Little Italy, I was so high on the violence, the crack of the lights and the crack of his knee, and the whole glory of having power over a bigger man, the glory of having power itself.

"We gotta do this again sometime," I said. My mouth was dry from panting so hard.

He gave me a funny look. "That was some ugly shit, Ray."

"What do you mean, ugly?"

He looked pale and used up. "Forget about it."

We did do it again. A lot. Stuff like that and stuff worse. Mikey, the deeper he got into the enforcement side of the business, the more serious he got. One night, drunk, he told me this life was worse than he had dreamed and feared when he was a boy. Much worse. He hated it.

The family business.

Marriage and children for both of us.

Twelve years went by.

———— . — . — . ————

During that time, Mikey's father, my Uncle Jimmy, took a RICO fall, along with Matty Maglione. They got ten years for bribing, then trying to extort a Pennsylvania trucking company owner who turned out to be wearing a wire. Mikey's mom, Christina, died of cancer. My pop, Dominick, became acting head of the family business. Paul Castellano got whacked just before Christmas of '85, and the so-called Mafia Commission Trial dragged on. Junior Persico was running the old Colombo outfit, which of course affected us LiDeccas, not exactly fans of the late Joseph.

Personally, I thought the worst part of those years was all the Chinese swarming into Little Italy. Overnight, it seemed. Weird people. Glass tanks of live fuckin' frogs and turtles to cook. All these signs you couldn't even read. Not hardly any Italian left. Just Italian for tourists, which is different. I hate change.

Personally, I tried to bring some style to things, the same way Joey did. I blew lots of money on clothes and dinner parties. I got to know the tabloid photogs, and they liked me. I have good, straight teeth and a kinda round face, so when you put both of them over an eight-hundred-dollar suit, I looked kind of lovable and wicked at the same time. Which is exactly what I was. Girls on my arms, but never my wife, of course. And I'd pop off to the reporters, give 'em good copy. I'd tell 'em what sports teams and casinos I liked, and what movies, and what the good wines and restaurants were, and I'd bad-mouth the feds every chance I got, take pity on 'em for being so dumb. The cops were okay, but the feds hated me. They harassed my family and threw charges at me to prove it, but what they couldn't prove was me being guilty. I left courtrooms with a trail of dropped charges and not-guilty verdicts behind me. I loved every minute of it.

Mikey went the other way. Hardly saw him. Regina dumped him outta nowhere, took off on tour with a Jersey bass player. That killed Mikey, having tried to be a musician once himself. Which was exactly her purpose, I pointed out. She left their children—Danny and Lizzy—with him, which was the only good thing Mikey seemed to get out of those twelve years.

He called me Christmas Day of 1986. He sounded happy and desperate at the same time. "We're going to California to live," he said.

"Danny and Lizzy and me. I'm out, Ray. I've worked it out with Pop and Uncle Dom and—"

I hung up on him because I was furious.

Later that day, Christmas Day, Pop told me they'd arranged to let Mikey out of the family for as long as Jimmy was alive. So, Mikey didn't exist no more. Obviously, this was out of respect for Jimmy, and not his coward of a son. All I could say on the phone to my own father was, "I'm sorry, Pop—I'm sorry I was the one brought Mikey along and couldn't teach him one bit of sense or even the most basic rules." Mikey was my failure.

Not long after, in the summer of 1987, Mikey did something even worse.

The video was sent to me by a friend in L.A. At first, I figured it was some more good San Fernando Valley porno, but no, this was a PBS news story showing some meatball walking across the stage at something-or-other junior high school in Irvine, California. And the meatball is Mikey.

The auditorium is full of children. Mikey's got himself a cheap-looking suit and a white shirt but no tie. He's put on some weight. He's got a real serious look on his face. A fat lady introduces him as Michael Ticci, and Mikey goes to the podium and takes the microphone.

And he tells the students he comes from a prominent crime family in New York, where he was born and lived for all his life until a few months ago, when he quit crime, moved to California, got straight. He doesn't name the family business. He tells about growing up in Little Italy, how it was a wonderful place for a kid, but he always thought there was something wrong about it. Then he tells how his great-great-grandfather built up a "wholesale food and produce" business before not-completely-honest men took it over. He's standing up there with this kind of frown on his face, talking shit about his own family. In public, on TV, to a bunch of children!

And you could see the emotion in him. His eyes go kind of squinty and he gestures with his hands and his voice cracks when he talks about "beating that man until he nearly died," and "Uncle Lou coming back from prison white as a ghost, with black hatred in his eyes," and how difficult it is to get the smell "of another man's blood off your hands," and "what it's like to live in a world where men substitute love of money for love itself, where money and power are all that matter, where there are no laws or limits." He said Little Italy was gone now, it was just a skeleton of what it used to be, because organized crime had eaten it out "like a cancer."

I watched the whole thing with my guts in a knot. Mikey had finally found something to say. I'd have gotten on a plane to California that day if it wasn't for the family. I'd have choked him to death bare-handed and pissed on his face when I was done. But the arrangement was the arrangement, and there was nothing I could do about Mikey while Uncle Jimmy was alive.

Ten years went by, and I'd like to say I didn't think about Mikey out there in California, but I did.

I thought about him a lot.

———— · — · — · ————

People like to think God lets things happen for a reason, and they're right. Why else would the family decide to have a sixty-fifth birthday party for Uncle Jimmy? And why else would Mikey LiDecca decide to sneak back and see his father? And why, when Mikey went to his old house on Grand that morning to see his old man for the first time in eleven years, walked right up and rang the intercom on the gate outside, and when Jimmy heard his son's voice, of course he let him in, why, when they sat in the old kitchen with Christina and the girls long gone, did Jimmy's heart just give up? Why did he die in Mikey's arms right there, one day before he was going to turn sixty-five? Answer me that.

I offered Mikey a ride home from the hospital, where the medics had rushed Jimmy and Mikey, just in case there was a miracle waiting for the old man. There was not.

Mikey gave me a long, kind of foggy look. "Thanks, Ray."

I parked my Caddy near the house on Grand. "You gotta see this, Mikey."

"What's that, Ray?"

"It's not far."

We walked down Grand, past Elizabeth and Mott and Mulberry. Like we'd done a million times as boys. It was still sunny out, but cold. Mikey shuffled along next to me, looking down.

"You said on TV that it got eaten up by a cancer," I said. "But I say, fuck that, Mikey. It's smaller, that's all. It's still a place for people like us."

"What do you mean?"

"This. Little Italy. You say it's dead, but it isn't. It's alive. Here. Look at this."

I led the way down an alley behind the Museum of the Chinese in the Americas. There were puddles of rain from the night before. I hopped around them, got out ahead of Mikey, then turned and faced him.

The alley was long and we were halfway down it, protected by the tall buildings. Mikey stopped and looked at me, and I saw that he got it. He finally *got* something. A little surprised, I think.

"With Jimmy gone, I can speak for the family now," I said. "This isn't just business. It's personal, too."

He did it right. Didn't even put his hands up. I shot him, and he went down hard. Twice more.

I walked back the way we'd come, around the puddles, back toward the house on Grand. I felt like some long misunderstanding was now understood. Like the thing he wanted to say was said.

I felt bad for Mikey, but this was always our thing, and finally he'd gotten that, too.

T. JEFFERSON PARKER *is the author of twenty crime novels, including* Silent Joe *and* California Girl, *both of which won the Edgar Award for best mystery. His last six books are a Border Sextet, featuring ATF task-force agent Charlie Hood as he tries to staunch the flow of illegal firearms being smuggled from the United States into Mexico. His most recent novel,* Full Measure, *is about a young man who returns from combat in Afghanistan to pursue his dreams in America. He lives in Southern California with his family and enjoys fishing, hiking, and cycling.*

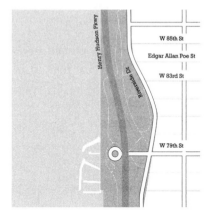

EVERMORE

Justin Scott

Stark ran west on Eighty-Fourth Street.

Starry-eyed gentrifiers had renamed the shabby old block Edgar Allan Poe Street. He crossed Riverside Drive against the light, gave a bus the finger and a cabbie a look that made the man reach for the tire iron he kept under the German shepherd on the front seat. It was the winter of 1981; life was already harsh in New York, and just when it seemed the city couldn't get more dangerous, Stark was on the lam.

He cut into Riverside Park, turned off the tarmac path, frightened a child, and climbed an enormous rock. It stood high as the fourth floor of the apartment buildings across the drive. He sat beside an old steel door someone had stolen from someplace and glared at the

Hudson River.

On the lam came in two varieties. Holed up in a four-star Bahamas hotel with a suitcase full of dough was good lam. The job gone wrong, a woman gone south with your getaway stash, and witnesses reporting which way you'd gone was bad lam. Bad lam meant you had to pull another job, like right now. But spur-of-the-moment heists promised jail or the morgue. So did sitting on this rock until the cops caught up.

The old door slid aside, and a cadaverous long-haired man climbed out of the hole it had covered. He sat on the door, gazed at the river, sharpened a pencil with a penknife, and scribbled in an ancient leather-bound notebook.

"You going to be here long?" Stark asked.

"I beg your pardon?"

"I said, when are you going to haul ass outta here and leave me in privacy?"

Dark, mournful eyes drifted over Stark's tough and battered face. They took stock of his clothing, the small rip in one knee, the solid lightweight assault boots, and the bulge under his sweat-stained gabardine jacket, which suggested either a firearm or an alarming pectoral. "I would imagine I'll be here another seven or eight hours. And you, sir?"

Stark said nothing. He glared at the Hudson, instead, and wondered if he was losing his touch.

"Poe."

"What?"

The cadaverous fellow extended a bony hand and said again, "Poe. The name's Poe. Edgar Allan Poe. And you, sir?"

Stark jabbed the top of the first page of the guy's notebook. "If your name's Poe, why'd you write, 'Ravings,' a Short Story by E. P. Allan?"

"Allan's a nom de plume."

"Huh?"

"A pen name. I had to change my name to sell my stories."

Stark nodded. He, too, had changed his name. This morning. Owing to the mismanaged bank job on the East Side. The connection pleased him, and an unusual sense of human fellowship warmed him like a restaurant exhaust fan blowing grease in a winter alley. He stuck his hand out. "Stark. Pleased to meet you."

"Delighted," said Poe, closing icy and surprisingly strong fingers around Stark's.

"I've already admitted I'm a writer. May I ask how you make *your* living, Mr. Stark?"

"Banks and armored cars."

"Do not expect me to be frightened by an armed robber. I'm accustomed to agents and publishers."

"I could be a writer," said Stark. "I could write a hell of a book about my work."

"And what would you write for your second book?"

"I could write ten books. I've pulled jobs you couldn't dream up. Some good, some bad. Human situations, mistakes, betrayals, revenge, scruples. All that stuff."

Stark, who had put prison time to good use reading, was impressed to be meeting a writer. He began to tell Poe about jobs he'd pulled—leaving out names, dates, and venues. Poe listened, politely. Now and then he made a note in his book. Stark was wrapping up a redacted version of the morning's disaster when Poe interjected, "Forgive me, sir, but I've got to finish this mystery before the Xerox place closes. They've got a special overnight rate, three copies for the price of two. One for my editor. One for me. And one for the girl who lives across the hall."

Stark displayed some inside knowledge he had picked up somewhere. "What about your agent? Doesn't he get a copy?"

Poe gave a small sad shrug, bent over his book, and resumed scribbling. Stark watched and when his pencil stopped moving figured it was okay to ask another question. "Why'd you have to change your name to sell your stories?"

Poe looked up, blinking. "What? What? Oh . . . I write different kinds of stuff. Poems. Novels. Short stories. I mean there's no way I can write a love poem, a horror novel, and one of these *Mystery Magazine* pieces with the same name."

"What does a name have to do with writing?"

Poe considered that a moment, and it seemed to make him un-comfortable. "Not writing. *Selling*. Marketing. You can't confuse the readers."

"I don't get it."

"The publishers say you can't confuse the readers."

Stark had spent enough time behind bars to understand the merci-less logic of the power behind the rules. "I get it."

Color rose to Poe's cheeks. He closed his notebook on his pencil and said, "It's more than that—here, I'll show you." He swung his legs over the edge of the hole in the rock and dropped into it. "Come on! I'll show you."

Stark peered over the edge. Poe was climbing down a rickety ladder.

"Come! I don't have all day."

The hole looked like the lowest form of on the lam where you huddled in the dark, curled in the fetal position. Still, you took your chances when you saw them; maybe it contained a tunnel that led un-der Riverside Drive into an apartment shared by Pan Am stewardesses.

Stark followed Poe down the ladder. The hole wasn't as deep as it looked. He caught up at the bottom. Poe led him down a rock-sided alley and into a narrow street of low brick row houses. A carriage pulled by horses clattered past. The sunlight was dulled by coal smoke. "What is this?"

"Greenwich Village, last century—there! There we are."

And there was Edgar Allan Poe, walking head down with a group of thin men who were listening to a plump, prosperous-looking busi-ness type with a thick gold watch chain draped across his belly.

The Poe standing at Stark's elbow said, "The gaunt men are Em-erson, Thoreau, and Hawthorne. The youngster is Melville. That's our literary agent doing the talking. Listen to what he says."

"How did we get here?" asked Stark.

"Listen—"

"Can we get back?"

"Of course."

Stark looked up and down the street and back at the stone alley and saw opportunity. His sharp cheekbones and granite jaw dissolved into a dreamy expression that had last crossed his face when his mother breast-fed him.

Poe smiled. "Would I be far off the mark?" he asked silkily, "to guess that you are speculating, what if you knocked that agent on the head and took his watch and chain back to Riverside Park in 1981?"

"I'm a heist man, not a mugger."

"Forgive me. I meant no insult."

"Any banks nearby?"

"Plenty downtown," said Poe. "But when we return to 1981, good luck spending currency issued by the Savings Institute of Butchers' and Drovers."

Stark's expression changed to that of a man grappling with the concept of attempting to pay a four-star hotel bill with a sack of gold coins.

Poe said, "Listen to the literary agent instruct the writers."

"The publishing business is changing," the agent was saying. He tugged his watch chain, checked the time, and shoved his thumbs in his vest pockets. "No more little books. No more medium-size books."

Emerson and Thoreau and Hawthorne and Melville started snickering. They exchanged superior looks. Then all talked at once.

"Absurd!"

"A good book's a good book."

"Who cares if it's big or little?"

"Long, short, you're done when the story's done."

Stark nodded. Emerson, Thoreau, Hawthorne, and Melville seemed to have a point.

A gleaming lacquered coach drawn by a matched team of four black horses came down the street. The agent raised his arm in a languid wave, and the coach stopped. A liveried footman jumped down and held the door for him. "Change," he called as he climbed inside. "Change or disappear."

"We've heard enough," said Poe. He led Stark back through the stone alley and up the ladder and out of the rock.

Stark squinted at the Hudson a while, digesting events. Tugboats and barges and heating-oil tankers headed to Albany were all signs of here and now. "Your buddies were right," he said. "A good book's a good book."

"No," said Poe. "Our agent was right. Look at Emerson, Thoreau, and Hawthorne. Dead as doornails. Melville went sailing. Took him forty years to get *Moby-Dick* noticed. Nobody would touch *Billy Budd* with a barge pole until the poor man was a generation in his grave."

Stark nodded. Put that way, Edgar Allan Poe had a point. "What about you?" he asked.

Poe hesitated a long moment before he answered. "I was terrified of disappearing."

"So, you changed."

"I wrote a big book—still a mystery at heart, but with thriller elements, and sort of multigenerational, almost a saga. My agent called it a saga and took me to lunch. Then he informed me he could not sell my big book under my little-books name."

"What's a little-books name?" Stark asked.

"I'd written some gothics. But gothics, like all genres, come and go, nice and steady for a while, not much money—four grand and a promise of lead book of the month sometime down the road—then your month finally comes along just in time for bodice rippers or sci-fi fantasies to knock gothics for a loop. Anyhow, my agent told me to use the pen name D'arcy de Chambord. The publisher who bought the mystery saga asked me to shift into big family sagas. D'arcy de Chambord cleaned up. Sold one to the movies, which paid for a house with a swimming pool in Connecticut."

"Just there on weekends?" Stark, who liked empty houses, asked.

"A fellow comes by to feed the wolf hounds."

"Well . . . if you're making so much money writing sagas, what are you doing these E. P. Allan short stories for?"

"I'm a *writer*. I like short stories. . . . My agent hates them. My book publishers hate them. So, I write them secretly as E. P. Allan."

"Which means, you don't have to pay your agent's commission?" Stark, whose mind ran along such lines, remarked.

Poe took offense. "First of all, the commission on forty-nine dollars a story isn't a hell of a lot of money. Second of all, as soon as I started making big bucks with the sagas, my agent raised his commission to fifteen percent."

Stark nodded admiringly.

Poe said, "The short stories feature the same character. A detective named Block. I figure, when I publish about eighty of them, E. P. Allan will start to get a following. Maybe even an offer for a full-length paperback original. But at the moment, they're just nice little classy stories that are fun to write."

"And thanks to your family sagas, you can afford to write for fun," said Stark.

"I wish that were so. Unfortunately, family sagas have gone out of style again. My agent couldn't give away the last one. If I don't come up with some new kind of big book, I'll go broke."

"You can always sell the Connecticut house."

"Mortgaged to the hilt. I really need another big book deal."

"I know the feeling," said Stark. "I really need another big heist. You know that alley we took to Greenwich Village? Where else does it go?"

"Funny you should ask," said Poe.

———— · — · — · ————

This time when they went down the rickety ladder, Stark reached up and pulled the door over the hole. "So we don't get interrupted."

Poe led him into the stone alley. "Where to?"

"There's a branch of the Emigrant Savings Bank on Third Avenue I was casing before I went away for a few years. If we went back there in 1971, I know it cold. Two-man job. Everything planned, prepped, and rehearsed. In quick, out fast."

Poe shook his head. "That's only ten years ago. Witnesses, cops, guards will still be around to finger us."

"Let me get a look at the job. If it's still like I remember, we'll be in quick, out fast, no one will see us."

"What if it's not like you remember?"

"Then we try a better one."

"The problem is," said Poe. "I can't keep doing this all day. We've already gone back to Greenwich Village. If we go to Third Avenue in 1971 and it doesn't work out, I'm done for at least twenty-four hours. Exhausted."

"Okay. Let's go so far back all the witnesses die of old age."

"Ahead," said Poe. "We go ahead."

"Why?"

"They can't come back for us."

"Nice. Where? When?"

"Place I visited once."

Stark followed Poe through the stone alley with a funny feeling that Poe had a plan. They emerged on the waterfront at the corner of Twelfth Avenue and Fifty-First Street facing Midtown skyscrapers ablaze in light, and their backs to the Manhattan Cruise Terminal piers. Disoriented, Stark looked up. Overhead, he saw only the night sky. "What happened to the West Side Highway?"

"They tore it down in '89."

Stark looked around. The shapes of the cars did not look familiar. "When is now?"

"Early two-thousands. Oh-five or oh-six. Before they changed the currency."

"What are they doing to the currency?"

"Making it harder to counterfeit."

Stark shrugged. Counterfeiting was indoor work. You might as well slave in a factory.

Poe said, "What we take here, now, we can still spend in '81."

Across the many lanes of car and truck traffic, a two-story stucco structure stretched a full block wide from Fifty-First Street to Fifty-Second. It managed to look vaguely Roman, an impression heightened by the stucco and a columned portico on its roof. It didn't appear to have any windows, and Stark, who maintained a professional interest in buildings without windows, assumed it contained something valuable. Must have been a warehouse many years ago when the waterfront was still active, which meant a lot of big, open space inside. Might even connect to the tall loft building behind it. Which was also blank walled.

There was a single door on the street corner at the downtown end. "What's that?"

"That is where guys making fortunes on Wall Street spend it."

Stark noted limos pulling up. Laughing men in suits reeled through the door. He said, "A strip club."

"For the highest rollers. They call it a gentlemen's club."

"Cash," said Stark.

"Mostly," said Poe. "There's some credit cards, but most use cash. Private from their wives."

"How many girls?"

"At least a hundred, a busy night like tonight," said Poe. "Plus hostesses, cocktail waitresses, and bar maids."

"Did you case the joint, or were you just hanging out?" asked Stark.

"Research. I'm a writer."

"Right," said Stark, and ran the numbers aloud. "Five hundred customers spending five hundred a head. Quarter million in that one building. Minus a hundred grand stuffed in the girls' drawers, we're still looking at a hundred and fifty thousand."

"Drawers these days," said Edgar Allan Poe, "don't hold that much."

"They'll find someplace to put it."

Poe looked troubled. "You wouldn't rob the girls, would you?"

Stark returned a look that would freeze vodka. "Even if we wanted to, can you imagine parting cash from a hundred women who worked that hard to get it? No, we're not here to rob the girls. We're here to rob the club's cash room."

"They have heavy security," said Poe.

"I would, too, in their position."

"I should tell you that the mob owns a piece of the business."

"The mob controls a strip club?" asked Stark. "I am shocked."

"I'm just warning you."

"Wait here."

"Where are you going?"

"We need chauffeur uniforms," said Stark, and he stalked across Twelfth Avenue.

———— · — · — · ————

Poe waited anxiously, wondering whether he had underestimated or overestimated the heist man. But surely Stark couldn't just rob the club and leave him stranded? How would he get back to 1981? An hour passed. A second crept by, and Poe reflected gloomily that the crook had decided to stay in 2005 forever and rob the club on his own.

A long limousine stopped at the curb. Stark was at the wheel, wearing a chauffeur's uniform that fit perfectly and licking blood from a knuckle. "Get in back."

Poe slid into the passenger compartment, and Stark steered the limo into traffic. On the seat were a chauffeur's jacket, pants, and visored cap. They fit perfectly.

"Got a gun?" Stark asked once Poe was dressed.

"No."

"Good. Have you ever pulled a job like this before?"

"I've written it dozens of times."

Stark glowered in the mirror.

"This is my first. In real life," Poe said.

"Listen up. When we get in there, your job is to keep your eyes open and watch my back. You see trouble, tell me who to shoot."

"Are we just barging in there?"

"No. We are entering on a mission to retrieve our criminal bosses, because the feds got the word they're in the club. The feds are going to bust in in ten minutes. Our criminal bosses are armed. There will be gunfire and innocents will die, which means the cops will shut down the club for a very long time unless their loyal limo drivers get their bosses out quietly."

"Security will ask what our bosses' names are."

"Our bosses use assumed names in strip clubs."

"Security will ask why we don't just text them."

"What?"

"It's the year 2005. They have cell phones that receive voice and text messages."

Stark digested this information and said, "We can't 'text' them because the feds are wiretapping their cell phones."

"The feds can't exactly wiretap cell phones. They have no wires."

"They can call it whatever the hell they want to call it, but I can guarantee you the feds are still tapping the phones. In your day, they would have netted homing pigeons."

Poe said, "The club has security cameras covering the whole place. They'll probably make us go to their office and look for our bosses on their video screens."

"Now you get it," said Stark.

———— · — · — · ————

Stark had driven down Twelfth Avenue while Poe put on his chauffeur uniform, and he talked the writer through the job. Now he turned the limo around at Fourteenth Street and headed back up toward Fifty-First. Two blocks from the strip club, he pulled to the curb and switched on the hazard blinkers.

"What?" asked Poe.

"Cops."

Patrol cars with flashing lights had converged on the corner of Fifty-First. A phalanx of men in blue charged in the door.

"Now what?" asked Poe.

"We wait 'til they leave."

"What are they doing in there?"

"Whatever they want to."

"Security won't believe our story if the cops have already been there."

"They'll believe it more," said Stark.

An ambulance pulled up. Men and women rolled a gurney across the sidewalk.

"Oh my God, it's a shootout," said Poe. "We better—"

"Just relax." Stark thought that Poe was getting dangerously nervous for a man who was supposed to be watching his back. Yet another reason not to pull a job without rehearsing. He kept his eyes on the scene two blocks ahead and tried to distract the writer before he got too frantic to be of any use at all. "What kind of book will you write next?"

"Mysteries are coming back big time," said Poe. "Best sellers, even. So, my agent thinks we can find a publisher willing to shell out big for the right book. He's trying to talk me into writing one. I have an awful feeling I'm going to have to."

"You don't like mysteries?"

"I like them. But I know I'll never win an Edgar."

"What's an Edgar?"

"MWA Edgar Allan Poe Award."

"MWA?"

"Mystery Writers of America. They organized to promote mysteries and protect writers. They've got a clever motto: Crime does not pay—enough."

"Bull," said Stark. "Crime pays top dollar. But you gotta put the work into it. Plan. Prep. Rehearse. If you don't, you're a two-bit stick-up artist broke and in the slammer—wait a minute. Did you say they named the award after you?"

"Writers think I invented the mystery genre."

"Hell of an honor."

"I suppose."

"Suppose? They don't call it a Herman or a Ralph or a—what was Hawthorne's name."

"Nathaniel."

"They don't call it a Nat. They call it an Edgar. How much dough is the prize?"

"No dough. Big honor, and you get a little statue of me. But I'll never win one."

"Why not?" said Stark, who tended to feel optimistic halfway into a heist.

"Too perverse."

"But genres come and go. You said so yourself. Sagas, gothics, bodice rippers. Perverse will come back, too."

"I meant I'm personally perverse. I always write whatever I feel like writing. I never build on one thing. Which the winners tend to. The comedy guys do comedy, the hardboiled guys hardboiled, and they keep doing it over and over and over until someone notices. I'm all over the place—detective, science fiction, horror. Perverse."

"Sounds more like feckless," said Stark.

The ambulance crew and the cops trooped out of the club wheeling a gurney on which lay a bulbous shape covered with a sheet. A nurse was holding an oxygen mask to his face. *Cocaine*, thought Stark. *Some things never change. Cute girls, martinis, coke, mortgage trader, no gym.* "Okay, here we go. You up to this, Edgar?"

"I think so," said Poe. "Can you give me any advice?"

"In quick, out fast."

———— · — · — · ————

Stark parked the long black Lincoln precisely halfway up the block between Fifty-First and Fifty-Second. They walked the half block to the door of the strip club and skirted the line the bouncers had established behind a red velvet rope. The sharp-eyed doorman cracked a joke at their expense. "Yo, limo drivers! You forgot your limo."

"Around the corner," Stark said quietly, then he leaned in close so only the doorman could hear. "Our bosses are in there. The feds are coming for them. We're supposed to get them out."

"Oh, yeah? What's their names?"

"Mine's name is Smith."

The doorman rounded on Poe. "What about yours?"

"Smith."

The doorman cast a dubious look on his reservations book. "I got eighteen Smiths tonight."

"We only want our two," said Stark.

"Text 'em you're here."

Stark said, "Text them? On what? You think they carry cells?" The doorman gave a small nod and several bouncers, big men, larger than the doorman even, gathered around. The doorman said, "Your problem ain't our problem."

"It's about to be," said Stark. "Just 'cause they don't carry cells, don't mean they don't carry."

"What?"

"I'll paint a picture for you. In red. That's going to be the color of your club when the shooting stops."

"Nobody shoots at feds. Let the lawyers handle it and stop blocking my door."

Stark took off his visored cap and said calmly, "Guys whose asses lawyers can't save shoot at feds."

The doorman spoke urgently into a shoulder mike, listened in his earpiece, spoke some more, and listened some more. Then he said to Stark, "I'm turning you over to the inside guys. Tell them your story. Do exactly what they tell you if don't want your face broken. That goes for you too," he said to Poe.

"We'll be in quick and out fast," Poe promised.

It looked like it might go just as well indoors, a huge room crowded with guys with their suit jackets draped over the back of their chairs and shapely naked women wearing high heels. They had arrived just in time for the March of the Ladies, where every woman in the joint formed a dancing line that snaked slowly about the room, accompanied by thundering music and flashing lights.

The head inside bouncer said, "I can't let you go wandering around gawking at the customers. You'll throw everybody off their game."

"Is there someplace where we could look for them without bothering people?"

The bouncer snapped his fingers. "Right. Right. Good idea. Come on. We'll scan the place. You can watch on the security monitors."

"Let's go," said Stark. "The feds will be here any minute."

"Got to clear it with the boss." He spoke into his shoulder mike and listened to his earpiece. Stark remained expressionless. He was pleasantly surprised when the boss bought it.

Led, flanked, and followed by bouncers, Stark and Poe were hustled along the edge of the main room, up a back stairway to the second floor and down a hall toward an ordinary-looking door that swung open as they approached. Stark was thinking that security was pretty light up here. The head bouncer ushered them into an office that had a wall of video monitors. In one corner stood an enormous funnel.

The music from below shook the floor. Women wearing not much more than they were downstairs were wandering around, drinking and joking with a fit guy in a suit whom Stark pegged for the mobster who owned the strip club.

"Make it quick. Find your guys and we'll send 'em out the back."

Stark and Poe paced along the wall of monitors, pretending to hunt for their limo passengers. Stark stopped suddenly, signaled Poe, and pointed at a monitor. "Look at this, Ed. These our guys?"

"They all look the same," said Poe.

"See the funnel?" Stark growled quietly.

"What's it for?"

"That funnel is why winging it is for stick-up artists. That's why they let us in here. That's why girls are wandering in and out. Stuff you pour into the funnels goes straight down a pipe to the cellar."

"Do you mean the room in the cellar is a vault?"

"You got it, Sherlock. So they don't have to unlock the cellar room every time someone brings up a deposit, which they do regularly so there's not a lot of cash on the floor to attract guys like you and me."

"What do we do?" asked Poe.

"Stall until the next load of cash comes up here, and then grab it before they pour it."

"But that will be only a tiny fraction of what's in the vault."

Stark stared. "You want a fraction or nothing?"

"Hey!" yelled the mobster. "Where are your guys?"

"Still looking, sir."

"Look faster."

The office door, which had been opening regularly, opened again, admitting two mostly naked women—a brunette who carried a canvas bank sack toward the funnel—and a beautiful bright-eyed blonde who walked straight up to Poe.

"Edgar?"

Poe, already paler than a bed sheet, turned white as snow.

The beautiful bright-eyed blonde looked confused. "Edgar? What are you doing in that uniform? You're not a limo driver."

"We were at a costume party," Poe stammered, adding in a whisper through clenched teeth, "I didn't realize you were working tonight."

The owner crossed the office in a bound. "Costume party? What the hell are you talking about? Annie, you know this guy?"

"Sure," said the beautiful bright-eyed blonde. "He's one of my regulars." She flashed Poe a dazzling smile. "My most generous regular. He's promised to buy me a beach house right on the ocean. Listen, hon, when you're done whatever you're doing up here, I'll be waiting for you in the Champagne Room."

To Stark—who now understood why Poe's Connecticut home was mortgaged to the hilt—the strip club owner said, "What are you pulling?"

"A Smith & Wesson," said Stark, moving very close to the boss while shielding the short-barreled .38 from foolish attempts to grab it. "Edgar, grab that sack before she dumps it."

Poe hurled himself toward the brunette as she threw the sack into the funnel. He caught it, and they ran out the door.

The head bouncer blocked the hall. He laughed. "I've been shot by a lot bigger guns that didn't stop me."

"It's not only a gun," said Stark. Before he had finished the sentence, the revolver and the bouncer's head had collided. Stark grabbed Poe and jumped him over the bouncer's body. He said, "Hang on to that sack," and dragged Poe to the stairs.

"Not up," cried Poe. "Down. Downstairs."

"We're going up."

Somewhere behind them, someone fired a gun.

Women started screaming. More guns popped. Men yelled in terror.

Stark dragged Poe up the stairs, outdoors into a columned portico, out between two columns, and across the flat roof to the low parapet that rimmed the edge. The limo was parked where he had left it, thirty feet below.

"How do we get down?"

"Rope," said Stark, uncoiling a heavy rope that was tied around a roof vent. He tossed it. The end fell within five feet of the sidewalk.

"Where did that rope come from?"

"Plan. Prep. Rehearse." Stark swung his legs over the parapet, grabbed the rope, lowered himself hand under hand to the sidewalk. "Throw me the money."

Poe threw the money and slid down the rope. By the time he was darting across the sidewalk, blowing on his burned palms, Stark had the limo unlocked and the engine started. Poe jumped in beside him.

"Put on your seat belt," said Stark, and he floored it, screeching into the late-night traffic, up Twelfth Avenue, and onto the Henry Hudson Highway, checking his mirrors repeatedly.

"All clear. Take us back to 1981."

"I can't from here."

"Why not?"

"We have to go back from the same spot we entered."

"Fifty-First and Twelfth Avenue?"

"Right across from the club."

"I wish you'd told me that earlier."

Stark checked his mirrors, for the tenth time, and turned off at the Seventy-Ninth Street. He circled under the highway, up the ramp, floored the big car back downtown. "We'll have about three seconds at Fifty-First for you to get us the hell out of there."

Poe's answer was an unreassuring, "I'll do my best."

Stark hit the brakes. "Now!"

They piled out the doors. Stark's estimate had been overly optimistic.

In one second, a club bouncer howled, "They're back!"

In two seconds, numerous large men were running across Twelfth Avenue full tilt at Stark and Poe, yanking pistols from coats and trousers.

In three seconds, several stopped running to take careful aim.

Stark raised the hand not holding the money sack, with a hopeless feeling it wouldn't change their minds. He heard Poe say, "Step back."

They were in the stone alley and, just as suddenly, at the foot of the rickety ladder.

———— · — · — · ————

Up on the rock, a cool fresh breeze was blowing off the river and the sun was sinking low. A siren, faintly audible at first, grew loud. Poe gazed at the river. "That's not an ambulance, Mr. Stark."

"I didn't think it was." He started to stand up.

Poe said, "There's a jeep patrol in the park. I wouldn't run for it unless I were very young and athletic."

"I thought you said they couldn't follow us back."

"Those aren't bouncers, they're cops. And they didn't follow us from 2005. They followed you from this morning on the East Side."

Stark's face assumed the flat hard lines of a man unamused as he scrutinized the rock for fields of fire. Three or four police cars converged on the Eighty-Fourth Street entrance, and Jeep with riflemen roared up the bank from the promenade.

"Okay, get us out of here. Back, forward, I don't care. Just away. Now."

"I'm sorry," said Poe. "I shot my wad getting us back from 2005. Being shot at didn't make it easier, you know. I can't budge us until I've drunk some wine and slept a full a day and night."

"In that case, Mr. Poe, I need a hostage."

"I am no longer famous enough to be a hostage. Too many pen names. They'll shoot me and blame you. No, we need a more creative solution."

"Any bright ideas?' Stark asked. He felt himself running on empty.

"One," said Poe. "I've used it before, but hopefully they don't read. Give me your gun."

"Fat chance."

"Lay it down, over there. I'll tell them you dropped it when you ran. Quickly, they're out of the cars. Do it, man! One gun won't make a difference."

Poe was right about that. The cops were hauling shotguns from their trunks.

"Give me your gun and take the dough down in the hole. I'll cover until they're gone."

Shaking his head dubiously, Stark slid the gun across the rock and slithered into the hole. The ladder chose that moment to break and he fell hard, but not far enough to do any damage. Overhead, the sky went black as Poe shoved the door over the hole.

"*In pace requiescat!*"

"What?"

Poe's answer, if indeed he had answered, was drowned out by clanging and banging. It sounded like he was covering the door with heavy stones. Stark heard the cops scrambling up the steep rock, calling to each other, shouting at Poe.

"He went that-a-way!" Poe cried. "Look! He dropped his gun."

Stark heard grunts, curses, the thump of rubber-soled shoes. Sirens. Then silence.

He waited a long time.

"Can I come out, now?"

Silence.

"Hey! Poe!"

Again silence.

"For crissake, Poe!"

He couldn't reach the door. He wrapped his garrison belt around the broken ladder rail and climbed the rungs gingerly. The repair held until he pushed up. The weight of the rock was too much; the ladder twisted and he fell again. He landed flat on his back and in that position pushed the unbroken ladder rail against the door like a pole. The rocks were really heavy. Stark pushed up with all his might. Nothing. He took a deep breath and concentrated his considerable strength by imagining he was using the ladder to impale Edgar Allan Poe.

Slowly the door lifted. He could hear the rocks sliding off, a noise like fingernails on a blackboard. Suddenly the door felt light and it flew away and the sky poured in. Stark patched the ladder again, picked up the suitcase, and very carefully climbed out. The sun had set behind a Jersey condominium and the Hudson River was mauve and fading fast. The cops were gone. So was Poe.

Stark smiled. Not a bad deal. It was a mystery why Poe had split, but now all the money was his. The only thing he had lost was his gun, and he could afford to buy another.

About a year later, Stark was pretending to read magazines in a news-stand across the street from a lightly guarded Connecticut National Bank, when he spotted the name E. P. Allan embossed in shiny foil on a fat paperback mystery novel. His old friend Poe, who had saved his ass in Riverside Park and helped bankroll a memorable winter at a Bahamas resort.

The book, *In Quick, Out Fast*, was touted as the first in E. P. Allan's new series of "astonishingly realistic" mystery thrillers featuring a brilliant armed robber who hit banks and armored cars. This first volume, of a projected ten, had already sold to the movies. A bunch of best-selling writers had given it glowing blurbs, but the one that speared Stark's eye was lifted from a *Kirkus* prepublication review:

> *"More, much more, than an action-packed, crackerjack, unbelievably realistic yarn about a bank robbery on New York City's East Side that goes bad. It's as if you were there, shoulder to shoulder with a quick-thinking, fast-acting hero you will want to read about again and again and again. Read it and cheer. Read it and wonder how E. P. Allan could know such things. Read it and weep."*

JUSTIN SCOTT *(aka Paul Garrison, aka J. S. Blazer, aka Alexander Cole) was nominated for the Edgar Award for best first novel and best short story. He writes the Ben Abbott detective mysteries set in small-town Connecticut. He cowrites the early-twentieth-century Isaac Bell detective adventure series with Clive Cussler;* The Assassin, *their latest Isaac Bell novel, debuted in March 2015. His novel* The Shipkiller *is honored in the International Thriller Writers anthology* Thrillers: 100 Must-Reads. *His main pen name is Paul Garrison, under which he writes modern sea stories and, for the Robert Ludlum banner,* The Janson Command *and* The Janson Option.

CHIN YONG-YUN
MAKES A *SHIDDACH*

S. J. Rozan

I have four sons and a daughter.

All my children are filial, even my daughter, Ling Wan-ju, whose American name is Lydia. She is a private investigator. This is a profession I do not approve of. I also don't care at all for my daughter's partner, the white baboon. In addition, it does not make me happy that her work requires that she associate with criminals. I would object to her associating with police also, but her childhood friend Mary Kee is a police detective, an important position. But all in all, I may say—only because it is true—that my daughter does her work with great competence. Often she is quite successful. She is young. She will find a more fitting profession as she matures.

Especially now that she has time to consider her future, since I have begun helping her with some of her cases.

She tells me she doesn't want me involved, but in fact she is just trying to protect me from the low atmosphere of the detecting world. Like my other children, my daughter has no real idea of my life in China, or in Hong Kong, before I came to America with my husband. Nothing in her world is new to me. This is why I've attempted to discourage her from being involved with the sort of people I myself have always tried to avoid. But, as I say, she is young.

Of my four sons, the older two are married to lovely Chinese women. Each has given me two grandchildren. My third son is in love with a man. They think I don't know, but I do. I regret the lack of grandchildren this situation will produce, but my son is an artist, a photographer, probably too distracted by his art to have been a good father in any case. And his partner is a charming, polite young man who takes good care of him.

This leaves my youngest son, Tien Hua, who prefers to be called by his American name of Tim—although I, of course, don't call him that. He is a partner in a large corporate law firm. Many young men his age have settled down to raise families, but my son is still single. This is unfortunate. A young man alone in a large apartment is not a natural thing. He makes a good deal of money, but he works long hours, leaving him little time to search for a girlfriend. If he were to pay more attention, he would find one immediately because, although his manner might be regarded as too formal (my daughter, with a roll of her eyes, says, "He's a stiff"), my friends assure me that Tien Hua is quite a catch. Handsome, intelligent, earning a very good salary, with advancement possibilities at his firm. I've offered to take him to Old Lau, the matchmaker, who could introduce us to any number of lovely, accomplished young ladies. The Jewish grandmothers at the senior center also have this custom. They call it "making a *shidduch*." I've told this to my son, that this is a time-honored way in many cultures for young people to meet.

He thanks me but says he is too busy to date.

I believed that was true, until the phone call from him that started this case.

I was in my kitchen, measuring rice into the electric cooker, when the red telephone rang.

"Ma, I need to talk to Lydia right away. She doesn't answer her phone."

"Your sister isn't here. She's working."

"That's no reason for her not to answer her phone."

"Perhaps it is."

"Ma! I need her."

My son's voice, usually controlled, was surprisingly distraught.

"What's wrong?"

"I can't tell you. I need Lydia."

My two youngest children are not close. Even as upset as he obviously was, Tien Hua would not call Ling Wan-ju to unburden himself. A suspicion took hold of me. "Are you intending to hire her professionally?"

"What if I am?"

His tone said everything I needed to hear. "The last time you did that, things did not work out very well."

"I've got to talk to her. This is really important. I'm about to go into a meeting. I know she'll answer the phone if you call her."

"Maybe she will, or sometimes not. Tell me the situation."

"No. Call her. Tell her to call me."

"I might not be able to reach her before you go into your meeting. Tell me why you need her."

He sighed. A voice in the background spoke. Someone else also going into his meeting, no doubt. I remained silent. Finally he said, "Valerie Lim's been kidnapped."

I didn't speak immediately. Many questions jumped into my mind. In detecting, it's essential to ask the most important question first.

"How do you know what's happened to Valerie Lim?"

"We're dating." As I feared. Though he could not see me, I frowned. But he hurried on. "Well, I mean, we went out. Twice. I think she thinks I'm too nerdy or something. She likes, you know, jocks. But I'm hoping . . ." His voice trailed off. My son is not only unable to lie, but he has always had a compulsion to tell more of the truth than necessary. I sometimes wonder how he has become such a success as a lawyer. "Her mother called me right after the kidnappers called her."

"Why?"

"She wants me to make the drop. That means, to give them the money."

"I know what that means!" I had not, but what else could it possibly be? "You'll do no such thing!" Lim Cui intended to put my son in such a dangerous position? This angered me, but I was not surprised. That's the kind of person she is. "How much money do they want?" I was curious.

"Two hundred thousand dollars. I will if I have to," he said. "If it's the only way to get Valerie back. But why would they give her back? If they have the money? If she's even still . . . even still . . ."

"Even still alive, yes, yes. Why are you calling your sister?"

"I want her to find Valerie."

"That's ridiculous. This is a crime, a police matter. Call Carl Ting."

Carl Ting was a friend of my son's when they were very young, until one day in the sandbox, when Carl Ting dumped a bucket of sand over my son's head. Ever since, they've been rivals. This is odd, because they are so similar. They both grew into very stolid young men, Carl Ting even more humorless than my son. Carl Ting, however, is also, like Mary Kee, a police detective.

"No police!" said Tien Hua. "The kidnappers said if the Lims call the police, they'll kill Valerie for sure."

"The Lims will not call. You will call."

"They'll still know."

"How?"

"I don't know! But it's too risky." He paused. "Ma, if Valerie's mom found out I did that, even if nothing bad happened, *she'd* kill *me*." Another voice spoke in the background, sounding more insistent this time.

I sighed. "All right, give me the details, then go to your meeting."

"You'll find Lydia?" The background voice came once more.

"I think you'd better hurry."

My son gave me all the details he had. I wrote them down in a little notebook I bought for cases. After he hung up, I sat. I looked at the notebook. I looked at my watch. I looked at the rice cooker, poured in water, then set the timer in case I didn't come home in time to turn it on before dinner. For half an hour after, I folded the laundry and did the ironing. When my daughter's blouses were hung in their proper closet, I put on my sneakers. Locking only the two top locks on my door—leaving the bottom ones open so that any lock pickers would pick them closed—I went downstairs to the street.

My destination was the Mott Street branch of Sweet Tasty Sweet. This is the original location of this bakery chain that now has three Chinatown shops—two in Flushing, Queens; one in Sunset Park, Brooklyn; plus two in Jersey City, New Jersey. The menu tells you that there are *More coming soon! In Manhattan! Queens! Brooklyn! Westchester! Long Island!* The Sweet Tasty Sweet chain, apparently soon to take over the world, is owned by Valerie Lim's father.

Two hundred thousand dollars is not so very much money in America, where they have television shows about wanting to be millionaires. It is a great deal of money to a Chinese immigrant poor enough to have smuggled himself into this country, however. In detecting, it is important to understand all the clues you find. In my experience, a person's enemy is most often a former lover, a business rival, or someone who feels misused. If Lim Xiao's enemy were an ex-lover or a rival, the amount of money demanded for the return of his only daughter would, I felt, have been much higher. But to a new immigrant, two hundred thousand dollars might seem the highest mountain Lim Xiao could possibly be asked to climb.

I don't care for Lim Xiao, any more than I do for his wife. Or his daughter. They're clay pots trying to sound like thunder. Lim Xiao started in the kitchen of another man's restaurant, working alongside my late husband. Fortune smiled on each of them in different ways. My husband and I had five smart, handsome, accomplished children.

The Lims had only one, their daughter Valerie. My family remained in Chinatown. Although my husband died fifteen years ago, our lives have been happy. My children properly revere their father's memory. The Lims became wealthy. They moved away to the kind of neighborhood my daughter says is called "upscale." Valerie Lim went to an exclusive school. She's never worked in a restaurant. Perhaps if she had, she wouldn't pout so often. Her profession now is "party planner." All this is their good luck, but the Lims have chosen to act as if it was all expected, no more than they deserved. They pretend they were never peasants. In America you can do this, but that doesn't make it true.

"Chin Yong-Yun!" Fay Di, the manager of Sweet Tasty Sweet, smiled from behind the pastry counter. "You're looking well! Have you come for a sweet?"

"A sweet tasty sweet. Are the red bean buns fresh?"

My old friend leaned forward with a sparkle in her eye. "Yesterday's," she whispered. "The lemon tarts are better."

"I'll have a lemon tart, then. With a cup of tea. Not black tea, real tea. Also, I need the answer to a question."

"From me?"

"Yes, of course, from you, that's why I'm asking you."

I took my plastic tray to a small table near the server's counter. Fay Di spoke to the young girl who was working at the cash register, then came around the counter. "Luckily, we're not busy right now. I'll sit with you a moment."

This was not a matter of luck. It was why I had delayed coming out until the lunch rush was over. But we had no time to go into that. "Excellent. Now tell me who would want to do harm to Lim Xiao."

Her eyes went wide. "No one."

"You mean, everyone. But I'm referring to a particular person."

"Who?"

"If I knew, why would I ask?" Really, Fay Di is kind-hearted but sometimes she is slow. "Lim Xiao is in a difficulty. I'm looking into it."

"What do you mean?"

"You know my daughter is in the investigating business. I sometimes work with her on her cases."

"You do?"

I narrowed my eyes over the steam from my tea. "We have no time for so many questions, Fay Di. Because of the nature of Lim Xiao's trouble, I believe the wrongdoer may be an employee of Sweet Tasty Sweet. Now, please. This is urgent. Can you think of someone who has reason to dislike Lim Xiao more than most?"

Fay Di's gaze went to the tabletop. In detecting, it is important sometimes to let the suspect think in silence. I do not mean I suspected Fay Di of this kidnapping, but the principle is the same. I bit into the lemon tart. It was lemony but too sweet, unlike my own, which have the perfect amount of sugar.

Fay Di rose without answering. I was surprised at such rudeness but did not speak, for my mouth was full of lemon tart. I watched as she went behind the counter to speak low words to the girl at the cash register. The girl shook her head. Fay Di spoke again. She put her hands on the girl's shoulders, propelling her—the girl's nametag read "Sarah"—to my table, where she sat her down.

"This is my friend," Fay Di said. "Tell her what you told me."

The girl turned to say something, but Fay Di went back behind the counter. A young man came from the kitchen with a tray of pastries. Fay Di busied herself with putting them in the proper cases, refusing to look at the girl.

"Sarah?" I said. "Is that your name?"

The girl whipped her head back to me. She didn't answer, as though I had asked a dangerous question. She was very pretty, with smooth skin. Unlike my daughter, she wore a touch of lipstick, a modest pink, very becoming. Her white bakery cap sat fetchingly on her shining black hair.

"My name for America," she said, eyes downcast.

"Sarah, this is very important. Do you know something about someone who would perhaps enjoy causing trouble for Lim Xiao?"

Again, she didn't answer. She seemed very nervous. I have lived in Chinatown many years, so I thought I might know why. Leaning forward, I whispered, "You are in America illegally, am I correct?"

She started to jump up, but I put my hand over hers. "Don't worry. I haven't come to cause you problems. In fact, if you help me, perhaps I can help you."

She looked around again to find Fay Di staring calmly at her from behind the counter. She turned back to me, then looked down at the hands in her lap. "Li Qiu," she whispered, so quietly I almost didn't hear her.

"Li Qiu? Who is that?"

"He comes from village close mine, in Fukien." Her Cantonese was poor, but I thought it enterprising of her to attempt to learn to speak it, just as it was for her to take an American name. All dialects of Chinese are written with the same characters, but they are spoken different-ly. Most of the new immigrants now are from Fukien province, not Guangdong, as my generation was. Their language is Fukienese. Many of them also speak Mandarin, but that's not much use in Chinatown, either. These people can get only the worst jobs until they learn either English or Cantonese. Most decide on English because it's a simpler language, Cantonese being very subtle, very complex. This Sarah, I decided, must be hardworking, hoping to better herself, plus she must be intelligent.

She spoke up again. "Li Qiu, not a nice man." She squirmed a little in her seat. "Thinks, because I Fukiense also, I friends of him. Tells things I do not want to hear."

"What sorts of things?"

"Tries impress me, make me think he's big. Not big, just nasty. Takes job at Sweet Tasty Sweet only so to learn things about rich owner. Says, rich owner going make him rich also. Says, I go with him, we be rich both."

"Do you know what he meant?"

"No. But since yesterday, Li Qiu doesn't come to work."

From the records in the tiny office in the back, Fay Di showed me a photograph of Li Qiu. I asked for his address. "I shouldn't be doing this!" she hissed. "I could get fired!"

"You are the manager. Unless Lim Xiao comes here himself, who'll fire you? Right now Lim Xiao is worried about other things." I tried to sound reassuring. Often in the course of a case, an investigator must convince people to do things they probably should not do.

Shaking her head, Fay Di quickly scribbled some Chinese characters on a counter check.

The address for Li Qiu was a rundown building on East Broadway. Standing outside looking at it, I cannot say I approved of the condition it was in. It was probably owned by a Hong Kong Chinese. They are investors who take very poor care of their buildings. I am not someone who likes to tell other people what to do, but the Hong Kong Chinese should go back to Hong Kong, taking their money with them.

I had many ideas of how I might gain entry to the building, but I was not forced to use any of them. The lock on the front door was broken. As I might have expected.

Li Qiu lived on the third floor. I myself live on the fourth floor, so climbing these stairs presented no difficulty. An investigator must be prepared to expend physical effort at any time if an investigation requires it.

When I found apartment 3D, I stood for a moment to catch my breath. I wouldn't have done so, but I needed the full power of my lungs. Finally, I pounded on the door, screaming, "You make too much noise! All the time, noise, noise, noise! You have to stop! Be quiet!"

I went on like that until the door opened. It was only a tiny crack, but I shoved the door, still screaming, waving my arms. I am not a large woman. The man peering through the crack seemed startled when I pushed. "I live downstairs! How can I sleep? How can I play with my grandchildren? How can I do anything? Much too noisy up here! You shut up! Shut up! Shut up!" I ran out of things to scream, but I just started over.

Now I could recognize Li Qiu, standing at the half-opened door, glaring at me. He must have thought I was crazy. If I'd been able to understand him, I might have learned whether I was right, but he replied in angry Fukienese whispers. It was clear to me he didn't want me to disturb the neighbors.

He tried to shut the door, but I jumped up as though to scratch out his eyes. Out of instinct he leapt back, as I'd planned. I was able to see into the room. No one else was visible, but I could see a closed door leading to another room. The place Li Qiu lived was quite untidy, with a bad smell. Clothes were strewn on the couch, take-out containers on the floor. The windows, which looked out onto a brick wall in any case, were covered by bed sheets hammered onto the frames.

The place was disgusting. I'd be humiliated if any of my children lived like this, even for five minutes.

Yet a Chloé handbag, open, its contents scattered, sat on a pizza box on a rickety table.

Chinatown is New York City's center for knock-off designer goods. I've seen them all my life. I am not a person who likes to boast, but I can tell the real from the false on sight.

This handbag was real. It had cost its owner a good deal of money.

Li Qiu pushed my shoulder. I stopped screaming, as though he had frightened me. Shaking my head, I backed away. I walked down the stairs muttering.

Out on the street, I almost used the small telephone in my purse to call Carl Ting at his police precinct. Then I remembered my daughter telling me she had been able to find lawbreakers by their telephone numbers. I was not a lawbreaker, of course, but I didn't want Carl Ting to find me. I called from a public telephone with a roof like a pagoda.

"A woman has been kidnapped," I told Carl Ting. "She is in an apartment on East Broadway. You must hurry." I gave him the address.

"Who is this?"

"A neighbor. The kidnapper is Li Qiu. He lives upstairs. He is a bad man."

"Is this a joke?"

"Is it the kind of thing policemen think is funny?" I'm sure there's nothing Carl Ting thinks is funny, as he has no sense of humor at all. "You must hurry to save her." Remembering what my son had said, I added, "This information comes from Chin Tien Hua."

"Tim Chin? What does he have to do with this?"

"Nothing. He wants someone to rescue her. He thinks you're the best man to do it."

"Why didn't he call me himself?"

"He's in a meeting. You cannot reach him. Rescue the woman. Then call my—call Chin Tien Hua." Quickly, I hung up the phone.

Valerie Lim was rescued within the hour. I learned this because my son called me later, very upset.

"The cops told the Lims I was the one who told them! They're furious!"

"But it was not you. Was it?"

"It must have been Lydia! I'll kill her."

"It could not have been your sister. She knows nothing about this case. I never reached her."

"Then why do they think that?"

"I have no idea. It must have been someone whose name sounds similar. But why are the Lims upset? Their daughter was returned to them."

"That's a disaster, too! Do you know who rescued her? Carl Ting!"

"Did he? I think that's lovely. I must congratulate his mother that her son is a hero."

"That's what Valerie thinks, too." I could hear the disgust in my son's words. "All she can talk about is how brave he is. How scared she was, but then how safe she felt, tied up in the bathroom, the minute she heard his voice. The only reason she called me, besides to thank me for telling the police—which her parents will never forgive me for, even though I didn't do it!—is to find out if I know Carl. She wants to know everything about him."

"How lucky for Carl Ting. Now, I have something I must ask you to do."

"Ma—"

"There is a young woman who calls herself Sarah who works in Sweet Tasty Sweet on Mott Street. She has come to this country to start a new life. She does not have whatever papers she should. She needs a lawyer to help her."

"I—she needs an immigration lawyer. That's not the kind of work I do."

"Then it's time for you to begin. You'll find her a charming young lady, also pretty. I'll meet you at Sweet Tasty Sweet at six p.m. to properly introduce you."

"What? I can't leave the office that early."

"I will see you there."

I hung up the telephone. I was about to invite Tien Hua to come to the apartment for dinner after his meeting with Sarah, but they might need to further discuss her situation, perhaps over noodle soup. Also, this case had been an intriguing one. My daughter, I was sure, would want to hear the details.

S. J. ROZAN's *work has won multiple awards, including the Edgar, Shamus, Anthony, Nero, Macavity, and Japanese Maltese Falcon. She has published thirteen books and four dozen short stories under her own name and two books with Carlos Dews as the writing team of Sam Cabot. S. J. was born in the Bronx and lives in lower Manhattan. She teaches fiction writing in a summer workshop in Assisi, Italy (artworkshopintl.com). Her newest book is Sam Cabot's* Skin of the Wolf.

THE BAKER OF
BLEECKER STREET

Jeffery Deaver

His call to action, to avenge the terrible crimes done to his country, came in the form of a note tucked into a neatly folded dollar bill.

Standing behind the glass cases in his bakery, Luca Cracco avoided looking directly at the man who handed him the cash. The customer was a tall balding fellow with liver spots on his forehead. No words were exchanged as the customer, whose name was Geller, took the crisp brown paper bag containing a loaf of Cracco's semolina bread, still warm, still fragrant. If any of the other patrons in the store noted that Cracco pocketed the bill, rather than wield the brass crank of the red mahogany National cash register to deposit the money in the drawer, they didn't pay it any mind.

Cracco, a man of thirty-two, curly haired and with a proud and imposing belly, rang up another sale. He glanced toward black-haired and voluptuous Violetta, who was replenishing the bin of wheat bread. She would understand why the sale had not been registered, why her husband had not returned change for the dollar when the loaf cost fifteen cents. Their eyes met, hers neither approving nor critical; she knew of her husband's other activities, and though she would have preferred him to stay true to his role as the best baker in Greenwich Village, she understood there were things a man had to do. Such matters among them.

Cracco did not immediately turn his attention to the message within the bill—he knew largely what it would say—but instead continued to sell to customers from his dwindling stock of goods: the signature semolina loaves and whole wheat, of course, but also more sublime creations: *amaretti, biscotti, brutti ma buoni* ("ugly but good," as indeed the cookies were), *cannoli, ricciarelli, crostata, panettone, canestrelli, panforte, pignolata, sfogliatelle*, and another of Cracco's specialties: *ossa dei morti*, "bones of dead men" biscotti.

A rather telling name, he reflected, considering what now sat in the pocket of his flour-dusted slacks, the note embraced by a silver certificate.

Situated in a building that dated to the past century, Cracco's bakery was shabby and dark, but the cases were well lit and the pastries glowed like jewels in Hedy Lamarr's bracelet. Cracco believed he had a calling beyond merely baking bread and *dolci*; in this city filled with so many Italian immigrants, he felt it a duty to provide solace to so many who had been derided and mistreated for their connection, however removed, to the black-suited icon of the Axis: Benito Mussolini.

He glanced out the window at Bleecker Street, overcast this icy January afternoon. No sign of anyone in trench coat and fedora, pretending not to surveil the store while doing just that. There wasn't any reason to believe he was under suspicion. But in these days, in this city, you could never be too careful.

Cracco rang up another sale, then gave his wife a brief nod. She dusted her hands together with sharp slaps and stepped to the register. He went into the back room, the kitchen, where the ovens were now cool. It was noon, late in the daily life of a bakery; the alchemy of turning such varying ingredients—powders and crystals and gels and liquids—into transcendent sustenance occurred early. He arose every morning at 3:30, swapped pajamas for shirt and dungarees and, careful not to wake Violetta and Beppe and Cristina, descended the steep stairs of their apartment on West Fourth Street. Smoking one of the four cigarettes he allowed himself each day, *primo*, he walked here, fired up the ovens, and got to work.

Now, Cracco pulled the apron over his head and, as was his nature, folded it carefully before placing it in a laundry bin. He took a horsehair brush and swiped at his slacks and shirt, watching the flour dust motes ease into the air. He reached into his pocket and retrieved the dollar bill that Geller, the liver-spot man, had given him. He read the careful handwriting. Yes, as he'd guessed. This was the moment: the final piece of the plan, the last stage of the recipe to bake revenge into bitter bread and force it down the enemy's throat.

A look at his Breil watch, crafted in Italy, a present from his father, also a baker. The timepiece was simple but elegant, the numbers bright and bold against the dark face.

It was time to leave.

Cracco lit a cigarette, *secundo,* and before the match guttered out, he set fire to Geller's note and let it curl to ash in one of the ovens. He pulled on his greatcoat and wrapped a scarf around his neck, then topped on his gray fedora. His gloves were cloth and threadbare, worn through completely on the right thumb, but he could not afford to replace them just yet. The shop provided only a modest income, thanks to the war. And, of course, he did not undertake his work for Geller for money, unless you counted the spy paying him one dollar for a fifteen-cent loaf of bread.

Luca Cracco stepped outside as flurries began to fall, frosting the walk, just as he himself might sprinkle powdered sugar on a *bigné di San Giuseppe*, the Roman puff pastry baked just before St. Joseph's day in March.

———— · — · — · ————

"You have confirmation? You really do?"

But Murphy was being Murphy and that meant he wouldn't be rushed. The man continued in a quick, staccato voice: "I was following him last night. All night. And he goes into the Rialto on Forty-Second Street. You know, *Gaslight* was still playing. After all these months. You can't get enough of her. Who can? She's bee-u-tiful. Dontcha think?" Ingrid Bergman, he was speaking of. "Of course, she is. Come on, Tommy. No actress prettier. Agree."

Jack Murphy worked for Tom Brandon and, when they'd been in the army, had been lower in rank. But another man's superior status, boss or commander, never figured much in Murphy's reckoning (except for the one time he was given a decoration by President Roosevelt himself. Murphy had blushed and used the word "sir." Brandon had been there. He was still surprised at the show of respect.)

Murphy rocked back in the chair. Brandon wondered if the agent would plop his flashy two-tone oxfords, black and white, on Brandon's desk. But he didn't. "And whatta you think happens, boss?" The small curly-haired man—taut as a spring—didn't even seem to be asking a question. "So, the host at the theater does the four-piece place setting giveaway—trashy stuff from Gimbels—and the organist plays a few tunes, then the lights go down and, bango, time for the newsreels." Murphy ran a hand through his locks, which were red, of course.

"We were talking about confirmation," Brandon tried.

"I hear you, boss. But listen. No, really. The newsreels, I'm saying. There was one about the Battle of the Bulge."

Terrible, the German offensive that had started in December of '44, a month ago. The Allies were making progress, but the battle was still raging.

"And what does he do?" This tiny pistol of a man pointed his finger at his superior and said, "The minute the announcer mentioned the German high command, he takes off his hat."

Brandon, who resembled nothing so much as a balding shoe sales-man at Marshall Field's in his native Chicago, was perplexed.

But Murphy didn't notice. Or, more likely, he did. But he didn't care. He said to the ceiling, "Does that mean Hauptman's a spy? Does that mean he's a saboteur? No. I'm not saying that. I'm saying that we need to keep watching him."

The *him* was a German American mechanic who lived in Queens and who had had some nebulous ties to the American Nazi Party be-fore the war and had recently been seen wandering past the Norden, as in bomb-sight, factory, not so very far from where the men now sat.

And so Murphy was on the case like Sam Spade after a cheating husband.

Brandon, of course, agreed: "Okay. Sure. Stay on him."

Outside, snow fluttered down and wind rattled the panes of this large, shabby room—the office that didn't exist.

It was situated in a six-story limestone walk-up in Times Square, overlooking the Brill Building, where so much wonderful music was made. Major, *retired* major, Tom Brandon loved music, all kinds. Tin Pan Alley—much of it written in the Brill Building—and classical and jazz and Glenn Miller, God rest his soul, who'd died just last month, flying to entertain troops. Jack Murphy liked, guess what, Irish tunes. Pipes, whistles, bodhrams, concertinas, guitars. He sang sappy ballads, too, after a round or two or three of Bushmills. He had a terrible voice, but he picked up the bar tab for all the boys, so Brandon and the rest of them in the office could hardly complain.

The office that didn't exist.

Just like Brandon and Murphy and the other four men who shared this austere paint-peeling room didn't exist. Oh, the Operation for Spe-cial Services, the intelligence agency, was as real as its colorful founder and head—Wild Bill Donovan (the name said it all)—but the OSS had been born from military intelligence and was supposed to take a backseat within the country's borders. Here, spy catching was the prov-ince of J. Edgar and his not-so-special agents. The OSS's bailiwick was overseas.

But a few years earlier, there'd been an incident. Once war broke out, Hitler wanted to strike Americans at home. He ordered his head of intelligence to come up with a sabotage plan, and Operation Pastorius was born, named after the first German settlement in America. In June of '42, German U-boats dropped Nazi commandos on the East Coast. One team on Long Island, one in Florida. They had a large store of explosives and detonators with them. The saboteurs were to blow up economically important targets: the hydroelectric plant at Niagara Falls, some of the Aluminum Company of America's factories, the Ohio River locks near Louisville, the Horseshoe Curve railway stretch in Pennsylvania, Hell Gate Bridge in New York, and Penn Station in New Jersey, among others.

The plan fell apart and the spies were detected—though not by the FBI, which denied there was a conspiracy at first and then finally accepted the Coast Guard's word that enemy troops were on U.S. soil. Still, the bureau had no luck whatsoever tracking the spies down. Indeed, they didn't even believe the head of the German saboteurs when he confessed. It took him days to convince the agents that he and his men were the real thing.

Roosevelt and Donovan were furious over Hoover's ineptness. Without telling the Justice Department, the president agreed that the OSS could open an office here in New York and run its own operations. Brandon handpicked the brash Irishman Jack Murphy and the others, and they set up shop.

He and the team had had some successes. They'd caught an Italian flashing an all-clear signal to a skiff bringing in a load of dynamite off Brooklyn, meant to sink ships taking Jeeps and other vehicles overseas. And stopped German and Japanese citizens from photographing military installations. There'd been an attempt to poison the Croton reservoir—a joint endeavor by Mussolini- and Nazi sympathizers.

They'd get Hauptman, too, if he was a spy and not simply too rude to take his hat off when he first sat down in the Rialto.

But now Brandon was tired of the movie theater incident and turned toward the Big Deal. He said firmly, "You said confirmation."

"Our man just got to town," Murphy said with a gleam in his eye. "Well."

Murphy was speaking of a German plan that he had uncovered a week or so ago, known as *Betrieb Amortisations*.

Or, in English: Operation Payback.

One of the wiry Irishman's sources in the field had learned that a brilliant spy from Heidelberg, Germany, would soon be arriving in the United States. He was bringing in something "significant." Whatever that was wouldn't win the war for the Axis, but it could give Hitler bargaining power to sue for peace and keep the Nazi government intact.

"Swell, that's swell!" Brandon wasn't known for his enthusiasm, but he couldn't contain himself.

Murphy pulled an apple from his pocket. He ate a lot of apples. Two or three a day. Brandon thought it gave him rosy cheeks, but that might have been because he associated apples with Norman Rockwell's paintings on the *Saturday Evening Post* cover. Murphy explained, "Don't know where he's staying. But I do know that he's picking up his special delivery tonight. I have an idea where." He polished the apple on his sleeve and chomped down. Brandon believed he ate the stem as well as part of the core.

Brandon said, "I'll get some boys together."

"Nope. Let me handle this one alone. They smell a rat and they'll scram. That damn leak, you know what I mean?"

Brandon sure did. It seemed that over the past few months somebody had tipped off several Nazi spies and sympathizers, who'd skipped town just before the OSS could get them. Evidence pointed to someone within the FBI itself. Brandon's theory was that Hoover wanted them out of town because they'd learned about Hoover's extensive network of illegal spying on citizens solely for political reasons. Better a little espionage than a lot of embarrassment.

"Get on with it, then," Brandon told his star agent.

"Sure deal, boss. Only, keep some of the boys at the ready."

"What's this guy's game?" Brandon mused.

"No idea yet. But it's bad, Tom. The Battle of the Bulge isn't going the way the Krauts hoped—they're getting their keisters kicked. And now they want to hit back. Hard."

Payback . . .

The agent regarded his gold pocket watch, which would be a pretentious affectation on most anyone else, certainly an intelligence agent. For Murphy, though, it seemed completely natural. Indeed, to see him strap on a Timex would be out of place. His next accessory, too, was right at home in his sinewy hand: he took his 1911 Colt .45 from a desk drawer and eased back the slide to make sure the gun was loaded.

Murphy rose, pulled on his dark gray overcoat, and slipped the pistol into his pocket. He winked at his boss. "Time to go catch a spy. Stay close to that phone, boss. I've got a feeling I'm going to need you."

———— . — . — . ————

The two men were sitting on metal chairs upholstered in red vinyl at the Horn and Hardart automat on Forty-Second Street. The atmosphere was loud; voices and the collision of china reverberated off the glossy walls and the row upon row of small glass doors in the vending machines, behind which an abundance of food sat.

A sign on the table read:

HOW AN AUTOMAT WORKS

FIRST DROP YOUR NICKELS IN THE SLOT

THEN TURN THE KNOB

THE GLASS DOOR OPENS

LIFT THE DOOR AND HELP YOURSELF

Luca Cracco was eating pumpkin pie. The custard wasn't bound with enough eggs, which were strictly rationed by the Office of Price Administration. He suspected gelatin as a substitute. *Mamma mia* . . . The OPA had also rationed butter and other fats since 1943. Margarine, too, was on the list. But lard had been okayed a year ago, in March of '44. Cracco could tell, from the coating on the roof of his mouth, that, yes, pig fat was the shortening in the crust. With a pang, he remembered when he and his brother, Vincenzo, would stand at their mother's hip on Saturday afternoon and watch her cut flour and butter into pastry dough. "Butter only," she'd instructed gravely. Her son's own output at his bakery was far less—and his income much smaller—because he refused to compromise.

Butter only . . .

The tall blonde man across from him was eating beef with broad noodles and burgundy sauce. Cracco had tried to talk him into H & H's signature chicken pot pie, a New World original, but he was sticking to something he was more familiar with. A dish similar to what he might have at home. *Like spaetzel*, Cracco imagined. Heinrich Kohl, presently Hank Coleman, had just snuck into the country from Heidelberg, deep in the heart of Nazi Germany.

They sipped steaming coffee and ate in silence for a time. Kohl often looked around, though not, apparently, for threats. He simply seemed astonished at the variety and amount of food available here. The Fatherland was in the throes of crushing deprivation.

In whispered conversation that could not be overheard, Cracco asked about the man's clandestine trip as a stowaway on the freighter that had brought him here just last night. About life in Germany as the Allies inched toward Berlin. About his career in the SS. Kohl corrected that he was *Abwehr*, regular German army, not the elite "protection squad."

Kohl in turn inquired about the bakery business and Cracco's wife and children.

Finally, Cracco leaned forward slightly and asked about Vincenzo. "Your brother is fine. He was captured near Monte Casino, when the Americans made their fourth offensive there. He was sent to a POW camp. But he managed to escape and made his way north—he knew that Italy would fall soon—and was not willing to let the war pass him by. He still wanted to do more."

"Yes, yes, that's my baby brother."

Kohl continued. "He met with some people and expressed that sentiment. Word came to me, and I met with him. He said that you and he had been in touch and you expressed a passion about getting revenge for what had happened to your country. That you could be trusted completely." The German ate a robust spoonful of noodles and sauce; the meat had disappeared first. "We contacted your handler, Geller, and he, you." The handsome man looked down at the dish before Cracco. "Your pie?"

"Lard." As if that explained it all. Which, of course, it did.

A laugh. "In the Fatherland, we would be lucky for lard." He took a packet of cigarettes from his pocket and lit one, inhaled slowly, enjoying the sensation.

Cracco joined him. *Terzo.*

Kohl examined the Chesterfield. "At home, we make cigarettes from lettuce leaves. When we can find lettuce. And your country, Italy, is no better. Ah, what those bastards have done to her." Then, a shrug. He smoked half the cigarette down, stubbed it out, and put the rest in his pocket. "The shipment will arrive this evening. You and I will pick it up."

"Good, yes. But Geller tells me we have to be very careful. The ones we need to be particularly wary of are the FBI and the OSS, the intelligence service."

"There is a specific threat?"

"It seems so. But he doesn't know what, exactly."

"Well, if this is to be my last meal, I'll have another." Kohl laughed and nodded at the empty bowl before him. "You would like some more pie, yes?"

Lard, thought Luca Cracco and shook his head.

———— . — . — . ————

After the late lunch, Heinrich Kohl vanished into the forever-migrating Midtown crowds. Gray and black greatcoats and fedoras for the men, overcoats and scarves for the women, some of whom wore trousers against the cold, though most were in cotton lisle stockings—which had replaced silk after the start of the war.

Luca Cracco descended beneath Grand Central Station and caught the subway shuttle for the trip of less than a mile to the Eighth Avenue IND line. He took a southbound train to West Fourth Street and walked to the bakery, which Violetta was closing up. It was a quarter to five and the shelves were nearly empty—only a few loaves remained. She would now return home. Beppe and Cristina were in the care of Mrs. Menotti, the woman who lived in the basement of their apartment building. A widow, she earned money by doing laundry and overseeing the children of the couples in the building who both worked, as many families now had to do.

Luca and Violetta had met ten years ago at the Piazza di Spagna, near the bottom of the famed steps. He had approached and asked if she knew which house the poet John Keats had lived in. He knew exactly which dwelling it was, but he was too shy to directly ask if the raven-haired beauty would have a cappuccino with him. Three years later, they were married. Now, they were both heavier than then, but she, in his opinion, was more beautiful. She was quiet on the whole but spoke her mind, often with a coy disarming smile. Cracco believed her to be the smarter of the couple; he was given to impulse. Luca was the artist, Violetta the businesswoman. And woe to any banker or tradesman who tried to take advantage.

He told her about Kohl and the meeting.

"You trust him?"

"Yes," Cracco said. "Geller vouches for him. And I asked certain questions that only the real Kohl would know the answers to." A smile. "And he asked me questions, too. I passed the test. The dance of spies." He thought, as he often did: Who would have guessed, when he came to America—to avoid the looming war, for the sake of his future children—that he would become a soldier, after all.

"I need to get the truck."

He could have gone directly to the parking lot from lunch with Kohl, but he'd wanted to stop by the bakery. And see his wife.

She nodded.

Nothing more was said of the assignment. They both knew its danger, both knew there was a chance he might not be coming back this evening. He now stepped forward and kissed her quickly on the mouth and told her he loved her. Violetta would not acknowledge even this glancing sentiment and turned away. But then she stopped and spun around and hugged him hard. She went into the backroom quickly. He wondered if she was crying.

Cracco now walked out the door and, hands in pockets, turned and headed east to collect his bread delivery truck; you could spend an hour finding an empty place to park in this neighborhood, so he paid a warehouse $3 a month to leave the vehicle there. He maneuvered carefully as he walked; the streets and sidewalks here were not as meticulously cleared of ice and snow as the more elegant Upper East and Upper West Sides. And, as always, there was the obstacle course of people, all ages, bundled against the freezing air and hurrying on errands this way and that.

His walk took him through the complex panorama of Greenwich Village, a pocket of nearly 80,000 souls three miles north of Wall Street and three south of Midtown. Nearly half the inhabitants were immigrants of varying generations. In the west, where the Craccos lived, the majority was Italian. Whereas the family was lucky enough to have their own modest apartment, many residents lived in shared units, two or three families together. It was a bustling world of shops and coffeehouses and clubs from which jazz and swing music escaped into the streets though open windows on hot nights, blending into a hypnotic cacophony. In this area you would also find bohemians—and not necessarily real ones from Czechoslovakia. It was the term used to describe New York's intelligentsia, painters, writers, socialists, and even a communist or two. The Village had become their home.

In the north—from Washington Square College of New York University and the park, which Cracco could now see on his left, to Fourteenth Street—were the elegant apartments of financiers and lawyers and heads of corporations. Some of those inhabitants earned as much as $7,000 a year!

The East Village, his destination now, was populated by Ukrainians and Poles and Jews and refugees from the Balkans. The men were largely laborers and tradesmen, the women wives and mothers and occasionally washerwomen and shop tenders. Their homes were tenements, tall and grim—outriders of the Lower East Side, to the south, where the early immigrants to New York had settled. The perfume of those streets was cabbage and garlic.

Soon, after only two near-misses on the ice, he arrived at the snow-filled parking lot near the Bowery. He climbed into his Chevrolet and after five minutes bullied and tricked the engine to life. The gears protested as he sought first, and, when they finally engaged, he pulled out of the lot and drove north.

———— · — · — · ————

At seven p.m., Cracco collected Heinrich Kohl in front of a flophouse in lower Hell's Kitchen, west in the Thirties.

The man climbed into the passenger seat.

"Anyone follow?" the German asked.

"No. I'm sure."

Amid the dense traffic, Cracco piloted his truck south and west until he hit Miller Highway, the main thoroughfare along the Hudson River shore.

He heard a snap of metal and looked to his right. The German's deft hands were slipping cartridges into the cylinder of a revolver. He put it in his pocket and loaded another gun.

Cracco thought: War is raging on virtually every continent on earth, a thousand people at least have died in the time it took this truck to drive from the hotel to the highway, yet that horror was distant. More shocking was the pistol he was now staring at. Six small bullets. The baker wondered if he could actually point the weapon at another man and pull the trigger.

Then, he pictured his country being so savagely attacked and decided that, yes, he could.

The truck eased slowly along the highway, through the northern portion of the West Village. He could see, now dark, the famed West Washington and the Gansevoort farmers markets—the city's main meat packers and produce venues. Mornings here were beyond chaos, with purveyors and restaurateurs and individual shoppers mobbing the stalls. By eight a.m. the cobblestones grew slick with blood and fat from the sides of beef, the split-open pigs, and racks of lamb hanging from hooks in the open air. Poultry could be bought here as well. Not much fish; that market was in the Bronx. And at the produce market, every vegetable, legume, and fruit God had created could be found.

Now, glancing to his right, Cracco noted the many piers and docks striking out into the Hudson. Another memory: he and his brother Vincenzo and dozens of other boys leaping off the docks in Gaeta, south of Rome, a beach town where the Cracco family would drive in their Fiat on summer days. That is, they would make the trip *if* the sputtering temperamental vehicle didn't overheat—which both brothers prayed at Mass would not happen, Cracco suspecting it was a minor sin to bend His ear for something so selfish. (Though He seemed to grant the supplications with blessed frequency.)

Here, too, in the sweltering days of summer, boys—and the occasional girl—would launch themselves into the gray Hudson River, not the most aromatic or clean body of water. But what did youth care?

He realized that Kohl was speaking to him.

"*Si?*" Then corrected himself, angry at the slip. He was, after all, supposed to be a spy. "Yes?"

"There. That's it."

A listing freighter was docking beside a pier, the structure and the ship equally dilapidated. The docks in Greenwich Village were not like those in Brooklyn or New Jersey, where the big cargo ships offloaded their valuable goods. Smaller ships plied these waters, like the hundred-footer that had carried their precious cargo into the country from Europe.

Cracco recalled the family's voyage here from Genoa in a state-room—an elegant but deceptive term for a three-meter-square chamber with one bare light and no windows. The only passenger in the family untroubled by seasickness was Beppe, yet unborn, and sleeping without care in the warmth of his own private ocean.

The men looked around carefully. The highway was crowded with traffic but the pier was hidden from view by a half dozen boxcars on a siding. No pedestrians here; there were no walkways and all the businesses nearby were closed for the night. Cracco noted boat traffic on the Hudson, of course, the hulls largely invisible in the dark but their running lights bright and festive. The massive black expanse of river was dominated by the huge Maxwell House coffee sign, with its forty-five-foot cup, tilted and empty (the company's slogan: "Good to the last drop"). It glowed brightly. Cracco believed there'd been a time when it had been shut off in the evenings—not to save money but so that it wouldn't serve as a beacon to enemy bombers. Now it was lit again, the country apparently no longer believing that the enemy would bring the war to its home shores. Erroneously, of course.

He pulled the truck up alongside the ship. Kohl handed the pistol to Cracco. It seemed hot, though that would be impossible on a night like this. He looked at it once, then put the weapon in his pocket as well.

"Are you ready?" Kohl asked.

For a moment, he wasn't. Not at all. He wanted to hurry back home. But then he thought again: *Payback.*

And Luca Cracco nodded.

They stepped out into the cutting wind and walked to the edge of the pier, watching the crews secure the ship with ropes. A few minutes later the captain hobbled down the gangway.

"*Bonsoir!*" he called.

As it turned out, the guns were unnecessary. The captain, a grizzled fellow, wrapped in scarves and two jackets and chewing on a pipe, didn't seem the least suspicious that a man who looked Italian and one who looked German were picking up cargo from war-ravaged Europe. And to the crew, these were just harried workers collecting a mundane shipment for their business.

Cracco spoke only marginal French, so it was Kohl who conversed with the man and pointed to Cracco, the consignee. Stomping his feet against the cold, the captain offered the bill of lading. The baker scrawled his name and took a carbon copy. Kohl paid the man in cash.

Five minutes later, seamen winched a one-by-one-meter crate to the pier and then muscled it into the back of the truck. Kohl tipped them and they hurried back to the warmth of the vessel.

Inside the bread truck, Kohl clicked on a flashlight and the two men examined the crate marked with *Etienne et Fils Fabrication* on the side. The German said, "Port of entry was New Jersey. Customs cleared it there."

Cracco imagined a lethargic civil servant glancing into the packing crate at the device and not bothering to inspect further. Perhaps he hadn't bothered even to look inside. Kohl pried the top off and they looked down at the small bakery oven, painted green. The only difference between this and a real oven was that the one they now examined included a large metal tank, as if for gas, to fire the burners.

Cracco whispered, "That's it?"

Kohl said nothing but nodded, and his eyes shone as if he were proud of what was contained in the canister. As surely he was.

"I would have expected bigger," Cracco said.

"Yes, yes. That's the point, now, isn't it? Let's get back. We've been here too long as it is."

Jack Murphy was deciding that shivers were creatures unto themselves. He couldn't stop them. They roamed his body, from neck to calf. Some playful, some downright sadistic.

His teeth chattered, too.

The OSS agent was hiding behind the switching station where an old Hudson and Manhattan R. R. track split off from the New York Central main line. The spur ended on a shabby pier, about fifty yards south from where the two spies were taking delivery of the shipment that one of his better intelligence contacts had alerted him to. Murphy had been staking out the place since he'd left OSS headquarters that afternoon, battling the tear-inducing cold.

His contact had told him that the shipment was arriving on this dock on this vessel today, the only delivery in Manhattan, but had said nothing more. Hence his long and arduous vigil. Finally, to his relief, he'd watched the bakery truck come into view along Miller Highway and then turn onto the service road and ease carefully over the icy ground to the pier.

Cracco's Bakery
Luca Cracco, Prop.
Est. 1938

Bakery truck, of course; because the shipment was an oven.

A New York Central locomotive, towing passengers headed home from the day's work in Lower Manhattan, had just left the Spring Street terminal, south, to his left, and now passed by. The thick perfume of diesel fumes filled the air in its wake.

More shivers, which replicated and sent their brood to muscles he didn't know he had.

Thunder and lightning, Murphy thought in Gaelic, rocking on his numb feet, clapping his hands together. *Let's get on with it, you damn spies!*

How he wanted nothing more than to be back in his two-bedroom apartment on the East Side with his wife, Megan, and son, Padraig. Sitting before the fireplace. Sipping a whisky. And reading the book he'd started last night. A murder mystery—he loved them. It was *The Moving Finger* by Agatha Christie. Murphy was determined to figure out the villain's identity before the detective.

His hands grew even more numb. If it came down to it—and he knew it would—could he pull out the .45 and shoot accurately? Yeah, he could. He'd master any muscle spasms. Traitors to their country had to pay.

Finally, at long last, the spies were now leaving with the oh-so-precious cargo.

Murphy couldn't move in yet, though. He needed to find if they had accomplices. He staggered back to where his Ford Super Deluxe, dark red, was parked. It was the latest model available, '42. Ford had stopped production of consumer cars that year, shifting to military vehicles, but had produced a few Super Deluxes. Murphy had managed to find one of the elegant coupes.

He climbed in and started the engine, which purred. He engaged the three-speed transmission and clicked on the radio. It was set to Mutual Broadcasting, one of his favorite stations—he and the family would tune in regularly to listen to *The Adventures of Superman*, *The Return of Nick Carter*, and his favorite, *The New Adventures of Sherlock Holmes*. But now he wanted to hear the news about the war, so as he eased forward he used the car's floor button to change the channels to find a station he wanted.

As Detroit's diligent heater poured blessed warm air over him, Murphy crept along, several car lengths behind the truck as it made its way into the heart of Greenwich Village. Finally, it turned onto Bleecker Street, then into an alley behind Cracco's Bakery.

Murphy continued past the alley and around the corner. He parked the Ford down the street and slipped into the alley behind the bakery, where the truck was idling.

The tall blond man—German, of course—stepped out and took a look around. A shorter round man—Italian, Cracco undoubtedly—joined him. With much effort they managed to unload the crate and get it through the back door of the shop. The German stepped out, holding a pistol, and regarded the alley closely. Murphy backed out of sight. Then the OSS agent heard the doors slam and the truck's gears engage. A fast glance and he watched the Chevrolet leave. Murphy wasn't concerned; he doubted the two men were going far. Probably just to park the truck.

He waited several minutes, then looked again. The alley was empty. He slipped to the back door of the bakery. Peering through the window, he could see the kitchen. It was dark, as was the rest of the place.

He picked the lock and stepped inside, closing the door behind him. He squinted against the dimness, noting the ovens, the trays, the pots. And he inhaled the comforting smell of yeast and fresh bread (thinking again of his wife, who baked every Sunday). The front of the shop was empty and dark, too.

Who are you, *Signor* Cracco? And why are you doing this? Is it patriotism, is it money, is it revenge?

No matter. Motives were irrelevant to Jack Murphy. If you were an enemy, for whatever reason, you had to pay the price.

He walked silently over the concrete floor to the crate. The top had been pried open and he lifted it, shone the flashlight inside. Well, yes, it was what he'd expected: quite a special delivery, indeed.

Saints preserve us!

He looked around and found a chair in the corner of the kitchen. He sat down and drew the pistol from his pocket. Sooner or later, the German and the Italian would return, possibly with accomplices. And Jack Murphy would be ready for them. The smell of yeast wafted over him once more. He was hungry. Soon he'd be back with Megan and Paddy and they—

"You!"

Murphy gasped as the voice hissed from behind him, close to his ear: "You, don't move!" Italian accent. It would be Cracco. The man had been hiding in a pantry. A pantry Murphy hadn't bothered to check. A gun barrel tapped the back of his head.

Murphy's heart slamming fiercely, breathing fast. So both men hadn't left. Only the German. Perhaps they suspected they'd been followed and had arranged this trap.

Jesus and Mary, he thought.

Cracco snatched the Colt from Murphy's hand.

He started to turn, but the Italian ordered, "No."

Murphy thought: *He doesn't want to watch my face when he shoots me.* He heard the pistol in the spy's hand click twice as he cocked it.

The OSS agent closed his eyes and chose the Lord's Prayer for his last.

His posture ramrod straight, as always, Geller strode into the back of the bakery. The liver spots on his balding pate looked particularly prominent in the low yellow light. Luca Cracco was forever putting dimmer and dimmer bulbs into the kitchen's fixtures. Electricity, like all else during wartime, had grown increasingly dear.

"Ah, this is where you work your magic," said Geller, the man who'd set today's events in motion with the note wrapped in a one-dollar bill.

Cracco said nothing.

"In the months we've been working together," the man continued, walking up to an oven and peering into the open door, "I don't believe I've ever complimented you on your bread, Luca."

"I know I bake good bread. I don't need praise."

Words are never arrogant if they're true.

Geller continued, "The wife and I like it very much. She makes French toast sometimes. You know what French toast is?"

"Of course."

Heinrich Kohl, standing nearby, however, didn't. Cracco explained about the egg-infused bread dish. Then added firmly, "But you must make it with butter. Not lard. If all you have is lard, do not bother."

Geller nodded to the crate. "Let me see."

Kohl opened the lid. The men looked down at the canister attached to the oven. All three men were somber, as if they were looking at a body in a casket.

Cracco said, "Uranium. That small amount will do what you say?"

"Yes, yes. There is enough there to turn New York City into a smoldering crater."

I would have expected bigger . . .

This material, Cracco had learned, would be turned into what was called an atomic bomb, and it seemed like something out of the science-fiction *fumetti* comic books that were so popular in Italy. Kohl had been working on it in Heidelberg for several years, seven days a week, ever since the directive from the führer was handed down to construct such a weapon.

Cracco patted his pockets and then stopped abruptly. "Is it, I mean, can I smoke?"

Kohl laughed. "Yes."

He handed out Camels and the men lit up.

Cracco inhaled deeply.

Quarto . . .

At that moment another man appeared in the doorway of the bakery's kitchen. A trim man, with a military bearing like Geller's. He looked around, mystified.

"General," said the new arrival respectfully. He was speaking to Geller, whom everyone referred to that way, though he was retired from his job as the U.S. army chief of staff in Washington. Presently he was a civilian—second in command of the Office of Strategic Services. Wild Bill Donovan's right-hand man.

"Sir. I—"

"At ease, Tom. It'll all get explained." Geller then asked Kohl, "Do we need to do anything with it?" Nodding at the canister in the crate.

"No, no, it's perfectly safe. Well, if you open the lead casing, you'd die of radiation poisoning in a day or two, and, I promise you, that would not be a pleasant way to die."

"But it won't blow up, will it?"

"No. The uranium must be shaped carefully and machined to within micromillimeters and the vectors arranged in such a way that critical mass—"

"Fine, fine," Geller muttered. "Just need to know if our boys drop it, we don't incinerate the Western Hemisphere."

"*Nein.* That won't happen."

"Sir?" Brandon asked again.

"Okay. Here's the scoop, Tom. Luca Cracco and Heinrich Kohl. This is Tom Brandon. Head of the OSS office here in New York. Even though we don't technically *have* an office here in New York."

Cracco had no idea what this meant.

Geller continued, "Colonel Kohl, of the Abwehr, *formerly* with the

Abwehr, was a professor of physics at the university in Heidelberg before the war. He's spent the last four years working with a team there
to make one of these atomic bomb things. We knew Hitler wanted
one, but we weren't too worried. Everybody in Washington thought
the crazy bastard'd shot himself in the foot with his Law for the Resto-
ration of the Professional Civil Service. You know, the law that kicked
all non-Aryan professors out of colleges in Germany. Including most
of their top atomic physicists. Felix Bloch, Max Born, Albert Einstein,
and—"

Kohl said with a wry grin, "Yes, yes, how ironic it was! Hitler lost
the very men who could determine the precise measure of mass to turn
uranium 235 into a fissile material. And that is—"

Geller cut him off before the professor/colonel got technical again.
"And they fled to the West. But *der Führer* insisted the work go on—
with people like Heinrich here. Of course, he happened to have a
conscience, unlike some of his colleagues. His goal all along was to
keep working on this . . . what do you call it again?"

"Fissile material."

"Yeah, that. But smuggle it to us, through the underground." Geller
glanced at Cracco. "Enter our amateur spy, here. About two months
ago, Luca's brother, Vincenzo, a soldier with the Italian army, was captured by the Nazis and thrown in a POW camp."

Many people thought the Italians and Allies were enemies throughout the war. But that wasn't the case. Mussolini was deposed in 1943,
and the king of Italy and the new prime minister signed a secret ar-
mistice. Many Italians then began fighting alongside the American,
English, and Indian forces against the Germans in Italy.

"Vincenzo escaped from the Nazi camp and headed to Germany
to fight with the underground. When they learned about Luca, they
put Vincenzo in touch with Heinrich, and they came up with a plan to
smuggle this fashionable material—"

"Fissile."

"—to America. Luca jumped at the chance to help. So they disguised the . . . material as part of an oven. And had it shipped to his

bakery."

Brandon said, "But, all respect, sir, why didn't I hear about it? We could have . . . " The agent's voice faded. He scowled. "You couldn't tell me because you suspected the double agent we've been worried about might've been in *our* office here."

Geller nodded. "German intelligence learned what Heinrich had done and that the shipment was on its way, when and where it would arrive. They alerted their agent in place. But we didn't know who it was. It looked like the traitor could also be in your office here, Tom. So Luca and Heinrich were the bait. The double agent followed them— and they caught him."

Brandon snapped, "It's Jack Murphy, isn't it? Jesus. Hell. I should've guessed. He never told me where his leads came from, how he knew about the operation. And he wanted to run it alone. So he could kill the two of them and ship the stuff back to Germany."

Cracco said softly, "I wanted to shoot him. I nearly *did*. But that is what the Nazis would do. Americans would give him a fair trial. So, I spared him, tied him up." He smiled. "I was rough with him, however, I have to say that."

Brandon added, "I always wondered why Jack had a two-bedroom apartment."

General Geller laughed harshly. "In Manhattan? On an OSS agent's pay?"

"And had a fancy pocket watch. Oh, and he drove a '42 Ford Deluxe."

Cracco felt wounded. "You mean he did this for money?"

"Looks that way," Geller said.

"Where is he?" Brandon's voice was thick with pain.

"Paddy wagon's taking him to federal lockup." Geller offered a smile, which Cracco had learned was a rare occurrence. "Bill Donovan's talked to Attorney General Biddle. We're keeping Hoover in the dark. He'll find out about Murphy's indictment when he reads it in the *Times*. *If* he reads the *Times*."

"What are you going to do with this?" Brandon indicated the canister in the crate.

"You didn't hear this from me, but it's going out west. New Mexico. There's a project going on that's pretty hush-hush. There've been some setbacks, and they need more of this fissile stuff. That's it? Fissile?"

"That's right."

Brandon was looking at Kohl when he asked with a frown, "They're going to use it, that bomb, against Germany?"

Geller said, "Naw. I told Heinrich and Luca right up front: It won't be dropped in Europe. No need, for one thing. Hitler's done for. The Bulge was his last gasp. Germany'll fall by May, at the latest. It's the Japs that're the problem. The Pacific Theater could go on for another year, we don't stop 'em. This will." A nod at the crate.

"Sir?" a crisp voice called from the doorway. "The team's here."

Geller said, "Inside, boys."

Three large men in overcoats stepped into the kitchen.

Geller said, "All right, get this to Fort Dix, over in New Jersey. We've got a special train headed to New Mexico tonight. Colonel Kohl will go with you. There are some scientists there who can use his help. Oh, and whatever the colonel says, I'll have the stripes of anybody who drops it."

"Yes, sir!"

Cracco watched three soldiers lift the crate off the floor and stagger outside with it.

Kohl turned to Cracco. "Well, my friend, it's been a short acquaintance, though a productive one. I think I am going to like this country. The politics, the freedom, the culture . . . And, more important," the man said with a serious frown that soon blossomed into a smile, "restaurants where you can find an entire meal behind little glass windows. This clearly is a paradise on earth!"

Cracco and the colonel embraced, and the German stepped out the door of the bakery into the alley to accompany the uranium, with all his potential for horror and for good, to New Mexico.

Tom Brandon stood partly at attention, partly slumped, a difficult pose to achieve.

Geller said, "We'll talk later, Tom. Oh, and if you hear from J. Edgar

Vacuum or his boys, send 'em to me."

"Yes, sir." The younger OSS officer nodded, then walked through the door, pulling his coat about him.

Geller turned from the empty doorway. "I got word this afternoon: Your brother's safely back in Italy, behind Allied lines." The general reached forward and shook his hand. "Ah, Luca. You've done a good thing here."

The baker shrugged. "It was my duty. The attack by the Japanese on Pearl Harbor was inexcusable. I would do anything to avenge that crime against my country."

His country.

America.

It had been Cracco who'd suggested the name Operation Payback. For, indeed, it was.

Geller added, "Oh, and here." He handed Cracco a dollar bill, open, not folded, as in the past.

"What is this?"

"When I told President Roosevelt about the operation, he asked me to thank you. And when I told him what a fine baker you were, he asked me to bring Eleanor and him a loaf of your bread."

"The president of the United States wants a loaf of *my* bread?" Cracco blinked.

"Semolina, of course."

"I'll bake some now. At once."

Geller said, "Don't have time. I've got to leave for Washington in a few hours. The first train out."

"Sit," Cracco said. "Have a café, which I'll make myself, while I bake." He picked up a metal bowl of risen dough, covered with a damp cloth.

"No, don't bother. I'll take one of those." He pointed to a bin of a dozen loaves.

Cracco frowned. "No, no, that's day old. Good only for turkey stuffing and pudding."

"Roosevelt won't care."

"But I would." And Luca Cracco pulled off his jacket and took an apron from the stack of cleans ones that Violetta had laundered and carefully folded. He slipped it over his head and tied the drawstrings around his girth.

"Sit," said the baker once more.

General Geller sat.

A former journalist, folksinger, and attorney, JEFFERY DEAVER *is an international number-one best-selling author of thirty-five novels and three collections of short stories. He's received or been shortlisted for dozens of awards.* The Bodies Left Behind *was named novel of the year by the International Thriller Writers Association, and the Lincoln Rhyme thriller* The Broken Window *and a stand-alone,* Edge, *were also nominated for that prize. He has been awarded the Steel Dagger and the Short Story Dagger from the British Crime Writers' Association and the Nero Wolfe Award; he is a three-time recipient of the Ellery Queen Readers Award for best short story of the year. Deaver has been honored with the Lifetime Achievement Award by the Bouchercon World Mystery Conference. His most recent works are* The Starling Project, *an original audio play from Audible.com,* The Skin Collector, *and* The October List, *a novel in reverse.*

ABOUT
MYSTERY WRITERS
OF AMERICA

Mystery Writers of America is the
premier organization for mystery writers,
professionals allied to the crime writing field,
aspiring crime writers, and those who
are devoted to the genre. MWA is dedicated to
promoting higher regard for crime writing
and recognition and respect for those
who write within the genre. We provide
scholarships for writers, sponsor MWA:Reads
(our youth literacy program, formerly known as
Kids Love A Mystery), sponsor symposia and conferences,
present the Edgar® Awards, and conduct other
activities to further a better appreciation and
higher regard for crime writing.